To Kill the Pope

An Ecclesiastical Thriller

Tad Szulc

A LISA DREW BOOK

SCRIBNER
New York   London   Toronto   Sydney   Singapore

SCRIBNER
1230 Avenue of the Americas
New York, NY 10020

SCRIBNER and design are trademarks of Macmillan Library Reference USA, Inc.,
used under license by Simon & Schuster, the publisher of this work.

DESIGNED BY ERICH HOBBING

Set in Bembo

Manufactured in the United States of America

1 3 5 7 9 10 8 6 4 2

Library of Congress Cataloging-in-Publication Data

Szulc, Tad
To kill the pope: an ecclesiastic thriller/Tad Szulc
p.   cm.
"A Lisa Drew Book"
1. Attempted assassination—Fiction. 2. Rome (Italy)—Fiction.
3. Jesuits—Fiction. 4. Popes—Fiction. I. Title.
PS3569.Z8 T6 2000
813'.54—dc21   00–028466

ISBN 0-684-83781-1

This book is for my grandson
JOHN DAVID

Contents

To Kill
the Pope

✠

Prologue

IT HAPPENED FASTER than the blink of an eye.

Indeed, for a split second, the excited, adoring crowd had not comprehended that *anything* had happened at all.

One moment, the white-clad figure, holding on to the iron bar at the back seat of the white Jeep with the left hand, was blessing the faithful in a slow, circular motion of the right hand as the vehicle advanced gently through the human mass filling St. Peter's Square in the Vatican under the azure-blue sky of the May afternoon.

The next moment, the figure in white was slumped, seemingly lifeless, in a pool of crimson blood sloshing in the rear of the Jeep. Those nearest to him thought they had heard that very instant sudden dry reports of a gun—*crack!, crack!, crack!* Astonished pigeons, aroused in their quiet perches in the baroque, seventeenth-century Gian Lorenzo Bernini colonnade that maternally embraces the square, fled to safety behind the basilica, their gray wings in flight a sinister loud beat.

Then the savage, desperate cry from thousands of throats in a hundred tongues rose to the heavens: "They killed the Pope! They killed the Pope! . . ."

However, Gregory XVII, the greatly beloved but often irritatingly controversial French pope of the Roman Catholic Apostolic Church, the ruler of a billion souls, went on living—most happily—although one of the three bullets fired at him at close range had passed within millimeters of his aorta, exiting below the right shoulder blade. The second had perforated the abdominal cavity and had to be excised. The third bullet had missed the pope altogether.

Yahweh, the Lord, evidently had not yet been ready to summon him. It obviously would be done in God's good time. Gregory XVII, who was an Old Testament scholar and had both deep faith and a philosophical bent of mind, was always quietly and joyfully resigned to accept the Lord's will.

The instant he had regained consciousness in the hospital bed, the pope remembered that Yahweh had once attempted to kill Moses, his best friend and conversation partner, then changed his mind, but, after the forty years in wilderness, did decree his death. Gregory XVII had memorized from the Book of Deuteronomy the Lord's words to the 120-year-old Moses: "Behold, your days approach that you must die . . . Get up into this mountain, unto mount Nebo, and behold the land of Canaan, which I gave unto the children of Israel for a possession, and die in the mount whither you go up, and be gathered unto your people . . ."—and the passage in Deuteronomy: "So Moses the servant of the Lord died there in the land of Moab, according to the word of the Lord . . . and no man knows of his sepulchre unto this day."

So Gregory XVII said to himself, "This time Yahweh changed his mind about me," grimacing with satisfaction even as sharp pain shot through his body. "The Lord chose to spare me today," he mused, "but perhaps he will not the next time. Behold His mysterious ways."

In his penumbral condition between anesthesized, sedated sleep and half-consciousness, the pope wondered, once more, whether Moses really ever existed. It was something of an intellectual hobby for Gregory XVII, since young priesthood, to discuss Moses with Jewish Bible scholars; it covered the whole range of Jewish scholarship and beliefs, with all the contradictions contained over thousands of years in the Torah and the Talmud, and the Rabbinical Commentators in the Talmud and the Midrash, the collections of storytelling. It included, of course, Christian scholarship, which often tended to be more rigorous faith than actual scholarship, and even Freud's *Moses and Monotheism,* and his doubts about the historic Moses. That *Yahweh* existed was beyond question, and Gregory XVII's inclination had always been to conclude that there had been *a* Moses.

Now, immobilized in bed with intravenous lines and mouth

and nose intubations and staring through narrowed eyes at the blinding ceiling light, the pope asked himself whether his lifelong secret penchant toward comparing himself to Moses was not sacrilegious, blasphemous or, at least, unspeakably arrogant? Gregory XVII had never forgotten that Christian theology always saw Jesus as "the new Moses," and this late afternoon the martyred pope, sedated as he was, allowed his mind to wander—wondering whether God, in sparing his life, had confirmed that he *was* the second Moses, preparing the world from the throne of St. Peter for the coming of the Messiah.

He was sufficiently conscious to know that he would have to rethink it all more deeply when he felt better and stronger—and in firmer command of his mind—though the image now flashed in his memory of Michelangelo's Carrara marble statue of Moses in Rome's Church of San Pietro in Vincoli, Gregory's favorite art object in the whole world. He kept finding excuses to stop and pray there as often as possible: Just seeing the massive Moses, the pope felt invigorated.

And, half dreaming, Gregory suddenly remembered an amusing fantasy he had read decades ago about the Plagues of Egypt, with the Lord casting an *eleventh* Plague in the form of a pharaonic pop song, *Take Me to the Nile, Mamma!* which had spread like wildfire across the land. The subliminal power of the song had paralyzed all activity as the entire population stopped working to hum it everywhere day and night, with Ramses having been warned that the *Mamma* epidemic would never cease unless he let the children of Israel go—led by Moses. In absolute desperation, Ramses caved in, *Mamma* instantly vanished, and Exodus was on.

This Mosaic obsession is ridiculous, Gregory thought as he slid back into deep sleep. But, unquestionably, Yahweh was testing him. But for what? And who was the human agency, the tool or instrument of the Lord's will, who had struck at him on St. Peter's Square? Someday the truth would come out—or will it?

What had saved the sixty-one-year-old pontiff apart from God's will were his powerful athlete's constitution and robust health, the speed with which he had been rushed in an ambulance to the Gemelli Clinic barely two miles away, and, ultimately, the extraordinary skill of the Italian surgeon, Dr. Francesco Crucitti, who happened to be on duty in the Emergency Room that lazy afternoon.

To Gregory XVII, of course, those magnificent but profane facts were *sacred*—divinely ordained by Yahweh when He chose to save him—and he never tired of pointing out publicly and privately that the assassination attempt had occurred on May thirteenth, the day of Our Lady of Fátima. The pope felt a special veneration for the Fátima Virgin at whose shrine in Portugal the following year he had placed the bullet that had nearly shattered his heart. It had been recovered from the hand of a young American nun into which it had penetrated after traversing Gregory's body. She had stood in the crowd ten feet on the other side of the white Jeep when the assassin, a mysterious Turk in his early twenties, had fired his gun at the pope at almost point-blank range. Our Lady of Fátima, Gregory believed, had been watching over him in fulfillment of God's will. She had performed the miracle of protecting his life when the Turk had squeezed his three shots from a sturdy Walther automatic pistol just as the pope was completing his relaxed tour of St. Peter's Square after holding his regular Wednesday General Audience.

In those days, the public audiences took place in the afternoon in the open, in front of St. Peter's Basilica, with a minimum of security. It had never occurred to anybody, even in this age of terrorism, that the pontiff could be the target of a murder plot. As was his custom, therefore, Gregory rode in his Jeep along rows of pilgrims, Roman faithful, and tourists from all over the globe, blessing them and waving smilingly in response to enraptured shouts and hand-clapping of applause: *Viva il Papa ! Vive le Pape! Long Live the Pope!*

The French pope, just three years on St. Peter's throne after his surprise election as the first "foreign"—non-Italian—pontiff in four and a half centuries, was convinced that frequent direct contact with his flock was essential to his pastoral mission. There had to be a flow of emotion and immediacy between him and the believers if the Church and religion were to have any lasting meaning as the new century and millennium approached. Besides, the gregarious Gregory, who was an extrovert as well as a mystical, introspective, but also highly pragmatic personality, thrived on rapport with people—the more the better—and lost no opportunity meeting with crowds on every conceivable occasion. It recharged and rejuvenated him.

The Wednesday General Audiences were the most natural such occasions, and the vast square in front of St. Peter's Basilica was always filled with thousands upon thousands who hoped for a glance from the pope from just a few feet away, perhaps a split second of eye contact with him, perhaps a chance to touch his garments as he drove by ever so slowly. It made Gregory visibly and palpably human to them, and made the crowd, to him, more than just a faceless abstraction of the faithful—not the way it had been not so long ago when the pontiff was carried on a palanquin during public appearances, looking down on his people.

But it also made it possible that day for the young Turk, who after his capture gave his name as Agca Circlic, to remain unnoticed within the ranks of pilgrims massed on the right side of the square, as one faced the basilica, excitedly awaiting the approach of the papal Jeep. He was the "human agency," as Gregory would put it later, who had carried out the will of the Lord toward him— though only up to a point. There was no reason for anyone to pay attention to the Turk, unshaven and wearing an ill-pressed, food-stained baggy light suit.

Circlic had arrived at the square two hours before the General Audience, standing patiently on the spot he had selected as the best for his purposes after observing on two previous Wednesday afternoons the pattern of the pope's Jeep tour among the pilgrims. His heavy pistol was snugly concealed in the left inside pocket of his suit jacket. Circlic's meticulous training in Turkey as a professional hit man—a political terrorist—had taught him how to measure precisely the distance to his target and the bullet's velocity before producing the pistol from the pocket and firing. He was a fine shooter and he knew that it had to be accomplished in a single graceful fluid motion, based on an instinctive mathematical calculation.

A few minutes before five o'clock, as the sun began to descend toward the western horizon, brushing with gold dust the churches, monuments, and roofs of Rome, Gregory's Jeep had turned toward the row where Circlic stood, and the Turk began calculating the distance for the optimal moment as the vehicle approached among even louder *evvivas* rising to a crescendo and cascading applause. The General Audience, held on the great wide stairs of the basilica, had ended some twenty minutes past, with the pope greeting the foreign visitors in a score of languages.

When the Jeep was exactly eleven feet away, with Gregory facing him for an instant, the pistol materialized in Circlic's hand. At the precise moment—three minutes after five o'clock, the Turk fired three times at an upward angle. He was cool and collected, mindful of his instructions, a finely tuned human machine. It was like target shooting at the Anatolia training camp back in Turkey: Circlic's hand was steady, his aim true, and the pope collapsed, wordlessly, in the back of the little vehicle.

It lasted less than a second, a frozen frame, that at the same time was an eternity. The French monsignor, Gregory's private secretary who had been sitting in a back seat, next to the pontiff, had thrown himself on top of him to shield him from any more gunfire, his black cassock turning even darker from papal blood. As it happened, the Jeep had been very close to an ambulance routinely parked on the square, and Gregory XVII could be instantly transferred to it. With the monsignor screaming to the driver, "*à l'hôpital, à l'hôpital!*" the ambulance veered violently to the right, dispersing the stricken crowd as it raced out of St. Peter's toward Gemelli Clinic, oblivious of the thick traffic ahead. The ambulance driver knew where to go: Standing orders were to rush to Gemelli in the event of an accident in which the pope might have been hurt. Miraculously, cars and buses made way for him. *Carabinieri* and police cruisers, sirens blaring and lights flashing, roared in the wake of the ambulance.

In the square, where pandemonium now reigned, Circlic had dropped the pistol on the spot on the pavement from where he had fired. It landed near a drying pool of blood, alongside a bouquet of white carnations that had turned bright red, one of the hundreds of bunches of flowers pilgrims had tossed toward Gregory moments earlier. Free of the gun, the Turk had turned in the direction of the shelter of the Bernini colonnade, trying to escape via that route.

But, immediately, he was a captive of the enraged crowd. Men and women had rushed at him with terrible imprecations, pinning him down on the ground, barely letting him breathe.

The sanctity of St. Peter's Square may have saved Circlic from being literally beaten to death, his flesh torn into shreds. Instead, the crowd drew back to let the *carabinieri,* posted as usual along the colonnade, grab and manacle the Turk and throw him inside their cruiser. Circlic looked strangely at peace though he seemed quite surprised at being captured and taken away. He must have been assured by his patrons that somehow he would be able to get away, scot-free, and he must have trusted them. In any event, the young Turk had acknowledged at once in broken Italian that, indeed, he had attempted to kill Gregory XVII, not making the slightest effort to deny, dissemble, or protest. He gave the *carabinieri* his name. Then he plunged into complete silence.

Exactly eight minutes after the affray on the square, the telephone rang shrilly and urgently by the bedside of Cardinal Diarmuid Hume, the octogenarian Irish Dean of the College of Cardinals. In the event of a pope's death, the daily conduct of the Vatican's administrative affairs is directed by the college until the election of a new pontiff. Today, the responsibility was placed personally on Hume. It had therefore been necessary for an official of the Papal Household to interrupt the cardinal's afternoon nap and notify him of the situation so that he would be ready to act at once if needed.

Moreover Hume, who always described himself, jocularly but truthfully, as "the only nondrinking Irishman," happened to be the wisest, most experienced, and most cynical figure in the Roman Curia. Indeed, he *was* a Holy See institution himself, highly respected and frequently feared in that crucible of piety and intrigue. Hume realized immediately that the Holy See and the Church might face an insoluble crisis if Gregory XVII remained alive indefinitely, but was incapacitated physically or mentally. Told of the extent of the pope's injuries, the cardinal could not rule out incapacitation, and it was an awesome dilemma. He could not and would not wish Gregory dead—for one thing they were warm personal friends—but since Canon Law does not make any provisions for incapacitation, and there is no such thing as "Deputy Pope," all decision making in the Church, such as naming bishops or formulating theological or political policies, is paralyzed *ad infinitum,* until there is a new pope elected. And incapacitation could last indefinitely. The prospects were frightening.

"Keep me posted every minute on the Holy Father's condition!" Hume shouted to his assistant, who had called him from the office of the college at the Apostolic Palace. "And now let me get dressed!"

Ten minutes later, as Hume was completing his toilette in the high-ceilinged bedroom of his *palazzo,* the telephone rang again with word that Gregory was fighting for his life at the clinic and that there were high hopes for his survival. The Irishman sighed with relief. "Praise the Lord," he said to his assistant, "and I mean it . . ."

"And, Eminence," the assistant told him, "the gunman was captured and taken away by the *carabinieri.* He is a Turk . . ."

"What ? A Turk? What kind of Turk?" Hume asked impatiently.

"I have no idea, Eminence," the man replied. "All we know is that he is young—and that he will not talk, except to state his name."

Hume turned the information over in his mind. He never took anything at face value.

"Hmm," he said to himself. "A Turk . . . Why would a Turk wish to kill Gregory? Because he is a fanatic Muslim, if that's what he is? No, it makes no sense. It's got to be more complicated. There must be more to it . . . Well, we'll find out sooner or later . . . or not. Meanwhile, I want Gregory back on his feet, running the Church."

Hume was still shaking his head in puzzlement as he entered his black limousine to be driven to his office in the Vatican to stand by for further developments.

"There's something else to this whole business," the cardinal muttered, thinking of urgent telephone calls he would make as soon as the emergency was over, either way, and of questions that had to be asked.

Rome, Italy, and the world hung for hours in a state of shock on whatever sparse news emerged that afternoon, evening, and night concerning the condition of Gregory XVII—and concerning the identity and background of the Turkish gunman. Would the pope live? Who *was* this Turk? Why did he try to kill Gregory? Who was behind it all? Of course, it had to be a conspiracy! RAI, the Italian radio and television network, remained on the air with continuous, excited reports on the events of St. Peter's Square—including breathless interviews with real or alleged eyewitnesses—though it had precious little new to say as the evening wore on. It interviewed, as did foreign journalists, anyone that could be located who knew the pope well, slightly, or not at all, or knew something or other about the papacy, all aspiring gravely to appear as experts on Gregory XVII and international terrorism.

From his private office at the American Embassy in Rome, his radio and television sets blaring, the CIA Station Chief was attempting in the early evening—it was early afternoon in Washington—to brief the Director of Central Intelligence over a secure telephone line at Langley headquarters. The CIA, the president, and the entire officialdom back home had learned of the attempted assassination within minutes of its occurrence—the wire services had flashed the news moments after Circlic had fired his gun and Gregory had collapsed—and now they all demanded fulsome answers and explanations. The president had ordered the Director of Central Intelligence to come up with "a full picture" as rapidly as possible; he feared, not unreasonably, a global crisis if the pope died and blame and responsibility had to be apportioned. The United States had to be prepared to act credibly and fearlessly in any contingency, and to make or weigh accusations. What if the Soviets had been behind it?

"No, sir, we have no clue about the Turk's identity," the Station Chief was telling the director, striving to keep his own impatience and frustration in check. "No, we don't know whether the Soviets are behind it . . . No, I know nothing about notorious Palestinian terrorists turning up in Rome . . . God, it only happened a few hours ago . . . Yes, the shooter remains in custody . . . And, yes, the pope is still alive . . . He was hit by two high-velocity bullets . . . Yes, we have our people at the Clinic . . . Of course, sir, we'll do everything we can to get you all the answers ASAP . . ."

*   *   *

The radio was on as well three blocks from the Vatican, in the tiny office of an American Jesuit in his early forties named Timothy Savage. He was a leading Vatican specialist on Islamic affairs. Savage, informally clad that afternoon in slacks and a polo shirt, had learned about the shooting from a fellow Jesuit who had burst into his office, shouting the fearsome news.

The American had just greeted a visiting retired French archbishop who had served for decades in West Africa, acquiring deep-seated suspicions about everything connected with Islam. He had requested a meeting with Savage to discuss dangers he believed were posed by the Muslim world. The elderly archbishop, severe in his old-fashioned black cassock and redolent of mothballs, had told Savage as they shook hands that he had arrived from his retirement home at the foothills of the Pyrénées in the south of France only two days earlier on a long-planned visit to Rome, probably his farewell one. Savage received him as a courtesy.

An emaciated, stooped figure with deep-sunken ice-cold blue eyes, the archbishop had arched his thick eyebrows and crossed himself silently as he was apprised of the attack on Gregory XVII, a fellow Frenchman. But the two men had talked only about Islam for nearly three hours as the old man would not let go of the subject. The archbishop was curiously reluctant to depart, and Savage tried desperately to listen to his visitor with one ear and the radio broadcasts with the other. Darkness had already fallen outside when the RAI announcer broke in to read a medical bulletin from the Gemelli Clinic that, after six hours in surgery, it appeared that Gregory XVII would live.

Rising from his chair, the archbishop crossed himself again, mouthing silently, "God's will," as he took leave of Timothy Savage.

BOOK ONE

Monsignor

Chapter One

1986

"THE HOLY FATHER wishes to learn the whole truth about that attempt on his life," Monsignor Romain de Sainte-Ange announced quietly in his French-accented English.

The monsignor, the pope's private secretary, paused for effect, fussed with his rimless glasses, brushed an invisible speck from the front of his elegantly tailored cassock and the violet sash, and leaned forward to fix the American Jesuit with a trusting, conspiritorial stare.

Father Timothy Savage nodded pleasantly, uncertain of how else to respond. He had no idea why he had been summoned so urgently by Sainte-Ange, whom he had never met before, and why he was now being informed of this wish of Gregory XVII. But the corpulent monsignor with soft features, a pouting mouth, and diamond-hard black eyes, was the pope's closest adviser and confidant—and the most powerful man at the papal court. Everything he did had a precise purpose, and Tim Savage assumed that it included his own meeting with Sainte-Ange this morning.

"You see," the Monsignor went on, shooting his gold-and-diamond cufflinks as he spoke, "the Italian authorities decided last week to discontinue their investigations of the assassination attempt because Parliament chose not to extend the period of the investigatory mandate, as required by law. Do you know why?"

"No, Monsignor, I do not know," Tim replied, increasingly perplexed by what he was hearing.

"It was because in the years since the attempt the Italian investigators have failed to come up with any new clues or evidence to indicate who had ordered the attack on His Holiness—and why,"

Sainte-Ange said. "As you know, today is the fifth anniversary of that attack, and we still know absolutely nothing of what was behind it. This is not acceptable! . . ."

The private secretary took a deep breath and continued: "Yes, the culprit, that demented Turk, is in prison serving a life term, but, apart from confessing, which he later recanted, he told the Italian tribunal absolutely nothing. And when the Holy Father visited him in his prison cell to forgive him, the Turk insisted he was Jesus Christ. And you know what?"

Tim shook his head, watching the monsignor turn red with anger.

"I am almost convinced that there is a conspiracy of some kind to prevent the discovery of the truth," Sainte-Ange hissed. "Everybody seems afraid of the truth. Despite President Reagan's promises, your Central Intelligence Agency obviously has made no real effort to help the Italian investigating judge. The same goes for Interpol. Can you understand that?"

"No, I can't," Tim answered. He was completely at sea. This was a surreal conversation, he thought, on a subject he had utterly ignored and that was none of his business. But, mysteriously, it was being made his business.

"For five years, we've been stuck with the same tired old theories nobody can prove," the monsignor told him. "That the Turk did it because he's a Muslim and Muslims are supposed to hate Christians. What nonsense! Or that the Turk had been sent by the Bulgarian secret police on orders from the KGB, which is idiotic, too, because nobody in the Kremlin is mad enough to want to kill the pope. My God, we are in secret negotiations with the Russians!"

Tim nodded again, praying for an explanation of what his meeting with Sainte-Ange was all about. In all his years at the Vatican, he had never had an experience even remotely resembling today's. Still, the Vatican was famous for strange and mysterious happenings.

Now the monsignor had regained his calm, smiling encouragingly at the American Jesuit across a small table from him in the minuscule but beautifully appointed square sitting room next to his office on the second *loggia* of the Apostolic Palace. It was one of the magnificent *loggie* designed by Raphael in the sixteenth century when St. Peter's Basilica and the adjoining holy edifice were being rebuilt after the Sack of Rome. An antique Venetian clock ticked on a marble-top table in a corner. The scent of Saint-Ange's expensive aftershave lotion, probably Hermès' Equipage, wafted richly around him. Tim thought idly that it was more pleasant than the smell of incense that seemed to permeate permanently the great halls and galleries of the Apostolic Palace. The odor of piety.

"Under the circumstances," the private secretary declared in a solemn voice, "the Holy Father has determined that we must rely on our own resources to discover the truth. He feels morally and legally that we must do what must be done. It is vital that we fully understand the dangers that may face the Church in the future, that we know who is the enemy . . . As in the past . . ."

He paused again and his smile was beatific.

"And," he said softly, almost seductively, "we have selected you to undertake this mission on behalf of the Holy Father. To find the truth. We hope that you will accept . . ."

Tim Savage stirred uneasily in his chair, trying desperately to dissemble the shock produced by the monsignor's words. He knew, of course, that the Vatican had its own secret service and even a department of "dirty tricks," but he had always succeeded in keeping his research work apart from subtle papal intelligence enterprises. And now this! At forty-four, Tim thought, he had lived through all imaginable surprises, yet he had been wrong.

And there was no way he could turn down Sainte-Ange's "invitation." As a Jesuit, he had taken a vow of obedience to the pope. He felt he was dreaming, that he was living a fantasy, that he had suddenly been trapped in an iron cage. A thousand alarms sounded in his mind: It was like the Kennedy brothers decades ago, murders never definitively solved, like Dag Hammarskjöld, the United Nations secretary general, whose death in a fiery plane crash in Africa may or may not have been an accident, like the much loved Swedish prime minister, Olof Palme, shot by unknowns in the street. What chance did he, Tim Savage, have to succeed in investigating the attempt on Gregory XVII?

Tim slowly inclined his head in assent. A minute had not elapsed since Sainte-Ange had spoken the fateful words.

"Yes," he said, "I am always at the service of the Holy Father. But why me? I'm just a simple American Jesuit working in Rome. I know nothing, absolutely nothing, about the assassination attempt. You have the wrong person."

"No, we have the *right* person in you," the monsignor replied firmly, pointing his immaculately manicured stubby finger at Tim. "Please believe me, Father, that much thought has gone into our decision to entrust you with the investigation. Much thought and deliberation. We are very familiar with your background, your special talents, and your experience. You are not 'a simple Jesuit . . .' Ah, it is a case of 'it takes a thief to grab a thief,' as you Americans say . . ."

"Actually, we say, 'to *catch* a thief,' " Tim Savage remarked politely, wondering immediately what made him correct the older man and realizing it was a silly little stab at asserting himself in this impossible situation.

The monsignor ignored it, making a steeple of his tiny hands and lowering his voice to a whisper as he continued to address Tim:

"I am so glad that you have accepted the mission. But your investigation must be conducted in the most confidential, not to say top-secret, manner. Your profile must be very low. That's why it must be a one-man investigation. As you are doubtless aware, the Vatican has its own prosecutor and Civil Court, but we have chosen to bypass them as well as the secret agents of the Swiss Guard. And we do not propose to take any action if we—you—discover the truth. We just want to *know* the truth.

"There is very little we can tell you to get you started," Sainte-Ange went on. "Just the obvious things. Because the Turk who fired the bullets, Agca Circlic, is a Muslim and a dedicated terrorist, we must envisage a Muslim connection, whatever it may be, though it's nothing more than a theory. But this is where your knowledge and background make you so perfect. And your special type of experience may fit some of the other theories kicking around to this day. Besides, few would suspect an American Jesuit scholar to be a detective for the Vatican . . ."

Tim again inclined his head in agreement. There was no point insisting on his uselessness as a sleuth for the Holy See. The pope and Sainte-Ange had decided his destiny. Well, so be it, he told himself. Others had done it before.

"One more thing," the monsignor added with a frozen smile. "You will be completely on your own. You can work any way you choose. Should anyone learn of your mission, or suspect it, we shall simply deny that you have anything to do with us. Our Press Office director, the Spanish psychiatrist, is unaware of your assignment anyway and he won't be lying in his denials. He'll say that you are a crazy American with delusions, a renegade priest . . . On the other hand, you will naturally have logistical support from this end through special channels I am creating. In fact, let me start you immediately."

Sainte-Ange picked up the telephone, whispering a few words in French.

"Just a moment," he said to Tim.

There was a discreet knock and the door behind Tim opened. He looked back, rose from his chair, and experienced his second shock of the day, a greatly more pleasing one. Standing before him was a petite nun in a white habit, smiling modestly.

"Father Savage," the monsignor said without getting up, "this is Sister Angela. She belongs to the order of Augustine Sisters of Notre Dame of Paris and, like me, she is French. She has been with the Papal Household for quite a few years, helping with the Holy Father's English-language paperwork and, sometimes, with foreign visitors because she speaks such excellent English. And this is why I decided to designate her as your direct contact with me. The sister has been briefed about your mission and she will be the liaison between us—you will see me only in emergencies or on special occasions. Sister Angela will provide you with funds, documentation, and anything else you need. You will have her direct telephone number and you will call her as required. If necessary, you may come to her office, but try to keep your visits down to an absolute minimum. You shouldn't be seen around here too often."

Listening to Sainte-Ange, Tim stared with total fascination at Sister Angela. He had instantly decided that she was uncommonly pretty, reminiscent of a delicate Matisse painting. And he decided, just as quickly, that she could be no more than in her early thirties.

He liked the way she looked calmly and directly into his eyes as the monsignor made the presentations. Most European nuns Tim had met tended to stare intensely at their feet or their hands in the presence of a man, even a priest. Damn impure thoughts, he told himself—it's the price you pay for being a man as well as a celibate. But he had to say something to her, to break the silence after the monsignor had introduced them. Sainte-Ange had already raised his eyebrows questioningly.

"Tell me," Tim asked her, "where did you learn your English?"

"I went to school at the Convent of the English Augustine Sisters in Paris," Angela replied in accentless English. She had a pleasant, low voice.

"English sisters in Paris?" he inquired incredulously. "I didn't know they had a convent there."

"Oh, yes," the sister answered. "It's on the Left Bank, in Faubourg St. Germain. It was established in 1653 by Augustine sisters who fled England to escape the persecution of Catholics by Cromwell. You know, he wrote that the great question was 'whether the Christian world should all be popery.' Anyway, the convent has been there ever since. George Sand, the famous novelist of the nineteenth century, studied there."

"But how did you wind up there?"

"In my case," Angela said, "it was because of my parents. My father was English, an expatriate in Paris . . . He was a Jew. My mother came from a long line of devout Catholics. They met during the German occupation; she fell in love with him and helped to hide him from the Nazis. Then they were married and I was born ten years later. My father died when I was a little girl, my mother brought me up as a Catholic, and the rest must have been predestined . . . But here's my telephone number, Father. Don't hesitate to call if you need anything."

She bowed to Sainte-Ange and left the room. The monsignor stood up, extending his hand to Tim Savage.

"Thank you so much for coming," he said. "I know the Holy Father will be most gratified . . . Please bear in mind that if you don't track down the truth, the pope will never be safe. His enemies will never give up. That's why your mission is so vital in immediate terms. It's not simply historical research."

*   *   *

"What did you think of the American?" Gregory XVII asked Monsignor Sainte-Ange. "Is he really the man for the job?"

They sat in the pope's private study on the third *loggia* of the Apostolic Palace, enjoying the quiet of the late morning before the noontime meal. Gregory XVII had bidden farewell to his last visitor of the day—there rarely were audiences in the afternoon—and Sainte-Ange had come up after Tim Savage's departure from his office. In the distance, they could see the sun's rays lighting golden fires on Rome's roofs across the Tiber as far as the Aventine Hill.

"Yes," the monsignor said. "Yes, I think he will do fine. I liked what I already knew about his past, and he made a good impression on me. My instinct tells me that we made the right choice."

Gregory XVII trusted Sainte-Ange without reservation. He was his oldest friend. It had been forty-five years since both entered the seminary at the age of twenty-one, near Clermont-Ferrand in the Vichy-governed zone of France. They remained there when, soon afterward, the Germans occupied that part of the country too. Both men discovered to their surprise how many priests sympathized with Vichy, collaborating with its police and subsequently with the Gestapo; many had denounced to the authorities Jewish families hiding in the countryside and *maquis* Resistance fighters defying the Nazis. Because neither the future pope nor Sainte-Ange was willing to join the right-wing "integrist" priests' organizations, they were shunned and isolated in the seminary. But, in the process, they learned much about the French Church's many hidden faces. They never forgot it, even when Church integrists paid homage to Gregory XVII upon his election to the papacy.

Now, at the age of sixty-six, the pope and his private secretary formed a perfect team, oddly paired and seemingly unmatched as it was. While Gregory XVII, tall, thin with a regal bearing, was cerebral, visionary, and immensely captivating, Sainte-Ange was purely pragmatic, and essentially cold. He was the classic French *homme des coulisses,* more comfortable in background shadows than in the limelight Gregory XVII adored, and a genius in the manipulation of power, which he exercised, often mercilessly, in assuring the Roman Curia's unquestioned obedience to his master and friend. It was logical that Sainte-Ange alone had devised and managed the investigation of the 1981 assassination attempt, convincing the pope of the urgent need for it, and, in effect, discovering Timothy Savage for the mission. In all of the Vatican, only Sister Angela, who had to perform the vital function of liaison and whom the monsignor decided he could trust, largely because of her own personal background, knew about the Timothy Savage undertaking.

"Well, I'm glad the mission is now under way," Gregory XVII said, savoring a sip of his favorite Gavi di Gavi white wine. "But does the American know about de Marenches' warning and that it was not heeded?"

"No, I thought it was premature," Sainte-Ange replied in his careful manner. "He has to do a lot of homework before he can understand it and all its implications. But I hope that our Father Savage will not be wasting time. You're never certain of being safe, perhaps more now than ever."

"True," the pope told him. "This is why I ask Our Lady of Fátima for protection in my every prayer."

Even as Gregory XVII and Sainte-Ange chatted in the papal study, two men greeted each other warily at a small table set against the wall at Roberto, a busy restaurant on Borgo Pio, just three blocks east of the Sant'Anna Gate, the principal entrance to the Vatican. Borgo Pio, a narrow street of eateries and small shops, starts at Sant'Anna Gate and is commonly known to Romans as the "Vatican Ghetto." Roberto is patronized mainly by foreign tourists and foreign priests, especially Americans, working at the Vatican.

The two men arrived at the restaurant within minutes of each other. The first was a solidly built, grizzled man with a malevolent face, its hard features frozen like a Notre Dame gargoyle, and bloodshot eyes. He looked to be in his mid-sixties and seemed to be more accustomed to a military uniform than the ill-fitting brown sports jacket and flowery shirt he wore today. He had commandeered the table by the wall, and now he rose at the approach of a much younger man in a well-tailored dark suit.

"It's a lovely day, isn't it, Mister Kurtski?" he said in English, which he spoke with a pronounced French accent. "And it's a pleasure to see you again."

"Sure," the older man replied curtly, "but you're not here to talk about the weather." His English came with an Eastern European accent and intonation.

"Then let us get down to business and waste no time," the Frenchman suggested. "When we first met in Paris, I told you how impressed we were with your reputation."

"Yeah, let's talk business," Jake Kurtski said. "But first, I want a cold beer. And what do you have in mind, anyway?"

"It is simple. We wish to see the pope dead," the elegant young man explained. "And we understand that you would know how to go about it."

Kurtski's expression did not change. The waiter had brought the beer and the old soldier took a deep draft from the bottle.

"Never mind what I know," he said. "Tell me *your* ideas . . ."

The Frenchman smiled engagingly. "Let me quote from your famous compatriot, Joseph Conrad, on the subject: '. . . The attack must have all the shocking senselessness of gratuitous blasphemy,'," he told Kurtski. "And Conrad was alluding to bombs. That's from *Heart of Darkness* . . . That's our idea."

"I don't know who the fuck Conrad was," Kurtski announced gruffly, pronouncing "fuck" as "*fock*." He went on: "So you want to blow him out of the sky? You want me to bomb the plane when the pope next goes traveling?"

"That's right," the young man said. "We want to blow him right into heaven. Can you do it?"

"I don't know. I have to think about it. You know, it's not all that easy with all the security around him and the airplanes," Kurtski observed.

"Oh, we understand. That's why we're offering you a million dollars if you make it happen," the Frenchman whispered.

"I'm not sure I can take it seriously," Kurtski told him. "You guys, whoever you are, seem to *fock* it up every time. "Your Turk *focked* it up on the square. And I know that you tried and failed to get a bomb aboard the Alitalia plane when the pope was going to Portugal: It was really stupid to stick the bomb in the food that was being loaded on the airliner. Of course, it was found. And wasn't that crazy Spanish priest with the bayonet at Fátima one of your people?"

"Well, yes, and that's why we're now turning to professionals," the younger man said. "And we also know that, as they say at the Vatican, patience is a cardinal virtue. So we can wait for your answer and your detailed plan as long as necessary. I'll contact you in exactly one month to arrange for another conversation."

Kurtski nodded and walked out of the restaurant without a word. Passing a fruit stand in front of a food store, he grabbed a *clementina* and began to peel it.

As the sun set over Rome, the Frenchman locked himself in his hotel room a block from Roberto to compose a long coded letter. Then he walked over to the tiny Vatican post office to mail it to an address in a small town in the south of France, not far from the medieval walled city of Carcassonne, a region where road signs read *Pays des Cathars,* the Country of Cathars—those "pure" thirteenth-century battlers for religious freedom.

Naturally, it never occurred to Tim Savage or Kurtski that they were in Rome at the same time, so near one another—and again on a collision course. Vietnam, after all, was such a long time ago.

Chapter Two

TIM SAVAGE STEPPED OUT of the somber mustiness of the Apostolic Palace through the Bronze Doors and into St. Peter's Square, serene in the warm sun of the May morning. The basilica and the imposing *Scala Regia*—the regal staircase—were to his right, the architectural centerpiece of the oval square.

Halting briefly, Tim removed his celluloid dog collar from its neck slots and stuck it in the breast pocket of his black cotton shirt under the short wool jacket of his black clergy suit. Jesuits, as a rule, almost never wear cassocks. With his shirt now open at the neck, he breathed easier as he tried to sort out and compose his thoughts and calm his emotions after Sainte-Ange's thunderbolt had hit him. Passersby glanced at Tim with more than casual interest: He was handsome in a pleasant Black Irish sort of way, standing at six feet, slim and broad-shouldered, with warm, deep blue eyes, high cheekbones, and an aquiline nose. His jet black hairline was beginning to recede, not unnatural past forty. Tim was an affable man who liked people, and even strangers felt it at once.

The piazza before Tim was rapidly filling with groups of foreign pilgrims shepherded by their tour leaders, sloppily dressed tourists from America and Spain and Germany—many of the women in tank tops and unbecoming shorts and men in T-shirts and jeans—and parochial schoolchildren in their neat uniforms playing around the fountain in the center of the square and chirping excitedly like the spring's swallows from Capistrano.

Nie biegaj tak!—Don't run like this!—a Polish mother was admonishing her knee-pants son. A teenage American girl, her blond tresses impeccably arranged, wondered loudly, chatting with her parents, "Are we going to see the pope in the window?" An elderly South American woman pilgrim, enthralled by the majesty of the basilica, kept exclaiming, *Por Dios, que maravilla!* Priests in black cassocks and wide-brimmed hats favored by the Italian clergy and dark-robed nuns darted importantly to and fro.

It was very peaceful, but Tim's memories of the day five years ago surged back in a flood. Having been charged with the task of bringing back the past—the real past—he felt great fear that he would not be up to the assignment, not knowing where to turn, how to begin. And an even greater fear was of disappointing the pope whom he admired as a human being, even though he disagreed with some of his stands. Tim had been introduced to Gregory XVII during a Jesuit group visit to the Vatican—the contact lasted one second—and he knew precious little about the pontiff: only that he was a mystic in the twelfth-century tradition of St. Bernard of Clairvaux and a rigorous intellectual in the highest French Cartesian tradition. Tim therefore saw the logic in Gregory XVII's desire to *understand* the mystery of death as well as to *accept* it and that, consequently, he *needed* to know the truth. As Sainte-Ange had pointed out, he needed it to stay alive.

Urgent thoughts raced through Tim's mind as he left St. Peter's Square, passed the famous Vatican bookstore and the Holy See's pretentious modern *Sala Stampa* press office, and entered Via della Conciliazione. The broad avenue led, west-east, to the Vatican from the Tiber and Castel Sant'Angelo, where a head of the Jesuit order was imprisoned by Pope Clement XIV over 200 years ago. The street was a triumphal gift to Rome from Benito Mussolini, and had required the razing of hundreds of ancient houses. Tim walked slowly toward his office, meditating every step of the way, wondering how he was going to carry out his instructions. It would not be in his nature to admit failure, particularly on a mission for this particular pope.

Gregory XVII had the reputation of being a very exacting man. As the first foreign pope in almost half a millennium, he also was the *tenth* French pontiff in history. It once made France the "First Daughter of the Church," but now an often disobedient one, and the second-largest purveyor of Roman popes after the Italians. Gregory XVII was the first French pope in 607 years, following in this Gallic tradition Pierre Roger de Beaufort, who had taken the name of Gregory XI and reigned for a year from 1370 to 1371. The immediate previous two popes were also Frenchmen, Urban V and Innocent VI. The first French pope was Urban II, né Oddone di Lagery, who ruled for eleven years, between 1088 and 1099, and was famous for proclaiming the First Crusade in 1095, a papal precedent many French would come to curse before very long. Gregory XVII took this name because Gregory the Great, who straddled the sixth and seventh centuries, was his role model. He also wished to honor the previous French Gregory, the eleventh, and his predecessor of this name, Gregory XVI, a pleasant Italian who occupied St. Peter's throne from 1831 to 1846, just before Europe's "Spring of the Peoples." The present pope certainly would not choose to be identified with Gregory IX, the thirteenth-century Bolognese lawyer who endorsed legislation authorizing secular powers to burn convicted heretics at the stake and who instituted the Great Inquisition in 1231. It was another papal precedent that would martyr much of France. Eight centuries later, it was history Gregory XVII could not afford to ignore.

Tim Savage himself had experienced memories and mysteries of death that he could not erase from his mind.

Displayed in the place of honor at his office was the neatly folded Stars and Stripes that had been ceremoniously handed to Tim's mother by an Air Force general after his father had been killed in a fiery crash of his B-25 bomber during World War Two. Tim was two years old at the time, and he already understood death. His father's bomber had been shot down by the Germans over Monte Cassino, the site of the hilltop Benedictine monastery where the Nazis long resisted the Allied advance across Italy. It was one of the most stubborn battles of the war, and the monastery was leveled along with its famous medieval libraries. After he had come to live in Rome, Tim made a pilgrimage to Monte Cassino every year, leaving flowers over ruins that still lay there. He had no idea where exactly his father's body reposed.

Then, very much later, there was the Arab youth, his throat slashed, in a narrow Cairo alley. Tim was twenty-six at the time. And, still later, when he was thirty-two, there was the haunting face of the dead peasant woman, a tiny cross on a chain around her neck, outside her burning hut in that little village in Vietnam. And there had been others whose deaths had been part of his life.

But now that he was a middle-aged Jesuit in Rome, neither feeling nor looking the age that follows youth, Tim remembered that past though he was no longer condemned to live and relive it. His quiet sense of humor had returned. His intelligence was as intense as his penchant toward independent thought, not an uncommon Jesuit trait. He was calm and relaxed most of the time. Courtly and friendly, Tim was likable in the eyes of both men and women. He was, of course, aware of his attraction to women, and, on occasions, he was strongly tempted to reciprocate—even all the way. Prior to his vows of chastity, Tim had enjoyed a reasonably active sex life, in college and then overseas, but it was one-night stands or brief affairs. No romantic involvements or commitments. Anyway that was the past, he kept reminding himself.

On this day, walking to his office from the Apostolic Palace, he was oblivious to his surroundings, overwhelmed as he was by his conversation with Monsignor Sainte-Ange. Via della Conciliazione overflowed with motorized and foot bound humanity, but Tim neither noticed nor heard in his concentration on what lay ahead in his new role. What with all the May religious feasts, uncounted thousands of pilgrims and tourists from every corner of the globe converged every day on the Vatican, like invading armies of yore, to stare at the window of the papal apartment high in the Apostolic Palace on the west side of the piazza where Gregory XVII appeared at noon every Sunday he was in Rome to bless the multitude, and to line up at the massive doors of St. Peter's Basilica, waiting to enter or just to gape. The square itself was little changed since Gianlorenzo Bernini had reshaped it—with the Baroque colonnade and the *Scala Regia*—in the second half of the seventeenth century under the patronage of Pope Alexander VII.

Tour buses with Italian, German, Austrian, French, Spanish, Portuguese, Polish, and other license plates that had brought the faithful and the curious to the holy sites lined both sides of Conciliazione, belching black clouds of diesel exhausts. The engines were kept running to assure that the returning sweat-drenched visitors would find their vehicles perfectly air-conditioned and super-cool. Little yellow taxis, private cars, and the motorcycles and *motorinos* responsible for the permanent high-decibel hum that is Rome's identifying sound streamed down the via toward the square, creating a perpetual traffic jam.

Pilgrims and tourists battled their way along the narrow sidewalks, conversing and shouting in every language of the Tower of Babel, stopping at the shops along the avenue to ogle and buy cheap, plastic, tacky Holy See memorabilia—Our Ladies (of Everywhere), Jesus Christ (on or off the Cross), crosses, rosaries, and framed color photographs of a bemused-looking French pope. They sat down, if they could secure a chair and a table, at the outdoor cafés for an *espresso, cappuccino,* a cold soft drink, a beer, or an ice-cream cone. In Tim's learned opinion, the hole-in-the-wall shop in the traditional Columbus Hotel, the pilgrims' favorite nest, made the best pistachio ice cream in the world.

The whole scene added up to faith and devotion, curiosity and recreation, and a never-ending business bonanza. Foreign currency bank exchange counters—the modern-day money changers in their temples—adorned both sides of Conciliazione. The trivialization and commercialization of religion was absolute. And the Vatican, too, participated in it, selling tickets to the Sistine Chapel and Holy See postage stamps, and charging foreign television crews for filming inside its walls. It was reminiscent of the selling of indulgences once upon a time. Perhaps not surprisingly, the Vatican had been enmeshed earlier in a mind-boggling scandal involving its own bank, along with Italian banks, with one top executive found hanging under a London bridge and other officials, including priests, under a dark cloud.

Tim Savage, feeling the rising heat of the late morning through his black ecclesiastic uniform, followed Conciliazione for two long blocks, then turned left into Via dell'Erba, a narrow street consisting entirely, on its western side, of an ancient *palazzo* that had been turned into a Roman Curia office building. The headquarters and offices of some of the Holy See congregations, pontifical councils and commissions, and other organizations forming the government of the Church under the pope are outside the Vatican proper, spilling out to adjoining avenues and streets, even as far away as the beautifully historic Santa Maria in the Trastevere neighborhood. The State of the Vatican covers only 109 acres, taken up mainly by St. Peter's Basilica and the square, the Apostolic Palace, the Vatican Library, the vast Paul VI Auditorium where the Wednesday General Audiences are now held, the magnificent Vatican gardens, several administrative palaces, a tiny railroad station, and the duty-free shop for Vatican employees, and, quietly, their secular friends.

The building at Via dell'Erba 1 houses the Pontifical Council for Inter-Religious Dialogue, the Pontifical Council for the Promotion of Christian Unity, and the Commission for Religious Relations with Jews. The Commission for Religious Relations with Muslims functions under the Inter-Religious Dialogue Council, both headed by a highly respected Third World cardinal. The Muslim Commission has offices on the ground floor of the Via dell'Erba building, and this was where Father Timothy R. Savage, S.J.—Tim to his friends—has been working for nearly two years as a full-time consultant—*consultore*—in recognition of his expertise in Muslim and Arab religious and political affairs, and his command of spoken and written Arabic, though mostly as spoken in Cairo.

Tim was one of the very few English-speaking priests who were Islam experts—English having only recently replaced French as the scholarly and political language in the Muslim world—and the president of the Muslim Commission had been overjoyed at recruiting him from the Gregorian University to which he had been attached. And now, Tim realized, it was the pope's turn to recruit him. He allowed himself to be pleased—and challenged—by the assignment as the first shock of the meeting with Sainte-Ange began to wear off. But of course Tim would resist the sin of pride, even in his mind.

There was a pleasantly international atmosphere in the Via dell'Erba building and its councils and commissions—something like a Ministry for Foreign Religious Relations—that was unlike the other musty Curial congregations and institutes where mind-dulling Italian Church provincialism still prevailed. Here, people continuously came and went on missions, overt and covert, to and from every continent and nation where the

Vatican had an interest, which meant virtually everywhere. Just before entering the main door, Tim noticed with a touch of wistfulness a young man in jeans leaning against the building wall, one hand around the waist of a pretty young woman, the other holding a cellular phone to his ear and talking away. "I hope it works for you," Tim said silently to the boy.

Inside his office, Tim removed the jacket of the suit, rolling up the black sleeves. For his visit to the Apostolic Palace today he dressed up in full Jesuit attire; he had even pressed the crease in his black trousers. Tim had been summoned only the previous evening when, without any further explanation, the general superior of the Society of Jesus, his top boss, had instructed him by telephone to be at Sainte-Ange's office at ten o'clock the next morning. He further instructed Tim to enter the Vatican through the Bronze Doors, used mainly by pilgrim groups, rather than through the Sant'Anna Gate. "It's less ostentatious that way," the general said.

Tim had met the French monsignor only once, just before Easter, when he accompanied the rector of the Saudi Arabian Islamic Theological University to a private audience with Gregory XVII. Their entire conversation consisted of Sainte-Ange ordering him not to follow the rector into the pope's private study. Escorting Muslim dignitaries, clerics, and scholars who had business at the Vatican of one kind or another was among Tim's duties at the Commission, and when the general called him, he assumed it concerned a similar occasion.

In the morning, as he dressed in his room on the top floor of Villa Malta, the Jesuit residence perched atop steep Via di Porta Pinciana in downtown Rome, Tim's only concern was to be free as soon as possible to go to his office and to get on with his current work—an analysis of the situation in Iran seven years after the Islamic revolution had toppled the shah. The Secretariat of State had ordered it as a top priority in preparing a confidential mission to Teheran. Relations with Muslim countries were very much on Gregory XVII's mind, especially after the Iranian upheaval that had followed his election to the papacy in 1978 by a few months. As a Frenchman and long archbishop of Marseille, he was familiar with Muslim North Africa and its religious and political problems, and now he was absorbed by the situation in the Middle East and along the Persian Gulf. The papal desire to be fully informed on these matters had kept Tim busy ever since he joined the staff of the Commission for Relations with Muslims two years earlier, the only American there.

Normally, Tim took the bus from Via del Tritone to Via dell'Erba. But today he decided to travel in style to the Apostolic Palace—in a taxi—even if it took a bit longer in the suffocating Rome morning traffic and cost more.

"*Buon giorno, Padre,*" the smiling driver greeted him after Tim asked to be taken to St. Peter's Square. "Are you on your way to see the Holy Father?" Returning the smile, Tim said, "Yes, of course . . . I see him every day!" Both men laughed happily.

BOOK TWO

Timothy

Chapter Three

1942

FOR A CHILD of a traditional, middle-class American Catholic family, a personal visit to the "Holy Father"—or, at least, to the power center of the church that commands one billion faithful—was an amazing occurrence. Tim Savage was keenly aware of it as he had walked past the black-and-orange–clad Swiss Guards at the bottom of the Bronze Doors on his way to see Monsignor Sainte-Ange. He felt the frisson of adventure.

Tim was the youngest of three Savage children. His sister Julia was a Foreign Service officer who had attained the rank of ambassador of the United States and now served as envoy to Brazil. The middle child was Anthony, who had graduated from the Harvard Law School and was a partner in a well-connected Washington law firm, specializing in powerful foreign clients, ranging from multimillionaire Palestinian contractors living royally in London to Asian finance ministries. The family of Captain James W. Savage, killed in combat over Italy, had done superbly.

Tim Savage was born in Washington at the end of the first full year of America's entry into World War Two, a year after Pearl Harbor. His father had come back on short home leave just before Tim had turned two years old: he saw his youngest only that one time before dying. Tim, of course, had no recollection of it. Two years after the end of the war, Tim's mother married Jim Stella, an Air Force officer who had been Captain Savage's best friend. Highly decorated for service in World War Two and Korea, he had retired as brigadier general by the time Tim entered the priesthood.

With Stella as his stepfather and his devout mother, Tim's childhood and adolescence, like Julia's and Anthony's, were years of strict, traditional Catholic upbringing. He attended a parochial school a few blocks away from the family home, a rambling old house off Reservoir Road below Georgetown, near the Potomac, which had belonged to his mother's wealthy parents. Next, Tim went to the Jesuits' fashionable Gonzaga College High School on "I" Street in the Northwest. That was the period of the "Catholic Ghetto" in Washington, as it was called, but Gonzaga catered to the capital's Catholic elite.

And for Tim's family it was Mass every Sunday, confession at least once a month at the Holy Trinity Church in Georgetown, their church for decades, and the observance of all the religious feasts: Ascension and Corpus Christi, not just Christmas and Easter. His elementary education, before the parochial school, had been at the Holy Trinity Grade School.

Graduating from Gonzaga with both athletic and scholastic honors, Tim entered Georgetown University. It had always been assumed in the family that he would apply—and be accepted—at the great Jesuit University in Washington, just as Julia and Anthony had done. At first, Tim was not entirely certain about his major though he knew that his inclination ran toward humanities, not sciences. He had selected ethics as an elective course—it attracted him intellectually, and it addressed the ancient Catholic concern, back to Aristotle and St. Thomas Aquinas, with concepts of good and evil. As luck would have it, it brought him into the classroom of Father Hugh Morgan. That opened wide horizons for Tim—and the fascination with Islam would follow, Father Morgan being an Islamic scholar as well as an ethicist.

The early sixties were a bracing, exhilarating time in Washington. Young John F. Kennedy, the first Catholic to be an American president, had launched the "New Frontier," and the nation's new generations were swept up in a wave of idealism. The new president promised peace, racial equality, and, among other ambitious initiatives, launched the Peace Corps, the most exciting expression of youthful American idealism in a rapidly changing world. That the Bay of Pigs invasion of Cuba, organized by the Central Intelligence Agency, had failed and Kennedy had dispatched the first military "advisers" to Vietnam were tiny clouds over the "New Frontier" and its euphoria.

It seemed to be a time of universal renewal. In one of their increasingly frequent chats, Father Hugh called Tim's attention to Vatican Council II, which Pope John XXIII had just inaugurated in Rome. John XXIII and John Kennedy were the world's most popular and attractive leaders.

"The idea is to streamline and modernize the Church," the priest had told Tim. "This is the first great Council in nearly a century—since 1870—and I'll bet you that the Catholic Church will never be the same again. Nor will the papacy. It was heroic on the part of the Council, for example, to replace the Latin Mass with Mass in the vernacular . . . So I think that the renewed Church will be in dire need of brilliant young priests, superbly educated, to carry out the decisions of the Vatican Council . . . And, you know, we in the Church need idealism, too. There will be powerful forces, even within the Church, fighting us and there will be great battles . . ."

Father Morgan had refrained from direct suggestions that Tim turn toward priesthood; they had an unspoken agreement not to return to the subject after Savage had declined the original hint to make the Church his life. Nevertheless Tim was very much interested in the Vatican Council as a significant event in history, and Morgan supplied him with a steady flow of information and documents over the Council's duration—a period parallel with Tim's Georgetown undergraduate studies. In his senior year, Tim had added a course in Church history to his curriculum.

One afternoon, a few weeks before graduation, when the Georgetown campus was a sea of azaleas, tulips, and dogwood, Tim was invited to tea by the dean of the School of Foreign Service to which he had applied for postgraduate studies. His sister Julia, then just starting up the hierarchy of her spectacular State Department career, had been pushing him in that direction. Entering the dean's office, Tim was introduced to a middle-aged man in horn-rimmed glasses, expensively casual gray slacks, a tweed jacket, white shirt, and rep tie. He wore it like a uniform.

"This is Mr. Billington from the Central Intelligence Agency," the dean said. "He asked to meet you."

Tim nodded, mystified. He had never encountered anyone from the CIA. But Billington wasted no time on small talk.

"The CIA is actively recruiting employees, a lot of them on the best campuses in the country," he briskly informed Tim. "Your name came to our attention as a promising prospect, and the Dean here was kind enough to arrange for us to meet. I hope I can interest you in a CIA career. You know, as the President said, it's 'what you can do for your country.' "

Tim had heard vaguely that while the Federal Bureau of Investigation was partial to Catholics, the CIA preferred White Anglo-Saxon Protestants and Ivy Leaguers, like those who had created the Agency from the wartime Office of Strategic Services veterans.

"But I'm a Catholic, you know," Tim said, instantly regretting it as a sophomoric remark. Billington laughed expansively, filling his pipe.

"That wouldn't surprise me at Georgetown," he replied. "That's why I'm here. You won't believe how many of your fellow students we've been able to hire here. All first-rate. Actually, I'm glad you mentioned religion. The Agency is very shorthanded on Islamic and Middle East specialists; we've been concentrating heavily on Europe, Asia, and Latin America. What we have in mind is to turn you into a Mideast expert, if it's okay with you. I am aware of your interest in the subject and I understand that you have applied to the Foreign Service School here. But I can assure you that the Agency will look very well after your education. I'm sure the Dean will agree . . ."

As Tim thought about it afterward, the idea appealed to him. He was to call Billington with an answer within a week at a special number he was given. The CIA seemed to be offering him the best of all worlds: advanced education, service to his country at this time of idealism, and a lifetime career surely full of exciting action. The Bay of Pigs fiasco notwithstanding, the CIA was still regarded with a touch of awe as a glamorous, mysterious elite service. The next day, Tim consulted Father Hugh Morgan, trusting his Jesuitic discretion. Billington had asked him not to discuss the CIA job offer with anyone except his parents and the closest of friends, if absolutely necessary to help him make up his mind.

"I'm all for it," Morgan told him, all smiles. "You know, intelligence work is what we Jesuits used to do best for centuries. Maybe we still do. Who knows . . . So I'm glad you're joining the

CIA though you wouldn't join the Society of Jesus. I guess it's the next best choice."

General Stella, his stepfather, naturally was delighted. That evening he opened a bottle of champagne.

"Let's celebrate—you, your mother, your brother, and me!" he exclaimed happily. "To your service to your country and to the future ace of the CIA!"

Tim spent two months at the CIA's Langley headquarters in Virginia, just outside Washington, learning the basics of the craft of intelligence·at the Training Division. He was assigned briefly to the Directorate of Plans—the clandestine, or "black," side of the agency that ran its worldwide covert operations. He had meetings with Directorate of Intelligence analysts who specialized in the Middle East, most of whom held doctorates from top universities, acquiring a general knowledge of the current political situation in the region. Next, Tim was shipped out to The Farm way south in Virginia to undergo the exceedingly tough training—physical, mental and psychological, and paramilitary—for future "case officers." The Agency never refers to them as "agents," a designation reserved for foreigners working secretly for the CIA abroad.

Late that autumn, Tim was summoned to a meeting with the chief of the Middle East Division in the Directorate of Plans.

"Well, it's time for you to go back to school," he was told. "I'm really hurting for good case officers in the Middle East, and you are being sent back to Georgetown, which, we think, has the best program in this field. You don't need a cover: you are simply working on your advanced degree at your alma mater. And I don't need to see you until you have your doctorate in hand. Naturally, we pay your tuition and expenses and you stay on the payroll. We're investing seriously in you . . ."

At Georgetown, Tim enrolled in the Faculty of Arabic Language Literature and Linguistics and at the Center for Muslim-Christian Understanding at the School of Foreign Service, which took him exactly where he had hoped to go in the first place. And, once again, he came across Father Morgan, this time in his incarnation as Islam scholar and teacher. Working seven days a week, Tim earned his master's degree in Middle East History late the following spring. Within six months, studying all summer with Morgan's careful guidance and without a free moment for himself, he gained his doctorate in Islamic Studies in record time. The CIA was pushing him to be ready for field duty as rapidly as possible; the Six Day War between Israel and Arab states had just been fought, and the U.S. government was hungry for fresh intelligence. Tim became astonishingly fluent in Arabic during the short time at his disposal. He was on the verge of collapse from exhaustion by the time he was awarded his Ph.D., the youngest in Georgetown history. He was twenty-six. People in the know said, "What a fantastic career young Savage is making!"

In mid-January, 1969, Tim was ordered by the chief of the Middle East Division to leave immediately for Cairo, where he would join the CIA Station. It was the largest CIA outpost in the world, responsible not only for operations in Egypt, but across the entire sweep of Islam in Africa and the Middle East, from Mauritania on the Atlantic in the west to Syria and Iraq in the east, and including Jordan, Saudi Arabia, and the Arab Emirates on the Persian Gulf. Non-Arabic Iran was a separate CIA jurisdiction. But the Cairo Station was, in effect, a regional CIA command, and its chief held more real political power than all the American ambassadors in the area put together, whether they realized it or not. CIA operatives were also active in the Israeli-occupied territories of the West Bank of the Jordan River and in the Gaza Strip on the Mediterranean to keep an eye on Palestinian militants.

Well over one hundred case officers were assigned to the Cairo Station. Some had diplomatic cover at the American Embassy, as the Station Chief did—and the Egyptians, of course, were aware of his real identity. Those with deep cover were spread all over Egypt and the region as businessmen, engineers, technicians, consultants, professors, and even journalists. Only the Station Chief knew their identities. The Station's section, concentrating both on the analysis of Islamic affairs and covert operations ordered by Langley or conceived by the Station Chief, was located in an office building housing the mission of the Agency for International Development and located two blocks away from the old Shephard's Hotel on the Nile. The AID mission in Egypt, as in many other countries, provided cover for "black" CIA operatives. Tim was officially listed as an AID mission member.

He threw himself into his work with boundless enthusiasm. He studied Arabic language newspapers, magazines, and periodicals for clues in changes in the patterns of behavior of Islamic groups, including the nascent radical movement beginning to turn to terrorism. Then Tim began to establish personal contacts with Islamic scholars. His AID cover rendered his interests perfectly legitimate: the mission funded and supported cultural and educational projects while infiltrating the intellectual and scholarly community.

Soon, Tim developed friendly relations with several professors of theology at Cairo's Al-Azhar University, the oldest university in the world and still the most important in Islam. The professors were impressed with Tim's fluency in Arabic, his understanding of Islam and its *sharia* laws, and, above all, with his sincere interest in the subject. Except for a few American theologians, they had never met an American, and such a young one, who was so much at home with their religion and culture. Tim loved every moment of it. The only disturbing event in which he was peripherally involved related to "termination with extreme prejudice," in CIA parlance, of a young Arab informer who turned out to be a double agent for Syrian intelligence and may have compromised some of the Station's far-flung activities. Tim had occasionally used him as a source, and was informed of his "termination" in a dark alley—with very gory details.

Tim Savage's love affair with Islam scholars and Egyptian intellectuals came to an abrupt end in less than a year. On Thanksgiving Day, 1969, the Cairo Station Chief informed him that the Agency had ordered his transfer to Vietnam in the shortest possible time—ASAP in bureaucratic jargon. Tim was indignant.

"But what about my training in Arabic and Middle East affairs?" he asked, his voice rising. "The Agency has invested a fortune in my education. And what about my contacts here? Haven't I done well? This is absurd! Aren't you going to protest?"

"No," the Station Chief replied quietly. "No, I am not. It is 'not ours to reason why' . . ."

Chapter Four

1969

SAIGON WAS DRENCHED after three days of monsoon-like down-pour when Tim Savage landed on a Sunday in December at fog-bound Tan Son Thut Airport. In Vietnam, pilots landed and took off virtually regardless of weather, sometimes with spectacularly catastrophic results, sometimes smoothly. Tim crossed himself when the huge Air Force C-141 troop carrier came to a stop at the military terminal.

He was met at the foot of the ramp by a tall, thin American in a yellow slicker over a Hawaiian sports shirt and slacks who said, "Savage? Follow me," and did not utter another word until the unmarked car, awaiting them a hundred yards away and driven by another silent American, had reached a three-story building in downtown Saigon. His escort led Tim inside and up the stairs to the top floor where he left him at the door to a large, carpeted office, with air-conditioning units humming below the windows.

A thin-lipped, unsmiling man who appeared to be in his fifties and wore a suit and tie, rose from behind his desk and extended his hand to Tim.

"I am Roger Stephens," he announced. "Welcome to Vietnam. You will be working directly for me in CORDS, attached to a special pacification unit."

Tim had heard back at the CIA in Langley that Stephens, something of a legendary figure in the Agency, had served as Saigon Station Chief in the first years of the war in Vietnam, Stephens regarded himself as the greatest American authority on Vietnam, tolerating no disagreements with his views, even from the Director of Central Intelligence, his nominal boss, who usually deferred to him. An ardent Roman Catholic from Boston, Stephens felt deep affinity with South Vietnamese Catholics, starting with the president and his top generals, in their battle against the ungodly communists from the North and their southern Viet Cong minions. Buddhists had no say at all in Saigon, though they were the religious majority in the country, and their saffron-robed monks gained fame for burning themselves alive in protest against their dictatorial, American-backed government.

Now, as Tim learned, Stephens had the sonorous title of Deputy Commander for Pacification, COMUSMACV, and the personal rank of ambassador in the immense, convoluted American military-intelligence-civilian bureaucracy that was running the war from Saigon. COMUSMACV stood for United States Military Assistance Command, Vietnam, to keep alive President Kennedy's original fiction about "advisers" and "assistance" because America had never actually declared war on anybody in Vietnam. The Command, MAC-V for short, was commonly known as "Pentagon East" and its commander-in-chief was a four-star Army general from Washington who had never grasped the nature of the challenge he faced, including the question of what made the Viet Cong fight so stubbornly in the first place. MAC-V was ostensibly a dependency of the American Embassy in Saigon, as was the huge, powerful, and totally independent CIA Station there.

The fourth pillar of the American establishment in Vietnam was CORDS, linked with the military Command, the Embassy, and the CIA, and this was Roger Stephens' fief for which Tim Savage was being recruited. CORDS stood for Civil Operations and Revolutionary Development Support—all parties in Third World internal conflicts claimed the fashionable "Revolutionary" label for themselves. Technically, CORDS answered to the MAC-V Command, but Stephens enjoyed nearly complete autonomy. CORDS' official "cover" was economic development and, indeed, it ran a number of civilian programs, employing AID personnel.

The heart of CORDS, however, were Stephens' intelligence and elite "search and destroy" operations under his Pacification Program. Though using AID officials and American military officers as cover, the massive CORDS structure was dominated by senior CIA officers and staffed in the field by junior Agency officers. For all practical purposes, Stephens had the run of the Saigon CIA Station, its chief unquestioningly making his resources available to him. The military likewise were at Stephens' disposal in providing Special Forces and Army Rangers for his operations.

Central in his clandestine enterprises was Stephens' brainchild, christened by him "Operation Phoenix" and designed as the principal American counterinsurgency weapon. And it was to Operation Phoenix that Tim Savage was assigned the moment he reached Saigon. Because the Vietnam War continued to go from bad to worse day after day—nine years after President Kennedy had dispatched the first American soldiers as "advisers" and started the buildup that finally reached a half-million troops—Stephens and his lieutenants conceived Operation Phoenix as a means of undermining the enemy. It was to complement the American war-fighting campaign that, at its peak, engaged hundreds of thousands of troops, tanks, heavy artillery, jet bombers and fighters, gunship helicopters, mountains of bombs, and rivers of napalm in support of the utterly incompetent and corrupt South Vietnamese Army.

Stephens was convinced that the communists would be defeated, the war won and Vietnam "pacified" only when Viet Cong guerrillas in the south—formally known to Americans as Viet Cong Infrastructure (VCI)—were liquidated. Their leaders and fighters, Stephens believed, had to be identified, captured, interrogated, and "terminated" in the villages where they ostensibly lived as peaceful and defenseless peasants, but, in reality, plotted and planned their guerrilla war, expanded their vital communications even as they tilled their soggy land, and turned into murderous nocturnal insurgents.

Vietnamese villages were theoretically controlled by South Vietnamese and American forces: "theoretically" because they were controlled in daytime, becoming Viet Cong country after dark. In Stephens' opinion, this disastrous reality could be reversed only by the operation he had named Phoenix after Phung Hoang, a huge bird that, in Vietnamese lore, could fly everywhere, anytime. To him, Phoenix was a quintessential CIA undertaking, and he would not trust anyone else with it.

This was why Stephens demanded that the Agency in Langley—and, through his Washington friends, the White House itself—

expand the CIA contingent in Vietnam with as many promising young officers as possible. And this was precisely why Tim Savage had found himself in Saigon the week before Christmas.

The formal designation of Phoenix was Provincial Reconnaissance Units (PRU), another euphemism intended to make the Pacification Program appear constructive and benign. But, as much as anything else, Phoenix teams—usually ten men—were assassination squads, pure and simple. Tim realized it as he listened to Stephens explain Phoenix in the course of a briefing in a spacious, air-conditioned CORDS conference room for CIA officers newly attached to the operation.

"What we have to do is smash the Viet Cong infrastructure, no more and no less," Stephens had said in his oddly squeaky voice, addressing his audience from a podium in front of a huge map of Vietnam divided into military and CORDS regions, provinces, districts, and grids that showed the areas of Phoenix activities.

A short, balding, bamboo-thin man with sharp features, Stephens was more at ease when he was looking down on the officers. He was very high strung, and eye contact made him nervous. He avoided it whenever he could, sometimes brusquely removing his rimless glasses as if to spare his pale blue eyes the experience of facing another human being.

"And it isn't really all that complicated," Stephens had gone on. "We locate the cadres, interrogate them about their networks, neutralize them, and before long we finally break Charlie's backbone. It should have been done this way years ago, instead of wasting time and resources on those Strategic Hamlets and the vast search-and-destroy Army missions and misleading body counts."

Stephens had stressed that his overall pacification concept included "resettlement villages" where peasant families, not suspected of enemy contacts, were transferred after their homes in clearly identified Viet Cong territory had been burned down by Phoenix teams or regular American or South Vietnamese army units to "eliminate centers of infection and contagion and teach them a lesson," as he put it. Stephens recognized that *all* peasant families were not Viet Cong operatives. He had paused, then added:

"Among your responsibilities, gentlemen, is to identify enemy villages and erase them, if necessary, after you have dealt with the cadres and the leaders—preferably terminating them. And I don't have to remind you that everything related to Phoenix is grave-yard. Never a word to anyone outside the operation. We don't need a My Lai kind of publicity in our line of work . . ."

What Stephens had told them that day made sense to Tim Savage. Son of a wartime hero, a practicing Catholic from childhood and a dedicated CIA officer, Tim believed in the righteousness of the anticommunist struggle in Vietnam and the American engagement on the side of Saigon. After all, it was JFK, the man he so greatly admired, who had first decided to involve the United States in Indochina. In Tim's mind, it fitted into the idealism of his generation.

Tim understood, of course, that people died in wars and that supreme cruelty was part of war. He belonged to a political and religious culture that accepted these realities, morally and ethically, if a war was a "just cause" and thereby a "just war" in the ancient Christian sense. And there was no question in his mind at that point that this certainly was the case in Vietnam. America was in the middle of the Cold War, communist expansion had to be checked at all costs, and the long-suffering Vietnamese given a chance at freedom, independence, and democracy. This was the American tradition and the American way. And Tim agreed with Stephens that the Viet Cong infrastructure had to be eradicated if the insurgency were to be stamped out. There was no other way and, Tim thought, Phoenix was the natural instrument. He had no qualms about the mission. Notions like "neutralizing" Viet Cong cadres were abstractions in his mind as he listened to Stephens that first morning on his new job.

Consequently when he was given his Phoenix marching orders, Tim did not see himself as a prospective assassin. The word did not even enter his consciousness. He was not senior enough in the CIA to be familiar with the Agency's own secret culture of polit-ical assassinations that went back to the Fifties, right after its cre-ation under President Truman's National Security Act. Perhaps astonishingly, the CIA's founding fathers—the cultivated, wealthy,

God-fearing men from the Eastern seaboard elite—had no moral qualms about such assassinations as a weapon in furthering what they perceived as the goals and interests of the foreign policy of the United States. To them, it was not even a question of "just causes," but of pure pragmatism and effectiveness. Planning and ordering political murders fitted smoothly into the romantic knighthood aura surrounding CIA covert operations. Covert operators saw themselves as a noble and heroic brotherhood, their excitement often heightened by the extreme secrecy surrounding the tasks of "terminations with extreme prejudice."

As Tim Savage would learn in time, this mindset had been reflected in the CIA's role in Guatemala in 1954 in overthrowing the elected president, a leftist named Jacobo Arbenz Guzmán, who had instituted land reform policies and was believed to be developing close ties with communism and Moscow. As it happened, the United Fruit Company, powerful in Central America and splendidly connected in Washington, was the principal target of land reform nationalizations. Rapidly, the CIA put together a Guatemalan paramilitary force to oust Arbenz while its Technical Services Division developed detailed assassination guidelines. They were embodied in an assassination training manual that stressed that "the specific technique employed will depend upon a large number of variables, but should be constant in one point: death must be absolutely certain." The instructions added helpfully that "absolute reliability is obtained by severing the spinal cord in the cervical region." In the end, no assassinations were required in Guatemala—Arbenz collapsed quickly—but the CIA remained faithful to this policy-making option. Tim Savage came upon a copy of the training manual in the small library at CORDS Saigon headquarters, but lacking the background of CIA operations, he was not particularly impressed or disturbed by it.

He did not realize, for example, that in the early Sixties, the CIA had virtually taken over all the decision making in the Congo, which had just been granted its independence by Belgium, with Patrice Lumumba, a young leftist who had attended Moscow's "Friendship University," becoming its first leader. Washington therefore feared communist influence in the Congo—in addition to the fact that the huge African country was exceedingly rich in uranium, the nuclear bomb raw material, plus cobalt, copper, gold, and diamonds. Lumumba immediately appeared on the CIA assassination list and was soon terminated by an unknown shooter.

Still in the Sixties, Fidel Castro, too, made that list. In the case of Cuba, American national security—"Ninety Miles from Home"—as well as the interests of great American corporations whose properties were being nationalized by the victorious revolutionaries, and those of organized crime syndicates owning Havana casinos, happened to converge. This brought the CIA's Technical Services Division and Mafia murder specialists together in shaping surrealistic scenarios for doing away with Castro. They all failed.

Not surprisingly, asassination as a political and counterinsurgency tool was adopted by the CIA in Vietnam and refined by Roger Stephens. By the time Tim Savage reached Vietnam, Stephens' Phoenix had been operating for years. He fully grasped its significance when he took up his assignment in the Mekong Delta.

Chapter Five

TIM SAVAGE'S ASSIGNMENT was Can Tho, the capital of Phong Dinh Province in the southern Delta, which served as the headquarters of the Pacification Program for all of the Mekong Delta, well south of Saigon. The Delta formed part of IV Corps—South Vietnam having been divided into four military Corps regions—and Can Tho was the home of CORDS IV, which, among other responsibilities, coordinated Phoenix operations in that section of the country. The command of the South Vietnamese Army's IV Corps forces was also located in Can Tho along with the command of its Twenty-first Infantry Division, probably one of the most useless in the whole war.

A Blackhawk gunship helicopter had transported Tim from Newport heliport on Saigon River in downtown Saigon to Can Tho on a misty morning early in January of 1970. He traveled in the company of two other junior CIA officers seconded to Phoenix and Jake Kurtski, the IV Corps CORDS chief, who was returning to his base after several days of intensive "Pentagon East" consultations with Stephens and senior American military commanders. Kurtski was Tim's immediate boss.

Kurtski was a completely bald, short, solidly built man with a thick neck, a perpetually red face, and strangely green slits of eyes—he was always chomping on a dead cigar. Born in Poland, he had come to the United States at the age of twenty-three in 1947, from a Displaced Persons camp in Germany. His sponsor was a colonel in Army Intelligence who had been impressed by the young man's toughness and talent for manipulation, and had him attached to his personal staff as a local hire. During the war, Kurtski had belonged to the anti-German armed underground in Poland—the Home Army—but had fled west ahead of the advancing Soviets. He hated the Godless communists. In America, Kurt-ski had spent a year or so working as a civilian with an Intelligence unit at Fort Benning, Georgia, before being co-opted by the infant CIA.

The Agency was eager for truly tough officers, especially if they had wartime experience and spoke foreign languages; Kurtski was an ideal candidate, fluent in Polish, Russian, German, and French. DP camps were superb do-it-yourself language schools, what with fellow refugees of a dozen nationalities. At the CIA, Kurtski soon discovered that his superiors were quite partial to Europeans, par-ticularly Eastern Europeans and Germans, and prospered rapidly in his new environment. His underground know-how was another plus. Assigned to the "black" Directorate of Plans, Kurtski was sent back to Europe to help deploy CIA networks across the continent, working out of stations in Vienna, Bonn, Berlin, and Helsinki.

When President Kennedy resolved to involve the United States in Vietnam, Kurtski was among the first senior CIA case officers to be sent to Saigon. He was not familiar with Southeast Asia, but his bosses—notably Station Chief Roger Stephens—found him to be an adaptable quick study. Kurtski's only request was to be allowed to remain indefinitely in Vietnam: in his mind, it was the greatest challenge of his career, a real war instead of the indecisive Cold War. He was determined to help make America victorious there— in gratitude to his adopted country.

Kurtski rapidly learned enough Vietnamese to deal with native friend or foe and mastered guerrilla war concepts faster than his American chiefs, who still were trying to comprehend what national insurgencies were all about. When the time came, Kurtski was on hand to help Stephens give birth to Operation Phoenix. He was a bachelor, a loner, had no friends other than Stephens, and was genuinely disliked and feared by his CIA colleagues, which suited him just fine. He went on solitary drinking binges—bourbon— once a week. He had a violent temperament. He had killed people without hesitation or remorse.

At Newport heliport, Kurtski barked at Tim, the first time he had addressed him, with a Polish-accented sentence: "You better get your act together right away or Charlie will have your *focking* head." He repeated it for the benefit of the two other case officers.

Kurtski carried a .45-caliber Colt pistol under his flowing Hawaiian sports shirt, the CIA's sartorial trademark hot weather civilian attire. Most CIA officers in the field despised Army fatigues, and the Vietnamese working with or near Americans could usually spot the "spooks" by their taste in dress. Tim, who had brought colorful sports shirts from Cairo, this morning wore his best flowered product of Egyptian bottom-of-the-line designers to be in tune with the Agency's idea of a uniform. He had been issued a sidearm, but the Blackhawk's crew chief handed him an M-16 automatic rifle as Tim climbed aboard the chopper.

"You never know," the boyish-looking crew chief remarked casually. "The bastards like to take potshots at us. Or we could crash . . ."

Presently, the rotors came alive, the helicopter shuddered on the pad, bolted forward like a thoroughbred out of the gate, and the crew chief installed himself comfortably behind a swiveling heavy machine gun at one of the open sliding side doors.

Leaving Newport behind, the Blackhawk climbed to three thousand feet through the morning haze, the pilots setting it on a southwestern heading. The crew chief explained to his passengers over the intercom that helicopter pilots preferred to fly above the range of light arms' fire from the ground.

"Why, just the other day a pilot lost his balls when a bullet hit the chopper's undercarriage, penetrated the craft and hit the guy in the scrotum," the chief shouted into his mike, sounding vaguely amused. Tim gently fingered through the fabric of his sports shirt the silver St. Christopher medallion on a thin chain around his neck. The relic, personally blessed by Pope Pius XII, had been given to him by his mother on her return from a group audience at the Vatican shortly after the war. She assured Tim that St. Christopher would keep him safe no matter where he went.

With the morning's rising sun on the Blackhawk's portside and its oblique rays coloring the countryside pink and red—the haze had dissipated—Tim could discern the features of the landscape below. First came the western slice of the Plain of Reeds, a badly burned-out fire zone. Then, immediately past the provincial capital of My Tho, there was the silent immensity of the Mekong

Delta. The mighty Mekong River, born in the Tibetan highlands and known to the Vietnamese as Me Nam Kong, actually becomes two separate rivers as it splits just below the Cambodian border into the Tien Giang, forming the northern boundary of the delta, and the Hau Giang, the southern divide. Between the two rivers lies the Delta proper, an oblong stretch of land blessed by the most extraordinary fertility due to the annual overflow of the Tien Giang and the Hau Giang that empty themselves into the South China Sea.

Even before crossing the Tien Giang, Tim could see the green waterlogged rice paddies to the north of the swollen river and the tiny black shapes of water buffaloes already at work under their wooden yokes. Sunbeams lit the wet surface of the paddies like giant windowpanes. Tim knew that the Delta had two elements in great abundance: rice and the Viet Cong. Its Vinh Long and Vinh Binh provinces were the granary of South Vietnam, which might have starved without the delta rice. But this rice also sustained the Viet Cong and therefore the whole guerrilla war in the strategic region of IV Corps.

Tim also was aware of how precarious was the overall Vietnam situation, apart from the Delta problem. Two years earlier, the Viet Cong fighters had smashed their way into Saigon in a desperate gamble that crowned their Tet Offensive. Repulsed and mauled by the overwhelming firepower of the Americans and the ARVN, they quickly rebuilt their cadres, never yielding the control of the Mekong Delta. CIA battlefield maps Tim had studied in Saigon indicated that the guerrillas had new bases in the western delta, linking them with Cambodian sanctuaries where arms and supplies were moving down the Ho Chi Minh Trail from North Vietnam and from the Cambodian port of Sihanoukville along the Sihanouk Trail.

The phantom Viet Cong underground headquarters—the famous COSVN, an American acronym for Central Office for South Vietnam—were believed to be located somewhere west or northwest of the delta, but they could never be pinpointed by Intelligence. Roger Stephens insisted that COSVN was the grand prize for his Phoenix teams to snatch or, at least, help locate through interrogations of captured Viet Cong commanders.

"I don't care what it takes or how many Charlie you've got to kill," he had told his new Phoenix officers. "I must have COSVN . . ."

The Blackhawk had traversed the delta in less than a half hour and crossed Hau Giang. This was the southern Delta, the Viet Cong–infested Phong Dinh and Ba Xuyen provinces. The helicopter banked sharply to the right and dropped down on a concrete landing pad.

"This is the end of the line—Can Tho," the pilot announced over the intercom. "Please disembark. I've got to refuel and head the hell back."

Squatting on the southern bank of Hau Giang, Can Tho was a beehive of activity. Jumping out of the Blackhawk, Tim saw six or seven other helicopters in the landing area, among them two heavy-lift Chinooks, in various stages of unloading supplies and refueling. Helmeted South Vietnamese soldiers drove trucks in and out of the perimeter, watched by bored G.I.'s, beer bottles in hand, in Jeeps parked alongside. Down a rutted highway, beyond the landing zone, Tim could see clusters of houses, smoke curling lazily over the roofs. Mosquitoes buzzed contentedly. Well, Tim thought, this is my new home.

More precisely, his home in Can Tho was a comfortable room in a two-story house in the barbed wire fence–protected CORDS compound on the western outskirts of the town. It was assigned to him by Jake Kurtski, who occupied a nearby spacious villa belonging to a wealthy South Vietnamese landlord who had fled to Saigon when the Viet Cong began to assert themselves in the Delta. For company, Kurtski had two black-and-tan rottweilers and, in daytime, two Vietnamese women servants. The women's every movement was watched by armed CIA guards to assure that they did not try to poison Kurtski or otherwise kill him. Charlie often used women as underground operatives. Besides, Kurtski was convinced that the maids would steal from his stash of Jack Daniel's Black Sour Mash bottles. At night, Kurtski's home was guarded by a heavily armed CIA squad and all the approaches were bathed in floodlights.

No such security measures protected the house where Tim had

been billeted. His landlord, so to speak, was Joseph Ryan, a civilian AID official who served as Kurtski's deputy. Two other CIA Phoenix officers also had rooms at Ryan's home, which was the nearest thing to an American boardinghouse in Vietnam. The men took their meals there between field missions and had access to the living room and its television set that easily picked up the powerful signal of Saigon's Armed Forces broadcasting station relayed south by microwave towers. Presiding over the household was Ryan's wife, Sonia, the only American dependent in Can Tho.

Can Tho was a reasonably desirable location, certainly for American military and CIA officers and CORDS personnel. Overall, it was protected from frontal attacks by a U.S. Army Rangers detachment, the South Vietnamese troops and gunship helicopters stationed there—and jet air support could be called in on a moment's notice. Among Americans in the Delta, Can Tho was famous as "Palm Springs" because the CORDS compound featured a swimming pool and a well-stocked officers' club. Americans at war, as Tim was learning in Can Tho, have a talent and penchant for escapism verging on the surreal. The first time he went to the cabana-fringed swimming pool, he joined fellow officers splashing about in bathing suits, their M-16s and their sidearms in holsters on the concrete deck within easy reach.

"Hey, isn't this a neat place for planning Pacification?" a deeply tanned Rangers captain clutching a beer bottle shouted to Tim. "Man, this is the life—if we live long enough!"

The Rangers' primary assignment in Can Tho was participation in Phoenix teams. Tim had met all the Phoenix officers—CIA and Rangers—the day he reached the delta headquarters at a meeting chaired by Jake Kurtski. Chewing on his unlit cigar between deep drafts of gin and tonic—his noontime drink—Kurtski encouraged the new arrivals to enjoy "all the joys of our Palm Springs."

Squinting and winking obscenely, he told the men: "You better listen to me! Drink, swim, and get laid while you can—and there's plenty of native pussy here—and some not so native. You might as well face the fact that Phoenix has a hell of a high casualty rate. When the cocksuckers catch us, they kill us—just as we kill them. Just bear it in mind . . ."

Tim kept Kurtski's advice very much in mind around the Ryan household. In fact, the thought had occurred to him the instant he set foot at the house and saw Sonia Ryan. She was a pretty and remarkably well-sculpted woman in her late twenties, her olive hue, liquid brown eyes, and high cheekbones revealing her Latin, perhaps Aztec, ancestry. Sonia moved with perfectly natural sensuality, and Tim's first reaction was that Joe Ryan, who must have been twenty or more years her senior, had to have been out of his mind to bring her to Can Tho to live among exceedingly horny men who never knew whether they would be alive the next day. Ryan was away a lot on inspection trips to the "Resettlement Villages," one of his principal projects, often gone for several days at a time, and there was no lack of opportunities for infidelity, if Sonia so desired.

As it happened, she did, wasting no time. Ryan having left on an inspection tour the third morning after Tim had moved into the house, Sonia appeared in his room just after midnight, her hair down and a flimsy peignoir over her naked body. She slid into bed next to Tim, kissed him deeply in the mouth, and whispered, "I want you to fuck me . . ." It was all over in ten minutes. Sonia planted a kiss on his cheek, patted him on the head, and was gone without a word.

Tim felt somewhat amused and pleasantly violated; it had not been very romantic, but what the hell! He had had sexual experiences, good ones, bad ones, and indifferent ones, starting with his Georgetown college days and continuing happily, if more discreetly, after he had joined the CIA. The Agency had no interest in the heterosexual life of its officers so long as it did not endanger national security. Not obsessed by sex, Tim had always been the initiator—the aggressor—because it came naturally to him, and Sonia's wholly utilitarian approach was an innovation. Sonia performed her brief pilgrimages to Tim's room whenever Ryan was away, and their sex life acquired the relatively satisfying regularity of evening meals. Her orgasms came with the precision of Swiss watchworks, lasting exactly ten seconds. She performed oral sex on Sunday afternoons. As Kurtski had pointed out, Can Tho did offer its own brand of joy.

Chapter Six

TIM SAVAGE HAD SPENT the first month in Can Tho organizing and training his Phoenix team, studying the intelligence traffic and trying to familiarize himself with the geography of the Mekong Delta from available South Vietnamese and U.S. military maps, unreliable as they were. Kurtski had also ordered Tim to undergo intensive exercises in jungle warfare, survival skills, and interrogation techniques. Rangers and CIA veterans of Phoenix were his instructors, among them Paul Martinius, a wiry son of Sicilians, who was completing a year at Can Tho and whom Tim found to be the most thoughtful and intelligent of all the Agency officers there. South Vietnamese intelligence officers attached to CORDS and Regional Forces' unit commanders taught Tim all they knew about Viet Cong movements, tactics, and concealment practices. But from the very outset, Tim had the disturbing feeling that what the South Vietnamese knew about their Vietnamese opposite numbers amounted to very little.

"What did you expect?" Martinius asked Tim, who had been complaining about the quality of South Vietnamese intelligence. "Einstein and James Bond wrapped into one?"

The most complex aspect in organizing Phoenix teams was to integrate their members as closely as possible, notwithstanding their basic differences in backgrounds, cultures, and languages. To succeed and survive, they had to get to know and trust one another and be able to function together like a fine-tuned instrument. It was a tall order, but after a month Tim believed that it was as ready as it would ever be. There were ten men in the team, code-named by Kurtski as "Romeo," from the military designation for the letter "R" (they were the "R Team").

The two other CIA officers in "Romeo" had participated in

previous Phoenix missions, but they were primarily counterinsurgency classroom experts with little actual military experience. The three Rangers under Tim—a young gung-ho lieutenant and two sergeants—had each gone on only one foray. The four South Vietnamese were drawn from the Regional Forces, a militia operating in its native region and ostensibly familiar with the delta jungle and its trails and with local villages and peasants. They had worked with Phoenix in the past, and their command of English was just sufficient for them to act as interpreters in interrogating the Viet Cong captured by the teams. Tim had asked Martinius whether the South Vietnamese could be trusted as interpreters; his friend shrugged, replying, "Why should they be trusted? They, too, are Vietnamese. We always keep forgetting that . . ."

Jake Kurtski, for his part, knew exactly what he expected the team to accomplish. His Phoenix detachments were deployed in a generally random fashion for sweeps in areas where intelligence suggested that Viet Cong leaders were active under the cover of peaceful villagers. A sweep could last a week or two or longer, depending on the results, fresh intelligence acquired in the field, food supply, and the condition of the men. It was always something of a lottery whether a team would actually locate Viet Cong leaders, but Kurtski operated on the probably correct theory that there were *some* Viet Cong in every village and should be treated accordingly. He spelled out what he meant by "accordingly" at a briefing for the American members of "Romeo" the evening before the team set out on their assignment.

"This is a three-step operation," he said. He sat behind his desk in the living room of his villa, mauling his cigar and sipping Jack Daniel's from a short, fat glass. "The first step, obviously, is to move into a village—it doesn't matter which one. The second step is to flush out the cadres. They could be village elders. Or they could be women. You begin interrogating them about how many guerrillas there are in the village or in the immediate vicinity, who are the chiefs, how they communicate among their groups, where they stash weapons and food, and so on. It's okay to hit them, beat them, torture them, or whatever, but you gotta be patient. Dead Viet Cong don't talk. The third step is to liquidate them *after* finishing the interrogation; you can do it any way you like. There is no point in letting them live—after all, they are the enemy. And, yes, it's up to you whether you want to torch the village when you're done . . . Good luck and good hunting, gentlemen!"

Tim's first mission was a sweep in the southern Delta in an area of several hundred square miles roughly between the district towns of Duc Long and Khanh Hung, some thirty miles south of Can Tho. Kurtski had told Tim that the sweep should take about two weeks. The team could radio Can Tho only in dire emergencies: if it was in serious jeopardy or if it had obtained information of an urgent nature requiring that it be communicated instantly—in code. The Viet Cong had learned how to intercept American radio traffic, and it was much safer to maintain radio silence.

Aerial reconnaissance had indicated that there were dry patches of land among dikes and rice paddies near Duc Long, the town nearest to Can Tho, where helicopters could drop the men. At dawn, Tim and the team were driven to the Can Tho landing zone, boarding two Huey gunships for the flight. Tim was in the lead chopper with a CIA officer, the two Ranger sergeants, and two Vietnamese Regional Forces troopers. The Hueys flew low, taking advantage of the morning ground fog below them, and twenty or so minutes later they landed, a minute apart, atop a small hillock overlooking waterlogged paddies. A stand of trees was discernible through the mist.

"Okay, move out!" the pilot of Tim's helicopter shouted over the intercom. "I can't risk being a sitting duck here . . . There must be Charlie all around . . . Be sure you have marked the coordinates of this spot on your maps . . . This is where I'll pick you up when we get word that you're ready to go home . . . And, yes, have a nice day, you guys. . . ."

The birds were gone and "Romeo" were left in what seemed like the middle of absolutely nowhere, assembling their weapons, radios, and supplies. "So where the fuck do we find the Viet Cong?" the Ranger lieutenant asked Tim softly. "Do we ask for directions or what?"

Checking his compass and maps, Tim determined that their operational area was confined to a narrow rectangle between their landing spot and Khanh Hung, which lay approximately thirty miles to the southeast. A dozen or more villages were within that perimeter, and South Vietnamese Intelligence had identified it as a major center of rising Viet Cong activity. Tim had already learned enough about Vietnam, though not from his CIA superiors, to assume that the Delta was very far from being "pacified"— indeed that for all practical purposes the entire countryside was controlled by the Viet Cong. He also knew that, in most cases, the villages led that double life: they were the home of peace-loving, land-cultivating families in daytime and Viet Cong strongholds after dark. Friendly Army types had given Tim private briefings.

Although it was easier and safer for the team to move at night, Tim feared that a nocturnal incursion might lead to a lethal confrontation with a vastly superior enemy, with heavily armed Viet Cong deployed around the cluster of houses forming a village. A daytime sweep would also present serious dangers inasmuch as the farmers would immediately shed their civilian identity and turn into a fierce fighting force, exchanging plows for Soviet-made Kalashnikov assault rifles, mortars, and rocket-propelled grenade launchers hidden in attics, cellars, and under rocks and boulders. Tim therefore decided to go for the only other alternative: a surreptitious attack just before dawn when, he hoped, most of the inhabitants would still be asleep and the armed sentinels relaxed and unsuspecting. They would be tired and sleepy after their nocturnal vigilance. It was the best approach Tim had learned from hearing about Viet Cong tactical habits.

Romeo's first target was Truc Thien village, about four miles east of the landing area. It had long been on the Phoenix hit list. Tim kept his detachment back in a gully obscured from view by trees, giving the men all day to check their equipment and concentrate their minds on the approaching action. They broke out K rations for the noon and evening meals. At nightfall, the team moved out, advancing silently in Indian file behind Tim. They were imitating the Viet Cong's stealthy ways.

Tim had spent the daylight hours trying to memorize the detailed map Kurtski had handed him before departure from Can Tho, but now he had to keep rechecking it with a tiny flashlight. He wore infrared goggles for night vision, as did all the team members, striving to match the terrain's features with the map's indications. Of course, Tim was uncertain how accurate was his South Vietnamese Army map, adding to his mounting tension. It was a typical, humid, oppressive Delta night, and the men were bathed in sticky sweat. Truc Thien village was immediately west of the old French Colonial Route 4, which helped Tim in orienting himself toward the objective: The map had to be right, if nothing else, about the location of Route 4.

The trick was to advance atop the grassy tracks of the connecting network of dikes, avoiding the swampy trap of the rice paddies, though every once in a while one of the men would slip down, returning sheepishly to the column, covered with mud. It adds to the camouflage, Tim thought after falling himself into a paddy, as he spat mud out of his mouth. They covered three miles in eight hours of walking virtually on tiptoe in their heavy boots. The safety catches were off their weapons: The men were ready to fire if they suddenly ran into a Viet Cong unit returning to one of the villages from *its* nocturnal raids. Viet Cong attacks on "pacified" villages were almost invariably at night. But the silence now was broken only by the cries of night birds and the chatter of monkeys.

A few minutes after four o'clock in the morning, Romeo reached the cover of a small forest. Truc Thien, according to the map, lay immediately behind the woods. He signaled the team to halt and crouch down to rest on its western edge. It was blackness ahead, but Tim could discern through the infrared goggles the village's houses and huts. He saw no movement.

At five o'clock, the roosters came awake, a dog barked here and there. Now it was dawn, not like thunder, but like the lazy end of a gentle spring night's dream. Romeo had mastered the art of communicating by hand signals; when it was to dark, the men conveyed signals by touch, whispering only if urgently required. Slithering through the forest floor muck to the first line of trees, his M-16 in his left hand, Tim hid behind a clump of thick bushes, the rest of the team taking up positions on either side of him. It was already light enough for him to observe the village through his high-powered binoculars. He made out six or seven one-story houses, some with narrow verandas, in the center of Truc Thien, and probably fourteen or fifteen thatched huts around the perimeter. He saw a tall, thin old man in a loose black garment stepping out on the veranda of his house, looking toward the rising sun, yawning and stretching.

"Go! . . . Go!" Tim shouted, leaping out from behind the bushes and running toward the village houses across a stretch of tamped-down, yellowish soil. The team raced alongside and behind him, a flying wedge.

Tim Savage, a CIA officer named Silva, and a Vietnamese sergeant rushed onto the veranda of the first house, knocking down the old man in black and hurling themselves inside through the open door. The Rangers fanned out to secure the approach to the village from the west—a rutted track emerging from rice paddies beyond—while the other CIA man, Gervasi, and the remaining South Vietnamese posted themselves around the house, their weapons raised in readiness against an attack.

Inside, Tim found the family at breakfast by a charcoal stove. The two men, three women, and four or five children froze with their rice bowls in midair as the Phoenix team burst in.

"Down on the ground, facedown!" Tim shouted, the South Vietnamese sergeant barking out the translation in his language. The villagers obeyed wordlessly. They were patted down for weapons; they had none.

"Okay," Tim said, "now get up and stand against the far wall, facing me." He instructed Silva to search the house for arms. The Rangers brought in four black-clad men at gunpoint.

"We grabbed them in the other houses," the lieutenant announced, "but others ran away, they just vanished."

Tim nodded, signaling for the Rangers' captives to join their fellow villagers at the wall. A straight-backed chair, the only one in the household, was placed in the center of the room, and Tim motioned Gervasi to lead one of the Vietnamese to it. The man was thrown into the chair like a rice sack.

"Let's have a conversation," Tim told him, and the corpulent South Vietnamese translated. "I'm going to ask a few questions, and if you answer truthfully, nothing will happen to your family. Do you understand?"

The Vietnamese, an emaciated man in his thirties, remained impassive and silent.

"How many fighters live in your village?" Tim asked.

The man in the chair stared at the ground, motionless. His facial muscles made his face hard like a mask. Tim repeated the question. Again, silence, expressively loud in its defiance and contempt.

"All right, have it your way," he said.

The South Vietnamese stepped up and backhanded the prisoner across the face, the force of the blow hurtling him out of the chair. He collapsed on the ground, and the sergeant kicked him viciously in the groin. The man uttered no sound. The South Vietnamese and Gervasi threw him back in the chair, tying his wrists with strong twine. The man's hands rested limply on his lap.

"This is the last time I'll ask you to answer," Tim said quietly.

The villager's face still betrayed no emotion. Tim raised his eyebrows as a signal to the South Vietnamese, who produced sharpened bamboo sticks from his backpack and deftly stuck two of them under the nail's of the man's right hand. The sticks tore off the nails, and blood spurted from the tips of his fingers. Now the villager howled in pain, then relapsed into silence. He will never talk, Tim told himself, but I guess we must keep trying. He felt nausea rising up from his stomach. God, is this what we should be doing? This is wrong, terribly wrong! How can *I* allow this to happen, let alone order it? It's inhuman! He clenched his teeth, letting the torture proceed.

The South Vietnamese sergeant yanked up the man's head, thrusting the sharp point of his curved knife into his right eye. There was a squishy sound and the eyeball slid down the villager's cheek onto his lap, then on the hard clay soil. Blood gushed out of the socket. A woman at the wall screamed piercingly. The man, her husband, fell forward, his bloodied face hitting the ground. He had lost consciousness. Tim ran out of the house, vomiting on the veranda.

Back in the room, the Vietnamese sergeant asked Tim, "Shall we dispose of him, sir?" Tim looked wildly at him and at Gervasi.

"What's that?" he gasped. "Oh, I see . . . Well, do your job."

Tim was in the doorway, fleeing again, when he heard the dry crack of a pistol. He did not look back to see the villager writhing in agony as his skull shattered. It lasted less than a second.

"Look, Tim," Gervasi said, "this ain't gonna work here. I mean the interrogation. Let's just get it over with. Let 'em see what happens when they refuse to cooperate. That we don't take any crap from them."

Tim Savage nodded weakly. Gervasi was an experienced Phoenix officer from the CIA's Security Division to whom the jungle sweeps were a totally impersonal assignment: his judgment was widely respected among the teams. Tim felt sick, lightheaded. What am I doing here? he asked himself as he stepped, blinking, into the sun that now shone brightly down on the Delta village. The Rangers herded the Vietnamese out of the house—the men, the women, and the children. It was very quiet. A minute or so elapsed, and the Rangers lieutenant looked questioningly at Tim.

"Shall we go ahead, sir?" he finally asked. "Er . . . you know, what's necessary?"

"No, let them go," Tim ordered the men. To the South Vietnamese sergeant he added, "just tell 'em to get the hell out of here."

"But, Tim," Silva, the other CIA officer, interjected, "they will run to their Viet Cong buddies, give away our position. There must be fucking Charlie all around . . ."

"Yeah, I realize that," Tim replied. "That's tough. But I'm not about to have a mass execution in the village only because we couldn't get answers from that guy. Anyway, he's already dead. Let that be an example."

The villagers had vanished from sight before he could complete his sentence. The Provincial Forces sergeant spoke out: "Sir, every village of this kind keeps caches of rice for the guerrillas. This village is no different. They usually hide the rice in cellars under their houses, under trapdoors. Shouldn't we . . ."

"Yes," Tim told him evenly. "Yes, we should. Set fire to every house and every hut. That will take care of the rice."

As Romeo retreated to the woods, flames were shooting up high from the village roofs and smoke was curling up around the structures. Then there were loud explosions.

"The sons of bitches had ammo stashed in their homes," Silva said. "We missed it when we searched the houses, but now they've lost it anyway."

It took Tim less than two hours to retrace their steps to the landing zone, marching rapidly in daylight. If there were Viet Cong in the area, they made no attempt to ambush or attack the team. In fact, the few peasants in conical hats they saw guiding their water buffaloes across the rice paddies seemed to pay no attention whatsoever to them, as if the Americans were ghosts. After all, they were peaceful farmers, tilling their land as their ancestors had done for hundreds or thousands of years. They knew nothing about wars, certainly not while the sun shone.

Halfway to the landing zone, Tim radioed Can Tho base in code for a helicopter pickup. Resting in the gully by the stand of trees, the men presently heard the clack-clack of the Hueys' rotors. The two birds sat on the hillock and Team Romeo climbed aboard. The pilot shouted to Tim as they were lifting, "I bet you guys had a great time! We saw the smoke in the distance as we were coming . . ."

"Absolutely," Tim told him. "Absolutely. We had a ball."

"You focked up!" Jake Kurtski screamed at Tim. His red face had turned wine-dark as if he had been struck with apoplexy. He had trouble breathing and his words tumbled out almost incoherently in his boundless fury. It enhanced his Polish accent pronunciation in English. In a strange sort of way, Kurtski must have sensed that, because of his strange European background and personality, he was an American caricature, and he seemed compelled to act it out.

"You focked up at that focking village, Savage!" Kurtski repeated in a primal scream. "We're not focking missionaries! . . . We're trying to win the focking war! You had no right to let them go scot-free . . . The motherfockers should've been executed. Every focking one of them . . . If you can't get information out of them, you kill them all. It's the only way we can get the focking Viet Cong to respect us!

"This is *not* what Phoenix is all about," Kurtski continued, growing somewhat calmer as he read again Tim's after-action report. "The idea is to destroy—yes, destroy—the Viet Cong infrastructure, *not* to play focking missionary or Good Samaritan. It's not enough to torch villages if the people are allowed to escape. This way, we'll never smash the cadres. So what's your excuse for this focking disaster?"

"I'm not making excuses," Tim answered quickly, controlling his rising anger. They were standing in the hallway of Kurtski's Can Tho villa, facing each other like gladiators.

"I am trying to explain why I acted the way I did. I just don't believe that executing peasants wholesale, including women and children, just for the hell of it, makes much sense. As you know, one of the villagers was killed when he wouldn't talk. I had to assume that the same would have happened with other adults there. Truc Thien obviously is firmly in Viet Cong hands. And I fail to see how mass executions are going to help us win the hearts and the minds of Vietnamese peasants. Isn't this what John Kennedy had urged us to do?"

Kurtski stuck the stump of his cigar in his mouth.

"Fock hearts and minds," he declared. "And fock Kennedy! . . . Anyway, Nixon is your boss now. . . ."

Chapter Seven

OVER THE NEXT two years, Tim Savage led scores of Phoenix sweeps across rice paddies and stretches of jungle. He lost count of the raids as if trying to forget each of them, the only way to preserve his mental equilibrium. Sometimes Romeo succeeded in capturing Viet Cong guerrillas, including, on a few occasions, regional chiefs, and extracting valuable intelligence after hours upon hours of persuasion, interrogation, and torture. Tim rebelled in his mind and heart against torture methods, but soon acquired enough controlled detachment to accept it as an operational necessity. It was astonishing how easily it came to the best of men in combat environment. Like others, Tim rationalized this acceptance, still believing to a degree in the cause for which Americans were told they were fighting in Vietnam.

But Tim never participated personally in applying torture in interrogations, leaving it to his Romeo subordinates. By the same token, Tim himself never shot dead a captured Viet Cong, though begrudgingly he accepted Kurtski's insistence that some prisoners had to be killed for their refusal to cooperate and the others *after* cooperating as an indispensable part of the eradication of the guerrilla infrastructure. One rationalization inevitably led to the next one.

When Romeo found villages empty, as if inhabitants had been forewarned in some fashion and fled in time, Tim had them torched. At the very least, it destroyed rice caches and arms and ammunition, usually concealed in cave shelters under sleeping platforms, and deprived the Viet Cong of local sanctuaries. When guerrilla sympathizers were identified, the villages naturally were burned down. To use Kurtski's word, it taught the enemy a "lesson." Tim felt sorry for the peasants—he assumed that old people, most of the women, and, presumably, the children had very little to do with the guerrillas—but it was war, after all, and the enemy had to pay a price. And, of course, the Viet Cong had their share of killing Americans, to say nothing of the South Vietnamese.

Unquestionably, Phoenix operations in the Delta were hurting the Viet Cong in important ways. Captured COSVN documents confirmed it to the joy of the planners in Saigon. But, overall, the war was going very badly for the South Vietnamese and the Americans. A major American incursion into the Parrot's Beak border area in Cambodia, just west of the Delta, had failed to halt the flow of supplies from North Vietnam to its regular Army units and Viet Cong guerrillas in the south. It had occurred a year or so after Tim had been assigned to Phoenix, and he remembered his shock and dismay upon hearing on the radio in his room in Can Tho about the student demonstrations back home against the Cambodian incursion—and about the four students shot dead by National Guardsmen at Kent State in Ohio.

And there was more and more death before his very eyes, and not only in the villages raided by Romeo. Tim had witnessed on innumerable occasions carpet bombings by the high-flying B-52s of suspected communist concentrations in the Delta and the spraying of the countryside by Marine Aircraft Wing jets with napalm and white phosphorus. Uncounted villages were erased from existence, thousands of peasants were incinerated, and Viet Cong guerrillas, when spotted, were turkey-shot strafed from Cobra helicopter gunships. Tim became sickeningly familiar with the stench of burned human flesh. But nothing seemed to work.

In Can Tho, the spring of 1971 was so stifling, with temperatures soaring well over one hundred degrees and Delta humidity just below one hundred percent, that even Sonia Ryan was too drained to engage in mechanistic sex with Tim Savage—and presumably others. Between missions, Tim spent most of his time in the swimming pool and the air-conditioned officers' club, drinking cold beer and wondering how much longer it would all last.

Then word had reached Can Tho that the Viet Cong had raided Khanh Hung, down Colonial Route 4, in a daring daytime attack, killing civilian district officials and massacring the small Regional Forces garrison, capturing arms and munitions. They came well armed with AK-47 assault rifles and B-40 rocket-propelled grenade launchers, gifts from the Soviets and the Chinese. American and South Vietnamese commanders in the Delta were uncertain whether the raid signaled a new communist offensive in the region, but they realized that it made no sense to engage, in response, regular units in search-and-destroy operations on a large scale. The guerrillas were too elusive and too well coordinated and the terrain was too forbidding to justify the use of armor, artillery, and even heavily armed infantry. Commando-type thrusts by Special Forces' Green Berets, Rangers, and Phoenix teams seemed to be the only way to cope with the latest Viet Cong initiative. Once more, the hope was to disrupt the guerrillas' infrastructure, an objective senior officers repeated over and over in briefings like a mantra.

Four Phoenix teams were based in Can Tho, and Kurtski, in consultation with Stephens in Saigon, decided to launch all of them simultaneously; normally, the teams rotated for rest periods. Team Romeo was ordered to operate as long as their supplies lasted in a grid area south of Khanh Hung where a half dozen villages were located. They were considered as sanctuaries to be liquidated. Briefing them before they boarded the helicopters, Kurtski told the team leaders that the operation simply had to succeed. He was beside himself with excitement.

"Go, go, motherfockers," Kurtski roared. "If necessary, I'll be there, too, to help out. Just radio me if you need me!"

At dawn of Good Friday—Tim had suddenly remembered that it was Easter week—Team Romeo reached a nameless hamlet in the heart of the southern Delta after a cautious nocturnal approach. They had been dropped by the choppers in a jungle clearing the previous afternoon. Moving into the hamlet at first light, the team came upon not only peasant families, the children hiding behind their mothers at the sight of the foreign attackers, but also an uncommonly large group of men, some of them with automatic weapons slung over their shoulders. Surprised by the Phoenix foray, the men fell back behind the houses, firing aimlessly toward the perimeter as they regrouped.

The team returned the fire, and, then, on Tim's orders, withdrew into the thick jungle undergrowth. Within minutes, he realized that he had stumbled, for the first time, into a Viet Cong command post, but also that Romeo were outnumbered and urgently needed reinforcements if they were to survive. Grabbing the radio transmitter from a Ranger, Tim called Can Tho for assistance, giving his coordinates and praying for a rapid appearance of the Hueys.

The Viet Cong and Romeo engaged in an exchange of fire though the guerrillas chose to remain inside the hamlet compound, clearly uncertain how large was the force facing them. This saved the team. Barely an hour had elapsed before three Hueys and a Cobra materialized overhead. Adjusting radio frequencies, Tim guided them to the hamlet proper. Instantly, the gunships raked it violently with rocket and machine gun bursts, leaving a dozen or so dead bodies on the ground. Then the choppers sat on grassy lots around the hamlet, letting out Rangers who rushed to surround the houses. Tim and his men raced to join them. As they came closer, Tim recognized Jake Kurtski in khaki pants, Hawaiian shirt, and a helmet liner on his head a step behind the Rangers, an M-16 rifle cradled in his arms, screaming commands.

"I told you I'd be here if you got into a focking fight," Kurtski shouted to Tim with enormous glee. "God, I love it! . . . I love it! . . . Now we'll show the bastards what's what! . . ."

He fired a burst from his automatic weapon into the nearest house, waving the Rangers to follow him inside. Tim was running alongside. Then Kurtski yelled, "Let's grab them!"

Three youngish men in black garments and an elderly woman, also in black, were crouching against the far wall of the front room as Kurtski rushed inside the flimsy house. He stopped for an instant, emitted a guttural sound, and sprayed the foursome with a torrent of bullets. Blood gushed up in fountains onto the walls and the low ceiling. The bodies writhed for a moment, then froze into the immobility of death.

"Let's see if they have any documents on them," Kurtski said, leaning down over the first corpse in his way, tearing off the man's blouse and searching through the pockets. "If this is a command post, I'll bet we'll find COSVN documents on them. Come on, help me look . . ."

They found nothing on the three men. Kurtski cursed, "Sons of bitches, they must've gotten rid of the stuff . . . Let's check the old woman."

Her face was horribly smashed by the bullets, though her eyes were untouched, now seemingly staring at the blood-stained ceiling, the sky, the heavens of this Good Friday. Kurtski ripped open the top of her black blouse. Tim Savage looked down and saw a tiny gold crucifix on a thin chain around her neck, shining like a beacon in the darkened room. Curiously, there was no blood on the crucifix.

Tim was awestruck. He could not breathe or talk for a long minute. He did not hear Kurtski say, "Let's round up the others for interrogation." He just followed him mechanically to the next house, where the Rangers had assembled a half-dozen Vietnamese men. The interrogation session followed the usual routine: questions, threats, torture, execution. Kurtski had pulled the trigger on his .45-caliber Colt pistol to perform the final honors. Tim was now completely numb—he had no idea whether the murdered villagers had come up with useful information or just silence. All he had before his eyes was the smashed face of the old woman and the gold crucifix. The vision had been imprinted on his conscious memory like an image on a photographic plate.

Romeo were lifted back to Can Tho aboard the helicopters. During the short flight, Tim stared down unseeingly at the Delta landscape below—the jungle, the paddies, the dikes, the peasant huts on the edge of the watery fields, the occasional bent figure in black, the huge animals. The greenery dissolved in a blur, then into the old woman's face and the cross. He wished he had known her name. Tim began to shake uncontrollably, as though in the throes of malaria. His hands tightened on the web of the safety harness across his chest. The chopper hit a patch of violent clear-air turbulence, dropping down and rising, dropping again and struggling to regain altitude. Tim felt terrible fear. Were they going to crash? Was this divine punishment? Was he to pay for his unspeakable deeds? Was this retribution for the old woman? Was God exacting vindication for the desecration of the crucifix? And, he remembered, this *was* Good Friday.

The helicopter had steadied on its course, beginning its sharp descent toward Can Tho. Tim looked down once more at the green lushness of the Delta. What am I doing here? he asked himself. What am I turning into? "Oh, God, how have I sinned!" he cried aloud though his words were lost to others in the grind of the rotors. It was the first time, Tim realized, that he had uttered them since confession in his early teens. He had not been to confession since those days.

In the evening, he walked from his quarters over to the officers' club. He had taken a shower and put on freshly laundered and pressed khaki slacks and his Egyptian sports shirt. Spotting Kurtski at the bar, a drink in hand, he sat on a stool next to him. It was unusual for the man to be away from his villa at night.

"Kurtski," Tim said, "I want a transfer out of here. To Saigon or whatever."

"What's the matter?" Kurtski asked unpleasantly. "You afraid of focking up again or you're chickening out?"

"Exactly," Tim told him. "I am chickening out and I don't want to fuck up anymore. How soon can you get me out of here?"

On May thirteenth, Ascension Day, Tim Savage boarded a Blackhawk for Saigon. He was to report to Roger Stephens at "Pentagon East." He did not bother to take leave of Kurtski or Sonia Ryan.

"I wish to resign from the Agency," Tim informed Stephens, "as soon as it can be processed."

He sat in Stephens' powerfully air-conditioned office, trying in vain to force him into eye contact.

"But why? Why?" Stephens asked, sounding genuinely taken aback. "You've done a great job. You have a great future with us. Langley thinks the world of you . . ."

"Well, I'm not so sure about doing a great job," Tim said. "Certainly not by Jake Kurtski's standards."

"Kurtski is a madman," Stephens replied dismissively. "Pay no attention to him. He's a crazy Polack, but I keep him in Can Tho because he's fantastic at counterinsurgency. That's all. He's not a judge of people, especially not of *real* American Agency officers. But he isn't the reason you want to resign, is he?"

"No, of course, not," Tim told him. "It's much more complicated and much more personal. It is fundamental for me. I just can't stomach it any longer. I just can't go on condoning killings and taking part in them. I guess I should've realized it a long time ago, but I believed in what we were doing in this war. Then something happened a couple of weeks ago to make me understand how wrong it all is. It was the murder of an old woman in a village. It was not necessary to kill her. And, you know, she was wearing a crucifix on a chain around her neck . . . That hardly made her a communist guerrilla . . ."

Stephens was staring down at his desk, playing with a steel letter opener, as if ready to thrust it into an enemy. At length, he dropped it and looked straight at Tim. For the first time.

"You are a Catholic, aren't you?" he asked. "And you graduated from Georgetown."

"Yes," Tim replied, puzzled. "You've read my file, so . . ."

"Then you must be familiar with Catholic teachings on 'just wars,' *Ius Bellum,*" Stephens said. "They go back all the way to St. Augustine and St. Thomas Aquinas . . . You see, I went to Notre Dame . . . Anyway, in the fourth and fifth century, Augustine had proclaimed the legitimacy of military service. And St. Thomas, rediscovering Aristotle, developed the idea that, much as the Church is devoted to the sanctity of human life, war is acceptable in a just cause, even an offensive war for a just cause, if it is so declared by civil authority. And, as you must know, war *is* ethical if it causes less harm than *not* going to war. The Church calls it 'proportionality.' In the case of Vietnam, we are unquestionably fighting for a just cause: for democracy and against Godless communist tyranny. So we are not talking about good and evil in a basic sense. But, sadly, war results in deaths. For example, Cardinal O'Connor in New York, so admired by Catholics and others, is a doctrinaire supporter of the Vietnam War. He even wrote a book in its defense. So, Tim, don't think you are the only Catholic who has given thought to this whole philosophical matter. I have, too, believe it or not . . ."

As it happened, Tim had taken courses in ethics at Georgetown taught by Father Morgan, his friend and adviser, and had read his famous treatise on "just wars." Morgan also made his students familiarize themselves with Augustine's *The City of God.* It all came back to him in a rush as he listened to Stephens' tutorial on what was just.

"You are absolutely right about Augustine and Thomas and Church teachings," he said. "But, then, you surely remember what the Church has called the criterion of 'civilian immunity.' It affirms, as you know, that civilians must not be attacked even in the pursuit of a 'just war.' It is also called, I think, 'Non-Combatant Immunity.' But we have violated it, especially through Phoenix, because we *do* kill civilians, and kill them indiscriminately in the villages, and I am as guilty as everybody else here. It has finally dawned on me that I am an assassin, directly or indirectly, hiding behind political excuses, even though I never killed anybody personally. But I must share the blame. And now I hear you invoking *Ius Bellum* to justify killing old women and little kids. And, you know, I just read Cardinal O'Connor's new book in which he says that he had been wrong in supporting the war, having concluded that, in accordance with Church teachings, our use of more and more unjust means results in robbing ourselves of a justification for being in this war at all. Here, I brought a copy of O'Connor's book so that you can see for yourself. I bought it yesterday at the PX down the street."

Stephens seemed faintly amused.

"This is the first time in my career that I've had a theological argument concerning the work of the Agency," he told Tim. "But, as a fellow Catholic, I must say I totally disagree with your interpretation of *Ius Bellum*. Vietnam *is* a just cause, and collateral damage—what you call 'attacks on civilians'—is tragically, but inevitably the price for what I know will be a moral victory for our side . . . O'Connor's 'conversion' notwithstanding."

"You mean we have to destroy them in order to save them?" Tim asked sarcastically. "Is that what we are doing in Vietnam, in someone else's country? This is insane . . ."

"No, it's not insane, Tim," Stephens answered. "We Christians do not believe in killing—Thou Shall Not Kill and all that stuff—even to protect ourselves. But the Christian teaching is that if someone is attacked, we must go to the defense. This applied to attacks against barbarians way back and it applies to Vietnam today. We are defending the Vietnamese against barbarian communists who attacked them. Do you understand?"

"No, I really do not," Tim said. "I recall reading in college about the Albigenois Cathar heretics. If memory serves, it was the pope—I think it was Innocent III, in the thirteenth century—who had proclaimed the crusade against them in the south of France as a 'just war' and thousands and thousands of perfectly nice, decent people were burned at the stake. Was that really justified? And the Great Inquisition was born from it. Next, the use of torture was legitimized by Pope Innocent IV for flushing out heretics—it's in that O'Connor book. Is that something the Church is proud of? Are we replaying it in Vietnam, with Washington in the role of imperial Rome? We kill and we torture . . ."

"Look," Stephens replied, "this is not the time nor the place to debate Church history. We must deal with the realities of today."

He got up from behind his desk, standing almost at attention below a government-issue photograph of Richard Nixon in statesman pose.

"Well, you are the one who brought up this whole business of the 'just war' to make me accept, as a good Catholic, what is unacceptable," Tim said. "That's why I want to resign from the Agency and wash my hands of this thing. I believe it was Cromwell who said that in a war every king is convinced that God is on his side."

"Fine. Have it your way—if you really think you can put the last two years behind you and be pristine again, even if you never pulled a trigger yourself," Stephens declared. "You admit that once you believed in what we are doing here. So you can't be like Lady Macbeth and say, 'Out damned spot!' Yes, if you think we are sinning, you are just as much of a sinner as the rest of us. You're trapped, my boy, you're trapped by your own reasoning. But there's one more thing I want to tell you before you quit . . ."

"What? A new justification?"

"In a sense, yes. I'm going to let you in on a secret. Back in 1961, it was the CIA, on Kennedy's orders, that organized the assassination of that dictator Trujillo in the Dominican Republic. I was the executive officer on the project. Trujillo was a bloodthirsty tyrant and we all agreed that he had to go. And do you know what the Dominicans called this assassination? They called it *ajusticiamento,* which in Spanish means 'the bringing of justice.' Would you argue that it was not a 'just' act on our part? Don't forget, Tim, that there are all kinds of moralities and ethics and judgments in our lives."

Tim nodded.

"Of course, you are right," he remarked. "But one assassination does not justify another. I've made my judgment."

Stephens put out his hand to Tim Savage.

"Then, go with God," he said. "Godspeed."

Chapter Eight

1972

THE FIRST CALL Tim Savage made on his return from Vietnam to Washington, after seeing his family, was to his former professor Father Hugh Morgan at Georgetown, a cheerful, corpulent Jesuit. In addition to teaching him when Tim was an undergraduate student, Morgan later shepherded him through the graduate school in pursuit of his master's degree and his doctorate in Islamic history and culture and Arabic language studies.

In ways that would serve him so well in Cairo and then in Rome, Tim had developed an abiding interest in Islam and the Middle East under Morgan's tutelage at the university: Mecca and Medina, the Prophet and the Koran, the glorious days of the caliphates and the Arab learning in philosophy and mathematics, the Moorish conquest of Iberia, the greatness and the fall; the scholars, warriors, and poets; the modern age of kings and nationalists, and the incalculable wealth of petroleum destined to recreate the ancient power of Islam—or lead to another collapse.

In Father Morgan, Tim had found the perfect mentor. Himself an Islamic scholar, Morgan progressed from his own earlier work on ethics to the Christian concepts of "Just Wars" and, consequently, to the role of the Church in Holy Land crusades and, inevitably, to Islam proper. Now Morgan was president of Georgetown University's new Center of Islamic Studies. In his late fifties, he exuded energy as a teacher, administrator, and friend and adviser to as many students as time would allow.

And to Tim, Father Morgan had probably been the single most important influence from the day he had first entered Georgetown at the age of eighteen. In those days, Morgan was in the habit of inviting his most promising students to lunch or tea on weekends to sound them out on the possibility of joining in the future the Society of Jesus. At a time when Church vocations were already diminishing sharply, Father Hugh Morgan was a tireless recruiter for the Jesuits. He referred to himself in proud jest as "The Proselytizer," but he was extremely selective and discerning in his choices. He had made not too veiled a pitch to Tim at one of his lunches, encountering an absolute lack of interest. Morgan remarked, "well, it's too bad: you'd make a fine Jesuit," and never again returned to the subject. Nevertheless a deep friendship grew between the professor and his pupil. Tim seldom made serious decisions without consulting him.

Back in Washington, Tim had to decide—soon—what he proposed to do with the rest of his life. He had already lived a remarkably full one: a Ph.D. at an uncommonly young age, service with the CIA in Cairo, then Vietnam, the frightening backlash of Phoenix, and his crisis of conscience.

But to be with Morgan and unload on him loomed to Tim as the first step in his search for solutions. The process of resigning from the Agency was an impersonal, automatic experience. He had driven to the CIA headquarters in Langley, on the Virginia side of the Potomac and a short distance from Washington, to meet with Personnel and Security officials, and his resignation was formalized immediately. He was not even asked why he was quitting; nobody seemed to be interested. All he had to do was to sign a standard secrecy pledge that he would never reveal anything about the Agency and its "Sources and Methods" or anything secret he might have learned during his years with the CIA.

At home, however, Tim had to play it with extraordinary care. Jim Stella, his stepfather, was an unflinching patriot who never questioned his government's policies. Like so many professional officers of his generation, he was idealistic when it came to America's actions in the world and profoundly conservative in domestic politics. He had no use for "bleeding heart" liberals. In the 1964 presidential campaign, Stella had worked enthusiastically for Senator Barry Goldwater, a fellow combat pilot. He had applauded Tim for signing up with the CIA—though he might have preferred the Air Force for his stepson—and was whole-heartedly behind the American engagement in the Vietnam War.

A rock-ribbed Roman Catholic, Stella saw Vietnam as a quasi-religious crusade against atheistic communism and he was proud that Tim was serving in Indochina. To him it was exactly the same cause for which he had risked his life in World War Two, where he had lost his best friend. Stella, to be sure, knew nothing about Phoenix, a top-secret project, and Tim could not allude to it. The retired general no longer had security clearances. Personally, he was deeply offended when he realized that the Church in America was split over Vietnam and its morality; he was shocked to see priests on television demonstrating against the war, like the four who had poured their own blood onto draft files. He simply could not understand it.

This was why Tim was convinced that his stepfather would never understand or condone his disenchantment—and his resignation from the CIA. Stella might have regarded it as a virtually treasonable act, and Tim, determined not to trigger a bitter controversy within the family, chose to lie. During dinner at home the evening of his return from Saigon, he told them that he had been transferred back to Langley for another assignment, but, in the meantime, had a month's leave. This made it possible for Tim to live with his family during the transition period, at least for a while. He planned to tell them the truth after deciding on his future course. The general was too disciplined an officer to inquire about Tim's supposed new Agency assignment: In the military, one did not ask about classified work, even of one's own children.

"As usual, I need your advice," Tim said to Father Morgan. They were sitting on a rainy December afternoon in front of a blazing fireplace in the living room of the priest's tiny house on Thirty-fifth Street, just around the corner from Georgetown University's massive main tower–graced building.

"I have resigned from the CIA," he went on, "because I couldn't continue to be part of the assassination program our government runs in Vietnam. I had become an assassin myself though I have never actually assassinated a Viet Cong prisoner there. But I was the commander of a team that specialized in assassinations and therefore I must share in the guilt."

Morgan cleared his throat. "And now?" he asked.

"Well, I don't know," Tim said. "That's why I want your advice. Here I am, an unemployed Middle Eastern spook, a former Vietnam assassin. Oh, God! I guess I must first come to terms with my guilt, my sins . . ."

The Jesuit added a stubby log to the fire and flames burst out merrily, encouragingly, the wood crackling.

"Have you been to confession?" he inquired.

"The truth is that I haven't been to confession since high school," Tim replied, shifting uneasily in the armchair. "I'm not sure why, and I lied to my mother about going to confession. But I imagine it can't do any harm now, can it?"

"Would you like me to hear your confession?" Morgan offered.

"Here? Now?" Tim wondered as if to gain time, the thought not having occurred to him.

"Why not? I don't have to sit in a confessional to hear your confession," the Jesuit told him. "Even though I'm wearing blue jeans and a red sweater right now. I doubt God cares about my sartorial habits."

Tim Savage stared at length at Morgan, knelt in front of him, and crossed himself. For the next half-hour, remembrances, words, and tears poured out in a stream of consciousness. The beatings. The tortures. The executions. The image of the dead old woman with the crucifix.

Morgan was silent. Minutes elapsed. The fire began to die down.

"Tim," Father Morgan finally said. "God forgives you. I absolve you. But you have to start a new life. Perhaps you wish to do something for God. But what you need now, I think, is to occupy your mind, to be busy, make a transition to a normal life. I may have an idea for you."

The idea that Morgan refined in the days that followed was for Tim to return once more to Georgetown, this time to teach. As it happened, there was an open instructor's slot during the forthcoming semester at Morgan's Center of Islamic Studies, and

Tim—with his Ph.D. and his Cairo experience—qualified easily. Starting in January of the new year, Tim marched to Georgetown from his new quarters five days a week to explain the intricacies of Middle Eastern politics and the legal mysteries of *Shariah,* the canon law of Islam, to a dozen graduate students. He had told his stepfather and his mother that the CIA had assigned him to run an emergency course for its officers, and, of course, no questions were asked.

The semester at Georgetown was Tim's most peaceful and reflective period since he had reached adulthood. He had rented a small efficiency apartment off Wisconsin Avenue, a few minutes away from the university, looked up old friends, and created something of a social life for himself. He went to the movies and had occasional platonic dates; he eschewed romantic involvements to avoid distractions and commitments. But, most important, Tim had the leisure to think, meditate, and analyze. He also saw Father Morgan every week or so for long conversations—a form of therapy.

Having studied the Koran as a student of Islam, Tim now reread the Scriptures with deep personal attention, aware of the reverse order in which he, as a Christian, had delved into sacred religious texts. He was familiar with the *history* of the Church, but not with Christian faith; he knew about *Ius Bellum,* but not about the Gospels, having long forgotten what he had been taught at the parochial school and Gonzaga. He now read an account of St. Paul's conversion that Morgan had dropped off at his apartment one evening—without further comment.

Tim's bitter resentment, as an American and a Catholic, of the Phoenix enterprise in Vietnam gradually led him to meditation about what values were meaningful in his world. In one of his chats with Father Morgan, he asked, "How do I transfer my sense of idealism, the idealism I felt when I joined the CIA and I guess I still feel, to something else in life, such as, hypothetically speaking, the Church? Is it possible?"

"Well, everything is possible," the Jesuit replied. "In this case, have you considered setting aside your political ideas and ideals, and, instead, working to advance the cause of the Kingdom of God and the Gospel of Jesus Christ? I don't mean to sound like a catechism teacher, Tim, but there's an awful lot you can achieve applying your idealism and your talents to the glory of God, which, at least to me, means working for the good of people who need all kinds of help."

"Are you suggesting that I become a missionary?" Tim asked, half seriously. "I have no idea what God wants from me, but you say that God still loves me despite all the horrors of which I am guilty. Maybe what I need is some sort of illumination."

"Perhaps you do," Morgan said. "You could do much worse than being a missionary in Rwanda or in Paraguay. Albert Schweitzer was in fact a missionary, even if he wasn't formally a man of religion."

On his way home from Morgan's house, Tim always walked past the Holy Trinity Church on tree-lined Thirty-sixth Street, his family church. He never stopped there, but on that particular drizzly spring Sunday afternoon, with flowers blooming proudly everywhere, Tim slowed down, stared at the façade of the church as if he had never seen it before and, guided by an inner force, went up the broad white steps. The door had been left ajar. The big church he knew so well from childhood was empty at that hour, but Tim could smell incense from the noontime Mass lingering in the air. He advanced toward the simple, rectangular altar. He knelt, crossing himself, whispering long-forgotten words of prayer. He looked at the crucified Christ high up and crossed himself again. Images of remembered thoughts flashed through his mind: the " ecstatic agony" of the soul of St. John of the Cross in search of faith and its mystical experience of the night, St. Paul's instant of conversion, and the words from the Scriptures: "Come, Follow Me."

Tim shivered, his eyes shut tight. Is God talking to me? he wondered. This is absurd! It is theatrical! I'm engaging in cheap dramatics!

He was seized with terrible fear, then felt a sudden sense of peace and serenity he had never experienced before descending upon him. Now everything was crystal clear in his heart and mind. The answers were there. Had he just been blessed in that elusive moment of revelation? Something surely had happened. Tim wiped his tears off and laughed happily. His step was light and quick as he retraced his way to Hugh Morgan's house.

"You asked me once, a long time ago, if I wanted to take vows, become a Jesuit," he announced as Morgan opened the door for him. "Well, today I have an answer for you. Yes, I do!"

The priest embraced him. "Let us pray together," he said. They knelt and prayed in the living room under the sad, watchful eyes of an emaciated El Greco Christ on the wall.

Chapter Nine

As PRIESTHOOD WENT, Tim Savage's was a late vocation. He knew, for example, that Hugh Morgan's vocation dated back to the second grade, to his childhood. But late vocations were not all that unusual. The Jesuits welcomed them as their own numbers tumbled down along with other religious orders and diocesan clergy around the world. In fact, late vocations were on the rise in recent years, often because many men underwent something of a midlife crisis with deep spiritual overtones.

Father Morgan gave Tim a magazine article about the type of men who left their secular workplace for the Church and their ages: a sixty-five-year-old former lieutenant commander in the U.S. Navy, a forty-six-year-old gastroenterologist who had "traded a physician's white coat for a Roman collar"; a thirty-three-year-old advertising agency executive who had a chic condominium, a sports car, and a corner office in a New York skyscraper, but decided "there was something missing from my life"; lawyers, psychologists, and social workers; and, finally, the Spanish highways engineer who became a bishop and head of the immensely powerful and controversial *Opus Dei* society of priests and laymen (which the Jesuits cordially detested for its conservatism).

"So why not a former spook ?" Morgan asked rhetorically.

Tim's choice of the Society of Jesus as his future life path was natural—apart from Morgan's personal influence. He was a product of Georgetown and its ancient Jesuit traditions. His educational achievements turned him logically toward the Jesuits, a teaching order with a touch of intellectual, humanitarian, and scientific elitism—for which the Jesuits were resented by many others in the Church. But if Tim was to enter priesthood, that was where he belonged, he thought.

Now Tim embarked on the lengthy and tough admission process. Morgan had volunteered to be his spiritual director—it was a requirement that candidates be guided spiritually—and he began to teach Tim how to pray and read the Scriptures as they should be read: in depth. The next step for Tim was to report to the vocations' director for the Jesuits' Maryland Province, which included Washington. One late June morning, he drove to the provincial headquarters on Rolland Avenue in northern Baltimore, an unpretentious building not far from the Jesuits' Loyola College. The meeting was brief, but encouraging, with Tim gaining the impression that there was serious interest in him. He also realized that the Jesuits—like the CIA—knew absolutely everything about him.

Much of the initial burden of preparing Tim for priesthood was on Father Morgan as spiritual director. He had to help Tim decide whether he really did have a vocation to be a Jesuit, making him better understand the Society of Jesus so that he could reach an intelligent, informed conclusion before he actually entered the order. Morgan supplied him with materials about the history and the activities of the Jesuits, urged him to pray daily and go to Mass regularly.

Tim spent the summer concentrating on religious studies at home, learning the Spiritual Exercises of St. Ignatius of Loyola, the founder of the Society of Jesus in the sixteenth century, perfecting his praying habits, and preparing himself for the road ahead in the admission process. In the autumn, he returned to Georgetown to teach one more semester on Islam as he awaited acceptance as a Jesuit novice, another preliminary step.

Little had changed in Tim's day-to-day life, but he now felt he was a truly changed man. He was at peace with himself. He no longer had nightmares about the old village woman with the shattered face and the crucifix around her neck. The guilt of Vietnam no longer hung over him like a black shadow. That Christmas, B-52 Superfortresses bombed North Vietnam into accepting the American peace—and the American departure. The peace treaty was signed in Paris a month later. Tim watched the ceremony on television in his apartment. It all seemed unspeakably remote. But, he thought, that was the end of Phoenix, too.

*   *   *

The admission process went on slowly, carefully, relentlessly. The Jesuits wanted only the brightest and the brainiest in their midst, and they took their time in deciding whom to welcome to the Company of Jesus. At that point, there were only eight candidates for the novitiate in the Maryland Province, but, as Hugh Morgan told Tim, "we are not so anxious that we would cut corners in the selection."

On a cold winter morning, Tim was interviewed—separately—by three Jesuit "judges" who went meticulously over his past life, childhood, adolescence, university, the CIA, Vietnam, and everything else to satisfy themselves that he was making a positive choice in wishing to embrace priesthood and not merely running from the world. Much of it seemed to be designed to confirm what they already knew about Tim—and hear it from his lips. The vocation, he was told, must be a constructive, unselfish undertaking that would contribute to the work of the Jesuits as educators, scholars, and intelligent messengers of God. And, above all, one of the judges informed him, Tim had to know and fully comprehend what he was leaving behind in terms of personal secular life—from complete independence to sex—by entering priesthood.

Next, it was the turn of professional psychologists, one a Jesuit and the other a lay Georgetown consultant. Running a series of tests on Tim, from inkblots to the MMPI—Minnesota Multiple Personality Inventory—method to determine whether he had hidden emotional or psychological problems. The Jesuit helpfully advised Tim that "for example, if you say that you see your mother with a knife on an inkblot, then we'll know you *have* a problem."

At long last, Tim was admitted to Jesuit novitiate. He took the train from Washington's Union Station to Hershey, Pennsylvania, then a bus to Warnersville, a small town where the Jesuit Novitiate of St. Isaac Jogues was located. Jogues was one of the first Jesuit martyrs in North America, killed by Iroquois Indians who first cut off his fingers. The novitiate was a large H-shaped structure, rich in marble, built to serve Jesuit novices by a Mrs. Brady, an American Papal Duchess from New York who had been personally acquainted with Pope Pius XII. A chapel was in the center of the compound.

The Jesuit novitiate that Tim Savage entered was a two-year program. When he arrived at Jogues, there were ten novices in the second year of the study and Tim was one of six in the first year. Life there was less strict than it had been in the past, but the novices had to remain on the premises most of the time. Tim had, of course, informed his family early in the year about his intention of becoming a Jesuit, and they took it rather well, after the initial surprise, though General Stella would have preferred his stepson remain in government service, military or not. As good Catholics, they could not object to Tim's desire to serve God. The family threw a magnificent farewell reception for him, complete with champagne, and he was embraced tenderly as he left in a taxi for Union Station. His sister Julia telephoned from her ambassadorial post in Brasília to wish him well in his new life.

The novitiate, as Hugh Morgan had explained to Tim, was intended to confirm—again—a man's priestly vocation and to give the Jesuits an in-depth opportunity to get to know the candidate. With the Director of Novices, a serious middle-aged priest with a gift of communicating smoothly and easily with his charges, while supervising them, the novices studied the history of the Society of Jesus, read the biographies of St. Ignatius and other great Jesuits, like Jogues, absorbed the Society's constitution and the great decisions of past Jesuit congregations, and attended theology classes. There was one hour of mandatory prayer, work around the house, and visits to Jesuit communities in Pennsylvania.

Novices are usually directed to spend six months or so teaching at Jesuit schools, often abroad, to acquire experience with poor people at home and the Third World, but given Tim's Middle East and Vietnam background, this was not judged necessary. Instead, he spent several months in Washington's turbulent, crime-ridden inner city, working with the homeless and drug addicts—and dining on Sundays with his family. As is frequently the case with affluent white Washingtonians, Tim had never been exposed to the sprawling black districts of the capital—these are two worlds apart—and his service at a halfway house in Anacostia jolted him into the surprising realization that American inner cities can be as degrading to their inhabitants as the slums of Cairo or Saigon. The vacant eyes of sickly Anacostia children and needle marks on the arms and legs of teenagers were Tim's post-Vietnam culture shock.

Recounting his Washington discoveries upon his return to Warnersville, he remarked to the Director of Novices that he thought the Jesuits should be more engaged in the realm of social assistance.

"Why, yes," the Father told him, "that is exactly what we are doing, especially since Vatican Council Two. 'Faith and Justice' are our new marching orders, not that we weren't working with the poor before the Council. The problem in the Church is that not everybody sees it quite that way. We, the Jesuits, are being resented by an awful lot of people who should know better. You'll find out the hard way, Tim, when you are out there, fighting all kinds of enemies of the Church, inside and outside."

Perhaps the crucial moment of the novitiate for most Jesuit candidates is the "Long Retreat," a thirty-day period of intensive meditation in total silence, except for three "break days," halfway through the first year when the men must take the final decision about their future and the Church. To Tim, the meditations at the retreat, which forced him to rethink and relive his past life, were the greatest spiritual experience ever: the deep prayer, the acceptance of God's love and mercy in ways he had never felt or contemplated.

"I think I have found faith!" Tim exclaimed to himself as he prayed alone one winter night. It was not pathos: it was real, he believed. His second thought was that he must apply his faith in a very constructive fashion. That was what Hugh Morgan had been telling him all along, remarking on one occasion, "You're not the kind of guy who's going to be a nine-to-five priest; you'll want to do more, you'll find a challenge, and your unusual background will come in handy! You'll see! . . ."

Tim's background included, of course, the Middle East—both as a scholar and CIA officer. This past invaded his consciousness when, during his novitiate, Egypt and Syria attacked Israel on the Jewish Yom Kippur holy day—the Day of Atonement—in the fourth great successive war in the region since the Israeli independence a quarter of a century earlier. He remembered that his ambition during his Egyptian assignment, perhaps a bit exaggerated in his youthful exuberance, was to be able to project Arab strategic thinking so that he could predict with some accuracy what Arab leaders might do next in this never-ending conflict. Now the thought had come back, recalling what he had learned.

"Actually, it is quite simple," a Cairo University professor he had befriended had told Tim over Scotch and sodas in the magnificent lounge of the Mensa Hotel at the foot of the great Pyramids. Tim had asked him to explain the workings of Arab political minds.

Stirring his drink with his right forefinger, the professor continued: "Always watch for signs of resentment or bitterness among our leaders toward non-Arab foreigners, real or imagined resentments, because it doesn't truly matter what they are. Then you will witness an irredentist surge of nationalism and, finally, foolhardy decisions designed to demonstrate their valor—and clout—to *other* Arab leaders. As you know, they all compete for supreme Arab leadership, like Sultan Saladin in the twelfth century. History does repeat itself. And if there are serious domestic problems in a leader's country—perhaps too much political opposition and too much poverty—then grand gestures serve to establish him as a great patriot and a fearsome nationalist.

"That's what Nasser did when he nationalized the Suez Canal, capitalizing on the fact that it should have been given up by the British a long time ago," the professor said. "Obviously, there are deranged acts performed by deranged individuals, and we have our quota of them. But you cannot predict such acts, although an explosive political climate may produce deranged behavior. This includes political assassinations, like the assassination of King Abdullah of Jordan in Jerusalem way back . . ."

Watching at the Warnersville novitiate television reports and reading newspaper accounts of the fighting, Tim was seized with the notion that perhaps he could best serve God and the Church in the Middle East, as a Jesuit missionary—or something.

The two years of novitiate flew for Tim. In his second year, he was one of the four remaining aspiring Jesuits. The others had dropped out along the way upon discovering that, in the end, they were not prepared to abandon the secular world. The four men had formed a close friendship even though Tim was the oldest in the group at thirty-three; his friends were in their early twenties. But his intelligence, warmth, and permanent good disposition made him most popular and well liked in Warnersville.

On September 15, 1975, Tim Savage took the vows of poverty, chastity, and obedience before the Master of Novices in the chapel of the novitiate. These were perpetual "first vows," making him a Jesuit, but not yet a priest. He was formally designated as "Scholastic" and still being addressed as "Mr. Savage" or just plain Tim. Normally, the next step for a "Scholastic" is to spend two years studying philosophy to be followed by three years of theology before being ordained as priest. Tim, however, was placed on what Hugh Morgan was pleased to call the "fast track" in his career. The Jesuit hierarchy from the Maryland Province to the Society's seat in Rome, the latter always most watchful, was highly impressed by him and his progress, and anxious to put him to work.

Considering that Tim already held a doctorate and taking into account his teaching experience at Georgetown and his overseas exposure, it was decided by the hierarchy that he—already marked as the future Jesuit "superstar"—needed only one year studying philosophy. The Jesuits knew how to be flexible. Consequently, Tim spent a full academic year at Fordham, the Jesuit university in the Bronx in New York City, receiving his certificate in philosophy at the end of June, 1976. He never left the university during that year, never setting foot in Manhattan or visiting his family in Washington. It was an around-the-clock academic marathon, Tim being determined to complete his Fordham stud ies in record time.

For Rome and ordination beckoned beyond.

BOOK THREE

The Search

Chapter Ten

1986

WHEN TIM SAVAGE WAS selected, out of the clear blue Roman sky, to investigate the assassination attempt against Pope Gregory XVII, he had been a priest for eight years. He had been ordained in Rome at the Gesú, the Jesuits' principal church where St. Ignatius is buried, on Via del Corso, across the street from Italian Communist party headquarters, after three years of studying theology at the Pontifical Gregorian University, the Jesuit institution known to Anglo-Saxons as "The Greg." As an ordained Jesuit priest, Tim next had to take the "Final Vows," the fourth being the vow to go wherever the Holy Father might wish to send him. Now, as he began to work to shape his investigation, Tim was struck—and amused—by the realization of how literally the fourth vow applied to his mission. Only God, certainly neither the pope nor Monsignor Sainte-Ange, knew at that point where he might wind up in pursuit of the truth.

There was a touch of predestination in the choice of Tim to conduct this secret investigation. As a practical matter, he was picked because he happened to live in Rome when the pope and his private secretary had decided to open their own inquiry into the shooting of Gregory XVII by Circlic, a young Turk of bizarre origins—and because he was recommended to them as an outstanding and brilliant specialist on Islamic and Arab affairs. Agca Circlic, of course, was a Muslim, apparently connected in some fashion to murky Islamic politics. This convergence made it simpler for Gregory XVII and Sainte-Ange to find the man for the task.

Tim lived in Rome because his Jesuit superiors, seeing in him a future "superstar," had sent him there after his year of philosophy at Fordham for advanced studies in theology at the Gregorian

101

rather than, like most American "scholastics," to the Jesuit School of Theology at Berkeley, California, or the Weston School of Theology at Cambridge, Massachusetts. And Tim had become an admirer of the Jesuits' intellect and thrust. Their missionaries, for example, had reached Japan and China in the sixteenth century as teachers; that century's greatest mathematician, Christopher Clavius, was the inventor of the Gregorian Calendar. And that was only the beginning. The Jesuits had always been in the vanguard of thought, science, and theological adventure.

The three years Tim had spent at the imposing Gregorian edifice on Piazza della Pilotta in midtown Rome were heavy with courses on systematic theology (once known as "dogmatic"), Scripture, moral theology, and practical instructions on how to celebrate Mass in the vernacular—in English for him—since the demise of the Latin Mass, administer the Sacraments, and hear confessions. The latter included role playing by the scholastics, who invented "confessions" to be heard by colleagues pretending to be priests in the confessional. Tim, naturally, was extremely careful in his mock confessions. As Father Morgan, visiting Rome during that time, remarked to him, "You cannot very well say, 'Bless me Father—I was an assassin in Vietnam or an accomplice of assassins.' "

Tim lived sparsely but comfortably at the Jesuits' Bellarmino Residence, within walking distance of the Gregorian, and, as before, he had time for little other than studies. He managed to squeeze Italian language lessons in between theology courses, learning it quickly with the help of his Warnersville background in Latin, taken as an elective. Very occasionally, when he could not resist particularly beautiful weather, Tim allowed himself a stroll around Rome, to the Colosseum, the Aventine Hill, the Villa Borghese or, across the Tiber, to Trastevere and, of course, St. Peter's Square. On such occasions, he was sometimes gone all day. Once a year, Tim drove in a rented car to the Monte Cassino Monastery, where his father's bones lay scattered under wartime ruins.

Tim's ordination finally came on a June day after he had earned his Master in Divinity degree at the Gregorian. He chose to be ordained in Rome, rather than Washington, and his mother, stepfather, brother, and sister attended the ordination Mass at the

Gesú. He was ordained by an American bishop attached to a Curia congregation whom he liked and respected. The Mass, along with six of his Gregorian colleagues being ordained the same day, was profoundly moving.

Wearing a white alb over a clerical shirt and black trousers, Tim lay prostrate as Mass began. After the Liturgy of the Word and the preaching of the homily by the bishop, ordination began. The men rose. The bishop wordlessly placed his hands on top of Tim's head: when he removed them, Tim had become a priest. Then his hands were anointed with oil, and other priests at the Gesú, including Father Morgan, who had also come for the ceremony, imposed their hands on the heads of the men just ordained. It was Tim's first Mass as a priest, and he concelebrated it with the bishop and his own colleagues. It was the end of a long and arduous road that had begun in that Vietnamese hamlet — and the start of a new one.

This new road led to the resumption of his work on Islam, now expanded to the complexities of Christian-Muslim relations. On the advice of the Gregorian's Rector, a Dutchman who had spent long years in Lebanon, Tim joined the University's Pontifical Oriental Institute and its Faculty of Ecclesiastic Oriental Sciences, where he could best improve his specialty. The Rector had made a point of telling Tim that Gregory XVII had himself a particular interest in bettering communications between Christianity and Islam.

Working out of his office on Piazza Santa Maria Maggiore, near one of Rome's great basilicas, Tim was soon involved not only in theological aspects of the Holy See's relations with Islam, such as meetings with scholars from Al-Azhar University in Cairo and impressively learned Saudi mullahs, but in the Vatican's Muslim politics as well. Increasingly, he was assigned purely foreign policy tasks by the Secretariat of State, ranging from analyses of fundamentalist Islamic pressures in Egypt or Turkey, two very different propositions, to reports on the situation of persecuted Christians under radical Muslim rule in the Sudan.

Within a year, Tim was engaged as a part-time consultant to the Commission on Religious Relations with Muslims, established in the mid-Seventies by Pope Paul VI as part of the Pontifical Council for Inter-Religious Dialogue. He was there, chatting with the retired archbishop from West Africa, when Gregory XVII was shot on St. Peter's Square. Three years later, the cardinal heading the Council requested the Gregorian's Rector to release Tim so that he could join the Commission as a full-time staff member. Having consulted with the General Superior of the Jesuits, the Rector, of course, agreed. They all kept an eye on the future of their "superstar."

Tim felt very much at home in Rome. His Italian was now fluent, without distorting his command of French acquired at Georgetown, and he liked Italians, their music, their cheerful disposition, and their food. He was cozily comfortable in his room at the Villa Malta on Via di Porta Ponciana downtown with a superb view of the Quirinale and the Pantheon. Though he was consumed by his daily work, Tim made friends easily with fellow Jesuits in Rome and became acquainted with quite a few Italian families. He maintained pleasant contacts with a number of Americans, including several journalists and diplomats attached to the U.S. Embassy on the Via Veneto—inside of which the CIA Station was tucked away—just minutes away from Villa Malta. He also cultivated relationships with diplomats from Muslim countries and with Islam specialists at the Gregorian University and other institutions.

Given their professional pursuits and travel around the rim of the Mediterranean, Tim found many of them to be excellent sources of information. Conversely, diplomats and journalists sought *him* out, not only because he was good company, but because his work at the Vatican made him a valuable contact. In the Roman environment, information was the most precious commodity.

The Roman years were Tim's best. At forty-four, he had finally succeeded in exorcising the demons of his former life, or so he believed, and, in finding the fulfillment and serenity that had so long eluded him. Feeling relaxed, he took frequent, long, and enjoyable walks around Rome—often strolling from Villa Malta to Via dell'Erba and his office, and back home. He went to the Tuscan countryside and its hospitable little towns and took up mountain climbing, driving to the Dolomites during summer vacations, and enjoying long weekends in the company of a French Jesuit who had once been a guide in the high Alps. There Tim discovered the exhilaration of conquering the sheer face of a mighty granite peak. His sense of humor had fully returned and, most delightful, he was truly enjoying life.

At his small office, Tim shut the door tight and, following Monsignor Sainte-Ange's orders to embark immediately on the investigation, began to shape his plans. But, first, he had to reshape his life in Rome.

He telephoned the secretary of the Commission for Muslim Relations, an easygoing Belgian who had become a good friend, to ask to be received later in the day. Then Tim placed a similar call to the offices of the cardinal presiding over the Inter-Religious Dialogue Council. He could not simply vanish from work one day without some explanation to his superiors. Once again he needed a cover story, Tim thought with a touch of amusement. The Jesuit General Superior, of course, needed no contrived explanations: he most likely knew the *real* story.

Already evident to Tim from his morning conversation with Sainte-Ange was the fact that his investigation would be lengthy—it could run to many months, if not years—because, quite clearly, seemingly insurmountable obstacles had been erected by someone or some organization to keep the truth inaccessible. Tim planned to go first through all the available official documentation and, perhaps, he might be shown or told more at the Vatican. But this would not even begin, he realized, to point the way. In any case, he would have to be away for a long time from his regular job concerns with Islam—and concentrate on others. The only known fact was that Circlic, the shooter, was a Muslim Turk. What Tim faced was a vast puzzle with no clues, a classic situation in the craft of intelligence.

His Belgian friend accepted without question Tim's request for a leave of absence, which, he had warned him, could be a "rather long one." The excuse he presented was that his physician had ordered him to spend "some time" at a high mountain resort and to rest at Villa Malta because of signs that tuberculosis Tim had supposedly acquired in Vietnam had not been entirely cured.

That was the first idea that had occurred to him for his cover story, and at the Vatican, where questions were seldom asked, it did not really matter whether it was credible.

The secretary of the Commission refrained from commenting on Tim's splendid physical appearance, "tuberculosis" notwithstanding. He just nodded sagely, saying, "Yes, of course, Tim. Take the time you need . . . Ah, I'll work myself on that Iranian analysis project . . . Do not worry . . ." The Belgian knew him well enough to believe that there must be an excellent reason for Tim's leave of absence. His shop was often involved in what amounted to confidential intelligence work.

Tim found the same immediate assent from the elderly Nigerian cardinal who chaired the Council. He, too, was an expert on the world of Islam. Born in the Muslim region of Nigeria, he had served for years as parish priest in Catholic villages there before being named bishop, archbishop, and cardinal by Pope Paul VI. Before the conclave that had elected Gregory XVII eight years earlier, the Nigerian was himself considered a long shot to become the first African pope since Vittore I in 189 A.D. Now he was utilized as one of the Church's principal advisers on the Third World. Tim made a mental note that, as his investigation advanced, it might be worthwhile to consult the cardinal.

As a matter of courtesy and respect, Tim next visited the Jesuit General Superior at the impressive gray edifice on Borgo Santo Spirito, a quiet street two blocks from St. Peter's Square. He was greeted warmly by the scholarly Spaniard, who had been stationed for many years in Egypt and was a highly regarded specialist on Islam, with amazing contacts among Muslim theologians. Tim began to report on his meeting with Sainte-Ange, however, the General gently waved him off. "But I wish you all the luck in the world, my son," he said, blessing Tim.

What Tim had no way of knowing was that the General himself had recommended his appointment to the Commission for Religious Relations with Muslims after observing his work on Islam at the Gregorian. Similarly, Tim did not know that Sainte-Ange had consulted the General as well as the Nigerian cardinal about the best candidate for a vital secret but unspecified mission for the pope that required familiarity with Islam and the Middle East. The

General had told the papal private secretary, "I can think of nobody who would be better than Father Savage," adding some comments about Tim's past links with the institution in Langley, Virginia. The Nigerian cardinal had made a few private inquiries with a trusted bishop in Washington and the Pronuncio who headed the Apostolic Nunciature there; both had solid connections with the U.S. government. Sainte-Ange had not explained why he was making these inquiries, but it was rapidly reported back to him that, indeed, Father Savage had a most interesting background and experience.

Tim had decided from the outset that his Villa Malta room would be the best center for his investigations. The Jesuits running the residence did not need to be informed about his health "relapse" and "rest" plans. If Father Savage preferred to work in his room instead of his office and if he traveled a lot, it was his business alone. Villa Malta, where several other Jesuits in important Vatican positions also lived and worked, was a supremely discreet hideaway.

Starting on his inquiry, Tim devoted long weeks to educating himself about every conceivable aspect of his assignment. He read everything available about the Turkish assassin, his identity and past, about all the official and unofficial investigations conducted over the past years, and about the shooter's trial. At his request over the telephone—he did not think it wise to visit her office, much as he would like to see her again—Sister Angela provided him with masses of material. She sent him Italian police reports, newspaper clippings, the Turk's trial transcripts, and even U.S. Senate hearings concerning the CIA's knowledge of the attack on Gregory XVII. It was naturally necessary for Tim to absorb all this information, but it did nothing to tell him how to orient his investigatory work. On the other hand, it provided him with the justification for calling Angela fairly often to request still another document and to ask what other materials might exist—more and more he invented impossibly difficult requests. Their conversations became longer and longer. Tim loved the sound of her voice. Angela sounded most pleasantly polite, but Tim thought he detected a touch more than mere politeness.

Awaiting, though without much hope, a breakthrough bit of information, no matter how small, Tim resolved to learn more about papal history. He had been taught both at Georgetown and at the CIA, that one, especially a scholar or intelligence officer, could not deal with the present without a knowledge of the past. He already knew enough to be convinced that the Vatican probably had no equal—ever—when it came to the great tradition of intrigues, plots, and conspiracies over scores of centuries. And, as Tim was discovering with amazement and fascination, the attempt on the life of Gregory XVII had ample precedents, to say the least. Murders of popes, often in sinister and repelling circumstances, were nothing new.

The incredibly horrifying track record of the papacy had started with the first pope officially recognized as such by the Church: Peter the Apostle, the poor fisherman from Galilee, named Simon Bar Jonah at birth, who with Paul the Apostle founded the Catholic institution in Rome after they fled Roman persecution in Palestine; there already were Christian churches in Jerusalem, Antioch, Corinth, and Ephesus. But the primacy of the Church of Rome became legitimized by Christ's words to Peter in the Gospel according to Matthew: "Thou are Peter, and upon this Rock I will build my Church and I will give to thee the keys of the Kingdom of Heaven." These words appear in Latin, though they were originally pronounced in Aramaic and Hebrew, in tall letters on the dome of St. Peter's Basilica, and Tim Savage knew them by heart.

Peter had run into anti-Christian persecution in Rome as well and fled from it, too. He returned after having had a vision of Christ and was imprisoned on the orders of Emperor Nero, who did not take kindly to any form of dissent. He was crucified upside down on the Vatican Hill, probably in 64 A.D. The next pope to be killed was Clement I, the third pontiff after Peter, who was exiled to Crimea by the Romans in 97 A.D., tied to an anchor, and thrown into the Black Sea. Callistus I was lynched by a mob in the Trastevere suburb of Rome in 222. Fabian was brutally murdered in prison in 250, after fourteen years as pope. Sixtus II, a Greek, was beheaded by his deacons in 258. Persecution against Christians was so severe well into the fourth century that the Church subsequently declared all the thirty-two pontiffs, starting with Peter, who had served prior to 335 to be martyrs. The last one in that group was Silvestro I, overthrown and killed by political enemies after twenty-four years on St. Peter's throne. Murder, however, was not a prerequisite for martyrdom status. Official persecution of Christianity finally ended with Emperor Constantine's conversion in 337, just before his death.

But, as Tim kept learning with mounting horror, this was far from the end of papal assassinations and other forms of disgrace and indignity. Thus the next papal victim of Holy See intrigues was St. Silverio, arrested and exiled to Anatolia and demoted to the rank of monk in 537. He was the son of Pope Ormisda, who had lived out his reign in peaceful and saintly fashion; there had been five other popes between father and son. Silverio had been framed by Vigilius, the aristocratic papal ambassador to Constantinople, the seat of the Byzantine Empire, who had powerful ambitions to become pope himself, and Antonina, the wife of the Roman general Belisarius. The general had accused Pope Silverio of plotting to open Rome's gates to approaching Goth armies. Vigilius was elected to the papacy, but this was not the end of the story. Though Emperor Justinian secured a new trial for Silverio, brought back to Rome from Anatolia with the understanding that he would be restored to the pontificate if found to be innocent, Vigilius succeeded in having him arrested again and deported to the island of Palmaria, where he soon died of malnutrition. Not surprisingly, the Church declared him a martyr.

However, even intrigue-ridden Rome could occasionally produce poetic justice. Justinian had Vigilius arrested twice over complex theological disputes that triggered major political crises in the Roman Empire lasting ten years, until Vigilius died from gallstones as he traveled from Constantinople to Rome in 555.

Being pope continued to be an exceedingly unsafe occupation with no guaranteed job security. Pope Martin I was arrested on Emperor Constans II's orders in 653 in still another imperial-theological power quarrel over theology and politics. After brutal maltreatment in a Roman prison, he was deported to Constantinople, found guilty of treason at a hasty trial, dragged in shackles through the streets, and flogged in public. He died two years later in exile in Crimea.

Pope Leo III was attacked in 799 by a Roman crowd that attempted to rip out his tongue and blind him. The mob was led by Paschalis, the nephew of Pope Leo's predecessor Hadrian I; Leo recovered from his injuries, keeping both his speech and sight. In 864, Frankish Emperor Louis II had planned to have Pope Nicholas I assassinated for excommunicating his brother, King Lothair of Lorraine, on grounds of bigamy, but cooler heads prevailed and papal authority was respected. Pope John VIII was clubbed to death in 882 by former friends and acolytes.

Stephen VI fared even worse after presiding over one of the most revolting spectacles in Church history. In January 897, Stephen VI had ordered the trial of the desiccated corpse of Formosus, a cordially hated pope—though a remarkable diplomat—who had died in April of the previous year. Formosus was followed as pope by Boniface VI, who expired two weeks after his election for unrecorded reasons. It is a mystery why Pope Stephen had staged Formosus' "Cadaver Synod"; attired in papal garb and poised atop a throne, the body was declared guilty of multiple crimes, its fingers were cut off, and it was cast into the Tiber. So horrified were Romans by this sinister farce that Stephen was ousted by enraged mobs, then strangled in prison. He had been pontiff for a year and three months.

Reading a recently published history of the papacy, Tim was astonished to learn that "a third of the popes elected between 872 and 1012 died in suspicious circumstances." It was not very encouraging in terms of his own investigatory endeavor, he thought. But Tim plowed ahead with his macabre research. Leo V, it turned out, was murdered in 903 by a Roman bishop who succeeded him as Sergius III. The first millennium of the Christian era ended with the suffocation of John X in 928 and Stephen VIII's terrible death from mutilation in 931 after less than three years as pope.

In terms of violent or mysterious papal deaths or murder attempts, the second millennium opened with the unexplained demise of Sergius IV in 1012, although things were calming down around the Vatican. Benedict IX, young and given to debauchery, was deposed in 1044, but allowed to live, even staging a brief comeback. Gregory VI was removed peacefully in 1046, after a year and a half on the throne. Gregory VII, one of the great popes, died in exile in Salerno in 1085, victim of savage European politics and wars of his time. But mayhem returned to the papacy when Lucius II was killed in 1145, his second year in office, in a battle for the control of Rome. In 1452, Nicholas V, a venerated humanist, patron of the arts, and founder of the Vatican Library, survived a powerful conspiracy by Roman aristocrats led by Stefano Porcaro to overthrow him.

Pope Clement XIV, Tim read with awe, was said to have been poisoned by the Jesuits with a "dish of chocolate" on Holy Thursday of 1773. Clement had suppressed the Jesuits earlier that year, and this may have been their attempt at vengeance. The Jesuits, world travelers since the sixteenth century, had discovered *cacao* in the Brazilian Amazon and perfected the art of preparing hot chocolate. In the event, the pope did not die until the following year, presumably immune to poisoned chocolate—if, indeed, the Jesuits had tried to do away with him in such an elegant fashion.

There was no record of assassination attempts against popes in the ensuing two centuries, Tim saw with relief, but mysteries seemed to reappear in the second half of the twentieth century. John Paul I died after thirty-three *days* as pope in 1978, and the circumstances of his demise were never fully clarified. And now, Tim Savage told himself, he had to cope with the case of Gregory XVII, particularly disturbing because it now appeared that this plot or attempt to kill a pope, successful or not, had come from *outside* the Vatican and Rome—and not from *within*—or so it seemed.

Chapter Eleven

And when it came to Gregory XVII, what did Tim Savage know about his past, his connections, his commitments?

The fact was that he knew almost nothing about the French pope, now in his eighth year in power, beyond what was in official biographies, shallow newspaper and magazine articles—and usually unreliable Vatican gossip. Without deeper knowledge of Gregory XVII, Tim realized he would be incapable of effectively pursuing his investigation. He had to search for what this pope may have done or said—or stood for—publicly and privately to provoke an assassination attempt, even if the act itself stemmed from irrationality on the part of one or more actors in the drama.

Things never happen in a vacuum, and Tim increasingly doubted that the shooting in St. Peter's Square five years ago was simply the idea of a mentally deranged individual. Police and tribunal trial records made that quite clear. The guiding principle in the craft of intelligence, as he well knew, was to look for significant clues, no matter how seemingly small or irrelevant, before centering on trails to follow in order to arrive at the ultimate solution. Thus far, Tim had found none.

The official Vatican biographical sketch on a bookshelf at Villa Malta told him what he already knew: that Gregory XVII, now nearly sixty-seven, was the two-hundred-sixty-fourth Roman Catholic pope, that he was the tenth French pontiff in the history of the Church, that he was elected in 1978, and so forth. But Tim's pursuit turned more and more interesting as he worked his way through further material, as he began to develop something of a perspective on the pope's life.

*   *   *

Gregory XVII was born Roland de Millefeuille, the only son of parents descended from a long line of Provençal nobility, on November 11, 1918, the day of the signing of the Armistice ending World War One. As a child, he lived in great comfort at his parents' family mansion on the left bank of the Rhône, not far from Avignon, where seven French popes reigned for seventy-three years in the fourteenth century. It was near the Philippe-le-Bel Tower, a magnificent thirteenth-century structure. The mansion was his birthplace.

From a thick new biography of Gregory XVII, published in Rome the week Tim had met with Sainte-Ange, he learned that Roland was a most precocious youngster and student, amazing his teachers with his acuity. The boy, it seemed, was endowed not only with extraordinary intelligence, but was kind and friendly, pious and impressively mystical even at a very young age. His parents believed that his mysticism was atavistic, flowing from ancient Provençal traditions of religion and faith—and kept alive as a mystery by the disquieting mistral winds of the south, the mystical poetry of Frédéric Mistral, the great bard who composed in beautiful, romantic Provençal language, and the ancient ballads of the troubadours of the land. There was a hint that this mysticism also had roots in the thirteenth-century crusades against Cathar heretics in Languedoc, just north of the Pyrénées and between Toulouse and the Mediterranean, when uncounted thousands of God-fearing but independent-minded Cathars were massacred or burned at the stake by French armies on the orders of the pope in Rome.

Roland himself wrote his first poem—in French—when he still attended the parochial Catholic grade school. It was an ode to Our Lady of Lourdes, composed after visiting with his parents the Marian Shrine at the Massabielle Grotto, where great miracles were said to be performed in healing the sick through the intercession of Mary, who had appeared eighteen times in 1858 to a fourteen-year-old local girl. Roland's piety grew during his years at the *lycée*—he went to church every morning to pray on his way to high school—but he also excelled in Latin, French literature, and history, and was considered to be the best center forward on his Avignon school soccer team.

Tall, athletic, hawk-faced, with a darkish Mediterranean complexion, and known for his Provençal courtliness, Roland was highly popular at school and among his teachers and other adults. Reading the pope's biography, Tim continuously came across quotations from those who had known Roland in his youth, describing his "phenomenal willpower," his "determination always to be best at everything," and his "charm and charisma." None of these traits seemed to have changed over the years. Even his appearance at the age of sixty-eight did not betray too much the passage of time: he still stood tall and erect, the hawkishness of his strong face giving him a commanding presence.

Tim suspected that there was a touch of hagiography in Roland's depiction, and was therefore intrigued and surprised by the words of a classmate, quoted in the book, that "Roland de Millefeuille does not tolerate disagreements with his views and opinions." Actually, Tim had heard rumors and comments that Gregory XVII had placed the Jesuits on a short leash, theologically and politically, believing them to be too assertive, but there was no noticeable evidence of it. The General Superior naturally would not discuss the subject with subordinates like Tim, and the rumors continued to float around the Jesuit community in Rome. But, as he thought about it, Tim began to wonder whether Gregory XVII's frequent and stubborn rejection of views of others—if it was really the case—might have been a motive for someone to plan his assassination. He stored this idea away in the back of his mind.

After completing the *lycée,* Roland had opted for priesthood and entered a seminary. He was ordained in the spring of 1940, just weeks before France surrendered to Nazi Germany and nine months after the eruption of World War Two. Not quite twenty-two, and one of the youngest priests ever ordained in the French Church, Roland was assigned by the archbishop of Avignon to a small parish down on the Rhône, an impoverished hilly village of elderly peasant families.

Father Roland spent nearly five years at his parish, until the end of the war, looking after his flock as best he could and hungrily devouring volumes on theology, philosophy, and ethics borrowed from the Avignon archdiocesal library. But he also led something of a double life as an organizer of the *maquis,* the French anti-Nazi resistance, in his area. The priestly cassock was an excellent cover, and the Germans never suspected the pious young *abbé* and the old people of the somnolent village, to whom Roland was so devoted, of secret contacts with the Free French. He was subsequently credited with assuring safe passage for scores of Allied officers and men who had escaped from German prisoner-of-war camps and sought to make their way to Spain and on to England. Roland was very heroic and after the war he was awarded the Medal of Liberation.

However, he had also realized, with considerable shock, that quite a few priests in his region had turned over escaped Allied prisoners—and Jews hiding across Provence—to the Nazis. Roland discovered when records were opened by postwar French governments that about 75,000 Jews, including 12,000 children, were deported from France to Nazi death camps between 1941 and 1944 and that only 2,500 survived. He shuddered at the thought that some of the Jews—even a single one—might have been sent to slaughter by his fellow priests.

Roland was deeply disturbed to find out at the same time that after liberation many of these priests often provided safe haven to French war criminals, police officers, and other *collaborateurs* with the occupiers, tarnishing the Church in France with the brush of extreme rightist coloration. When his own pro-Allied activities during the occupation became known in the aftermath of the war, Roland's ultraconservative priestly colleagues launched a whispering campaign, accusing him of communist tendencies. Tim read about it with amazement in a magazine article Sister Angela had sent him from the Apostolic Palace in one of her frequent packets of materials. Could this charge loom behind the conspiracy against Gregory XVII after so many years, Tim asked himself, but rejected the notion as wholly implausible. The French Church could not be so deeply divided, its past notwithstanding, he thought. But it was the pope himself who, as a young priest, had delivered a devastating critique of his fellow Frenchmen, charging in a sarcastic sermon that "under the banner of Liberty, Fraternity, and Equality," they had transformed the monarchy into an evil empire. Roland was alluding to the prewar Third Republic with its corruption and immorality. That, too, could go for the French Church.

Studying papal materials twelve or more hours a day in his Villa Malta room, pausing only to sleep, eat, and run occasional personal errands, Tim saw Roland's ecclesiastic career unfold before his eyes. Thus, within a year of the war, the *abbé* was assigned to Marseille to minister to the faithful and their families in the tough, impoverished port district, the famous Canebière. The Archbishop of Marseille had been searching for an "inspired" priest, and his Avignon colleague, who owed him favors, instantly recommended Father Roland.

Roland spent a year in Marseille, discovering the despair of the urban poor and joining the new movement of worker-priests. In slacks, blouse, and jaunty black beret, Roland labored on the docks alongside the stevedores, helped to run soup kitchens, and at night taught adults literacy. Naturally, he performed his priestly duties as well: from hearing confessions to dispensing advice on family matters, and officiating at weddings, baptisms, and funerals. He also began to write articles about Christian ethics of social justice for progressive Catholic publications. The lay Catholic philosopher Jacques Maritain, who helped to redefine and modernize social thought in the Church, became his intellectual and spiritual hero. And Roland formed friendships with destitute Muslims from North Africa who, in quest of work, were settling in southern France by the tens of thousands—and creating one more social problem. Marseille was Roland's first contact with Muslims and Islam, and the beginning of his interest in the religion of Muhammad and His followers. Was this a first clue to what would happen so many years later, with a Muslim Turk firing his pistol at the Roman Catholic pope on St. Peter's Square? And if so, what did it mean?

There were so many dots to connect in the puzzle. What, for example, was the nature of the connection between Father Roland and the Grand Mufti of Jerusalem who, according to a one-sentence mention in the new biography, was "well acquainted with Father Millefeuille whom he saw often in Marseille"? Then there was a similarly passing remark suggesting that when the rebellion erupted in Algeria in the late 1950s, Roland, then studying in Rome, openly supported the National Liberation Front's demand for independence from France. This was not unusual among progressive priests in the French Church, but it left Tim with the impression that the young Father was sympathetic to Islam-linked causes, which, in turn, made it rather unlikely that a Muslim would try to kill him some twenty years later—when Roland already was Gregory XVII. On the other hand, however, Tim was aware that none of it led to logical conclusions, one way or another. He knew precious little at this juncture.

Another potential clue came Tim's way as he read Roland's articles on Mission de France, the worker-priest movement with which he had been associated in Marseille. He was struck by Roland's comments on the struggle between Roman Catholic and communist and socialist unions for the control of the Marseille docks—and his firm identification with the Catholic unions. Tim thought this was interesting enough to warrant further research, and he spent several days at Rome's National Library going through books on postwar labor problems and rivalries in Western Europe. He found no mention of Father Millefeuille's name, but what jumped out at him was the story of how the CIA and the American Federation of Labor secretly provided funds to Catholic trade unionists in Marseille—and their silent gangster-longshoremen allies—to fight and defeat the communists. It was, to be sure, ancient history by now, yet it coincided with Roland's presence in Marseille and his worker-priest involvements. The more Tim worked on his life story, the more of Roland's footprints materialized in seemingly unrelated and even contradictory contexts. He certainly was an activist in and out of the Church, and activists do tempt fate, even lethal fate.

Gradually, Roland's reputation spread throughout the Church hierarchy. One day, he was summoned by the Avignon bishop, still his ecclesiastic superior, to be "informed"—actually it was an order—that he would be attending the Sorbonne in Paris to earn his doctorate in philosophy; he already had the equivalent of a lower university degree through his *baccalauréat* from the *lycée* and his seminary studies.

"You are the hope of our Church," the old archbishop told him. "You have the mind and you have the heart . . . Today, our Church lacks both . . ."

Three years later, at the age of thirty-two, Roland received the doctorate: his dissertation was on Mission de France and its implications for the Church and secular ethics.

The 1950s were the heyday of Church intellectuals and Roland de Millefeuille was a rising star among them. His friends included a bishop from Orléans, himself a philosopher, who had converted from Judaism as a teenager during the war—his parents had emigrated from Poland to Paris and he was born there—and now was a leading thinker among Church liberals. On his advice, Roland applied to the Pontifical Gregorian University in Rome to work on a doctorate in theology. His bishop friend had warned him "that it's no longer enough to have just *one* doctorate." Roland's friendship with the "Jewish Bishop" won him still more hostility among the coterie of right-wing priests. This *is* interesting, Tim Savage thought, making a note in the fat ledger, the centerpiece of his growing papal dossier.

Roland remained in Rome for seven years, earning his theology doctorate and establishing a wide-ranging network of Curial friendships, a precious investment for the future. Elevated to the rank of monsignor, Roland de Millefeuille was drafted by the Secretariat of State as a speechwriter—in Latin—for Pope John XXIII. Early in 1962, the pope approved his nomination as bishop of the Fréjus-Toulon diocese, a choice appointment on the affluent Riviera; the diocese also comprised the great French naval base at Toulon and therefore high-level military connections.

Back in the south of France, Roland rediscovered his Provençal roots, addressing in Provençal the simple people in the fishing and hill villages, and his wealthier faithful in elegant French. Mass in those days was still said in Latin, the sixteenth-century Tridentine Mass inherited from the Council of Trent and Pope Pius V, its rigid implementor.

Roland, however, believed that for the Church to survive in the modern world, liturgy had to be modernized—and Mass celebrated in the vernacular, the language of the faithful in their country. He frequently wrote and spoke about it, winning further opprobrium among the traditionalist priests who began circulating letters in their dioceses sharply criticizing Roland. The letters attacking the bishop violated Church obedience rules, but the authors were prepared to be in defiance to make their views heard.

As soon as he was installed in Fréjus, Roland had arranged for his seminary friend Romain de Sainte-Ange to join him at the diocese as administrator. They had stayed in touch over the years, though separated by distance, especially during Roland's long stay in Rome where Sainte-Ange managed to visit him only twice, but as bishop in Fréjus, Roland had the power to choose his deputies for the management of the diocese. At the time, Sainte-Ange was the parish priest of the largest church in Honfleur in Normandy, and there was no problem in having him transferred to Fréjus. Roland could not be happier: not only could he entrust the actual day-to-day administration of the diocese to his friend, but he had also acquired a loyal and absolutely discreet interlocutor with whom he could discuss his ideas about the future of the Church— and his own.

In October 1962, Roland was back in Rome to attend, with 2,859 fellow bishops from all over the world, the Second Vatican Council, convoked by Pope John XXIII to force the Church to enter the modern age. The first Vatican Council had been held in 1869 and 1870, nearly a century earlier. Roland was assigned to the drafting of the Constitution of the Sacred Liturgy, which, for the first time, authorized the use of the vernacular in celebrating Mass—Roland's dream—and the drafting of the Declaration on the Relationship of the Church to non-Christian Religions. These were magnificent assignments for an ambitious intellectual prelate, and Bishop de Millefeuille turned into an outstanding figure at the Council. He formed strong friendships throughout the world Church, among Western and Eastern European bishops, North and Latin Americans, Asians and Africans. As he told a biographer many years later, "I was privileged to help build the *true* universal Church . . ."

Tim Savage found it extremely interesting that Roland had been a coauthor of the *Nostra Aetate* (*In Our Time*) declaration, which, in a historical breakthrough for the Church, had affirmed that Jesus' Crucifixion "cannot be blamed on all the Jews living without distinction, nor upon the Jews of today." He wondered whether this pro-Jewish stand could have triggered enough resentment among

Muslims to result in an assassination attempt, now that Roland was pope? Could it explain why the Turk, a Muslim, was the shooter? Tim knew that most Muslims were not viscerally or fanatically anti-Jewish in the religious sense, but Islamic fundamentalism was rising rapidly—the 1979 revolution in Iran, led by fanatic mullahs, was certainly a worrisome example—and a conspiracy against Gregory XVII could not be ruled out altogether.

But was it not equally plausible, Tim asked himself, that the plot had been hatched by extreme right-wing Catholics, priests, or laymen, who were fundamentalists in their own way? No, he decided, it was too absurd. We are not living in the Middle Ages, when popes were murdered at regular intervals for religious reasons, real or imagined. Tim still had no clues to point him in any convincing direction. He noted that Sainte-Ange had accompanied Roland to the Council, but there was nothing to indicate whether he had influenced his friend in any fashion or how he reacted to conciliar texts coauthored by the Fréjus bishop.

In the post-Council years, Roland was busy actively building his Church career. In 1967, he was named archbishop of Marseille by the pope. Not only was this familiar territory from his young worker-priest days, but now he had to live with the new realities of France—and of the Church. Algeria's independence, which Roland had supported from the outset, filled the French Mediterranean coast with *Pieds-Noirs,* French colonialists expelled from their North African ancestral homes, and still another wave of young Arabs fleeing to the urban centers to find work. Social tensions, already exacerbated by youth rebellions of 1968 across France, were barely controllable in Marseille and along the entire southern coast. The new archbishop had to act as pastor to the faithful; conciliator between employers and workers; adviser to the police, the *gendarmerie,* and local politicians; preacher of racial and religious tolerance; and executor of Vatican theological instructions. In 1970, Roland de Millefeuille became cardinal, the first name on the pope's consistory list that year. He was fifty-two years old, full of ideas, energy, and very strong opinions. He moved to Rome once again, this time to be prefect of the Congregation for Bishops, a powerful post rarely given to a newcomer to the College of Cardinals. But the old pope saw the future of the Church in Roland, a notion fully but quietly shared by the new cardinal.

Eight years later, the old pope died peacefully, and his duly elected successor died mysteriously after a month on St. Peter's throne. The conclave, back at work at the Sistine Chapel, found itself stalemated by the rivalry of two Italian cardinals, rapidly concluding that it had to turn to France, the country that had already provided nine popes. Turning to France meant electing Cardinal Roland de Millefeuille, the charm-blessed intellectual with a social conscience, two doctorates, a distinguished role at the Vatican Council, enviable political and diplomatic acumen, impeccable pastoral credentials, an impressive strength of character—and powerful friends in the College of Cardinals who elect popes.

At sixty, his age was perfect for the papacy: his pontificate would probably be neither too short nor too long, which was the way cardinals wished it to be. Thus Roland de Millefeuille of Avignon became Pope Gregory XVII, the pontiff of the enchanting smile and steel-trap mind. The cardinals explained that they had been inspired by the Holy Spirit.

Gregory the Great, as Tim Savage noted, wrote once: "I am ready to die rather than allow the Church of the Apostle Saint Peter to degenerate in my day." That was in the sixth century. Roland de Millefeuille would do no less in the twentieth century.

Tim Savage finally put down Gregory XVII's biography, having underlined what struck him as revealing passages, making copious notes in his ledger, and placing questions and exclamation marks wherever something had caught his special attention. In the ledger's section dealing with the pope's personal history, Tim wrote, CONCLUSION: MANY ENEMIES—MANY FRIENDS, then listed names, organizations, and governments in each column, assigning plausible but tentative motives under MANY ENEMIES. He chose not to put down comments under FRIENDS; his intelligence training had taught him that one could never be certain who might be on *his* trail, following him, possibly breaking into his room, and finding the ledger, though it was locked inside a safe Tim had bought. Mild paranoia is part of the craft of intelligence. His comments about ENEMIES were essentially obvious, and it would not really matter if they were read by one or another of the "enemies." Comments about "friends," however, should not fall into the wrong hands; it was none of the business of the "enemies" who were the significant "friends" of Gregory XVII and how they could be relied upon in the course of Tim's investigation.

Studying Church history at the Jesuit seminary, Tim had naturally become familiar with endless schisms and heresies, great and small, divisions, internecine battles, and conspiracies of every imaginable type affecting Christianity over the past two millennia, or nearly so, since the dawning of the Christian era. But now Tim was curious about the relations over the centuries between France and the Holy See, hoping that he might come upon some useful lead. It was uncanny how history, even fairly ancient history, could help one comprehend certain contemporary realities. Religions and nations have eternal memories, always ready to act upon them. Wars, civil or otherwise, over religion and its interpretations had been as common in the first Christian century as they were in the twentieth: they involved early Christian heresies; battles over the Protestant Reform; modern fundamentalism among Catholics, Protestants, and Muslims; conflicts between Muslims and Hindus; and so on and on. And in the case of France and the Roman Church, history was unbelievably intractable, contradictory, petulant, and violent.

It began in the second half of the fifth century when Clovis, king of the Salian Franks, converted to Christianity—his Christian wife, Princess Clotilda, had long urged him to do so—in gratitude to God for victory over his enemies, the Alemanni, the Germans of the day. Clovis was baptized by St. Remigius in Reims on Christmas Day of 496, along with three thousand Franks. Becoming one of Europe's most powerful rulers, Clovis made Paris the capital of his kingdom, erecting the Church of Holy Apostles, known later as St. Geneviève's. His soldiers were armed with battle-axes known as *franciscas,* one of France's early claims to glory. Today, as Tim learned, Clovis is still celebrated by the Church as the hero who made France its "First Daughter."

Urban II, the first French pope, who reigned for thirty-seven years from the late eleventh to early twelfth century, was a passionately obsessed and zealous Church reformer. He was determined to make the Church pure, excommunicating in the process Catholic sovereigns across Europe and savagely persecuting bishops and archbishops who resisted reform and insisted on corrupt practices. He was, of course, the same pope who had proclaimed the First Crusade against the Islam "infidels" of Palestine in 1095. Did Islam fundamentalists today remember that crusading Frenchman? Probably not, Tim decided, but made a notation under ENEMIES in his ledger.

At the outset of the thirteenth century, Pope Innocent III, an Italian, launched the European crusade against Cathar heretics—also known as Albigensians—in the south of France in alliance with the French king, Philip Augustus, whom he had earlier attempted to turn into his vassals. The Albigensian Crusade soon exploded into a civil war between northern and southern French aristocracy, with Innocent III fully in support of Philip Augustus and the northerners. Tens of thousands of the southern heretics, the "pure ones," were burned at the stake or otherwise liquidated with the pope's enthusiastic blessings. This put the French in Innocent's debt, not long after northern French priests and laymen loudly demanded independence from Rome for their Church.

Reading up on the Cathars, Tim was uncertain how they should be listed in his ledger: as FRIEND or ENEMY? He was now aware that this ancient heresy and its dreadful consequences had not been forgotten. Thus Frenchmen in the south may feel atavistic hatred toward Rome and the northerners may feel gratitude—or none of the above. Besides, this was Gregory XVII's corner of the world. Tim just placed a question mark over the episode; his instinct told him that it was not unimportant in the broad scheme of things.

A half-century later, France surged as Europe's superpower, forcing the papacy into submission to the French crown. Curiously, the French power had been consolidated by Louis IX, a pious king who was later canonized by the Church. During the fourteenth century, relations between the Roman Church and the French oscillated crazily. Elected in 1305, the French pope Clement V refused to reside in Rome because of internal Italian conflicts and, instead, established Avignon as the pontifical See for a long period of what was called the "Babylonian Exile" of the popes. The Church became even more submissive to France. With five more French pontiffs ruling from Avignon and the College of Cardinals packed with Frenchmen, the Church soon resembled a French institution. Only in 1362, Urban V, himself a Frenchman, returned the Apostolic See to Rome.

In 1404, cardinals in Rome elected as pope a Neapolitan who took the name of Innocent VII, but who had to compete with Benedict XXIII, a Spaniard and the second of the four "antipopes" elected by French cardinals in Avignon and who held court at Avignon. This was the time of the "Great Schism" in the Church, pitting Rome against France. Benedict, of course, had the support of the French crown. Gregory XII became pope in 1406 on Innocent's death, but he and Benedict could not come to terms. Meanwhile the French Church turned its back on Benedict, and Martin V, an Italian, was chosen in 1417, ending the "Great Schism." At that point, Tim Savage's head had begun to swim as he strove to understand the vagaries in the conflicts between France and Rome.

But, inexorably, the story went on. The French and the papacy could not leave well enough alone. Late in the fifteenth century, Charles VII of France occupied Rome on behalf of a clique of rebel cardinals, and threatened to depose Pope Alexander VI. For the next three centuries, Rome and Paris swung back and forth between conflict and collaboration—in power politics, not theology—until the milestone of the French Revolution.

The 1789 Revolution had declared a full-fledged war on the Roman Catholic Church, for which the Holy See has not really forgiven France—to this day. In fact, Tim knew an aging monsignor who spoke of François Mitterrand, then the French socialist president, in the same spirit as he spoke of Robespierre. Napoleon Bonaparte's Italian campaign led to the occupation of Rome by his armies and the capture of Pope Pius VI, who soon thereafter died in exile in France. But five years later, Pius VII anointed Napoleon as emperor, transforming the monarchy into an empire. Five years after *that* occasion, Napoleon annexed the Papal States in Italy and deposed his erstwhile friend Pius VII, removing him to France. It was a far cry from Christmas Eve in 800 A.D. when

Charlemagne, an earlier emperor, lay prostrate in St. Peter's basilica waiting for anointment by Pope Leo III. But when Napoleon finally fell from power after Waterloo, Pius VII returned to Rome in triumph. In the end, the Church always seemed to win.

Still, the rivalries continued. Pope Pius IX had been forced to flee Rome by the 1848 liberal revolution in Italy, but French armies restored him to power two years later. The papacy was protected by France until the Franco-Prussian War of 1870, when the defeated French had to concentrate on their own affairs. In 1901, the French Third Republic demanded that religious orders—from the Benedictines to the Jesuits—leave the country, closed 14,000 Catholic schools, and confiscated Church property.

A lot of this long history was plain power-hunger warfare, bloodshed, and intolerance among some of Europe's most civilized people. With rare exceptions, the kings and the popes were not shining examples of virtue—most were capable of unspeakably dastardly deeds. Tim marveled that so much mischief and criminality on the part of the enlightened rulers and their courtiers could belong to the same epochs as much of Europe's splendid culture and creativity in arts and human thought.

Evidently good and evil could coexist happily in the Dark Ages as well as during the Enlightment. But, then, Tim thought, things were not all that different nowadays. It was just as plausible to kill a pope today as at any moment in the history of mankind and religion. The mindset was always present and there were always plenty of devout volunteers—not just mercenaries—believing that they were God's instruments in doing away with popes they thought were betraying the Church. For Tim, papal history offered valuable perspective he had lacked, and quite a few key findings. They included periodic outbursts of protest, resentment, and even violence by extremist French clerics and their followers against the papacy, especially after the Second Vatican Council in the mid-Sixties. Tim duly noted them in his ledger. Now he had to consider that the assassination attempt against Gregory XVII could, after all, have come from *within* the Church, discarding the conventional wisdom that it had to be plotted, say, by Moscow or Muslims—to the exclusion of other possibilities. On the other hand, conventional wisdom might have had it right.

Tim's research fascinated him as he delved deeper and deeper in the materials he was receiving from Sister Angela. But he was totally exhausted when he finished reading the hundreds of pages on the history of the papacy in the early morning that June day. Despite the newly acquired perspective, he had no sense of having achieved any meaningful progress in his work. All he had after a month of study were half-formed ideas and suspicions. Suddenly, he felt hopeless and depressed.

The sun was already hot and bright when Tim stepped out of the Villa Malta gate to walk down Via di Porta Pinciana to the convent at the bottom of the street. He entered the chapel and prepared to celebrate the Mass of 6.30 A.M., the first of the day, for the few pious elderly women who attended it daily. Tim did this once or twice a week. Saying Mass and being in communion with God always cleared his mind and restored his inner balance. This morning, Tim Savage needed it more than ever, certainly since his tour in Vietnam.

Chapter Twelve

"MY GOD," I haven't seen you since 'Nam, since the Delta!" Paul Martinius shouted, bouncing out of the deep armchair at the chic Via Veneto bar near the American Embassy and hugging Tim Savage tightly. "I knew you had become a priest, but I didn't realize you were in the Eternal City . . . Boy, it's great to see you again!"

Martinius, an exuberant, powerfully built man, was the CIA Station Chief in Rome, a new-generation intelligence officer with a doctorate in political science. He and Tim had served together in Vietnam as young Phoenix operatives, and Martinius had gone on to build an impressive career with the Agency. Tim, trusting him as a friend, made an exception to his rule of total secrecy about his mission in deciding to get in touch. There was a chance, he thought, that Martinius might have some knowledge concerning investigations of the assassination attempt even though he had not been in Rome at the time. It would be normal for the Station to have kept files on the subject and, as a matter of course, Martinius would be informed of any new developments.

Tim had not explained over the telephone why he wished to see Martinius, and the Station Chief asked no questions. He was not surprised that Tim knew about his current assignment: Agency and ex-Agency people tended to keep track of former colleagues. They had agreed to meet the following evening at the bar suggested by Martinius, and Tim dressed with casual elegance in slacks, a polo shirt, and a sports jacket to fit the surroundings. The two men brought one another up to date on what they had done with their lives after their farewell beer in the Mekong Delta town, and Martinius proposed they keep the tradition alive.

"*Birra, prego,*" he told the waiter, then turned to Tim. "So, tell me, what *are* you doing here?" he inquired. "And what can I do for you?"

"I work on Islamic affairs at the Inter-Religious Dialogue Council over at the Vatican," Tim replied. "And I thought I'd touch base with some of my old pals. I figured you would be interested in my subject, and it gave me an excuse to call you."

"Oh, that's right," Martinius said, taking a swig of his beer. "Islam was the stuff you had been working on before they brought your sorry ass over to 'Nam. I almost forgot. And, yes, we obviously follow Islamic affairs in my shop. There's a lot of Muslim traffic through Rome; we worry about Muslim terrorism, and that sort of thing."

They chatted awhile about the rise in Islamic fundamentalism, Martinius repeating his concerns about terrorism. Tim saw his opening.

"Well," he asked, "do you think, for example, that Muslims were really behind the assassination attempt against the pope five years ago? I mean that Turk, Agca Circlic, who's now in prison?"

Martinius put down his beer carefully on the table. His eyes narrowed.

"Tim, my boy, is this a casual question, or what?" he asked.

"No," the Jesuit said. "I won't lie to you. It's not casual. It's professional. But that's all I can say now about my interest in it."

The Station Chief lit a long cigar, a Cuban Cojiba, a forbidden pleasure in the United States, where imports of Cuban cigars are banned by the embargo law. "Okay," he told Tim, blowing smoke. "I understand. What, exactly, do you want to know from me? I'll try to be helpful, but you realize that I, too, am under severe constraints on this one. It's graveyard . . ."

"I was hoping that you could help me make sense out of the attitude of the Agency—and of the U.S. Government—in this matter," Tim explained. "I find it very confusing, especially after reading the Director's testimony before that Senate committee last year."

Tim was referring to rather startling documents: the transcript of the CIA director's answers to questions at a Senate committee hearing on terrorism and the Agency's internal reports on the assassination attempt. The Apostolic Nunciature in Washington had secured the whole set of documents, forwarding it to Saint-Ange's office. Angela forwarded it to Tim at Villa Malta by motorcycle courier.

To Tim's trained eye, the CIA's overall performance in tracking down the attack on Gregory XVII was immensely disconcerting and disturbing. The accepted view in the White House and the public opinion in general was that Circlic had simply been an instrument of a Soviet-Bulgarian conspiracy to kill the pope because of his very active and effective support of dissident movements in Eastern Europe, much more so than support given by any previous popes, anticommunist as they all fervently were. This was particularly true and successful in overwhelmingly Roman Catholic Poland. But while the CIA seemed not to subscribe to the Soviet-Bulgarian scenario, it appeared to have none of its own and, indeed, acted in the most inexplicably detached and unprofessional manner.

And, of course, Tim was stunned to discover that the Agency had no opinion of its own on whether the assailant had acted alone or as part of a wider conspiracy—a running controversy among investigators everywhere. It was the eternal question, Tim kept repeating to himself, just like the Lincoln and Kennedy assassinations. Did John Wilkes Booth act alone? Did Lee Harvey Oswald almost one hundred years later? And did Agca Circlic nearly twenty years after that?

As for the CIA, which *always* had opinions on virtually everything, it was as caught up in the controversy as all the other players, Tim realized, but in a very strange way. Thus the Italian court that had found Circlic guilty and sentenced him to life in prison, had concluded in its fifty-one-page Statement of Motivation that "it was unthinkable" that the Turk "could have undertaken this difficult project in absolute autonomy." But the CIA Director informed the Senate committee that Circlic was "a known crazy . . . too unstable to be included in an assassination plot, let alone be trusted to do the shooting." The Director also testified in executive session that in the CIA's opinion the Soviets "were not so insane as to organize a plot to kill the pope, knowing full well that an assassination would almost certainly lead to uncontrollable popular explosions throughout Eastern Europe, notably in

Poland, and destroy their relations with us and everybody else. They could not have risked being caught red-handed. . . ."

Why was the CIA insisting, in effect, that the Turk had acted entirely on his own? Tim knew that in almost every instance the Agency's views and conclusions were linked to political considerations at home and abroad. So why was it taking this stance now? Tim had also found totally incomprehensible the Senate testimony by a senior Agency official that "in the first several years after the attempted assassination, CIA moved very awkwardly and slowly in trying to deal with the problem" and that "at least at the outset, it was due to a mindset that accepted the idea that a lone gunman was responsible." He read with growing disbelief that "while the inconsistencies in Circlic's accounts and the shortcomings of the evidence do not lend conclusive support to a Bulgarian-Soviet conspiracy theory," the CIA's own investigations "reveal some serious shortcomings." The internal critique stressed that "in the absence of evidence, [the CIA's] production was hamstrung, mindsets replaced evidence, and the issue became increasingly polarized."

Next, Tim learned that the CIA's "upper management had strong and in some cases conflicting views on the issue" and that "analysts and managers were reluctant to investigate alternative scenarios." And he discovered from the documents that a "knee-jerk approach was at least partly responsible for the spotty quality of current intelligence coverage of this subject." Tim was accustomed to battles within the Agency when National Intelligence Estimates, the NIEs, were being drafted—and the clash of views was often healthy—but this was pure insanity.

"What am I to make of all this?" he asked Martinius after summing up the reports he had read and the nagging questions they had raised.

"I am familiar with the material," Martinius said quietly. "I was briefed at Langley before I left for Rome. But there isn't a hell of a lot I can tell you. The fact is that I don't know the truth and I'm not sure that *anybody* on our side knows it. I'll tell you one thing for sure: in my opinion, my personal opinion, mind you, *nobody* really wants to find out what happened. *Nobody* wants to know the truth. *Nobody* wants to touch it. And this is a tip from your old buddy. . . ."

Tim sat petrified, staring at Martinius.

"What do you mean '*nobody*' wants to know the truth? How's that possible?" he asked incredulously.

"It means, in *my* opinion, that everybody who matters in this affair has concluded that knowledge of certain events is more dangerous than ignorance," the Station Chief said softly. "You see, Tim, if you discover the truth, whatever it may be, and this truth becomes widely known, you have to do something about it. And chances are that you are not really served by doing 'something' because it could lead to disaster . . . like a nuclear war . . . or whatever. . . ."

"Okay, okay," Tim said, "you are telling me that if, for example, it could be proven that Moscow was behind the assassination attempt because Bulgarian intelligence types were spotted near the scene, the United States would have to do something drastic about them? Like the nuclear war you just mentioned? And that the U.S. obviously was not prepared to launch a war over the life or death of Gregory XVII and that the crowd at the White House don't want it either?"

"Something like that," Martinius said, nodding. "But you are the one who drew that conclusion. I'm just agreeing with you . . . But I can tell you that my pal, the new Soviet KGB *rezident* here, whom I knew elsewhere in the past, thinks along similar lines. He is scared to death that somebody, like the U.S., will suddenly proclaim the 'truth' and all hell will break loose. He says that it would be a 'provocation' worse than the Cuban Missile Crisis, no matter who did the provoking. I told him he need not worry. We're not about to discover anything or proclaim anything. It's old stuff, best to be forgotten."

Martinius paused and finished his beer.

"I didn't tell him, but I'll tell you, old friend," he said at length. "Just for your ears. My instructions are *not* to investigate the pope business, not to ask questions, not to listen, not to report anything back to Langley."

"You mean, 'see no evil, hear no evil'?" Tim asked.

"You could say that," the Station Chief agreed. "But, if you care, you may wish to nose around the other Western intelligence people. Not the Italians. They threw in the towel a long time ago and they are happy with the way things are. Circlic in prison for life and all that. Don't bother with the Brits—they're on the same wavelength as us. I'm not sure, however, what the French may or may not know about what almost happened to their venerated compatriot. You know, the guy who ran their intelligence outfit, the SDECE, was a real genius. His name was Alexandre de Marenches. Have you ever heard about him? You should. . . ."

Martinius rose to leave, putting his arm around Tim.

"And, by the way, speaking of strange characters, did you know that our old friend Jake Kurtski is in Rome? I wonder why. . . ."

Back in his room at Villa Malta, Tim Savage pondered over what Martinius had told him. The CIA's behavior was certainly odd, and Martinius had no reason to invent explanations. What he had said was consistent with the CIA documents and Senate transcripts Tim had studied. Tim understood the policy rationale, astonishing as it sounded, but remained puzzled over the fact that the Agency had halted all investigations of its own. Whatever the White House may decide on policy, it is not in the nature of an intelligence organization to quit acting like one. And now Tim began to remember other little and big things that had perplexed him as he plowed ahead with his task.

It was perfectly plausible for Monsignor Sainte-Ange to complain, as he did to Tim that first day, that the CIA had not tried very hard to investigate the shooting on St. Peter's Square notwithstanding the U.S. government's promises to the Holy See. The private secretary was presumably unaware that the western powers, starting with the United States, had resolved not to risk a confrontation with the Soviets over the attempt against Gregory XVII—unless his French secret service friends had told him so, which was possible. Tim had no idea, but, he reasoned, the very perspicacious monsignor may have figured it out by himself. By the same token, Sainte-Ange would have understood that Interpol, the international police organization based in the French city of Lyons, had chosen—or had been strongly advised—to stay out of the papal matter altogether.

Under the circumstances, the pope and the monsignor were justified in launching their own secret investigation, even though Gregory XVII had announced publicly during a televised visit to the Turk's prison cell that he had forgiven him in Christian spirit and that the Holy See considered the subject closed. There was, of course, a profound difference between public pronouncements and private, secret enterprises, and Tim remembered that Sainte-Ange had told him at the outset that the decision to conduct the new investigation was taken after Italy had formally discontinued its efforts to arrive at the truth.

This constituted the perfect excuse, should questions ever be raised as to why Gregory XVII had reopened the subject after piously closing it for the benefit of world public opinion. Tim had now reached the conclusion that the pope and his private secretary had always been determined to find out who had ordered the assassination and why, but had to await the moment when they could quietly take matters into their own hands. And that moment had arrived. Tim wondered whether Gregory XVII and Sainte-Ange would reveal the truth, should he succeed in uncovering it, unless it happened to suit them for whatever reasons of the Holy See's interests as they saw it. Such as tying up the loose ends of the pontificate.

Tim's attention centered increasingly, especially after his chat with Paul Martinius, on all the bizarre pieces he was coming across as he sought to assemble facts that made sense. It struck him that Sainte-Ange had explained that the decision on the secret investigation had been made because "last week" the Italians had terminated their inquiries. But this could not have been entirely correct, Tim suspected, because his selection for the mission clearly had been made somewhat earlier: Sainte-Ange could not have suddenly picked him out of the air. Tim knew from both his CIA and Vatican experience that it took time to find the right person for a highly sensitive assignment, and Sainte-Ange obviously knew for weeks, if not longer, what the Italians were planning to do. So why had Sainte-Ange been imprecise or less than fully truthful with him?

Then, there was the strange case of *L'Osservatore Romano,* the official Vatican daily newspaper. Going through the mass of material Angela kept sending him, Tim was intrigued by an editorial in *L'Osservatore* a few months after the shooting in the square that "something keeps all this from adding up" and that Circlic's approaching trial "could carry us past the confines of surrealism because of the evident disparity between small questions that may perhaps never be answered and great ones that will assuredly never be answered." Tim was aware that the editorial contents of *L'Osservatore* had to be approved daily before press time by the Vatican's Secretariat of State, sometimes by the Cardinal Secretary of State himself, and that the newspaper spoke for the Holy See. This fact made it even more interesting to Tim that the bizarre editorial about Circlic had used the word "conspiracy."

Why, Tim asked himself, would the Vatican conclude publicly, even prior to the trial, that a "conspiracy" had been afoot, that it touched on "surrealism," and that "great questions" surrounding the Turk's criminal act would "never be answered"? Did Gregory XVII and Sainte-Ange know something, then or now, that the monsignor had not been prepared to share with Tim? Was he being used as a decoy or, in CIA parlance, as a "cut-out" to serve a purpose he could not decipher? Tim was beginning to think that if, indeed, there was a conspiracy, it was a conspiracy of silence on the part of all involved—including Sainte-Ange. Troubling Tim more and more, the crucial question was, what did the monsignor know and when did he know it?

Tim Savage was uneasy: Was it all smoke and mirrors?

Several weeks after his conversation with Paul Martinius, Tim attended a dinner at the Jesuit headquarters on Borgo Santo Spirito to honor an elderly French Jesuit priest on the fiftieth anniversary of his ordination. Chatting with him at the end of the evening, while they finished their cognac, Tim made a passing reference to the assassination attempt on Gregory XVII, remarking how fortunate it was that the pope, the old Frenchman's countryman, had survived it. He was just making conversation. But the priest stiffened, looked around, then whispered, "Too bad that they paid no attention to the warning!"

"The warning? What warning?" Tim asked, perplexed.

"Well, the warning from Alexandre de Marenches, of course,"

the Jesuit answered impatiently. "I thought everybody here knew about it . . ."

"I'm afraid I do not know," Tim told him. "I'm sort of new here. Can you tell me about it?"

"Certainly," the Frenchman said. "It's not a secret as far as I'm concerned. Less than two years after the attack on the pope, de Marenches, you know, the great French spymaster, spoke in a newspaper interview in Paris of the warning he had sent to the Vatican. I think it was *Le Figaro.* He said that he had warned the highest people in the Vatican two years *before* the assassination attempt that a plot was being hatched against the pope, but that nobody had paid the slightest attention. Imagine! Not to pay attention to such a warning!"

A bell rang in Tim's head. De Marenches was the French secret service chief that Paul Martinius had made a point of mentioning to him that night at the bar. Of course, Tim thought, Paul *was* pointing him in a direction that had not occurred to him. Perhaps pieces were finally beginning to fall into place. The next day, Tim telephoned Angela to request a copy or a Xerox of the interview in *Le Figaro,* though he was unable to provide a date. Twenty-four hours later, Tim had the clipping in hand. This is what de Marenches had to say:

"At the beginning of that year, two years before the attack, the threat was so serious that I sent a general and a top-ranking officer to Rome to warn the head of the Church."

After reading the article, Tim asked Angela whether there was anything in the files of the Papal Household about de Marenches and the warnings he had claimed to have sent. Angela called him back three days later.

"I can't locate anything about any warnings, except for that *Figaro* interview," she said. "De Marenches died a few years ago. But you might be interested to know that about two and a half years after the shooting on the square, one of de Marenches' principal aides, a colonel named Bernard Nut, was found mysteriously dead in Nice, in the south of France, and there appears to have been some kind of connection between his death and the conspiracy against the Holy Father."

Tim, who listened to Angela's voice with breathless attention and pleasure, noticed that she had used the word "conspiracy" in the most natural fashion. Was that an accepted "fact" in the papal entourage? But the warning story was utterly confusing as well. The next batch of materials from Angela included a newspaper interview with Ferdinando Imposimato, a judge on Italy's Supreme Court of Cassation, who at the time of the shooting was in charge of all investigations in the Rome metropolitan region. Imposimato's version was diametrically opposed to de Marenches' account. "De Marenches," the Italian judge declared, "did not cooperate at all with Italian justice . . . In fact, on three separate occasions we asked Paris for additional information and Paris replied: send us a written request. We sent a list of questions to SDECE and Paris answered with five lines, which said absolutely nothing."

So, Tim asked himself again, who was lying and who was telling the truth, if anybody? He was also surprised that, judging from the documents he had read, the CIA had missed de Marenches' *Figaro* interview, which was unlikely, or chose to ignore it, which would be consistent with what Paul Martinius had told him about the Agency's overall attitude toward the Gregory XVII situation. In fact, Tim now realized, Martinius had deliberately put him on the scent of de Marenches.

"The American knows about de Marenches and the warning," Monsignor Saint-Ange told Gregory XVII when they sat down at dinner at the pope's small private dining room, adjoining the pantry and the kitchen.

"How did he find out?" the pope asked.

"Well, Angela came to see me this morning to say that Savage had inquired whether we had anything in our files concerning de Marenches' warning," the monsignor said. "He had heard somewhere about the *Figaro* interview and, at his request, Angela had sent him a clipping. That was all right because he could have easily obtained the newspaper elsewhere. But, naturally, I informed the Sister that we had nothing among our papers that dealt with warnings."

"Does the American know that the warning wasn't heeded?" Gregory XVII persisted, "and why it wasn't heeded?"

"I doubt it," Sainte-Ange murmured. "But he may well come up with something along those lines now that he is aware that there was a warning. De Marenches may be dead, but there are others, still alive today, who may talk if Savage stumbles upon them. But, Holy Father, we chose in him the best investigator available for your mission and, consequently, we must assume that he will get to the bottom of lots of things we would prefer he ignored. We can't have it both ways, I guess . . ."

"Yes, I can see that," Gregory XVII mused. "Still, I have the uneasy feeling that, at this stage, it's not entirely clear who is investigating whom and what . . . We may wind up being investigated by the American before he discovers who had tried to murder me . . . Perhaps we should have left well enough alone . . ."

Romain de Sainte-Ange chose not to comment.

At his office at the American Embassy, Paul Martinius finished drafting a cable to CIA headquarters at Langley and called for the Station's cypher clerk to encode the message. The key sentence informed his superiors that "the Vatican, at the highest level, has opened a secret investigation into the assassination attempt against Gregory XVII" and that "it is being conducted by a former Agency officer, an old friend from Vietnam." Martinius added that he awaited instructions on how to deal with this situation, if at all, apart from watching it the best he could.

It was now mid-June. Rome was insufferably hot and the Vatican was drowning in pilgrims and tourists. Tim's room under the tile roof of Villa Malta was a furnace. Sitting by the window in an old stuffed armchair and sweating profusely, for the Jesuits somehow failed to discover air conditioning, Tim held his ledger and manila folders in his lap, the rest of his files spilling over onto a nearby small table and the floor. He was attempting to sum up what he had learned during the first month of his investigation. His conclusion was that, apart from history and some recent events, he knew precious little—and what he thought he knew was insufferably confusing.

Tim knew, for instance, that Agca Circlic was a twenty-three-year-old Turkish citizen of Muslim religion with a strange record and a mysterious past. Italian investigators had established that Circlic had once belonged to Gray Wolves, a fascist terrorist organization in Turkey. He had murdered a newspaper editor in Istambul for unclear reasons, then escaped from prison under unexplained circumstances though he had clearly been helped by someone in authority. Then Circlic had written a letter to a Turkish publication threatening to kill the pope, within a year of his election, just before Gregory XVII visited Turkey in order to display his friendship toward Islam. Actually, it had been a rather ill-conceived gesture inasmuch as Turkey was a completely secular state and, even though most of the population were of Islamic persuasion, a quiet one.

In any event, no evidence had been found to show that Circlic had pursued the pope in Turkey or, during ensuing years, anyplace else. Besides, Tim thought, the Gray Wolves were a right-wing outfit with no involvements with Islamic fundamentalists anywhere and therefore it would have been senseless to have Circlic, one of their "soldiers," kill the Catholic pope. His own threat to assassinate Gregory XVII in Turkey made even less sense, but Tim was curious as to what had made him do it. Circlic, of course, may have been deranged—his subsequent behavior seemed to confirm it—with a psychotic obsession about the pope.

On the other hand, Tim reasoned, Circlic's personal hatred of Gregory XVII, whatever demented causes filled his brain, did make him a perfect choice for assassin-for-hire on the part of whomever was aware of his disposition. With his criminal record, if captured, Circlic could easily be disavowed by the instigators of the plot—should he have named who had hired him—or, preferably, liquidated. Tim recalled that Lee Harvey Oswald was shot to death by Jack Ruby two days after he had murdered Kennedy in Dallas and that, in turn, Ruby died under strange circumstances, possibly of cancer.

In Circlic's case, however, his "employers," if they actually existed, had abandoned him to his fate. Nobody tried to do away with him and the Turk was easily arrested. That one or more Bulgarian officials, who may or may not have been their regime's secret police agents, were detained in the vicinity of the square shortly after the shooting proved nothing. The Bulgarian secret service was a dependency of the KGB, but Tim was inclined to accept the CIA's in-house conclusion that Soviet leaders were not mad enough to wish to have the pope assassinated. Thus Circlic either acted on his own or was "thrown to the wolves," as Tim had noted in his ledger before realizing that it was an involuntary pun on the Turk's erstwhile Turkish associates.

The Italian judiciary system proved no help, either. Although it had swiftly convicted Circlic, the Rome Court of Assizes had failed to go beyond the simple fact of proclaiming his guilt, which never was in dispute. The Turk had eagerly admitted to the police that he had shot Gregory XVII, then recanted and, most perplexingly, refused to testify at his trial. Italian law provides for trials even when defendants admit their guilt beforehand in order to determine the punishment to be meted out. Circlic had also undergone successive psychiatric tests, but, as Tim learned with dismay, Italian experts disagreed on the degree of his psychosis; some in fact did not find him to be psychotic.

There were only questions and no answers, and Tim was faced with the depressing discovery that each question arising in his mind served to raise additional questions. Why, for instance, Sainte-Ange had omitted to tell him about de Marenches' warning? And why he made a point of telling Tim that a "Muslim connection" must be envisaged? Only because Circlic was a Muslim? It was like being lost in a labyrinth.

Taking a deep breath, Tim started a new section in his ledger with three headings: SOVIETS—ISLAM—UNKNOWN. His instinct told him that the key to his investigation was under UNKNOWN. But where did UNKNOWN lie? All that Tim knew for sure was that the trail was turning cold. People were dying and people were lying.

The afternoon sun was beating down harshly on Santa Maria in Trastevere Square, one of Rome's most famous piazzas, as the thin, youngish Frenchman in his usual gray suit slid behind a small, round table of the crowded outdoor café and sat down in the chair next to Jake Kurtski.

"I see that you always like to be the first to arrive for a meeting," the Frenchman remarked in the form of a greeting.

"Right," Kurtski said, "I don't like surprises, like the wrong people awaiting me . . . So what's on your mind this time?"

The heat had turned Kurtski's fleshy face redder than usual, and his chest was sweating profusely under his sports shirt. The beer on the table in front of him was already warm. Kurtski was decidedly in a bad humor, worse than most of the time. He had returned to Rome the previous evening for the meeting with the Frenchman, but he disliked the city and was anxious to get back to his little beach house on the Algarve coast in Portugal, where he now lived from spring to autumn. Sex was good there if one had enough dollars, which Kurtski did, even if one were an oldish man. Algarve maidens had a solid business sense.

"Well, Mr. Kurtski," the Frenchman told him in a low voice, "my principals have thought it over and they wish you to proceed with the plan we discussed last time we met. And your price is acceptable. One million U.S. dollars, right?"

"Right. One million dollars, one half now and one half after the assignment is completed. If it fails, we each are out a half million: I don't get the second payment and you don't have to make a second payment. Of course, I keep the first half no matter what happens. In fact, I won't start the project without a down payment."

"Yes, we understand it and I am prepared to make the first payment even today if we work out all the details," the Frenchman said. "We think that the accident should occur, as I mentioned before, aboard the plane . . . We believe it's more likely to succeed."

"I guess you're right," Kurtski concurred. "Obviously, you can't try again to shoot him. It's too *focking* chancy. And we saw with the Turk how easy it is to get caught. It's a good thing he didn't know who was paying him . . ."

The Frenchman nodded. "How much time would you need to prepare what has to be done?" he asked.

"It's not easy," Kurtski replied, "and I would imagine that I might need two or three months ahead of a trip to get everything in shape. Do you have any idea when and where he is going next?"

The Frenchman consulted a small notebook he produced from his coat jacket.

"Well, let's see," he said. "Okay. He's off to France next month, but that would be too soon for you . . . In September, it's North Africa and in October it is the United States. What do you think?"

"I would prefer the trip to the U.S. because Alitalia would be laying on a larger plane with more people for the long flight, and it's easier to bring explosives aboard and conceal them on a 747 or a 707 than on a DC-9 or a 727 that would be used to fly to North Africa. And that would give me plenty of time to set everything in motion. We can blow him up over the Atlantic . . ."

"Fine," the Frenchman said. "It's a deal. We trust you. I shall deliver the money tonight if you tell me where you want it."

Kurtski gave him the name of a small hotel near St. Peter's Square and watched the Frenchman rise from his chair and walk away into the crowd of tourists massed in front of the exquisitely beautiful church of Santa Maria di Trastevere.

Chapter Thirteen

MONSIGNOR SAINTE-ANGE may have been right—or not—about the "Muslim connection" in the attack on Gregory XVII, but Tim Savage had to pursue this lead if for no other reason than that Agca Circlic was a Muslim and nothing could be ruled out. And the next logical step was to learn more about the young Turk.

Pondering on a hot summer afternoon how best to proceed and to which of his Islamic contacts in Turkey and elsewhere he might turn for assistance, Tim heard a knock on the door of his Villa Malta room. Opening it, he was handed by the porter of the residence a bulky green manila package. Inside, he found a personal file of the type used by the CIA, marked simply, AGCA CIRCLIC. A hand-printed note attached to the file said, "From your old buddy!" For the Rome Station Chief, "see no evil, hear no evil" was a flexible doctrine, even if it violated Agency rules.

Glancing excitedly through the fat file, Tim saw that he must have been given everything the CIA and its Rome Station had on Circlic and the Gray Wolves. And the file provided him with some gruesome facts. Circlic, it seemed, was a born thug and bully from a peasant family in a destitute Anatolian village. Psychologically and emotionally unstable, he had turned up in Istambul before he was twenty. There, he became notorious as a daring smuggler, black marketeer in alcohol and weapons, small-time drug dealer, and enforcer for Turkish organized crime bosses. These qualifications attracted the attention of the leadership of the Gray Wolves. Circlic was just the man for them.

The Wolves were squads specializing for the past twenty years or so in assassinations, kidnappings, and bombings on behalf of well-paying "clients" or for their own usually unclear reasons. These "clients," Tim read, included Turkey's secret service and

the Counter-Guerrilla Organization of the Army's Special Warfare Department, principally concerned with liquidating political
dissidents and Kurdish separatists. The Counter-Guerrilla Organization, which occasionally supplied arms to the Gray Wolves,
was largely funded by the Pentagon inasmuch as Turkey was a
NATO ally of the United States. And there surely was a CIA link
as well. The Wolves were, pure and simple, death squads. Tim
Savage shuddered: shades of Phoenix, he thought.

Soon after enlisting in the Gray Wolves, Circlic rose to a key
position under their chief, Abdullah Catli, a convicted murderer
and heroin trafficker who also was on the payroll of the Turkish
secret police. It was unclear, however, on whose orders and why
Circlic had assassinated the editor of the Turkish newspaper
Millyet. It could not have been his own idea, Tim believed,
because it simply made no sense—as so much in the investigation he had undertaken for the pope had not. But it was Catli
who helped Circlic escape from prison, a significant detail,
apparently dug up by the CIA, that Tim had not found in Italian
investigatory reports, and supplied him with fake identity
papers and money to travel around Europe prior to the attack on
Gregory XVII. And Catli had testified four years later at a Rome
trial of a group of Turks and Bulgarians accused of conspiring
against the pope that he had provided Circlic with the pistol to
fire at the pontiff. The world press had missed that story.

Tim was now virtually convinced that Circlic had shot at Gregory XVII on orders from the Wolves and had been paid by them.
But there was nothing in the CIA file to suggest *why* they had
wished the pope dead, and Tim was taking for granted at that
point that the Wolves had acted on behalf of a "client." Absent
fanatic religious impulses against the head of another religion,
they clearly had no interest in killing the Roman Catholic pontiff.
They were, first and foremost, professionals. That Circlic himself
had described the attack as "a desperate act to make history" in talking to the Italian police that afternoon was meaningless. Tim
doubted very much that the Turk had the slightest notion why he
had done the deed: someone must have told him that he would be
engaging in a "desperate act" and would "make history," and he
simply repeated it—believing every word. And, for that matter, Tim

could not be certain that Circlic's letter threatening to kill Gregory XVII had actually been written by him. It might have been part of a carefully prepared disinformation effort, a subject familiar to Tim from his CIA days.

Whatever Sainte-Ange had meant by "Muslim connection," Tim had to follow the thread—with luck it might lead him out of the labyrinth, like Ariadne's thread in mythology. The thread for now led to the Wolves and their friends.

Tim Savage was on a nonstop Alitalia flight from Rome's Fiumicino Airport to Istambul, looking for all the world like a conservative businessman in his well-cut gray suit from Brioni. He preferred not to call attention to himself on the plane though he felt pleasantly elegant with his silk blue shirt and dark blue figured necktie. Sister Angela, who disbursed funds for his expenses, did not bat an eye at the sky-high Brioni bill.

"Your vows of poverty do not preclude elegance when you are in quest of a greater truth," she told him lightly. "You have to make a good impression."

"Thank you," Tim said just as lightly. "But I do try to remember my other vows."

Angela blushed and averted her eyes. It had been the third time that Tim had visited her small office on the second *loggia* of the Apostolic Palace since he entered papal service to pass on his non-progress reports for Monsignor Sainte-Ange, request special materials he did not wish to mention even over the secure telephone line, and collect operational money. Each time, Tim felt pleasantly ill at ease in her presence, suspecting that the French nun was not wholly indifferent to him—as a man. But now he damned himself for his flip remark about chastity. I am flirting with her in the house of the pope, he told himself. I am sinning. This must stop.

And it was about Angela more than about Circlic that Tim was daydreaming as the jet airliner crossed the Italian peninsula, the Adriatic, a slice of Albania and Greece, and the Aegean Sea, before landing gently in Istambul. Yes, these *were* impure thoughts. He sighed and disembarked on Turkish soil.

At the reception desk at the Conrad Istambul Hotel on the bank of the Bosphorus, Tim was greeted cheerfully as "Mr. Savage" and assigned a room with a marvelous view of the straits, just east. Asia loomed across the waterway. Angela had made the hotel reservation through a Rome travel agent experienced in arranging sensitive Vatican trips. Paul Martinius had seen to it that Tim received a new U.S. passport with a photograph showing him in a civilian suit, shirt, and tie; his regular passport showed him in clerical collar. Details were essential in Tim's type of endeavor.

Seeking to uncover the truth about the Church's most recent near-tragedy, Tim stepped in Istambul into religious history and tragedies of a time long past. He remembered Machiavelli's dictum that one "should never take simple truths seriously"; complex truths were what mattered. When Istambul was still known as Constantinople—and "New Rome"—after Emperor Constantine, who founded the city astride the Bosphorus in the fourth century and embraced Christianity, the Schism of 1054 had come to divide the Latin and Greek Christian churches. It was over the issue of the Christians of the Roman Empire of the East—Byzantium—refusing to remain in communion with the pope and Rome. This separation has never ended, with Rome and Constantinople remaining at bitter odds over long centuries. Indeed, Constantinople was attacked at the dawn of the thirteenth century by the armies of the Roman pope in the form of the Fourth Crusade. And in the twelfth century, the mysterious heretical sect of Bogomils had been spawned just north of Byzantium proper, in Philippolis and Bulgaria, to spread west to Lombardy and then to the south of France. It led to the infernal Albigensian Crusade, ordered by the pope of Rome, that resulted in the deaths of hundreds of thousands of believers, massacred or burned at the stake.

Now, Tim reflected, how ironic was it that he was searching in Istambul—the new Constantinople—for answers to the mystery of a terrible tragedy that might have occurred in Rome just five years ago. Even today, the fate of Roman popes and the Roman Church could not be disassociated from Byzantium. There was obviously no connection between events more than nine centuries apart, but Tim was a believer in the endless power of history.

For instance, he considered, a truly demented Greek Orthodox fanatic, steeped in the memories of the schism and Byzantium's ultimate collapse four centuries later to make room for Islam's

Ottoman Empire while Rome thrived, might have conceivably masterminded a vengeance for the Fourth Crusade by killing Gregory XVII. Men possessed of religious fervor and undying memories are capable of savage deeds. For this, such a fanatic might have hired a professional assassin like Circlic, notwithstanding his Muslim identity. And a year to the day after the assassination attempt in Rome, a Spanish priest, belonging to an ultra-right-wing religious group, rushed at Gregory XVII at the Fátima shrine in Portugal with a bayonet in hand. It reminded Tim, once more, not to underestimate religious hatreds morphed into murderous psychoses.

Tim, of course, ruled out as preposterous the idea that he was dealing with a Byzantium act of vengeance: it was too Byzantine, and he had first thought of it as a hypothetical illustration of the power of religious history. Moreover the two churches had already begun a tentative march toward reconciliation when Pope Paul VI flew to Istambul almost twenty years ago to embrace Greek Orthodox Patriarch Atenagoras I at the lovely little church of St. George by Golden Horn Bay.

Still, *someone* had hired Circlic, Tim now being firmly convinced that the Turk had not acted on his own. The principal lead he was following, based on the CIA file, was in the direction of the Gray Wolves, and the fundamental question was whether, why, and on whose account they had planned the Rome shooting. And Tim knew that the plot had not been Turkish-inspired. The overwhelming majority of Turks were secular Muslims who had greeted Gregory XVII with respect and courtesy. There was no trace of anti-Catholic sentiment in Turkey, unlike, for example, in fundamentalist Pakistan where, Tim had recently read, a Christian Pakistani had been sentenced to death for blaspheming Islam.

In fact, a small Jesuit community functioned in Istambul as a scholarly religious research center and Tim was anxious to visit it. He thought that his fellow Jesuits could offer him useful guidance, preferring not to seek out his Turkish Muslim contacts to avoid unnecessary curiosity or suspicion. The Istambul community had been advised by the General Superior in Rome that Father Savage, a Vatican expert on Islam, would be coming to the city for his own research and they were requested to be of discreet assistance. It was a perfectly routine request.

The morning after his arrival, Tim took a taxi across the desperately traffic-choked Yeni Galata bridge over the Golden Horn to the Jesuits' quarters in a small house near Kapali Çarşi, the teeming Covered Bazaar of four thousand shops. On this occasion, he regained his casual Jesuit appearance, dressing in slacks and a sports shirt, ideal for the Istanbul heat and marking him in the street as a foreign tourist.

A young Polish Jesuit priest welcomed Tim, led him to a modestly furnished sitting room, offered him a cold soft drink, and inquired what he could do for Father Savage. He spoke English with a slight accent; he had studied theology at Cambridge.

"We are looking into terrorist organizations in the Muslim world," Tim told him, "because of the surge of terrorism in this whole region and the concern over how it might affect our Church. The explosions that destroyed the two Christian Maronite churches in Lebanon the other day—and forced the cancellation of the Holy Father's journey there—are examples of what worries us . . ."

"I'm afraid that we're turning into something of an investigatory and law enforcement agency in addition to all our other duties," he added with a conspirational smile, "and I was hoping that you could guide me a bit, at least as far as Turkey is concerned. I guess this is part of our Jesuit tradition . . ."

"Yes, I understand," the Polish priest said. "We share your worries and I have been thinking about it for some time. But I'm not sure you will find much in Istambul. Because Turkey remains so secular since the days of President Atatürk decades ago, we don't have *Jiddah, Hezbollah,* or *Hamas* type of religious-political radical organizations here. So far, anyway. Still, you never know. The Turks are given to incredible political and ethnic violence, as you must have heard: the massacres of Armenians and the Kurds, the more recent military coups, the hanging of Premier Adnan Menderes, the invasion of Cyprus, and so on . . . So one day it could be channeled into religious violence . . . The fellow who tried to kill the Holy Father was a Muslim, wasn't he?"

"Yes, I believe he is a Muslim, but I know very little about him," Tim replied. "It's not a subject I have followed very much . . ."

He hated to lie to his host, and hastened to change the tack.

"But what about Turkish right-wing terrorist organizations that are *not* religiously oriented? Is this something we should take into account? I hear that such organizations do exist . . ."

"You are absolutely right," the young Jesuit said. "They certainly exist, they are very active as part of the whole Turkish political picture, and I suspect that they have ties with the Turkish secret police. But, basically, they are freelancers. They are not a problem for us at the moment, but I try to keep track of them, just in case. You never know when a political terrorist finds it convenient to turn against a religion—his or ours. Anyway, politics and religion have always overlapped here in Turkey . . . For example, we have something called the Gray Wolves. I hear that the Turk who shot at the pope had once worked for them. Have you heard about the Gray Wolves?"

"No, not really," Tim answered. "What, exactly, are they?"

"It's a very strange outfit," the Jesuit explained. "They kill political opponents of the government, they hate leftists, they massacre Kurds in the mountains, they deal in drugs and weapons, and they make a lot of money. Nobody's quite sure who actually runs the Wolves these days. Maybe it's a committee of some kind. But I am fortunate in having a few contacts with them. It's one of my quiet research projects. For all I know, they may have serious Muslim fundamentalists among them."

"That's interesting," Tim remarked, trying to conceal his excitement and appear casual. "Do you suppose I could meet them? It sort of fits into my research as well . . ."

The priest pondered the question for a moment, slowly lighting his briar pipe. He tugged pensively at his lower lip as he put down the pipe on the table.

"I imagine it could be arranged," he told Tim, in turn sounding casual. "Let me see what I can do about it in a day or so. I've got to locate some of those guys. Where can I reach you? How long are you staying in Istambul?"

*   *   *

They met again at the Jesuits' quarters three days later as the sun was setting in the west over the fifth-century walls built by the Emperor Theodosius II to protect Constantinople from invaders. The Pole explained to Tim that he had arranged to introduce him as an American businessman, "a bit on the shady side," to an acquaintance of his. Tim knew better than to inquire how the Polish priest had come to be acquainted with Turkish Gray Wolves and why he was instructed to pose as a "shady" businessman. But Jesuits tend to trust one another's judgment, and Tim was glad he had invested Holy See funds in the purchase of the Brioni suit. His guide was wearing a light windbreaker over a sports shirt.

The priest drove the Jesuit community's small Japanese car in a zigzag fashion in the tangle of Istambul's downtown streets, often checking his rearview mirror. He was silent, just puffing on his pipe, as he navigated the fairly short distance east through the evening traffic. The car passed between Sultanahmet, the magnificent seventeenth-century Imperial Blue Mosque, and St. Sophia Basilica, which Constantine the Great erected in the fourth century, and then the Jesuit veered slightly to the right. Tim could see to his left the walled-in immensity of Topkapi Palace's buildings and courtyards overlooking the Bosphorus and the Sea of Marmara. The compound, he remembered, once included the *seraglio,* the harem for wives and concubines of Ottoman sultans. Only a few months earlier, Tim had gone to the Rome opera for a performance of Mozart's *Abduction from the Seraglio,* and found himself thinking of Sister Angela. Now he smiled in pleased reminiscence of the moment. St. Sophia under Byzantium and Sultanahmet under Turkish power had witnessed and sheltered awesome loves and plots, betrayals and carnages. Again, Tim thought, he was surrounded by history and millennial traditions of great conspiracies and great romances.

Presently they stopped in front of a dilapidated three-story house on Mehmet Aga Street, and the Pole led the way inside. Several boys kicked a soccer ball on the sidewalk, showing no interest when the two foreigners walked past them. A door opened on the second front landing, and the two priests were waved in by a short Turk with a grizzled short beard, wearing a checkered lumberjack shirt. It was breathlessly hot in the darkened apartment.

"This is Mohammed," the young Jesuit said to Tim. Turning to Mohammed, he said, "this is my friend from America, Mr. Savage."

Middle-aged with suspicious eyes and smelling richly of garlic and onion, Mohammed clapped his hands. A curtain was drawn open at the end of the room and a young woman walked in, carrying a copper tray with three tiny cups of steaming Turkish coffee. Mohammed gestured to the Jesuits to help themselves, then fixed Tim with an unfriendly stare.

"Is there anything I can do for you?" he asked harshly in Turkish. The Pole translated.

"Well," Tim said, "I am looking for some special business opportunities in Turkey, and the Father, whom I met the last time I was in Istambul, thought you could offer me some advice."

"What kind of opportunities?" the short man asked suspiciously.

"Well, I deal in arms and things like that," Tim informed him, smiling engagingly. Dealing in arms was a convenient cover because "negotiations" with a prospective buyer could be stretched out long enough to gain time and the trust of the Wolves and, Tim hoped, obtain the information he needed. In addition, his Vietnam experience made him convincingly knowledgeable about weaponry.

The Turk studied him, scratched his beard, and fixed him with another tough look.

"You wouldn't be with the CIA, would you?" he asked. "We don't need *provocateurs* . . ."

"Hell, no," Tim said truthfully, sounding offended. "What do you take me for? A fool? An amateur? I do business deals, and if you're not interested, I can go elsewhere. You guys are not the only game in town. And I don't like insults . . ."

He started to get up, but the short Turk waved him back into the chair.

"No insult intended," Mohammed said. "I'm just careful. We've had bad experiences dealing with Americans. But I trust the Father here. We checked him out a long time ago when he first came to Turkey. That's why I agreed to meet you when he asked me. So what's on your mind?"

"I'm in weapons as I said," Tim answered. "Right now, some friends and I would like to dispose of stuff that's stayed behind after the last war in the Middle East . . . and some stuff from Vietnam that's still available. You know, M-16s, grenade launchers, and even bigger items if I find the right customer—and get the price I want. For immediate delivery . . . I hear that you people might be in the market. Or have clients who are . . ."

"It's possible," Mohammed said. "It's possible. Of course, I have to discuss it with my associates. How long will you be in Istambul?"

"As long as necessary," Tim told him.

The Turk switched to English. "We'll be in touch," he said, rising. "I'll contact you through the Father if we decide to talk with you again."

On the way out, Tim had a quick glance of athletic young men, automatic weapons at the ready, behind the curtain from where the tray of coffee had come.

A week had elapsed before Tim's hotel room phone rang and the Polish Jesuit invited him to "dinner" at the community behind the Covered Bazaar. Tim assumed that Mohammed was consulting with his fellow Wolves, but he also took it for granted that he was being closely watched. It was elementary in the world of spying and terrorism. Tim's movements and behavior, accordingly, were designed to convince all concerned that he was a bona fide crooked American businessman, really trying to clinch arms deals in Istambul—one of the world's greatest arms bazaars.

Because of a special dispensation from his Jesuit superiors, Tim did not have to celebrate Mass every morning in his hotel room. He could not have risked traveling with liturgical paraphernalia or being surprised by a hotel maid—his cover had to be protected. He was sure that his room had already been searched. During the day, Tim took taxis in the midtown area, darting in and out of modern office buildings along Istiklal Boulevard and riding elevators up and down to impress the men presumably tailing him with his business activities. He also visited foreign banks' branches for lengthy conversations with vice presidents on financial topics of his imagination.

Evenings, Tim sat at the hotel bar, alone or with one of the young women always present there, nursing a Scotch on the rocks and making small talk. He was never tempted on these occasions to break his chastity vows, but the Wolves could not know it as they observed him marching toward a hotel elevator with a young woman whom he then dismissed, with *bakshish*—a bribe—on one of the floors. Tim thought this was comical—for a Jesuit.

He used his idle time as well playing the tourist, admiring the extravagant beauty of Istambul's great monuments, mosques, and museums. As an orientalist, Tim loved his stay in the city: it was a rich bonus. Well, bless Sainte-Ange, he thought gratefully the third time he strolled under the dome of St. Sophia. Along the Bosphorus, a tourist guide, spotting him as a rich American, pointed to the narrowing of the straits across which an American ambassador to Turkey had once swum from Europe to Asia to make an obscure diplomatic machismo point.

At the Jesuit community the evening of the "dinner," the Pole told Tim, "They're waiting for us. I guess they've checked you out to their satisfaction. I'll drive you over."

It was a long way from the Covered Bazaar, over the Golden Horn Bridge, to the Istambul downtown and across the suspension bridge to the Asia side of the Bosphorus and to the Üsküdar district to the south. Amidst Üsküdar's mosques, the Jesuit located a large, whitewashed house on narrow Aziz Mahmut Street. The front door opened before they had time to ring the bell, and Mohammed stepped out to greet the visitors. On the second floor, three men in cheap black suits, no neckties, awaited them. No introductions were made. A slim, bespectacled man with a scholarly mien, probably in his early thirties, went straight to the point as soon as the two Jesuits sat down on straight-backed chairs. There was no other furniture in the big room.

"What do you have to sell?" he asked impatiently in English. "In what quantities and at what prices?"

"Right now," Tim replied, having memorized his presentation, "I can offer you a lot of one hundred M-16s with spare parts and a reasonable supply of munitions. I also have ten .50-caliber heavy machine guns, a dozen grenade launchers . . . This is for immediate delivery. I have it in Izmir, near that NATO base, but more of it and other items can be brought to the country without much delay."

"We could be interested," the bespectacled man told him. "We could be interested in everything you have in Izmir. We can take delivery there. And we could be interested in more if the price is acceptable."

Tim and the Wolves' leader discussed prices for several minutes, both writing figures down. Tim had a Conrad Istanbul hotel notepad, the Turk wrote in a small black leather notebook. The money negotiation went well though Tim deliberately delayed it with unnecessary comments about the quality and reliability of the American-made arms he was offering. It was the crucial moment of his mission. He needed a better and easier rapport with this man. He was gambling everything on the Turk's reaction to the question he was finally about to ask.

"Well, I guess we're in business," Tim said at length. "You can take delivery a week from today in Izmir for a cash payment. But I have a question I'd like to ask you, if you don't mind. Or, rather, ask your advice about something very special . . ."

"Yes?"

"Hypothetically, where, or to whom, I would turn if I wished to have someone liquidated in another country. You know, in a very discreet way."

The men exchanged quick glances.

"Why do you ask us, Mr. Savage?" the leader inquired calmly. "Why should we know such things? We are not an employment agency for assassins."

"No, of course not," Tim said reasonably, keeping excitement out of his voice. "But we're all professionals in what we do, and there surely is no harm in asking a professional question. Is there?"

The Turk stared at Tim with cold curiosity.

"No, but there could be harm in *answering* a question like that," he remarked. "In any case, why do you bring it up with us at all? Why do you ask in Turkey, why not elsewhere?"

Tim said a quick, silent prayer. It was now or never.

"I shall be frank with you," he said. "It's impossible to find someone knowledgable in the United States these days because of all that crazy business in the past with the CIA trying to assassinate foreign leaders, like Castro in Cuba, and so forth. It's too dangerous. In Europe, all there is nowadays are dishonest people one cannot trust; the professionals or stupid amateurs from the old outfits like the Red Brigades in Italy who don't know what they're doing. The Palestinians are nuts. Okay?"

Tim took a deep breath.

"So why do I ask in Turkey?", he continued. "I ask in Turkey because I remember—you see, I, too, read newspapers—that it was a Turkish person who tried to kill the pope in Rome five years ago. He was a good shot; he hit the old man, but he was out of luck. The pope lives and the shooter sits in prison. Poor sonofabitch . . . So what I'm asking is whether you know, by any chance, another person like what's-his-name . . . And I'm asking *you* people because we're doing business together and I think I can trust you, at least enough to ask. Besides, you have quite a reputation for your contacts and your efficiency. Naturally, I have friends who would pay very well for advice. And, you understand, I'm putting myself at risk by even asking the question. But I trust you. . . ."

There was a long silence. The bespectacled man looked at the window. It now was very dark outside. There were no streetlights on Mehmet Aga. But they could hear the evening wind from the Bosphorus whistling through the neighborhood.

"Sit down," he said to Tim. "Let's talk a bit."

Tim felt a wave of relief washing over him. His nerves were steadier. He had not blown it—yet.

"I must explain something to you," the leader told him. "Yes, it's obviously true that it was a Turk who shot the pope. And you must know, just from reading newspapers, as you put it, that Agca Circlic—that's his name, in case you forget—had once belonged to our organization. This makes it clear to me why you ask how to hire a murderer. But I hate to disappoint you, Mr. Savage. The Gray Wolves, or whatever they call us, are not in the business of assassination for money. We are a political organization, a revolutionary organization—that's why we're doing business with you today to get the arms we need—and if we kill, it is for reasons of politics. Not for dollars . . ."

He paused briefly to let his words sink in.

"So you, Mr. Savage," the Turk went on, "are really asking why Agca Circlic, who may or may not have been one of us at the time, went to Rome to kill the pope, a project of no special interest to us."

Tim nodded. "Yes, I suppose so."

"Then I shall tell you in order to protect the good name of our organization," the leader said, peering at Tim intently through his thick glasses. "We did make Circlic available for that job because our brethren, our Muslim brethren—and don't forget that we *are* Muslims—had asked us for someone like him as a fraternal favor in the name of our religion. And Circlic was as good as they come as a shooter. He had proved it in the past. And he was just stupid enough to be trusted for that operation."

Tim listened tensely as the Turk kept talking.

"You will never understand our culture, but let me try to say to you that we are men of honor and when we kill, we kill as a matter of honor and duty. We are inspired by Allah and his Prophet to be pure and defend our religion and our nation . . . Yes, when Atatürk was president way back after the First World War, he turned Turkey into a secular state. He betrayed Islam. They call us criminals and terrorists because of what we do, but our first aim is to be faithful to Allah and the Koran. This is why we agreed to honor the request from our French brethren. By the way, I have a degree in theology and—"

"*French?*" Tim interrupted, uncomprehendingly.

"Yes, French," the Turk replied. "French Muslims. The people who came from Algeria and so on. They suffer a lot in France and we're often in touch with them. Sometimes we help. We helped with Circlic."

"But why would they want to kill a Roman Catholic pope in Rome?" Tim asked, now completely disoriented. "I don't follow . . ."

"Frankly," the Gray Wolf told him, "I don't know and I don't care. I don't need to know. It doesn't concern us. We have no problem with the pope. All we did was what our brethren desired. I have no idea whether they have a problem with him."

"Wait a minute," Tim broke in. "Why did this man write a letter to a Turkish newspaper that he would kill the pope? Why all this stuff about the Soviets, the KGB, the Bulgarians?"

The Turk smiled for the first time since they had met. He looked pleased with himself.

"Oh, this is what you Americans call 'disinformation,'" he said. "It was part of the whole arrangement with Paris that was nearly a year in the making. We sprang Circlic out of prison after he had assassinated that newspaper editor—it was at our suggestion for our own reasons—and we prepared and trained him for the work in Rome. Later, a weapon was given to him. And it was I who wrote the letter to the newspaper about planning to kill the pope and signed Circlic's name. Then we invented the thing about the Soviets and the Bulgarians so that, Allah forbid, our brethren would not be accused of anything. The pope, of course, is so strongly anticommunist that it was a very plausible deception. And did the press eat it up! It sort of worked. But nothing can be proven—so I don't mind telling you our end of the story. You know, Circlic was supposed to have been killed himself—like your Oswald in Dallas—but our other guy screwed up and ran for dear life. What the hell! . . . As you must have read, Circlic said nothing truly useful to the police. This was because he didn't know why he was doing it. He simply took his orders from us—and our money. So now, Mr. Savage, you know as much as I do. Or almost . . ."

"I see," Tim said. "You people were just doing the brotherly thing. It wasn't business."

"That's right. And that's why I cannot give you any advice—and I would certainly not procure a new Circlic for you. Please understand that we wouldn't do it for money. You Americans are not our brethren so we owe you nothing. Only the dollars for the arms when you deliver them in Izmir. . . ."

On his way to the airport, Tim stopped at the Jesuit house to bid farewell to the Polish priest and thank him for his assistance.

"But there's a loose end," he told him. "What about the 'arms' they think they'll be buying from me in Izmir? Will they feel deceived, betrayed, try to kill you, or what?"

"Oh, not to worry," the Pole said with an endearing smile. "We get along just fine for their reasons and my reasons. Exchanging information, you know, is a very valuable commodity in Istambul. I'll go over there to explain that at the last minute the Turkish Army, on a tip from the CIA, or somebody, had impounded your shipment . . . No big deal. They're not out of any money, which is what would mean the most to them. In their line of business, life is full of glitches like that. And I doubt they'll lose much sleep over telling you about the 'French Brethren.' The Wolves have no idea who you are and why you would be really interested in all that stuff. It had no significance to them. So forget it, Father Savage, and enjoy your flight back to Rome. I'm glad I could be of help. . . ."

Chapter Fourteen

A CLUE IS A CLUE is a clue, Tim mused as he flew home to Rome, but it is meaningless unless one knows what it means. Gertrude Stein knew, at least, that a rose *was* a rose. Tim did *not* know who were the "French Brethren" of the Gray Wolves and why the Turkish terrorists had provided them with an assassin. Yet, the French clue was crucial, he thought.

But if he ever were to run down the "French Brethren" and move ahead with his investigation, his next destination had to be France, Tim knew even before his airliner landed at Fiumicino. As he entered his Istambul impressions in his big ledger in his hot Villa Malta room, he noted that while, in a literal sense, a "Muslim connection" was part of the assassination conspiracy, the shooter being a Muslim belonging to a Muslim organization, the attack had not been a Muslim enterprise. The Muslims appeared to be intermediaries, not intellectual authors of the attempt against Gregory XVII.

In this sense, the Istambul conversations had been extremely useful to Tim, eliminating to his satisfaction the notion that Islam fanatics had been behind the plot. Having so concluded, Tim now wondered what, precisely, Monsignor Saint-Ange had meant by "Muslim connection." Was it just stating the obvious because Circlic was a Muslim, or did he know something else he was not telling? Inevitably, the question arose in Tim's mind whether there was some link between the mysterious "French Brethren" and de Marenches' "warning" from Paris? And should he tell the monsignor about the "French Brethren" before he had learned who they were? How did the violent history of tensions between France and the Holy See fit into this vast murky picture?

Needing even a momentary distraction from analyzing and

reanalyzing theories, Tim poured himself a glass of red wine and reached for *Panorama,* the Italian weekly newsmagazine. But as luck would have it, and Tim had to laugh when he opened the publication, the lead article dealt with the approaching trial of suspects in the kidnapping and murder of Aldo Moro, the very controversial but also very popular Italian prime minister, and his five bodyguards. Though the authorities had concluded that the deed had been perpetrated by Red Brigades terrorists, it remained a mystery who and why had ordered the murder. Given their obsessions with conspiracies, going back to the Borgias and before, most Italians were convinced that Moro had been the victim of a plot hatched very high in national power circles. The magazine reported that Moro had been killed because "powerful men had reasons not to keep him alive." There were charges of a cover-up, and a Red Brigades veteran had told *Panorama:* "I don't know whose hands were behind the scenes, but I know we were part of a much larger game."

The Aldo Moro story was no encouragement to Tim. It was another unsolved political assassination, another mystery. Moro was a Christian Democrat, close to the Holy See, but who were the "powerful men" who "had reasons not to keep alive" the French pontiff? And what chances did Tim, an obscure American Jesuit working virtually on his own, have to discover what had motivated the assault on St. Peter's Square? He felt a touch of helplessness and depression, but a touch of growing frustration and curiosity as well.

Two days after returning from Istambul, Tim called on Sister Angela at her Apostolic Palace office to present an oral report on his Istambul expedition. Angela took his words down in short-hand to pass on to Sainte-Ange, who, presumably, would inform Gregory XVII. The monsignor had insisted that there be no written reports; there should be no paper trail of any kind, he had said.

"Tell him," Tim instructed Angela, having decided to share with Sainte-Ange *almost* everything he had discovered in Turkey, "that now we have an enigma wrapped inside a mystery. It seems that the Gray Wolves, that Turkish terrorist group, had indeed supplied the shooter as a courtesy—if that's the word—to some

French Muslims for reasons they themselves do not know and, of course, would never inquire. I met with them in Istambul, and that's the way those things work. It's like the 'need to know' rule in intelligence communities. So now I have to track down those Muslim "French Brethren," and I'm not quite sure where to start. Why don't you ask the Monsignor if he has any ideas? He's bound to have some contacts with French intelligence people . . ."

"I'll see if he can receive me this afternoon," Angela told him. "Your work is top priority for him. Then I'll get back to you as soon as possible—if I have anything useful to pass on . . . By the way, how did you like Istambul? I was there once a long time ago, before I took the vows."

"Oh, I loved it," Tim replied enthusiastically. "It's extraordinary: the architecture, the colors, the Bosphorus, the Golden Horn . . . I wish I had more time to look around. But I did see the *seraglio* from a distance. It made me think of you. I don't know why . . ."

"I beg your pardon?" Angela asked, her cheeks suddenly gaining color.

"Well, it was some kind of a strange association of ideas," Tim said, his turn to be embarrassed by the conversation. "I can't really explain it."

He thought she looked especially attractive today, feeling like an adolescent. Impure thoughts again. Why does the Church make such a big deal of celibacy? Priests, after all, were free to marry in the opening centuries of Christendom, and they still were in many Catholic faiths in communion with Rome.

Just before St. Peter's bells tolled the Angelus, Monsignor de Sainte-Ange knocked lightly on the door of the pope's study before entering. Gregory XVII, writing at his long, narrow desk, looked up with a tired smile. Chopin's Scherzo No. 3 in C sharp minor, his favorite, played softly in the background.

"I had hoped to complete the draft of this speech for Paris before dinner, but I guess I was too optimistic," he remarked. "It has to be a perfect text, and one cannot hurry it. So let's take the dinner break now, and then I'll continue. Anything interesting?

"Well," the secretary said, "the American is back from Istambul with some startling news that I'm not certain he himself fully understands."

"Such as?"

"He has reported to me through Sister Angela that the Gray Wolves, the Turkish terrorists, had provided Circlic at the request of what he calls 'French Brethren,' meaning, I imagine, French Muslims," the monsignor told the pope. "He has no idea who the 'French Brethren' are, but he is, of course, determined to find out. After all, this is the mission we gave him. So now he's getting ready to go to Paris. And God only knows what he'll come up with. It makes me a bit uncomfortable. We always knew it had to do with Muslims in some way, but not with *French* Muslims . . . Maybe a Turk was used to confuse us."

Gregory XVII nodded thoughtfully, toying with his soup spoon.

"Do you think this was what de Marenches tried to tell us with his warnings? Was he referring to French Muslims?" he asked.

"Perhaps, perhaps," the monsignor answered. "And perhaps we should have listened, tightened security, gone public or something, rather than worry about political relations with Islam and even with France. It could have cost your life, Holiness . . . It was my fault. I should have thought more clearly."

"We were both at fault," Gregory XVII told him. "But now I can only pray that nothing of this comes out before we go to Paris. Things with France are already so complicated. Clovis and St. Bartholomew's Day and the mad archbishop. All I need now is a Muslim problem! . . . God, I hope the American is discreet . . ."

The pope's trip to France was scheduled for the following month—his third home since his election—and he was, as usual, prepared for unpleasantness there from all sides. Each time he was chastised and criticized for paying solemn homage to King Clovis I of Salian Franks who had accepted baptism in 496, turning France into a Christian nation. The criticism came mainly from masses of French atheists whose denunciations of the Church and its ties to Rome dated back to the 1789 Revolution— still a matter of angry debate by stubborn intellectuals nearly two centuries later—and still feared any threat to the separation of state and Church. Liberal Catholics were against Clovis' and

France's formal identification with the Holy See under Gregory XVII because they opposed what they regarded as Rome's conservative attitudes and policies in violation of the Second Vatican Council's modernization of the institution.

Still on the Catholic side, the pope faced a virtual rebellion by extreme right-wing priests and believers who considered that the Church had gone too far "to the left" at the Council, notably by sanctioning the vernacular Mass instead of the Latin one, and that Gregory XVII was guilty of abetting this "betrayal." Heading this increasingly vocal movement—the Fraternity of St. Pius V—was the aged priest from West Africa the pope had called the "mad archbishop," who had already defied the Holy See by ordaining four priests on his own—for which he had been suspended by Rome—and, now in effect, was inviting punishment in the form of excommunication.

The Pius V Fraternity was the rebirth, three centuries later, of the Secret Society of Pius V, a powerful organization of theological paranoia and terror. Pius V was the sixteenth-century pope who had enforced the Latin Mass as decreed by the 1545 Council of Trent's decision on the "Uniformity of Liturgy." His spirit was revived by Pius X whose reign between 1903 and 1914 had ushered in the Church's latest "Age of Intransigency," in the words of a famous historian. This pope had written that "the Church . . . comprises two categories of persons, the pastors and the flocks. The hierarchy alone moves and controls. The duty of the multitude is to suffer itself to be governed and to carry out in a submissive spirit the orders of those in control." The memory of Pius V and Pius X was still very much alive in France, with the fanatic archbishop leading the Fraternity. Pope Paul VI had already condemned the archbishop's attitude and his Fraternity in 1976, and Gregory XVII had made up his mind to excommunicate him—excluding him from the communion of the faithful until he repented—but Sainte-Ange had prevailed with the argument that this act should be postponed until the return from the French visit to avoid public protests there and further division of the French Church.

But resentments against the pope and his planned trip also came from French Protestants who had not forgiven the Church and Rome for butchering ten thousand or more Huguenots under the Catholic queen, Catherine de Médicis, during the St. Bartholomew's Day Massacre in August 1572. The massacre was carried out to prevent the accession to the throne of the Huguenot Henri of Navarre as Henri IV of France, resulting in the post-Reformation French Wars of Religion. Protestants remembered to this day that Pope Gregory XIII, an Italian, had celebrated the massacre with a majestic "Te Deum" Mass of gratitude; it was the year of his accession to the pontificate.

French Muslims, and particularly the new immigrants from North Africa, were basically indifferent to Gregory XVII and his impending visit. It had nothing to do with their lives and they held no animus against the Roman pope on religious grounds. The great Crusades were forgotten. If anything, Muslim leaders were grateful to the Catholic Church for standing up publicly in defense of the practice of their religion and culture in France and firmly opposing deportations of immigrants by Paris governments, which responded to pressures from jingoist rightist political parties and Catholic "Integrists." In the church of St. Bernard de la Chapelle, for instance, 210 Muslims, including women and children, had sought refuge from deportation until riot police violated that Parisian sanctuary and dragged them out.

The last thing Gregory XVII desired therefore at this juncture was to see Muslims rising against him and the Church in France, perhaps no longer remembering his stand in protecting them during his Marseille days. This is why he was worried now by Tim Savage's discoveries in Istambul that Sainte-Ange had described to him. If publicized in some fashion, the supposed role of the "French Brethren" in the assassination attempt could have unpredictable consequences and ruin his hopes for a serious dialogue with Islam.

Rome and Islam, to be sure, were open rivals for the souls of tens of millions of essentially religiously uncommitted Africans— Animists or "pagans" or people who somehow blended their ancestral religious traditions with either Christianity or Islam. For Gregory XVII, Africa represented, as he put it, the "last frontier" in the world for his Church to conquer. He hoped to sway African Muslims away from their faith to his; Nigeria, where he had gone twice, was a case in point as was the Sudan, with the populations divided between Islam and Catholicism. The pope also prayed to attract the "pagans" where neither organized religion prevailed. He had gone to the extreme of accepting "acculturation," a mix of traditional rites and Christianity, and allowed tribal singing and dancing inside St. Peter's Basilica during a recent synod of African bishops. Islam and Catholicism had made an effort to keep their rivalry low profile and avoid public confrontations. Hence the pontiff's concerned that Tim's findings, if disclosed and misinterpreted, could destroy this fine balancing act. That same concern had guided his decision over de Marenches' warning.

The most pro-papal religious community in France, after the Catholics loyal to the Holy See, were the Jews—the smallest of all these groups—because of the Vatican's pro-Jewish policy since the Vatican Council and, presumably, because the cardinal archbishop of Paris was a converted Jew and Gregory XVII's close personal friend. The memories of the Dreyfus affair a century ago and the wartime behavior of "Integrist" priests toward the Jews were, however, just below the surface, and the pope was aware of an explosive potential involving Jewish communities and anti-Semites. He was looking forward to a long private session with the cardinal in Paris, but he was becoming concerned, as he listened to Sainte-Ange, that if the "French Brethren" Muslim connection in the assassination attempt were to surface, it could damage the Jewish relationship, too.

"God," Gregory XVII sighed, "why can nothing be simple, just once, in my own homeland?"

"Amen!" Sainte-Ange exclaimed, a shade too piously.

Entering a restaurant he particularly liked just below the Angelicum, where Gregory XVII had once studied for his doctorate, Tim Savage crossed the main dining room, led by the owner, a good friend, to the small garden where he found Paul Martinius awaiting him for lunch at one of the four tables around a cool fountain. It was very private there in the shaded warmth of the early afternoon and under the protection of old Roman walls across the street.

"Sit down and taste my Gavi di Gavi wine, the pope's personal favorite," the CIA Station Chief urged Tim, pouring from the bottle he extracted from the ice cooler. "It's the best damned white wine in this country. Then tell me about Istambul."

Tim did both, savoring the Gavi and giving Martinius a detailed account of his contacts with the Gray Wolves and their claim that they had made Circlic available to honor the request from "French Brethren."

"What do you make of it?" he asked. "Do you believe it and what does it mean?"

"Yes, I do believe it, but I'm not quite sure at this point what to make of it," the CIA officer answered. "But do you remember what I told you about de Marenches? I'm beginning to wonder what sort of a strange triangle are—or were—these Muslims, the lamentably late de Marenches and your papal secretary. I have that awful feeling I'm missing something here. I assume you're going to France now? . . . Oh, shit, I wish you had stayed with the Agency! Your talents are wasted here . . ."

"Obviously, I'm going to France," Tim said. "As soon as I can get organized."

"And have you thought of touching base—gently—with Interpol? They're in Lyons, you know, and the Secretary-General there is an old pal of mine. A Frenchman who gets around a lot. Tell him I sent you. His name is Raymont Quindelle."

"Sure, but you know I can't tell him what I'm really after."

"That's alright," Martinius said. "Just stick to your interest in Islamic organizations in general because of the Holy Father's hopes for better relations with Islam and so on, and old Quindelle may surprise you. Muslim terrorists are very much part of his *dossier* these days and he may welcome the opportunity of chatting with a great scholar like you. He must have heard about you. Why, he may even know that you just came back from Istambul!"

The Station Chief laughed, poured them more Gavi di Gavi, and signaled a hovering waiter for menus.

"It's a very small world we spooks live in, remember?"

"You may have bitten off more than you can chew," Father Blás, the Jesuit General Superior, told Tim. "Or, to mix metaphors, you may have stirred up a hornet's nest."

They were eating alone in the General's private dining room at the Borgo Santo Spirito Jesuit headquarters. Tim had called to request an appointment at the office, but the Spaniard had invited him to dinner.

"We'll be more relaxed that way," he said. Their conversation was in English, Father Blás having studied in the United States for his doctorate in sociology, and being at ease with colloquialisms and Americanisms.

Sainte-Ange had insisted that the investigation be conducted in absolute secrecy, but Tim quickly realized that he could not function in a total vacuum. Especially after Istambul, he felt he required advice and guidance from a few men he trusted implicitly; Paul Martinius and Father Blás clearly qualified as confidential advisers.

Giving the General Superior a full report on his Istambul discussions, not failing to express gratitude to the Polish Jesuit who had put him in touch with the Gray Wolves, Tim wound up expressing his quandary over the meaning of the "French Brethren." He also mentioned having learned about de Marenches' warning at the anniversary party for the elderly Jesuit priest earlier in the year.

"Yes," Father Blás said, turning around in his hands his cognac ballon. He was a tall, thin man with melancholy eyes, oddly reminding Tim of Don Quixote. "We have known for a long time about the warning. And you should know that it came to us from our Jesuit brothers in Paris, long before the *Figaro* interview. De Marenches had many Jesuit friends, and I daresay that our brothers in France continue to cultivate their friendship with his organization. We are often interested in the same thing, but I must confess that we've never been able to establish what precisely de Marenches had included in his warning, whether he had provided names, identities, *modi operandi,* and so on . . . At this end, only the pope and Sainte-Ange may know what the warning contained. By the way, you should stay at the Jesuit Residence in Paris so that your visit there will appear to be routine. I'll let them know to expect you."

"Thank you, Father," Tim said, "but do you suppose that they also have contacts with the Muslim community in France, especially with religious leaders? I have my own *entrée* to French Islamic scholars, but I wouldn't mind having another access road."

"I would imagine so," the Spaniard told him. "Even so, I suspect that you will have a hard time identifying the 'French Brethren' who had hired the assassin among the mass of Muslims in France. Whoever they are, they must be very well hidden from view. I have to assume that they are dedicated terrorists of some kind and that they know how to cover their tracks . . . When I lived in Lebanon, I had a chance to become somewhat familiar with the operational tactics of groups like the *Hezbollah*—and they have to be taken seriously. These groups usually have very little in common with one another, but share tactical experiences. The most important thing is that they all are meticulous planners."

"Getting back to de Marenches for a moment," Tim asked, "did the Paris Jesuits who informed you about the warning mention anything about Muslims or 'French Brethren'?"

"No, not really," Father Blás replied. "There may have been a passing allusion to a vague possibility of de Marenches having some Muslim involvement in mind, but that was all. Sorry, my boy."

"One more question, Father: Did the Holy Father, as far as you know, pay any attention to the warning? Did he do something about it?"

"I don't think so," the General Superior said slowly. "He must have had reasons for choosing to trust the protection and the mercy of God. And about *that,* he was right in the end!"

The Spaniard rose from the table to signify the end of the dinner.

"What you have, Tim, is dynamite," he said. "Be very careful with it. *Vaya con Díos!*"

Past the passenger terminals and airline hangars at Fiumicino Airport near Rome, Alitalia's In-Flight Food Service occupies an indistinguishable, three-story whitewashed building with loading docks for its trucks delivering meals to planes. Late on a Saturday afternoon in early July, Jake Kurtski parked his small rental car at a side entrance, leaned comfortably against his seat, and lit a cigar, calmly awaiting a man he had not seen in over thirty years.

Presently, the side door opened and the man stepped out in the setting sun, looked around, and walked slowly toward the rental car. He was short and compact, probably in his fifties. He wore a driver's coveralls. Squinting, he approached the parked vehicle, peering at the figure behind the steering wheel.

"Holy God," he exclaimed in Polish. "This is really you, Jacek Kurtski?"

"It's *Jake*," Kurtski corrected him. "Get in. We have to talk.

"Thirty-five years ago, I saved your ass and your life at the Magdeburg camp," he went on. "Remember? The life at the D.P. camp? Fine. So now you are going to pay that debt, my dear Grochowski. You will do what I'll tell you to do, when I'll tell you to do it."

"How did you find me here?" Grochowski asked in awe. "After all these years?"

"That's my business," Kurtski told him. "Your business is to follow my orders and keep your mouth shut—if you want to hang on to your life. You'll hear from me again before too long. Now get out of the car!"

BOOK FOUR

The Discovery

Chapter Fifteen

PARIS APPEARED to Tim Savage to be a city abandoned by panicked inhabitants fleeing the Black Plague when he arrived there the first week of August, a day so hot that even pigeons hid under the eaves of Notre-Dame. Parisians themselves had vanished for a month along the Atlantic and the Mediterranean, in the mountains and in the countryside, from the Loire Valley and Dordogne to Lake Annecy and the Languedoc. The only human presence, it seemed, were foreign tourists, and Tim was convinced, from their sounds and appearance, that most of them were Americans.

Scanning *Le Monde* during the short flight from Fiumicino to Orly, Tim came across a short, page-one story about the forcible occupation of a parish church in Chamblac, a small town in Normandy, by followers of the Pius V Fraternity, which the reporter described as an "Integrist" organization and whose militant members evidently had not gone away on vacations. "Integrist," Tim knew, came from the Latin *integratio,* meaning a renewing or restoring, and it was used in connection with extreme conservative groups in Church opposing the reforms of the Second Vatican Council and other modernizing steps. It was just one more quarrel inside the French Church, a subject of no particular interest to him.

But the next two stories in *Le Monde* did command his attention at once. One reported another massacre of villagers in Algeria by an Islamic terrorist organization; this was a topic Tim had followed closely while working at his commission office. Algeria, even more than Egypt or the Sudan, had become the country to watch for every Islam scholar and African and Middle Eastern policy planner. The other story recounted the latest episode of violence between "young Arabs" and Turkish immigrants and the riot police in an industrial Parisian suburb that was home to thousands of Muslim families, mainly unemployed refugees from overseas. It was part of the "Muslim Belt," as the article put it, where even the toughest French *gendarmes* hesitated to enter after dark. Was this where he might have to go in his quest for the "French Brethren," Tim wondered uneasily.

After his return from Istambul, Angela had sent Tim a copy of *The Mystery of Marie Roget* by Edgar Allan Poe, the famous whodunit featuring Auguste Dupin as the detective hero. "You may find it amusing, if not helpful," she had written in an accompanying note.

Tim, who at this stage fervently welcomed anything helpful, had smiled with appreciation reading Dupin's admonition that "not the least usual error in investigations . . . is the limiting of the inquiry to the immediate, with total disregard of collateral or surrounding events. I would divert inquiry from the trodden and unfruitful ground of the event itself, to the contemporary circumstances which surround it." And he remembered from a Georgetown class in legal logic that "absence of evidence is *not* evidence of absence."

As the plane now began its approach to Paris, Tim suddenly remembered Dupin's words, struck by their immediate relevance to his own investigation. Yes, *contemporary circumstances,* he thought, but what were they—or what *are* they? Dupin seemed to be trying to tell him to look for broader horizons. Again, Tim was intrigued by Sister Angela: nuns were not habitual readers—or fans—of Poe, or admirers of the great Auguste Dupin. She certainly was a remarkable woman, with her most unusual mind, her literary knowledge, and her quiet sense of humor. Dupin, of course, fitted his mission perfectly. And there were other aspects of Angela's *persona* that Tim was finding exceedingly attractive, and more and more on his mind, not excluding impure thoughts. He enjoyed the thoughts. More than once he dreamed about her very beautiful face and, since they were dreams, about her very beautiful body. And he hardly knew her.

Dupin's advice notwithstanding, there was no pattern of *contemporary circumstances* surrounding the assassination attempt against Gregory XVII that Tim could discern. Alright, he admitted, there was the alleged Muslim connection and his discovery of the "French Brethren," but thus far it told him nothing about the crucial *circumstances.* And there were no clear *circumstances* surrounding other great contemporary acts of terrorism and violence, most of them unresolved—even apart from the American assassinations of past decades.

In August 1980, less than a year before the attack on the pope, for example, eighty-six persons were killed when a bomb went off at the Bologna railway station when a train from Rome had come to a stop. An organization identified as "Fascist" had taken the responsibility for this act, but nobody knew why the "Fascists" had done it. No visible *contemporary circumstances,* other than the entirely irrelevant fact that Bologna had a communist mayor and fascists hated communists. Some years later, the commander of the Vatican's Swiss Guards and his wife were shot and killed by a Swiss Guards corporal who then killed himself. This hit as close to home as imaginable, inside the Vatican perimeter, but, likewise, there were no signs of conspiracies and no *circumstances* surrounding the tragedy. It probably had nothing to do with Gregory XVII, but Tim felt he had to look into the Swiss Guards shooting, just in case he found a clue; all he found were hints that the commander and the corporal may have had a homosexual relationship.

Even when people "killed for God," or said they did, patterns—as distinct from personal motivations—could not be traced or established in a broader fashion. St. Stanisław, the bishop of Kraków in Poland, was killed in the eleventh century on the orders of the king whom he had denounced. In the twelfth century, Thomas à Becket was murdered at his altar on the orders of England's King Henry II—he was a "turbulent" and "meddlesome" priest in the eyes of the sovereign. In El Salvador, eight centuries later, Archbishop Oscar Romero was assassinated at his altar by right-wing military leaders to whom he was a politically "turbulent" priest. Was Gregory XVII, too, a politically "turbulent" and "meddlesome" priest to a sovereign or a madman, who had to be "killed for God?"

The room assigned to Tim at the Jesuit Residence on Rue St. Jacques on the Left Bank, not far from the Sorbonne, was spacious, pleasant, and comfortable. He had told the Jesuit brother who showed him to the room that he was not certain how long he would stay in Paris—perhaps a few weeks, he said—and was smilingly assured that he was welcome to remain there even for a few years.

"If you stay here until the middle of September," the brother remarked, "you will catch the visit of the Holy Father. I'm sure that you see him often in Rome, but you might find it interesting to observe him on his home turf. Parisians will be back from the holidays and we expect a huge turnout of the faithful. You speak French so well that you will not miss a word, not a nuance of the visit."

"Yes, that would be quite interesting," Tim replied, actually meaning it. Would the "French Brethren," whoever they might be, try to kill Gregory XVII in Paris, having failed in Rome? There was so much Muslim unrest in France these days, as had just been emphasized in *Le Monde* that morning, that one could not feel safe about anything, especially if it touched on religion.

In fact, the pope seemed to face new dangers even at the Vatican. Thus just before he left for Paris, Tim had been told by Sister Angela, on Saint-Ange's instructions, that a bomb had been discovered several days earlier in the Bernini Colonnade on St. Peter's Square, directly below the Papal Apartments. And that same week, the CIA Director had flown from Washington to inform the Cardinal Secretary of State during a most discreet visit that the Agency's networks were picking up signs, imprecise as they were, that unidentified terrorists were plotting to kill the pope. Unlike five years ago, Tim thought, the CIA was now paying serious attention to possible new conspiracies. He wondered whether the Agency was aware of any actual warnings, from whatever quarters, similar to de Marenches' warnings last time around, the ones that went unheeded by the Holy See.

The message from Sainte-Ange that Angela had delivered to Tim included a reference to the information communicated by the CIA Director. But, Tim noticed, there was no suggestion that an attempt against the pope would necessarily be made during the approaching visit to France. Yet, it could happen, he reasoned, particularly in the light of what he had learned in Istambul about the "French Brethren."

His discovery, of course, just happened to coincide with the bomb found in the Bernini Colonnade and the signs picked up by the CIA. Tim, after all, had gone to Istambul at a time of his own choosing and he had sought out the Gray Wolves—so it was a matter of luck, if that was the proper way of putting it. But then there was the uncanny coincidence of Tim's newly acquired knowledge about the "French Brethren," which forced him to pursue his investigations in France without delay, and Gregory XVII's visit to his homeland, just three weeks away.

It was all vague, elusive, and confusing. But Tim Savage suddenly experienced, on that first day in Paris, the eerie feeling that his efforts to unearth the truth about the assassination attempt were turning into a life-and-death race against new conspiracies directed at the pope. His investigation, Tim sensed, no longer was the exercise in historical sleuthing he had thought it to be at the outset, when Sainte-Ange had told him that Gregory XVII desired to know the "truth." There was sudden urgency about his endeavor, he startingly realized, and he knew he was back in action. As in Vietnam. Tim was now determined to remain in France for the duration of the papal visit, even without the encouragement of his Jesuit hosts on Rue St. Jacques, and, if all went well, to stay on as long as necessary to follow the Istambul leads and all the new information until he made real progress. It could not wait long, and there was much spadework to be done in France.

The private office of the Minister of Interior, facing the presidential Élysée Palace on deserted Rue du Faubourg St. Honoré, was filled with France's top security officials at the eight o'clock morning meeting. The tourists were not yet out in the street to admire the powerful black automobiles inside the courtyard and lining up along the sidewalk outside.

The minister, a fastidious and meticulous politician, had concluded that time had come to review all the imaginable security aspects of Gregory XVII's September visit. Planning security measures for such an occasion was a standard law enforcement procedure that in the past had not required the minister's personal involvement. This time, however, there was acute nervousness at the highest levels of the French government about the pope's safety, and the president had assigned the interior minister—in effect, France's top police official—to assume personal responsibility for the visit.

Rising Muslim unrest in the country was, of course, one of the reasons, and everybody at the morning meeting remembered that Agca Circlic was himself a Muslim. Conventional police wisdom, shared with conventional historians, held that history tends to repeat itself almost literally. But some of the officials assembled in the ornate ministerial private office actually knew and remembered some other significant facts about the 1981 assassination plot that, they believed, should be considered at this meeting. The minister had obviously been informed of the discovery of the lethal bomb in the Bernini Colonnade—it had not been made public—and, as a matter of sharing intelligence, at least in some situations, he had been provided with the same information that the CIA Director had just presented at the Vatican.

"What should I worry about?" the interior minister asked his advisers. He was an old-line Gaullist with an impressive military background—Indochina, Algeria, and the command of the Foreign Legion's parachute strike force—and a very effective and skillful politician who had saved his president on a number of potentially embarrassing occasions. Right now, all the men gathered in the minister's office knew that averting a frightful embarrassment to his president and to the French Republic was of higher priority for him than the actual fate of Gregory XVII. The minister was an nonpracticing Catholic from an old noble Catholic family claiming direct descent from Charlemagne. Tim had come across this gem of knowledge when he read up on French leaders in preparation for his expedition to Paris.

"Do we know of any *actual* threats, plots, or rumors of plots against the pope during his visit to France, other than the usual garbage?" the minister pursued. "Do we hear anything unusual from Muslim communities, apart from their normal antisocial behavior?"

"No, we do not," was the reply from Colonel Georges de Sainte-Ange, the red-mustached head of the SDECE, the French secret police, and first cousin of the papal secretary. He had replaced Alexandre de Marenches, who had died of a supposed heart attack three years ago. "But there's some history in our files that you may wish to hear about. It's quite germain, I think."

"So go ahead," the minister said. "Let's move on with it."

"According to our files," the colonel explained, consulting a folder in his lap, "Monsieur de Marenches, my predecessor, had secured information that a conspiracy to kill Gregory XVII was in the making. He took it very seriously, and dispatched one of his deputies to Rome to warn the Holy See. As a matter of fact, de Marenches delivered personally this warning to the pope's secretary, who, as you may know, is my cousin. I was at the time the chief of the SDECE section dealing with Soviet affairs, and my own interest in our very compartmentalized agency only touched after the event on whether there was any Soviet involvement in the assassination attempt. I had no previous knowledge of the warning to the Vatican."

"How precise was the warning?" the minister insisted. "Did de Marenches put his finger on somebody?"

"I cannot tell because sections of this particular file are mysteriously missing," the colonel said. "I only became aware of it yesterday, when you called this meeting and I requested the file to bring myself up to speed on this whole thing. This is how I found out that de Marenches had gone to Rome to warn my cousin. But there are notations in the file to the effect that some Muslims, somewhere, were involved in the supposed conspiracy mentioned by de Marenches. Unfortunately we cannot ask him."

"Did the SDECE actually discover the plot in France or elsewhere?"

"Yes, I believe it was discovered in France," the colonel replied.

"Does it follow, then, that it was a conspiracy by Muslims in France?"

"Not necessarily, *Monsieur le Ministre.* We have a worldwide operation, and de Marenches' people might have picked up the scent elsewhere. As you know, we watch Muslim organizations everywhere so it might have happened this way. I just don't know. But France might have been a convenient transit route for the killer, this and no more. Like Carlos the Jackal, who kept crossing and recrossing the country. Still, this is important history, flimsy as it is, and we should keep it in mind as the date of the papal arrival approaches. Believe me, my people have been working overtime on this subject since the visit was first announced, back in the early spring. And we are in constant touch with the security and intelligence people at the Vatican."

"Well, I do worry about Muslims, the pope or not," the minister declared. "I got to know them in the Algerian war. And I've just seen a report that of the twelve or fourteen million Muslim immigrants in Europe, most live in Paris, Brussels, Frankfurt, and Berlin. A total of five million are permanently in France—that's ten percent of our population! The Muslim ghettos keep growing. We're sitting on a time bomb, gentlemen. Gregory XVII may come and go—and I pray that he gets back home safely—but the Muslim threat will continue to hang over us. So when we think about security for the pope in France, let's be sure we think in broader terms of Islam. Nobody else in our country poses a danger to the Holy Father . . . Incidentally, did de Marenches have a history of heart disease? I was really taken aback at the time by his death. . . ."

Chapter Sixteen

Tɪᴍ Sᴀᴠᴀɢᴇ ᴛᴏᴏᴋ the *métro* from the St. Michel station on the Seine to an apartment building on Rue de Ménilmontant, where he was awaited by Professor Ahmed Al-Kutas, an Egyptian anthropologist from Alexandria who had come to see him in Rome several years ago as part of his research on a scholarly project. Both of equal age, Tim and Al-Kutas liked each other, keeping in touch through occasional letters after the Egyptian returned to Paris where he taught at the famous École des Sciences Politiques, the Sciences-Po as the French called it. Al-Kutas invited Tim to tea when the Jesuit telephoned him to say that he was in town and wanted to get together to chat.

Speaking in French, they exchanged pleasantries and comments about their respective health and families. Al-Kutas inquired about Tim's current work after telling him he was completing a book about social structures in Saudi Arabia and Islam's role in them.

"Basically, it's the same work I was doing when we first met," Tim said, "but right now it's a bit more political—my bosses are fascinated by the politics of Islam—and this is a little field trip."

In a literal sense, he was telling Al-Kutas the truth, smoothly skirting the specific nature of his mission. Tim had not expected the Egyptian to provide him with leads in his investigation or reveal to him the identity of the "French Brethren"—there was no imaginable reason for him to know anything about it—but he was hoping that Al-Kutas could share his knowledge of the mood and the politics in Parisian Muslim ghettos. *That* was the anthropologist's professional field. Like the best intelligence officers, though by no means all his former CIA colleagues, Tim deeply believed in absorbing as much as possible about the environment in which he was operating before making any serious moves. It would help him,

179

he thought, to understand better *contemporary circumstances,* whatever they were in this case.

"What the Vatican wants to evaluate," Tim told Al-Kutas, "is the degree of religious and therefore political power developing in great Muslim communities like Paris. This is obviously a significant new phenomenon, and my people aren't quite sure they know what it means in the long run. On the one hand, they worry about fundamentalism and terrorism, rightly or wrongly. On the other hand, as you know, Gregory XVII is very keen on maintaining a constructive dialogue with Islam, and he doesn't want to make any mistakes, especially as he is about to visit France again. And, as you also know, the Holy See, along with the majority of the French Church, has been quite outspoken in the defense of human rights of the Muslim immigrants here. It keeps protesting, for example, the deportations of Muslim refugees from North Africa by the French government. So, in a way, I'm something of an informal advance man for the papal trip."

This was a slight exaggeration, but Al-Kutas took it on face value. He poured them more of his exceedingly sweetened tea, reminding Tim of Cairo, and picked up a folder from a table by his armchair.

"Yes, I understand," he said, pulling pensively on his short, black beard. "It makes sense and it's a good approach. So I'll try to be helpful. What I have here are family statistics of Muslims in the Paris region. I was interested in the contrast between them and the data covering the traditional, conservative families that I'm studying in Saudi Arabia. What do they tell me? Well, first and foremost, that unless something is done about the horrifying unemployment among them, the ghettos will explode sooner or later, and I think rather sooner. You know, overall unemployment in France is around twelve percent of the labor force, which is a drama to the French, but among the Muslims here it is well over fifty percent, which is a veritable tragedy. And the overwhelming majority of adolescents and young people are almost entirely without work. There is no decent education, there are no social services to speak of, no health services—and no future. What there is in abundance, however, are drugs, alcohol—yes, our young Muslims *do* drink—and more and more crime. What you therefore have here is a recipe for absolute disaster. Does that answer your question?"

"Sure," Tim said, "but how does it all translate into politics and religious attitudes?"

"In many ways it still is an evolving process and you cannot draw categorical conclusions at this point," Al-Kutas replied. "And there are a lot of contradictions. Politically, for instance, those with French citizenship, born here or naturalized, vote for the Left, not ideologically, but in protest against what they see as repression by rightists in the government and the brutality of their police. Religiously, however, they are not only discovering that they are devout Muslims—which they probably were not in, say, Algeria—but they follow the most conservative imams who preach the kind of fundamentalism that I, as a Muslim myself, cannot accept. It's incredibly rigid and destructive. Yet, I have to understand reality. You can hear all that fundamentalist thundering at Friday services at the mosques in and around Paris, but you will also find that the fundamentalists are setting up social services, clinics, and schools. This gives them an immense range of power over their people. You know, it is like Hamas in Gaza. Social services, care for the children, a bit of help with money, a new sense of finally belonging to some kind of a rational society—and there you have it: virtually self-governing enclaves, where the French fear to tread, powerful Islamic fundamentalism, and an enormous potential for violence directed at the outside."

"Well," Tim asked, "should we be worried about any danger to the pope from Islamic militants when he comes to France next month? After all, the guy who shot him in Rome was a Muslim. What do you think?"

"No, I doubt it very much," the Egyptian answered. "Certainly not as anything spontaneous. I'm afraid that the pope is the last thing on their minds. I suspect most of them don't even know who Gregory XVII is. They will watch him on television, or not, and that will be it. I definitely see no reason for organized political violence against your man. The Muslims here don't see him as an enemy."

"I'm glad to hear that," Tim said. "I'll pass it on to headquarters. And, if you don't mind, I'll mention you as one of my founts of knowledge. You have a fine reputation in Rome, and they will be happy to know that we have your guidance, Ahmed. Meanwhile, I'll hang around Paris, talking to the French and our Church people to flesh out what you've told me."

"Fine, and, of course, I'm at your disposal at any time. But, you know, you really should hear it also from some of the Muslim leaders, a mullah or two. Would you like to?"

Al-Kutas smiled fondly and gave Tim a farewell embrace.

"I can arrange it fairly easily," he added.

Al-Kutas' invitation was a godsend for Tim. It had not occurred to him to ask the anthropologist for introductions to Muslim leaders because he thought it would be an improper imposition and might have appeared suspicious. But their conversation had flowed in the right direction and Al-Kutas had made it so simple and spontaneous. His introduction should make all the difference in the world in terms of how he would be received. His luck was holding up.

Al-Kutas called Tim at the Jesuit Residence several days later, suggesting a get-together with "a friend" after mosque services the following Friday. They met at the Egyptian's Ménilmontant apartment, then took the long *métro* ride north on the Yellow Line to the Stalingrad Station in the nineteenth *arrondissement*. It was part of the industrial suburbs' "Muslim Belt," between La Villette slaughterhouses and the factories of Rue de Flandre, and Tim felt magically transported back to the Middle East.

He could discern minaret towers in the afternoon haze of polluted air, the sun lurking somewhere above the dirty blanket that smothered the town. Store signs were in flowing Arabic script. Most of the women in the streets were in *purdah* or, at least, wore scarves tight around their heads, making them unrecognizable even at a short distance. Men with thick mustaches *à la* Saddam Hussein chatted idly on street corners. Barefoot children played soccer on the pavement and empty lots filled with uncollected garbage. The smell of cooking, the smell of the people, and the indefinable but powerful smell of the poor neighborhood were those of the Cairo slums Tim had known. Civilizations and cultures, the best and the worst of them, can be so easily transplanted, he thought.

With Al-Kutas leading the way, they walked down Rue de Tanger to a huge converted warehouse with an unmarked façade. The Egyptian explained to Tim that it was the Addawa Mosque—Addawa is Arabic for "The Call"—but known commonly as the Stalingrad Mosque because of the nearby subway station. It was, he said, the largest mosque in France, but, Tim saw, it was grim and depressing, compared with the elegant Paris mosque on the Left Bank of the Seine. Poor Muslims regarded the latter as "too much Establishment," and it was too far for them from their destitute northern *banlieue*. Al-Kutas pounded three times on a solid metal door in the back of the mosque and, at length, it was opened by an emaciated little boy who raised his eyebrows questioningly.

"Your father is expecting us," Al-Kutas said in Egyptian-accented Arabic. "I am the professor from Paris and this man is my friend. Please take us to your father."

The mosque proper was a large hallway on the ground floor, now empty with the prayer carpets rolled up against the walls. A rickety staircase led to offices on the first floor. A middle-aged man with a full, graying beard and infinitely fatigued eyes came out of a room to greet them. He wore the robe of an imam, prayer leader, over a business suit.

"*Salaam Aleikum,*" he said politely, bowing slightly before the visitors. "Please come in."

The imam's office was small and cluttered, his desk piled high with documents, pamphlets, and books. A shortwave radio receiver, an old-fashioned large instrument encased in dark, brown wood, sat on a table in the corner of the room. Al-Kutas made the introductions, and the imam invited the visitors to sit down on straight-backed chairs, installing himself behind the desk.

"How can I help you?" he asked Tim in French, in a low, pleasant voice. He was French-born and had a doctorate in theology, Al-Kutas had told Tim.

"I understand from the professor that you are concerned about the safety of the pope when he visits France next month," the imam went on. "But let me first welcome you here as the Islam scholar I am informed you are. I wish for more Christian scholars, particularly religious scholars like you, to share your interest in Islam."

"Thank you," Tim said. "I am honored, as a Jesuit and a student of Islam, to be under your roof. I appreciate your hospitality. And, yes, there is concern about the safety of the Holy Father. This is why I took the liberty of asking my friend, Professor Al-Kutas, how Muslim communities in France might react to this visit, and he suggested that you may give me the best answer."

The imam smiled, leaning back in his swivel chair.

"I suppose your question has to do with the fact that it was a Muslim who tried to kill the pope and your fear that it could happen again, this time here, because there are so many of us in this country," he said most courteously.

"It does, in part," Tim told him, "but I was wondering at the same time whether it would be a good idea if the Holy Father met with some of your elders during his stay in Paris. You are a major religious community and, as I'm sure you know, the pope is very keen on a positive dialogue with Islam. He likes to converse with representatives of all the religious communities in the countries he visits. In France, for instance, he will meet with the Jewish community and Protestant leaders, as he has done in the past. It was an oversight, I confess, that the Holy Father had not met with the Muslim community on his previous trips to France, and I think it should be remedied this time. After all, he had worked with Muslims when he was a young priest. What is your opinion?"

Proposing to the imam the possibility of an encounter between Gregory XVII and French Muslims was an inspiration that came to Tim in a flash. He was using his cover as the pope's advance man to the hilt to push forward his investigatory mission although he was not authorized to represent himself in this capacity. But the importance of his assignment surely justified a little improvisation, a notion that had been drilled into him at the CIA concerning the approach to secret missions.

Tim, of course, had no idea whether the pope would desire such an encounter. But it was quite plausible, particularly in the light of his active contacts with Muslims in his days on the Marseille docks. And it was public knowledge that it was on his orders that the Church in France had been vigorously protesting the deportations of Muslims back to North Africa. Tim now hoped that his sudden inspiration would help to create a better rapport with the imam in his search for the "French Brethren." His host was himself a Muslim "French Brother" in the broad sense and he might be flattered that the Vatican "envoy" had sought him out, an obscure imam in a Parisian suburb, for his opinions. And the imam appeared to be pleased as he listened to Tim, running his prayer beads through his fingers.

"I can assure you that the pope is in no danger from Muslims in France," he said solemnly. "As far as a meeting with the pope is concerned, I think it is a very good idea, but I must consult the others."

The imam paused, hesitated, smiled with a touch of embarrassment, and went on:

"Speaking of the pope and the Muslim who tried to kill him, I think that we owe you an explanation, now that you come to us in peace and friendship."

"An explanation?"

"Yes. And an apology. Meeting you, Father, is our first opportunity to do so. In our religion, as you are aware, truth comes first . . . and contrition. It is Allah's will that you are here today."

Tim tensed up. Excitement, anticipation rushed through his mind, like in the Mekong Delta with the chopper lifting his team to a mission.

"You see," the imam told him softly, "we are responsible in a way for that assassination attempt."

"What do you mean?"

"We are the ones, the Muslim elders' council in France—and I am one of them—who appealed to our Muslim brethren in Turkey to designate a person who would extract vengeance for an act of religious crime and sin . . ."

"What crime? What sin?" Tim cried.

"The shameful truth is that I don't know," the imam said. "We were not told that. We were simply honoring, as council of elders, our commitment to our brethren."

"I don't understand. What commitments? What brethren?"

"Well, we were asked by our brethren in Toulouse, down in the south, to use our contacts abroad to help locate such a person. The Toulouse brethren do not have such contacts. They indicated that it was a matter of faith. In such cases, one asks no questions.

One just does the best one can. On faith. And we were in a position to help."

"My God!" Tim sighed. "Then what?"

"Then we sent word to our contacts in Turkey and they responded affirmatively," the imam replied. "That was our last communication with them. And only when we learned of the attack on the pope and that the man with the gun was a terrorist from Turkey—and a Muslim—did we understand what horror had been perpetrated and how *we* made it possible. You see, we had no idea that the pope would be the target. We were never told and it had never occurred to any of us . . ."

"But this is monstrous!" Tim shouted, almost losing all control. "How could you?"

"Yes. I agree. It was monstrous. We sinned against Allah and the Prophet as well as against your church. We should have known better. I wish there was a way of expiation, of atonement."

Tim thought for a moment.

"Yes," he said gravely. "I think there is a way, if you wish to take it. I cannot absolve you though I am a priest. I know God forgives you, He who is God of all of us, but it is up to you to atone."

"How?" the imam asked. He was in tears.

"Put me in touch with your brethren in the south," Tim said. "Now I need to know the full truth of what happened—and why."

The *concierge* brother at the Jesuit Residence knocked on the door of Tim's room the morning after the meeting with the imam. Tim had stayed up late into the night working on his notes, and he was barely awake as the *concierge* shouted, "Father, there's a telephone call for you downstairs! Can you come down?"

Getting into a pair of jeans and throwing on a sports shirt, Tim trotted down the stairs to the reception desk on the ground floor and picked up the phone.

"*Oui, ici le Père Savage,*" he said into the mouthpiece.

"My, don't you sound like a native Parisian!" a woman's voice told him laughingly in English. "This is Angela. I'm in Paris."

Tim was speechless for a moment, utter surprise and a surge of joy delivering him to a touch of incoherence.

"You, Sister Angela? . . . You are in Paris? . . . Really? How come? . . ." he stuttered at length.

"Well, I arrived last night for our annual reunion at the Convent of the Augustine Sisters," she said lightly. "And the Monsignor told me to call you to see how you are faring here . . ."

Tim fell silent again, thinking furiously how to react, what to say. He was completely disoriented.

"Hello, hello, are you there, Father Savage?" Angela asked with concern. "Are you on the line?"

"Oh, yes! . . . I am . . . That's wonderful that you are in Paris. How long will you be here?"

"About a week, I think," she told him, very warmly. "We have our reunion at the Convent and I want to visit my relatives who live near Paris. But if you are not too busy with your work, perhaps we could meet for a cup of coffee."

"No, no!" Tim cried, "Of course, I'm not too busy. I'm not busy at all, as a matter of fact. It would be great to see you! Shall we meet somewhere? What is convenient for you?"

"Well, we're rather near each other," Angela said. "The Convent is just off Boulevard St. Germain, maybe seven or eight blocks from your Residence. And let us be a bit adventurous in a literary way. How about Deux Magots? Around noon? Do you know where it is?"

Tim hung up slowly, absolutely stunned. A get-together with Angela in Paris, and not on Holy See business, was the last thing in the world he would have ever expected. He let out a victory holler, like when one's team scores a touchdown on a Hail Mary pass—and raced back upstairs, laughing so loudly that doors opened at other Jesuits' rooms as he passed them. *Ah, les Américains! . . .*

In her room at the Convent of the Augustine Sisters of Notre-Dame of Paris, Angela said a quick prayer, quite pleased with herself, before starting to dress. Monsignor Sainte-Ange *did* suggest that she call Tim in Paris as a courtesy and to make sure he had everything he needed in his mission for the Holy Father. But he had not suggested that they meet for a cup of coffee. That was Angela's sudden inspiration when she heard Tim's voice over the telephone. She smiled with confidence at the image of the Virgin on the wall of her room: She was full of love, She would understand.

At noon sharp, Tim stood in front of Café de Deux Magots on the boulevard, staring hard up and down the sidewalk in search of a nun amidst the crowd of tourists on that hot, muggy day. As usual in the summer, there seemed to be no Parisians in the street. Minutes elapsed, and Tim grew tense with impatience and anticipation. What if she had changed her mind and decided not to come? It would, of course, make sense. Why would they be meeting in the first place?

"I'm sorry to keep you waiting, Father Savage." The quiet, melodic voice behind Tim made him jump as if a gun had been fired point-blank in his ears. Turning around, he saw a petite woman with straight dark brown hair and a lovely face looking at him with an amused smile. The face was even lovelier than he had remembered from their few Vatican encounters.

"I recognized you even from the back," Angela told him, "even in your civilian clothes."

Tim, who wore slacks and a dark blue short-sleeved shirt, saw that Angela was in plain but perfectly elegant street attire, a light-green dress just below her knee, a discreet silver necklace and tiny earrings. She had a touch of lipstick. This was the first time, Tim realized, that he saw her out of religious habit. Angela looked to him a completely different person and the same person, all at the same time.

"Oh, Sister, good morning . . . I mean good afternoon. No, you didn't keep me waiting. I just got here myself," he said, extending his hand in a formal greeting because he did not know what else to do. "Shall we take one of these tables on the sidewalk?"

They sat down, Tim feeling more awkward and tongue-tied than ever in his life.

"Did you have a nice trip?" he asked, embarrassed that he could not think of anything else to say. "How is the Holy Father? How is the Monsignor?"

"I had an excellent trip from Rome and the plane was on time," Angela answered, quite relaxed. "And they are very well. The Monsignor sends his regards."

They ordered *citrons pressés* from the bored waiter, making small talk about Paris, with Tim telling Angela about his previous visits.

"Shouldn't I ask how your work is proceeding? Any progress?" she inquired.

"Well," Tim said, "I think that a new avenue is opening up in the Muslim thing—you remember the 'French Brethren' from my Istambul trip?—but it's too soon to tell. I guess I'm mildly encouraged. I'll have to go to the south of France, probably later this week."

"Is there anything you want me to tell the Monsignor?" Angela asked.

Tim turned this over on his mind, deciding to trust his instinct.

"No, I believe it would be premature," he replied. "In fact, I'd appreciate it if you didn't mention to him what I just said about a possible new avenue. Okay?"

"Sure," she said, her eyebrows rising slightly. "By the way, are you familiar with the history of this place, the Deux Magots?"

Tim shook his head. "I've walked past it several times, that's all," he said.

"It's quite famous in French literature and the history of the Church," Angela explained. "It even plays a tiny part of my own history."

"How so?"

"Around the middle of the seventeenth century, Blaise Pascal, the great religious philosopher and mathematician, used to come to Deux Magots—it was an old Paris inn—to do his writing. He may have written his famous *Pensées* right where we sit."

"But how is the café a part of your history?"

Angela laughed. Tim loved the sound. It cascaded like water over a fall.

"It's very simple," she said. "Pascal was a Jansenist, a follower of Bishop Cornelius Jansen who had early in the seventeenth century launched a religious revival movement based on the teachings of St. Augustine. Jansenism proclaimed, as Augustine did, that spiritual religious experience, not reason, must be the guide in the life of Christians. The *Pensées* reflect this view. Now, because I belong to the order of Augustine Sisters, Pascal, the champion of St. Augustine, is our hero. When I was at the Convent, all of us—students, novices, and Sisters—had to pray for Pascal when we walked past Deux Magots."

"That's very interesting," Tim remarked. "I didn't know about Deux Magots and Pascal, but I do know about Jansenists. For example, they were in most violent conflict with the Jesuits."

"Oh, I won't hold it against you," Angela smiled, her green eyes sparkling. "Anyway, Pope Innocent X declared Jansen heretical later in the century. Which reminds me that Pascal had denounced Father Sainte-Ange, who was a Capuchin priest, for being unorthodox, if not downright heretical. I read that in school . . ."

"Was the Father related to Monsignor Sainte-Ange?" Tim asked.

"I have no idea. Maybe he was the Monsignor's great-great-great-grandfather or something," Angela said. "I had forgotten all about Pascal and Sainte-Ange the Capuchin, until I went to work for *this* Sainte-Ange. But I never questioned him about his ancestry."

"What a coincidence," Tom commented. "A Saint-Ange who was a heretic? How about that! But good for old Pascal to keep the faith even if he fought the Jesuits. And for having immortalized Deux Magots for us. He must have been quite a figure."

"He was," Angela nodded. "And do you know what else Pascal did at Deux Magots?"

"No, I don't."

"He wrote here his *Discours sur les passions de l'amour* . . . He was a romantic theologian . . ."

And, Tim suddenly remembered, St. Augustine of Carthage, after whom Angela's religious order was named, had lived with a concubine for fourteen years, until his conversion at the age of thirty-three. And as the great bishop of Hippo, he remained sex-obsessed—or so claim Church historians.

Chapter Seventeen

"WHAT IS TRUTH?" Pontius Pilate, the Roman procurator of Judea, asked Jesus before sanctioning His crucifixion.

What *is* truth? Tim Savage asked himself for the millionth time as he reflected about the causes and circumstances of the assassination attempt against the head of the Church of Jesus Christ. And the immediate and most pressing question on his mind—as the TGV, the super-express *Train à Grande Vitesse,* sped him southwest from Paris to Toulouse—was who exactly were the "French Brethren" and why had they sponsored and orchestrated the attack on Gregory XVII?

However, for the first time since he had accepted the investigatory mission, Tim had the sense that he was moving, promisingly, in the right direction—though he was still without a clear idea what it was. It remained a Muslim track, but it was now evolving away from Sainte-Ange's original if vague "Muslim Connection" concept.

Unquestionably, Tim was making progress. The Istanbul meeting with the Gray Wolves was a breakthrough as he learned about the mysterious "French Brethren." This had led him to Paris, where, through amazing luck, he was introduced by his Egyptian friend to the imam of the Stalingrad Mosque. Just as amazingly, the imam, grieved and contrite over the role his Council of Elders had inadvertently played in the conspiracy, had agreed to put him in touch with the Muslim "brethren" in the South.

True to his word, the imam provided Tim with names, addresses, and telephone numbers in Toulouse and other towns in the sprawling region at the foot of the Pyrénées. He also told Tim that he would be expected by those whose names he had been given.

"I am, of course, assuring them that you will be absolutely discreet and protect their identities from the authorities and everybody else," the imam had added.

"Of course," Tim said. "In my religion we respect trust as you do in yours. Besides, you too must wish to know the truth."

Tim and the imam had gone on to discuss Islam and its mutations and nuances in relation with the shooting on St. Peter's Square by Agca Circlic. The imam, who turned out to be an Islamic scholar as well as a mosque prayer leader, remarked that, in his opinion, the plot had most likely originated with fundamentalist Muslim groups or sects in the south of France rather than with religious moderates who were a majority there.

"I cannot tell you why fundamentalist leaders would have become engaged in such a plot," he told Tim, "but we have in the south a number of *mojtaheds,* you know, senior Shia theologians, who follow the Ayatollah Khomeini's teachings on how Islamic holy laws should be applied to modern life. Most of them came from Algeria where fundamentalism is quite powerful, and I suppose we cannot rule out some aberration that might have triggered the notion of killing your pope . . . Perhaps one of my friends in Toulouse might guide you better than I can. Your impeccable Islamic scholarly credentials that I mentioned to them will help you in understanding whatever had occurred."

"Could it have been motivated by the fact that the French Church is divided over the whole Muslim question and so many bishops and priests agree with the government on deporting Muslim immigrants back to North Africa?" Tim asked. "Would the *mojtaheds,* or some other Islamic leaders, want to take it out on Gregory XVII?"

"No, not really," the imam replied. "It just doesn't make sense. The pope has been most supportive of us. But, again, fundamentalists are a mystery even to a man like me. In some ways, you know, they remind me of Roman Catholic fundamentalists in France. They are mirror images. For all I know, they have a lot in common."

Tim may have been making progress along the Muslim track, as he now called it in his mind, but the warning from de Marenches to the Holy See kept nagging at him. All he knew about the late French spymaster was what the elderly Jesuit had told him in Rome, the interview in *Le Figaro,* Angela's remark about the "mysterious" death of de Marenches' top aide, and Paul Martinius' casual comment that Tim should look into the past activities of the SDECE chief. Everything he had heard and read about de Marenches was enormously intriguing, yet none of it seemed to fit the different variations of the Muslim track he was seeking to reconcile.

Although Tim hated wasting even a minute of his evening with Angela on papal business he raised the subject of de Marenches as they were both studying dinner menus at the little old bistro on Rue d'Odéon in their Left Bank neighborhood. After saying goodbye at Deux Magots, Tim and Angela had agreed, quite naturally, to dine on the eve of his departure for Toulouse. He had thrown out the suggestion, and she responded, "Sure, why not?" as if they had been friends forever, meeting unexpectedly away from home.

And, joining him at a corner table in the bistro, Angela was a sight to behold. Tim had dreamed about her every night following Deux Magots. He knew he was smitten as never before, and now she stood before him like a reverie. She wore a long skirt, a white blouse with short sleeves, and a cardigan over her shoulders, a touch of modesty. A light scent of *eau de cologne* wafted after her. On the ring finger of the left hand, Angela wore a wedding band: She was a bride of Jesus Christ. A pang of jealousy coursed through Tim.

The waiter came by to pour wine. Tim lifted his glass, saluting Angela, then said, "I hate to bring this up, but I am enormously puzzled by this de Marenches warning business, and I recall that you had mentioned something to me about the strange death of one of his aides. This could be really important, and I wonder whether you remember anything else?"

"Well," Angela said, "not really, not very much. When you requested the *Figaro* interview with de Marenches, I had asked the Monsignor whether there was anything else about it that you should know, that I should pass on to you. He replied that, no, there was nothing particularly relevant to tell you. He sort of seemed annoyed when I brought up de Marenches, so I dropped the subject."

"But how did you know about that Colonel, Bernard Nut,

you told me had been murdered or whatever in Nice?" Tim inquired.

"To tell you the truth," Angela answered, "I, too became curious, and I did something a bit out of school. When the Monsignor went to lunch with the Holy Father in the dining room upstairs, I spotted a file folder on his desk, marked 'de Marenches.' I peeked inside and saw some newspaper clippings about de Marenches, the interview and his death. But I also found a sheet of paper on which the Monsignor had written the name of the Colonel and a notation that he died 'mysteriously' after the de Marenches warning had been delivered to the Holy See by one of his deputies. De Marenches does mention in the interview, as you know, that he had dispatched a top aide to deliver the warning, and it might have been this Colonel Nut. That's all I know about it . . ."

"I see," Tim said, pensively. "That's very interesting. And I'm glad you mentioned it, but I still don't know what to make of it. Like who killed the Colonel and why? And why Sainte-Ange was annoyed when you asked him about de Marenches . . . Oh, well, let's not ruin our dinner with this whole mess."

Their evening elapsed in the blink of an eye. They each were eager to learn about their respective lives, their narratives flowing smoothly and quietly. Angela told Tim about her childhood, the convent school, her decision to take the vows and abandon secular life—more, she realized as she spoke, than she had ever told anybody, except perhaps her mother, a long time ago. Tim spoke of his youth, the university, the CIA, Egypt, Vietnam, and Phoenix, his rebellion against the Delta killings, his resignation from the Agency, and the process that had led him to turn to the priesthood and become a Jesuit. To Tim, if was like a conversation with an old friend, catching up on their pasts after a long separation.

As they said there good-byes, Tim said, "Of course, we'll keep in touch—and not only over my work." "Yes," Angela answered, "we'll *always* keep in touch."

Tim had informed his Jesuit hosts in Paris that he was planning to spend a vacation in the South to immerse himself in the beauty and romance of the ancient lands below the Pyrenees' chain, and visit medieval castles dating back to the days of the savage papal crusade against Cathar "heretics." Arrangements were made for Tim to stay at the Jesuit Residence in Toulouse, an edifice next to the Church of St. Stanisław that also housed a school as well as an excellent historical library. Tim found it preferable to a hotel, hoping that the local Jesuits might in some way assist him with his research in that corner of France. And he was curious about the contemporary Church in the south, given its tortured and violent history.

From the newspapers he read on the train en route to Toulouse, Tim also learned more about the increasing face-off between the official French Church and conservative Catholic rebels, the "Integrists." Tens of thousands of these "Integrists," the Catholic equivalent of Muslim fundamentalists, fought the full range of Second Vatican Council's Church modernization, from the decisions on religious freedoms and Christian ecumenism policies to the legitimization of the vernacular Mass instead of the traditional Latin. Their leaders were priests, like Archbishop Julien Leduc, who had been at swords' points with the Holy See for decades, earning a suspension, but still escaping excommunication, and Catholic intellectuals like Professor Jean Guitton, who had written in *The Spiritual Genius of St. Thérèse* that all the Church's troubles since the council were caused by "the extinction of the mysterious and mystical aspects of liturgical prayer."

Not only had the "Integrists," Tim read, occupied the church in the town of Chamblac in protest for a number of days, but thousands of them had marched eighty miles from the great cathedral in Chartres to Paris to celebrate a Mass of defiance in front of the Sacré-Coeur de Montmartre church. They carried signs calling for "A Prayer of Victory, A Rampart of Christianity" in tribute to the victorious naval battle of Lepanto against the Turks in 1751, "Down with the Muslim State!" and "Down with the Hypocritical Enterprise of Subversion of the Church!" The French were clearly addicted to lengthy messages on their posters. But Tim also learned that the Bishop of Evreux, a hero of "Liberal Catholics," had been deprived of his diocese for advocating artificial contraception, anti-AIDS measures, tolerance for Muslims, and acceptance of homosexuality. He was offered, instead, the post of a prison chaplain.

To the "Integrists," the true destiny of France lay in the wartime pro-Nazi Vichy regime, as Tim had been told by friends in Paris, and the rightist author Louis-Fernand Céline, actually an immensely gifted writer of the prewar years, was their ideological hero. This was the realm of Joan of Arc and the spirit of the Middle Ages. Yet, this was part of the French Church milieu that had produced Gregory XVII.

From the Toulouse railway station, Tim went by taxi to the midtown Jesuit Residence. There, he was stepping into history. Toulouse, called Tolosa by the Romans, was founded not later than the second century B.C., and ironically had a bad reputation from the very beginning. After its temple had been pillaged in 106 B.C., the famous Latin proverb, *habet aurum Tolosanum,* was coined as an allusion to ill-gotten gold. In the fifth century A.D., Toulouse, straddling the Garonne River, became the capital of the great Teutonic kingdom of West-Goths that spread from the Rhône to the Atlantic and from the Loire Valley to the Rock of Gibraltar. Soon, however, Toulouse was captured by Clovis, the first Christian king of the Franks, but it prospered nevertheless and was made the capital of South Aquitaine. Next, Charlemagne conquered it, appointing his son Louis the king of Aquitaine. In the mid-ninth century, Raymond I emerged as the count of Toulouse, launching the aristocratic dynasty whose successive heads were the most powerful lords in southern France and under whose reign some of the greatest horrors in contemporary Europe were to occur.

True to his professional conviction that he needed to know and fully understand the history of the places and the people where he pursued his mission, Tim Savage read volumes at the Jesuit Residence on the story of Toulouse, its emperors, kings, and counts, discovering in the process that the region was the birthplace of the romantic *troubadours* of the Middle Ages and their songs of love, passion, and courage. Reading their songs in French—he could not quite follow the original texts in the native Language of Oc, from which Langue*doc* derives—Tim found himself wishing that Angela were there to share the *troubadours'* romances with him. She was very much on his mind, even more after their Parisian encounters than before, in Rome. And the word *Oc* means "yes."

Languedoc, as Tim discovered, is both a legend, dating back to Roman occupation, and a modern-day reality, a most relevant fact to him. A vast swath of France, it stretches west from Montpellier on the Mediterranean, bordering on Provence, through Béziers and Narbonne to Carcassonne and the lands beyond Toulouse. It reaches the valleys of the upper Loire in the North. The foothills of the Pyrénées from Perpignan to Foix are part of Languedoc, which in many ways has always been a country unto itself. Belonging officially to France since the mid-ninth century and one of her oldest provinces, it was virtually independent of Paris until the seventeenth century, ruled by great aristocratic—quasi royal—dynasties like the counts of Toulouse, Foix, and Carcassonne.

The proud and stunningly beautiful province over the centuries had fought its own domestic political and religious battles as well as wars with France and England, survived a murderous papal religious crusade among its towns and castles, its own crusades in the Holy Land, a short-lived union with Catalonia, Moorish conquest, and Moorish defeat—the *reconquista*—and subsequent French royal and republican sway. Languedoc nurtured its own culture through the language of Oc, music, and poetry—and the tradition of being the oldest wine-producing region of France, with some rather remarkable wines.

Much as France remains rich in assertive regionalisms and nationalisms, Languedoc's may be the strongest though in its own quiet fashion: French men and women from elsewhere are simply called "people of the north," in a somewhat derogatory manner. Languedoc, however, is not inhospitable to the ever-growing Muslim immigrant populations, a significant contemporary political reality. It also is a land of deep religious mystery and mysticism.

Though Tim's immediate concern was to locate and contact Muslim leaders in the South, largely on the basis of information given him by the Paris imam, he realized that it was not as simple as swooping down on a Muslim mosque, office, or household, and proceeding like a common policeman with no-nonsense questions about the "French Brethren," the plot to assassinate the pope, and so forth. Such an approach, he knew as an intelligence officer, would guarantee suspicion, resentment, silence, and ultimately total failure. He first had to learn more about the Muslim milieu in that part of France to make himself acceptable in some fashion—the imam's introductions alone would not be enough—and to see how the Muslims there fitted into the broader picture of religious life in the South. His instinct told him again that nothing exists in a vacuum, including Muslims in the Languedoc and the adjoining Roussillon, and that homework was required before he plunged into active detective work. Tim, apart from being a history buff, believed that history and religion were vital in his pursuits.

Actually, Toulouse had rich religious roots. St. Sernin, or St. Saturnin to some scholars, the first preacher of gospels in Toulouse, was martyred in the third century A.D. His body had been dragged through the streets by a bull until he died. Tim was now so conditioned to the subject, that even a mere mention of martyrdom immediately aroused his attention. This, too, applied to the massive massacres in the thirteenth century during the papal Albigenois crusade against the Cathars. Strolling around Toulouse, Tim came upon the eleventh-century church of St. Sernin, the largest Romanesque basilica in the world, and St. Stephen's cathedral dating back to the same century. He found it interesting that St. Sernin was canonized by Pope Urban II, a Frenchman, in 1096. It began to dawn on Tim that, in more ways than one, Roman popes had touched on the destiny of Toulouse—or had been touched by it. Since his mission dealt directly with a pope, Gregory XVII, all that past was relevant to his endeavor.

A few days after his arrival in Toulouse, Tim was invited to dine at the residence by the very aging but remarkably clearheaded Jesuit librarian. When Tim entered the refectory, the librarian, wearing a black beret, sat at a small table, awaiting him.

"I hear, Father Savage, that you are an expert on Islam," he said, his pale blue eyes under white eyebrows centering on Tim. "We have lots of Muslims here, and we all get along just fine, but I doubt that they have much to teach you about Islam. So what brings you here? Are you *really* on vacation?"

The old man was most perspicacious and instinctive, Tim thought, which could be either very helpful or very damaging. He could, for example, turn out to be a great gossip as so many aging priests are. He was pleased to belong to this community of suspicious, perspicacious, learned, and gossipy men.

"Well, I *am* on vacation," Tim told him. "But there is no rule, I imagine, against learning something new, even during vacation, is there? And, yes, Father, I do specialize in Islam and I expect to be in touch with the Muslim community here. As you know, the Holy Father is most interested in interreligious dialogue, and the thinking is that with such a huge concentration of Muslims around here we ought to help in starting up such a dialogue."

"The Holy Father is absolutely right," the librarian said, "and, in my opinion, Muslim elders here would be open to dialogue. However, your problem may be with much of the French Catholic clergy here. The ones known as 'Integrists' don't have much use for the Muslims. They are frightfully right wing—they urge the government to deport the Muslims—and I don't quite see them sitting down with Muslim mullahs to debate monotheist religions. The South is an 'Integrist' stronghold just as it is the political stronghold of the right, the Front National and groups of that ilk."

They drank strong Languedoc red wine, and when the *cassoulet* was served, Tim said, "That's very interesting what you are saying about the 'Integrists' and their friends. I'd like to know more about them. Can you fill me in?"

"Sure," the old Jesuit said. "I'll be delighted. I can't stand the bastards. But I'll also tell you some things you may not know about Muslims and Christians in this neck of the woods . . ."

In the front room of an old abbey just below the hilltop town of Fanjeaux, once the home of St. Dominic, a young man in a gray suit knelt to kiss the old archbishop's ring in greeting and homage.

"Excellency," he said after he was invited to sit down on a straight chair, facing the archbishop, "I've just come back from Rome. I flew directly to Toulouse, then rented a car at the airport to drive to the abbey."

"Are you sure you weren't followed ?" the archbishop asked in his *basso profundo* voice. "We can't take chances."

"I am sure, Excellency," the visitor replied. "I'm pretty good at spotting tails and losing them. Years of practice, you know."

"Very well, then. What have you to tell me?"

"I had another very satisfactory talk with my friend in Rome," the young man said. "He is most interested in the subject and he thinks it's probably feasible. I offered him the money you had authorized, and he was satisfied, too. I assume he's now at work on it."

"So, when ?" the archbishop inquired sharply. "Can't wait forever."

"I would imagine it will be the early autumn, in connection with the voyage to the United States. I think it's very promising."

Chapter Eighteen

TIM SAVAGE SOON LEARNED that his idea for a Christian-Muslim dialogue in southern France—or, at least, his attempt to use it as a cover for his sleuthing—was not a very original one. At best, he was nearly nine centuries late with it.

The day after their dinner, the priest-librarian had dropped off at Tim's room a book by Professor Charles-Emmanuel Dufourcq of Nanterre University on *Islam and Christians of the South (XII and XIV Centuries),* in French, dedicated to the history of dialogues, in war and peace, between Christians and Muslims dating as far back as the middle of the twelfth century. These dialogues, Tim read with rising interest, had been initiated by Roman Catholic mendicant religious orders to establish contacts with Muslim Moors who had established themselves as conquerors in Spain and southern France in the closing centuries of the first millennium, with the Francs' town of Narbonne as the principal center. They first came in 719, and Al Samh Malik al-Khawlani, a Moorish chieftain, died in the battle for Toulouse in 721. But the mendicants had subsequently set in motion dialogues with Jews and Moors inhabiting the region, and in both cases the contacts were based on learning one another's languages—Latin, Hebrew, and Arabic—in schools known as "Studia Linguarum."

Thus Tim was discovering that Christians and Muslims in the south of France had active dealings and links long centuries before the appearance of the waves of North African Muslim immigrants in the second half of the twentieth century. That was one aspect of Islamic history that was wholly alien to Tim, but now, as he perused Professor Dufourcq's scholarly, if rather obscure, fat volume, it dawned on him that in this part of Europe old religious traditions never died—and that in some unsuspected way they might hold the key to the mystery of the "French Brethren." And it was quite a history.

The Koran, for example, had been translated from Arabic into Latin by Robert de Ketton, a scholar employed by Pierre the Venerable, the Abbot of Cluny, as early as 1143, under the title of "Dialogus." And what struck Tim the most was the translator's emphasis on violence as proscribed by the Koran, apart from the Holy Wars, the Jihads, and battle against Christian crusaders. Muslims also regarded Jews and Christians as "People of the Book"—the Old and New Testaments—thereby deserving Muslim protection. According to *suras* in the Koran, Muslims, too, venerated Christ though they refused to believe that Jews had killed Him and that resurrection had occurred. And under Moorish rule in the South of France, Christians were free to worship their God. Tim wondered whether Muslims there today were aware of this past of tolerance amidst frequent warfare. But, he felt, new vistas might be opening before him.

In the remote past, Muslims had been the powerful, noble rulers over the Christian majority in Languedoc and Roussillon. Today's Muslims there were an inferior, often unemployed and destitute and not infrequently violent, minority. It was among them that Tim hoped to locate the "French Brethren." It was most unlikely that the North African immigrants remembered, let alone knew about, the medieval Christian Crusades against the "Infidels" of the Middle East or about Muslim slaves held in Languedoc after *reconquista.* Or that their main oppressor was Guilhem-of-the-Curved Nose. There would have been more up-to-date reasons for involvement in the conspiracy against Gregory XVII.

On the first day of September, a clear, sunny day with a pleasant breeze blowing from the Pyrénées, Tim set out into the streets of Toulouse to track down the leads he had received from Al-Kutas in Paris and from the Jesuit priest-librarian at the residence. Together, they added up to a dozen names of individuals, several community associations, religious centers, one mosque, and a few business establishments. Muslims in Toulouse, some residing legally and others illegally, some born in France and some in North Africa, probably exceeded one hundred thousand, a signif-

icant and remarkably well-organized segment of the city's population. After Paris and Marseille, they were the largest Muslim
concentration in France, and their numbers grew continuously
from steady arrivals from across the Mediterranean and from their
high birth rate. Most were Algerians who had fled—and were
still fleeing—from the utter misery of a collapsed national econ-
omy and from the rising violence and killings by the military and
the police on the one hand and Islam fundamentalists on the
other. Their children and grandchildren, born in the Languedoc,
formed the increasingly radicalized—politically and religiously—
new Muslim generations. The youths were bilingual, in Arabic
and in French, and they congregated around Toulouse's mosques,
always in attendance at Friday services.

"You must bear in mind that there is a powerful strain of fundamentalism among Muslims here," the priest librarian told Tim
as they sat at a table among stacks of books. "It's a phenomenon
that predates Ayatollah Khomeini's revolution in Iran and the rise
of Islamic militancy in Algeria, but has been greatly influenced
and strengthened by both. It also feeds on poverty and despair, of
which there is plenty here. We, the Jesuits—or, at least, I—watch
this fundamentalism grow with concern because I fear that it
encourages other religious fundamentalisms, and there's a powerful Christian fundamentalist tradition in the Languedoc, a very
special one, with roots in the first millennium. And, inevitably, it
polarizes politics in the south in a dangerous shift to the right as a
reaction to 'these Arab troublemakers.' With your interest in
Islam, you ought to pay attention to it, too."

"Yes, I certainly will," Tim said. "It is, in fact, my top priority."

The Muslim presence in Toulouse and its nature were quite evident to Tim as he walked through the prosperous downtown and
penetrated Muslim neighborhoods, which existed painfully and
angrily as segregated and isolated fiefs. Crossing the vast Place du
Capitol from the marble-pillared town hall to the luxurious Grand
Hôtel de l'Opéra, where wealthy tourists stay, Tim gained a
glimpse of the city's social infrastructure. It was quite uncompli-
cated: Muslims dominated all that was menial or temporary in the
realm of breadwinning work. In the center of the beautiful Place
du Capitol, the pavement was being repaired by a crew of North

Africans in orange coveralls. Along Rue de Metz and Rue d'Alsace-Lorraine, the principal shopping streets with expensive boutiques, crews of immigrants swept the sidewalks with huge brooms. Luckier were the doorman at the Grand Hôtel, splendid in his medieval attire, and at least two waiters at the outdoor café under the arcades of the Place du Capitol: Their work was lighter and cleaner, and unquestionably better paid, what with tourists' tipping. They must have belonged to old-time Muslim families in Toulouse. North African men and women tended a row of rickety stands in front of the town hall, selling cheap clothes and footwear, ragged old paperback books, and fruit and vegetables. The priest librarian had told Tim that the best jobs to which the immigrants could aspire were as unskilled workers at the Aérospatiale, the immense aeronautical complex where the Concorde and Airbus were manufactured by the European consortium. And at the bottom of this social infrastructure lay, pure and simple, hopeless unemployment, bitterness, violence, and crime.

The Muslim neighborhoods stretched across a seeming labyrinth of narrow streets on the other side of Garonne River that bisects Toulouse, worlds away from the elegant midtown. In slacks and a windbreaker, not to arouse special attention, Tim strolled through these neighborhoods day after day to capture their character, mood, sights, and sounds. The streets were mainly chains of small houses with peeling paint, a few ill-maintained apartment buildings, and an infinity of tiny shops with signs in flowing Arab script. In one neighborhood, Tim counted five small mosques.

Women in cream-colored headscarves hurried to and from homes and shops. There were few men in the streets, but youths with nascent mustaches and insolent looks in their eyes congregated at street corners, smoking, chatting, cursing, and waiting for something—anything—to happen. As Tim walked past a group of four or five youths with menacing miens, the oldest of them pulled out a long knife from his jacket pocket, pointing it at him, and shouting laughingly in Arabic, "Go away, son of a pig! Next time we'll butcher you!"

Tim stopped, smiled warmly, and replied in his best classic Arabic, "And may Allah bless you, too." He left stunned silence behind him.

*   *   *

As on covert missions in Cairo seventeen years ago, Tim now began discreet visits to homes and offices in the Muslim districts of Toulouse. Again, his fluency in Arabic—though the language spoken by North African immigrants differed considerably from that of the Georgetown University linguistics institute and of Cairo—made a world of difference in how he was received after ringing the bell or knocking on the door. First impressions are crucial. Unlike in Cairo, however, Tim chose not to disguise his identity in Toulouse. In Egypt, he had to conceal his CIA identity under the cover of an American economic assistance official. In Toulouse, he had decided that honesty was the best policy, and he dressed in black Jesuit attire. Priests were a common sight in the Languedoc, and nobody, not the French, not the Muslims, seemed to pay any special attention to Tim—after his first slacks-and-windbreaker outing. And more than once, he spotted priests in long black cassocks in the streets of Muslim neighborhoods and at offices of immigrant social assistance associations. Islam, after all, Tim remembered, was the last frontier to conquer by the Roman Catholic Church.

He felt a sense of relief as he turned, at last, to legwork, dealing with live human beings other than librarians and scholars. As usual in serious intelligence pursuits, the bulk of research—call it sleuthing—was the mortifying tedium of seemingly endless hours in libraries, archives, and files, and exhaustingly guarded interviews and conversations. It was like constructing an intricate cryptogram or solving a crossword puzzle, slowly, painstakingly, until the last pieces, or words, fell into place. Excitement and romance in intelligence work—"action," as outsiders thought of it from reading spy thrillers—were a very small part of the overall effort. Increasingly, brains replaced brawn, and the agency now adored academics with multiple doctorates. Tim, of course, believed in the academic aspect of intelligence—that was what he was doing every day as an Islam scholar back at the Vatican—but it was invigorating to be back on the street once more.

Tim's first potentially promising visit was to the oddly named North African Beneficial Association of St. Sernin—the sign over the storefront was in Arabic—because of its proximity to the St.

Sernin Basilica; this particular Muslim community was in downtown Toulouse. Entering the cramped, seedy office, Tim asked to see the Association's secretary-treasurer, whose name he had been given in Paris by Al-Kutas. He had already gone to three home addresses, meeting barely concealed hostility. Tim knew that his Toulouse conversations would be exceedingly difficult—he had to ask directly at some point why the "French Brethren," who clearly were a Muslim group in the south of France, had arranged to hire Agca Circlic to kill Gregory XVII five years ago. He had, consequently, prepared himself the best he could for these interviews, to the extent of forcing himself to think in Arabic to formulate and verbalize his thoughts, not an easy mental task after seventeen years away from the language. In Vietnam, Phoenix's violence and village murders and torchings were the method of extracting information. In the south of France, persuasion, skill, subtlety, and empathy would be Tim's tools—in French and Arabic.

The young man at the desk in the storefront office had gone inside through an open, narrow passage to fetch the secretary-treasurer, and Tim looked around as he waited. The walls were covered with posters depicting impoverished women and children and urging donations in Arabic script, and a poster in French, exclaiming, *S.O.S. RACISME!* the name of the militant organization of all imaginable minorities in France and of many French themselves that quite effectively fought the pervasive, deep-seated racism of a society that had long ruled over a colonial empire. Liberty, Equality, and Fraternity did not apply to minorities and immigrants on the soil of metropolitan France—as it had not applied to the natives in Indochina before the French armies had been shattered and expelled after the battle of Dienbienphu in 1954. Tim had learned to appreciate it during his tour in the subsequent *American* war in Vietnam, and now all the images of the lethal action he had helped to trigger in the Mekong Delta came rushing back as he stared at the *S.O.S. RACISME!* poster in the small office in Toulouse.

A hefty, middle-aged man in a pink business shirt without a necktie and wearing a tight brown suit came in from behind, squinting at Tim with suspicious eyes. He had a deep scar across his left cheek, giving his olive-skinned countenance a slightly sinister appearance.

"Bonjour, mon Père," he said in French, then shifted to English to ask, "Are you English or American? I am the secretary-treasurer of this Association. What can I do for you?"

"I am American," Tim replied, "and I came to see you on the suggestion of a friend in Paris."

"Oh, yes, you are the American Jesuit I was told to expect," the man said flatly, without enthusiasm. "So, what can I do for you?"

Tim decided to take his chances with Arabic and openness. He had to assume that as a result of his Paris conversations, Muslim community leaders and elders in the South, to whom he was being sent, had some idea of his interest.

"The Stalingrad mosque imam with whom I had the great pleasure of speaking the other day," he said, "gave me the impression that I could learn in Toulouse important things about Agca Circlic, the Turk, and the attack on the pope. The imam believes that I should know the truth."

The secretary-treasurer lit a Gauloise, filling the room with acrid cigarette smoke. He silently thought over Tim's words, then stared grimly at him.

"I don't know what you should know or not," he said slowly in his guttural Maghreb Arabic. "It's not for me to say. And this isn't the place to discuss it."

"What, then, should I do?"

The Algerian raised his eyebrows and spread out his hands in a gesture of helplessness.

"Perhaps you would like to return here tomorrow after dinner," he said. "Perhaps you will then meet some other people, if they come. But it's possible that they will decide not to come. I can't promise you anything . . . It's up to you."

Tim bowed his head slightly in gratitude, ready to leave the office, but the man motioned him to stay.

"How is it that you speak Arabic so well?" he asked. "I never heard of American Jesuits who speak Arabic. I am curious . . ."

Tim brightened up. The question was a marvelous opportunity to break the ice, establish a personal rapport, and prepare for the meeting that might take place the following evening—if he was lucky and made a good impression now.

"Well," he answered with a conquering smile, "I was fortunate to be able to study the history of Islam as well as Arabic at a great Jesuit university in Washington many years ago. In fact, I have a doctorate in Islamic history and culture. I am very proud of it. You know, Jesuits are deep believers in learning and education, especially about other cultures and societies. We are teachers and often missionaries. Back in the sixteenth century, for example, the first Jesuits arrived in China, learned the language, and gave Confucius his world fame by latinizing his Chinese name, Kong Fuzi, which means the Very Reverend Master Kong, or Kongzi. I think the Jesuits were impressed realizing Confucianism to be a monotheistic religion as is Christianity—and as is Islam. I also lived in Cairo for a time . . ."

"My name is Fawzi," the beefy Algerian told Tim, "and, as it happens I, too, am an imam . . . What you said about Jesuits is very interesting. I hope you can repeat it for the benefit of my friends tomorrow. *Salaam Aleikum* . . ."

"*Aleikum Salaam*," Tim responded gravely to the salutation. "May peace be upon you."

"The five of us are the council of elders in Toulouse," the elderly man informed Tim as he was ushered into the room by a muscular young man in a track suit. "It is the council of the beneficial associations, and I am currently the chairman. I am also the imam from a mosque not far from here. My name is Faisal . . . And we were advised that you desire to ask about the events in Rome in 1981. But we wonder why?"

Faisal spoke in elegant Arabic. He was a frail, elderly man with a carefully trimmed short white beard, who sat behind a long table in a large room behind the storefront office of the Beneficial Association. Two men, one of them Fawzi, sat on either side of him.

Faisal spoke in pleasant, businesslike tones. There was no hostility in his attitude, and his curiosity about Tim's mission seemed genuine. Tim had already decided to be almost absolutely honest with the council—he would skip some operational details and he was glad he had not mentioned to Fawzi the previous day his Cairo CIA connection—simply because it was the only rational strategy at this juncture.

"We are both men of God," he told the imam, "and I shall speak the God's truth. I work as an Islam scholar at the Vatican, and our Holy Father has instructed me to learn all I could about the attack on him because Italian and international investigators had been unable to come up with adequate answers. I was chosen for this mission because the assailant is a Turk and, frankly, the Holy See suspects what they call a 'Muslim Connection' in this affair. And I am specialized in Islam."

"But why does your pope insist on an investigation now?" Faisal asked. "After all, God had saved him—and the Turk is safely in prison . . ."

"Honestly, I don't know," Tim answered. "The reason and the timing were not explained to me. Perhaps because the Holy See fears that the pope remains in danger if we do not find out what was behind the shooting, and is not in a position to defuse new conspiracies. I really don't know, except that it is a top priority for the Apostolic Palace."

"I see," Faisal said. "But I fail to grasp what has led you to Toulouse. Can you enlighten us?"

"Yes, of course," Tim assured him. "In a sense, I was working my way back, with quite a bit of luck—and help. Because Italian investigators had determined that Circlic, the Turkish shooter, had once belonged to the Gray Wolves, a terrorist organization in Turkey, I flew to Istambul in the hope of contacting the Wolves to confirm that this was correct—and to inquire why they had recruited Circlic, who is mentally unstable, for the job."

"You certainly take chances," Faisal remarked. "They could have killed you. We know something about them. And you are very imaginative in your pursuit. If I didn't know that you are a priest, I would have thought that you are a professional intelligence agent, the way you operate. But please go on."

"Thank you," Tim said. "To make a long story short, I found friends in Istambul who did put me in touch with top people of the Wolves. Once we had something of a rapport, I asked them if they knew anything about Circlic and why they had hired him to kill the pope. I pointed out to them that this whole thing was a mystery, that I couldn't understand what Turkish Muslims, even fundamentalists, had against Gregory XVII that they would want him dead."

Faisal leaned forward, enthralled. "And then what?"

"Well, I must confess that I was surprised that the Wolves did not deny hiring Circlic for the assassination. But they told me that it was really none of their business and they had provided the Turk on the request from their 'French Brethren.' They said that it was a request from fellow Muslims that simply couldn't be refused, that it was a matter of solidarity among Muslims around the world, and, consequently, they asked no questions. They had no idea who, exactly, the 'French Brethren' were, but they had been contacted through secret Turkish Muslim fundamentalist emissaries. And, yes, the money to pay Circlic and meet his expenses also came from the 'French Brethren' . . ."

The men behind the table gasped. " 'French Brethren,' " Faisal repeated almost inaudibly.

"The next logical step for me was to go to Paris, where I have Muslim friends, to try to figure out who are the 'French Brethren,' " Tim went on. "In Paris, an Egyptian friend introduced me to the imam at the Stalingrad mosque who encouraged me to go to the south of France, to Toulouse, to pursue my leads. You know the rest. The imam told you to expect me. So here I am."

Silence descended on the room when Tim finished speaking. Faisal, the imam, and his colleagues looked at each other confusedly, wordlessly. At length, the imam addressed Tim.

"This is terrible," he said. "I am at a loss for what to say to you. Everything you learned in Istambul and Paris is unfortunately true. We, this council, are the 'French Brethren' you were told about. It is true that we contacted Muslim brethren in Turkey to request the hiring of a man who would be prepared, for money, to undertake the assassination of a world figure. But we didn't know that the pope would be the target."

It was Tim's turn to be confused. He looked from one end of the table to the other, at the faces of the five members of the council, trying to comprehend what he had just heard.

"I don't understand," he said, his voice rising in indignation and puzzlement. "What possible interest would you, French Muslims in Toulouse, have in killing the Roman Catholic pope? My God, the wars of the Crusades ended over six centuries ago! What were you thinking? And what do you mean that you didn't know that the pope was the proposed victim? It doesn't make any sense!"

"No, it does not," Faisal said. "Except that we did not realize it at the time. We asked the people in Istambul for an assassin, may Allah forgive us, but we were not apprised that he was to assassinate your pope . . ."

"Apprised by whom?"

"By people here, in Toulouse, who had approached us to help them find an assassin. They convinced us that the death of that world figure, as they put it, would restore our great religions to the glories of the past, the glories of Allah and the glories of your Christian God. We didn't ask any questions; we agreed to help, and even to transfer funds to Istambul for this operation."

"But, for God's sake," Tim shouted, "*who* are these people?"

Faisal looked to the right, then to the left, at his fellow councilmen. He sighed and raised his eyes to the ceiling and heavens above.

"They are Roman Catholic traditionalists. Priests and bishops. They call them 'integrists,'" Faisal said hoarsely. "Or they are called fundamentalists. We are Muslim fundamentalists. And their fundamentalism and our fundamentalism are part of ancient traditions that are still strong, that unite us. We must stand together to preserve the essential values of our great religions. This is the reason we agreed to hire an assassin at their request. But, I swear, Father Savage, they never told us that it was the pope they wanted to kill. After we established the contacts with Istambul and Agca was hired, we were no longer in the picture. We were not told anything. These 'integrists' established direct lines of communication with the Wolves and, I presume, with the Turk himself to give him precise instructions. You can imagine, Father, our paralyzing shock when we heard that the Turk whom we had provided had attempted to kill the pope . . . Of course, we share the blame—this is why I am telling you the truth tonight . . . But the Catholics were the original sinners against the head of their Church. . . ."

At the Apostolic Palace in Rome, Monsignor Sainte-Ange summoned Sister Angela to his second-*loggia* office the day after her return from Paris.

"How was your visit home, my child?" he asked.

"Oh, fine, Monsignor, just fine. I saw relatives, did some errands, bought some books, and prayed at our convent chapel."

"And did you call Father Savage, as I suggested?"

"Yes, Monsignor," Angela replied. "Not only did I call him, but we met for a *citron pressé* on St. Germain one day. He seemed to be in good form."

She chose not to say that they had met at Deux Magots, not exactly the proper site, even for a platonic rendezvous involving members of the opposite sex who were also members of ancient religious orders. And she omitted mentioning their bistro dinner.

"Did the Father talk about his investigation?" Sainte-Ange inquired. "Did he have anything interesting to say?"

"No, not really," Angela told him. "He said he had seen an old friend from his Cairo days and visited a mosque in the Muslim suburbs. And now he has gone to Toulouse to follow whatever leads he thinks he has."

"Why Toulouse? What leads?" the monsignor asked. His voice was suddenly tense, alert.

"I have no idea," Angela said truthfully. "He didn't say."

In the papal study later that day, Sainte-Ange told Gregory XVII that Tim Savage had gone to Toulouse after conversations with some Muslims he knew in Paris.

"I wish I knew more about the Toulouse idea," he added.

"Yes," the pope agreed. "Me, too." "This is becoming a bit sensitive. And the Languedoc, believe me, is a can of worms."

BOOK FIVE

The Truth

Chapter Nineteen

IT WAS A GHASTLY can of worms, all right, Tim Savage, who had the same thought, said to himself. A fundamentalist can of worms, with Muslim and Catholic theological hard-liners in a lethal alliance.

It also was pure horror, the discovery he had just made that dissident or rebel Catholics, and priests of God at that, would arrange to assassinate the pope, the head of the universal Church, in the name of religious "glories of the past." And it meant that having failed once, the Catholic fanatics would unquestionably try again. Sometime, somewhere. Tim had no reason to doubt the veracity of Faisal's account. It followed logically from what he had learned in Istanbul and in Paris, and the Toulouse imam would have no motive to invent such a tale. It was common sense. Step by step, he thought, it was all beginning to fall into place. But only *beginning* to fall into place.

And as a purely practical and immediate matter, Tim realized, his duty was to defuse new conspiracies, if they already existed, or prevent them from being hatched. This was the classical responsibility of an intelligence case officer—to obtain thus far unattainable secret information and to act upon it.

Tim's information, however, menacing and sinister as it was, did not indicate how and where he should act. He was given no names, identities, or details about the Catholic fanatics. Tim could not have pressed them further at their evening meeting. He could not ask the Muslims to betray, in effect, their fellow fundamentalists. The Christian-Muslim history in southern France was very old, almost a thousand years, and traditional ties could not be severed so easily. The imam, caught up in his own moral dilemma, gave him the facts concerning his council's involvement—and conveyed his tormented regrets—but he would not go beyond that. He and his associates may have felt betrayed themselves by the Catholic group's failure to tell them that Gregory XVII was the intended target of the plot. Still, loyalties existed among fundamentalists of different faiths—Tim knew this was not confined to southern France—because they shared the vision of a collapse of moral order in a rapidly changing world, which emphasized materialism, contempt for tradition, and the abandonment of ancient values. Jewish fundamentalism and Hindu fundamentalism were as powerful in the new age as that of the Christian and Muslim faiths. In Iran, for example, after the Khomeini revolution, Shiite Muslim fundamentalists killed moderates. In fact, extremisms of one sort or another have existed since the inception of religions—because the world has always been changing.

Under the circumstances, Tim's investigation was very far from complete, and dangers to the pope still lurked. It was now late September, and Gregory XVII had come and gone safely without any reported incident during his visit to France. It did not surprise Tim. Killing the pope in France would have been too dangerous, too easily traceable. So it would be attempted elsewhere, in an anonymous fashion, along the general lines of Agca Circlic's attack. The event at St. Peter's had been perfectly planned, and it had failed only because the bullet had missed the pope's heart by millimeters—as Gregory XVII believed, God had saved him. But Tim had to worry about the *next time,* especially in the light of what he had learned in Toulouse, and the only questions were how soon and where?

Recovering in his room at the Jesuit Residence from the shock of his Toulouse discovery, Tim resolved that it would be premature to pass on the new information immediately to Monsignor Sainte-Ange. His instinct warned him against it. Besides, his instructions were to find the truth, the full truth, and all he had at this stage was very incomplete truth. He had too much to discover about the "integrists," whoever they were, the history of their movement—or movements—their milieu, and their backgrounds. He had to identify them, locate them, perhaps even confront them to obtain proof of their culpability. It was Tim's standard meticulous operating procedure to absorb everything possible before proceeding further ahead, just as he had learned in the CIA.

Emotionally exhausted, Tim wondered vaguely whether he would have confided his new knowledge to Sister Angela, had she been there, and what she would have thought of it, as a Catholic, a nun, and such an intelligent person? He smiled even as he fell into a troubled asleep.

After Tim Savage and his council associates left the room, Faisal sank into deep thought. The imam, now in the seventh decade of his life, never regarded himself as saintly, unlike many learned ulemas and bombastic mullahs he knew. But he did believe that he had always been an honest man in his secular activities and in his devotion to Allah. Tonight, however, he faced an awesome test, a moral dilemma and uncertainty that he must overcome and, if needs be, act on accordingly. As night turned into dawn, Faisal prayed to Allah for guidance and read the appropriate *suras* in the Koran, seeking inspiration and answers. His white goatee quivered and there were tears in his eyes.

Faisal had been profoundly shocked upon learning from the Jesuit priest that he and his fellow Muslims on the Toulouse council had been used—most dishonestly, he thought—by the Catholic believers in helping them to find through their Istambul connection a punishing hand, a murderer, to right a religious wrong. It had never crossed his mind that the intended victim would be the pope, the supreme head of another great monotheistic religion.

The imam and his colleagues had hesitated for long days before deciding whether to honor this request at all. They had been very troubled by the notion of providing assassins even for high religious reasons, although religion could justify murder in very special cases, as narrated both in the Koran and the Old Testament. In the end, they agreed to do so in the name of solidarity among those who wished to preserve the purity of their respective faiths. Christians and Muslims, after all, were children of Abraham, and, quarrels, wars, and crusades notwithstanding, they still had very much in common. However Faisal himself had remained most uneasy even after Istambul had been contacted and the arrangements made.

Now, though, he understood that he may have contributed to a tragedy of historical proportions. He was guilty of sacrilegious criminality in terms of his own cherished moral precepts as well as of religious and secular law. Muslims, who, along with Jews and Christians, recognize Moses as prophet, shared the admonition of the Commandments that *Thou Shalt Not Murder.* Faisal realized tonight how frightfully wrong he had been. Yet, it had happened—and it could not be undone, no matter how he chastised himself. And he hated himself for failing to connect the Turk's attack on Gregory XVII with the Catholics' request for a gunman. Where had his mind been? Was he becoming senile?

But Faisal's torment now went far beyond that dreadful act. Did he have the right to confide in the American Jesuit that the Toulouse council had played a crucial role in helping to recruit a murderer on behalf of the avenging Catholics? Had it been a violation of trust, had it been a betrayal—even after Faisal had learned the terrible truth from the Jesuit? Did he have the right to judge and to compound one immoral act with another immoral act? He sighed and prayed again.

It was already light outside when Faisal concluded that he could not live with such a breach of trust on his part, regardless of the sins of others. One could not be two-faced, it was mandated in the Koran and in the Bible. This left him with only one course of action, shameful and devastated as he felt about it—and about himself.

Faisal gathered his robes and left the store with a heavy step. It was early morning, but the street in the immigrant neighborhood was already teeming with men and women rushing to work—and those—the majority—who had no work, but faithfully congregated on street corners awaiting they knew not what. That would be their day, like yesterday and like tomorrow. From a nearby mosque, he heard the taped voice of the *muezzin* in morning prayer.

At the big intersection a block away, Faisal boarded the city bus, also already thronged, to ride to the other side of Toulouse, across the Garonne. He left the bus on a quiet, old-fashioned working-class street of identical houses and identical dwellers. He walked three blocks to the church of St. Adalbert, a smallish structure covered with the patina of time. The door was unlocked and Faisal entered. Incense wafted in the air from the six o'clock morning Mass, but the church was empty. Faisal crossed over to the sacristy.

"Good morning, Father," he said to the tall priest in a black cassock who stood in the center of the room studying the front page of the morning newspaper. He was the same priest, an old acquaintance, who had come to Faisal nearly six years ago, shopping for a murderer.

"There is something I must tell you," Faisal went on. "A Jesuit priest named Timothy Savage, an American, came to see us last night to ask us what we knew about the assassin who attempted to kill your pope. You hadn't told us at the time that it was the pope you wanted murdered. Thus it was my obligation, as a man of God, to tell him that we had acted on your request. Now it is my obligation, I believe, to inform you of what we have told the Jesuit."

Faisal bowed in courtesy and left the church. The tall priest had not reacted to his words. He had remained silent, his face stony. When he was alone again, he reached for the telephone on his desk and dialed an out-of-town number.

"I must see you with the greatest urgency, Excellency," he said softly and hung up. He was pale with anger.

In his room that morning, Tim spent long hours making notes and analyzing the information from the Muslims. What mattered the most were the motives of the Catholic fanatics: Was the assassination attempt an aberration by a few? Was it the work of a small splinter group in the Church? Was it a new schism or heresy? Was it the opening volley in a new kind of Catholic religious war? Did its roots wind all the way back to the Dark Ages and medieval times, back to the first centuries of Christendom?

It was one thing for those "integrists" to invade and occupy churches in France, as they were doing with rising frequency, to parade with posters and banners and to defy the Holy See by consecrating their own bishops and refusing to remain in communion with Rome. But to try to kill the pope was something else again, on a demonic scale. And this time it was not just unleashing rampant mobs, as in the past, to capture the power of the papacy—now it was theological and ideological, a religious cleansing.

Schisms and heresies, of course, dated back to the infancy of the Church, and Tim decided it would be useful to refresh his memory about this aspect of Christian history. It might help to create a context for today's "integrists." He found it curious that so much Christian heresy had occurred in France.

And the more Tim studied the history of heresy, the more he became convinced that the plot against Gregory XVII was the ultimate expression of a modern heretical defiance of the Holy See. The heretics, naturally, regarded themselves as the only true defenders of the faith, damning the Rome papacy for sullying the legacy of the Fathers of the Church. The Vatican, then and now, saw its theological challengers as heretics in the full sense of the term, the historical sense, and thereby subject to excommunication, a virtual expulsion from the Church, its priests banned from administering holy sacraments.

Heresies were so much a part of the Church's history that a formidable study of *Heresies of the High Middle Ages* that Tim used to teach himself the subject was an 865-page volume in small print. Some of the great minds of theology, he found, had been profoundly engaged in battles against heretics, including the famous St. Bernard of Clairvaux in the twelfth century; he had even gone to Toulouse to combat the influence of Henry of Le Mans, a preacher described by Church historians as "eccentric but highly popular" as he stirred an anticlerical uproar among the faithful.

Contemporary heretics like Henry of Le Mans and others rallied against the Roman clergy for its hedonism, insisting on the spiritual character of the true Church to the exclusion of its material attributes. Generally, heretics of that time considered themselves as "pure" and, as Tim noted, they were essentially conservative Christians, horrified by the behavior of the organized clergy and the papacy, prepared to kill and die for their beliefs, and in open defiance of Rome. The Church in those days often engaged in simony, which was the buying and selling of ecclesiastical preferment, such as high posts; it was named after Simon Magus, a Samaritan sorcerer. There was also lucrative traffic in indulgences and widespread corruption. There was a touch of heroism about these early heretics, Tim thought, and they were, in effect, the forerunners of today's Catholic fundamentalists. Still, this gave them no license to perform as radical an act as killing the pope: Today's Church was not corrupt, it was modernizing itself.

Christian heresies went back to Manichaeism in Persia, lasting from the third to the sixth century, and apparently spawning Gnosticism and later the Cathars. These were "dualistic" heresies and sects, proclaiming that two creative and irreconcilable forces—good and evil—operated in the universe. Mani, the father of the Manichaean doctrine, believed in two realms of being, Light and Darkness, each under its own lord, battling each other, and his Gnostic and Cathar descendants accepted this rejection of the idea that God was the Creator of all. Their unanswered question was, "if God is good, whence comes evil?"

Dualism in its many forms, Tim read, was probably the most powerful and the longest lasting of the great heresies—and it was still surviving to some degree in today's south of France as a Cathar tradition. But France also produced heresies in Châlons-sur-Marne, Aquitaine, Arras, and Orléans in the eleventh century; the Orléans heresy was the first "popular heresy"—a mass movement—a century before the advent of Catharism in the south. In the twelfth century, Waldenses heretics, named after Waldes, a rich merchant who underwent a religious experience, emerged in the city of Lyons—they became known as the "Poor of Lyons." But there also were Messalians in Armenia and Priscillians in Spain in the fourth century, Paulicians in Asia Minor in the seventh century, and the Bogomils, the ancestors of the Cathars, in Bulgaria and Macedonia in the tenth century. Joan of Arc was burned as a heretic in Orléans at the age of nineteen in the fifteenth century.

It was an extraordinary history that Tim was absorbing in great gulps, increasingly certain of its relevance to his investigation. But he had to find ways of relating the past Catholic heresies to the French Catholic "integrism" to understand what had led to the attempt to kill the pope. That France and the Holy See had been perpetually at war since the 1789 revolution—and that to this day both liberal and hard-line Catholic splinter groups were defying Rome—suggested that the conspiracy was French in origin. But Tim needed proof.

"If you're still interested in integrism," the Jesuit priest-librarian told Tim after the Angelus mass at the Toulouse Residence chapel, "come to my office tomorrow afternoon and we'll chat. I'll even make coffee for you."

Both Jesuits and both scholars, Tim and the priest-librarian soon discovered another bond between them: Vietnam. The librarian had been a career French Foreign Legion paratrooper, a *para* as the elite corps was admiringly known, and served as a captain with General de Lattre de Tassigny when Dienbienphu fell to the Vietminh communists in 1954. He had lived a wild youth in the best traditions of the Foreign Legion, but the horror of the Indochina war transformed him, and Jesuits he knew in Saigon after the defeat helped to guide him through the religious revelation. His parents, he knew all along, had been collaborators with the Vichy regime and the Nazis during the German occupation, and this inherited guilt was another reason he sought atonement. Like Tim's, the librarian's vocation for priesthood had been late, and similarly precipitated by Indochina experiences. Nearly twenty years older, the librarian appointed himself to be Tim's mentor in Toulouse and beyond; he seemed to divine his mission, though Tim had never mentioned it in so many words.

A bizarre wooden contraption on the librarian's desk looked to Tim like a prehistoric *espresso* machine, which it actually was, with a glass bubble for heating water inside, and it produced excellent coffee. "I brought it back from Vietnam," he said proudly, pouring cups for Tim and himself.

"But let's talk about 'integrists' whom some people call 'integralists' because they accept unquestioningly the most rigid, antiquated Church doctrines," the librarian said. "They are quite important and quite dangerous, in my opinion, given their access to powerful Church, political, and economic individuals and organizations. They work overtly and they work covertly. Their most visible and very militant religious institution is the Fraternity of St. Pius V, which may have between a half-million and a million adherents, mainly in France—it was naturally a French idea—but also in Switzerland, Germany, Austria, and even the United States. It is a full-fledged schism, with its own priests and bishops, and in full, formal defiance of Rome. In a way, it has already become a separate church, full of hate for the pope and the Holy See. Politically, it is in league with reactionary political parties like the Front

National here in France and extreme right-wingers, even neo-Nazis, elsewhere in Europe. The Fraternity is, of course, anti-Semitic and anti-immigrant. During the war, many of the priests who are today Fraternity members collaborated with the Vichy police and the Gestapo in rounding up Jews for transport to Auschwitz and other death camps. Believe me, I am very familiar with this subject: my parents, I regret to say, were *collaborateurs.*"

"But how could priests behave like this?" Tim asked. "I mean, they were betraying Christian teachings and all that . . ."

"Very easily," the librarian told him, bitterly. "Being a priest doesn't make a man a real Christian or even a decent person. In France, it is often just a profession. And after the war, they behaved even worse, providing sanctuary for criminals like Paul Touvier, a top official in the Vichy militia, who lived in parish houses with priests and was kept in ample funds by the Chevaliers de Notre Dame, another fascist religious outfit. Then there were the famous René Bousquet, who was secretary-general for police in the Vichy government, and Maurice Papon, who was in charge in Bordeaux. They were responsible for the deaths of thousands of Jews. For years, they, too, were protected by our Catholic clergy. Brossard was paid by the Chevaliers de Sainte Marie, whoever they were. Yes, our Church is rich in criminals. And, of course, they all hate Gregory XVII."

"But I must add," he went on, "that a group of French bishops recently issued a declaration that the silence of the French Church leadership in the face of the wartime persecution of Jews was a 'fault.' That was good. However, even Gregory XVII has refused to predict whether the Roman Catholic Church as a whole will offer a formal apology for this silence. The Holy See is still determined to protect the great silences of Pius XII. And here in France, the Fraternity and other integrists just love to keep it that way. They have a lot of power."

"Tell me more about the St. Pius V Fraternity," Tim asked the librarian. "Who runs it, or does anybody in particular?"

"Oh, yes," the old Jesuit said. "It's run, with an iron hand, by its founder, Archbishop Julien Leduc. Haven't you heard about him?"

"Just vaguely. Who, exactly, is he?"

"Leduc is a retired archbishop who spent long years in West

Africa, then, after formal retirement, decided to invent his own church, which, as I said, is a schism. Actually, I think it is a modern heresy. He represents the hard core of integrism. Leduc's role models are Pius V, who began implementing the straitjacket decrees of the Council of Trent held in mid-sixteenth century and thus earned sainthood, and Pius X who reigned until the start of World War I in 1914. You will appreciate why Leduc named his Fraternity after Pius V and why he venerates Pius X, who was a reactionary paranoiac and thought all intellectuals were heretics. I might add that Pius X was canonized after the war, in 1954, by none other than Pope Pius XII. When Pius X was pope, the future Pius XII was his diplomatic assistant. Yeah, Archbishop Leduc is quite a figure. You should meet him one of these days . . . Actually, he is our neighbor in Languedoc. But that's another story . . . And I think you should take a good look at the saga of the Cathars. You may find it most interesting—and useful."

"Is it hard to find the Archbishop?" Tim asked. "Does he see outsiders?"

"No, I don't think you will have any problems locating him," the librarian replied. "He lives somewhere near Carcassonne, not hiding from anybody . . . But there's something else you ought to know about the Pius V Fraternity. Do you remember that demented Spanish priest who had lunged at the pope with a bayonet, while he prayed at the statue of Our Lady of Fátima on the first anniversary of the shooting at St. Peter's Square?"

"Yes," Tim said. "Of course, I remember. What about the Spanish priest?"

"He was a member of the Pius V Fraternity," the librarian told him. "And when the pope was in France earlier this month, there was another strange incident that was kept out of the press at the request of the Holy See and the French authorities: A crude homemade bomb was found in a church near Paris where Gregory XVII was scheduled to concelebrate a Mass . . . and the bomb contained an inscription in Latin and French, reading, 'In the name of the pope, BOOM!' "

The following Sunday, Tim Savage happened to be watching television during a late breakfast in the refectory of the Toulouse Residence. With scant interest, he saw and heard Languedoc politicians, leftists and rightists, propound their platforms for the approaching parliamentary elections, when, suddenly, his attention was caught by images of a huge mass of people advancing along an *autoroute* with banners and crosses. The sound was of religious chants and prayers rising to the heavens from thousands and thousands of throats. Now listening closely to the live broadcast, Tim learned that it was the final stage of a seventy-mile, three-day march, under alternating hot sun and violent downpours, by members and followers of the Pius V Fraternity from the ancient cathedral in Chartres to the Sacré-Coeur de Montmartre church in Paris. The marchers had first attended a traditional Mass in Latin, according to the rite of Pope Pius V, at the Chartres Cathedral, then an identical Mass at the Montmartre church. A tall cross carried by the believers was dedicated, in big white letters, to St. Bernadette, a favorite of the traditionalists. Tim was surprised to hear that the Mass in Chartres had been celebrated by Cardinal Angelo Felici, once a papal nuncio to France and currently the president of the Pontifical Ecclesia Dei Commission, which looks after traditional Catholics. Indeed, Archbishop Leduc and his Fraternity had quite a following in France—and a strategic presence in Rome. It was Cardinal Felici who had announced to the world, from the balcony of St. Peter's Basilica, the election of Gregory XVII. But Leduc himself was not in the crowd.

Tim had heard the name of Archbishop Leduc and something about his controversial movement, but he was not a theologian and this whole subject was entirely outside his sphere of knowledge and interest. It would never have occurred to Tim to research Leduc and the Fraternity in the context of his investigation. The conventional wisdom, at least as relayed by Monsignor Sainte-Ange, was that there existed a "Muslim connection" in the assassination conspiracy, and that was in part the reason for recruiting Tim. The warning from de Marenches, about which he was apprised later, had not pointed, as far as he knew, in the French integrist direction. It was extraordinary, Tim thought, how powerful were the passions aroused within and around the Church over religious traditions, including the issue of the rite in which Mass in Latin or in vernacular should be celebrated, four centuries after the Council of Trent—and toward the end of the twentieth century—to become a schism and a heresy.

Fascinating as fundamentalist battles appeared to be, they ceased, however, to be abstract and theoretical to Tim Savage from the moment Faisal, the Toulouse imam, had admitted Muslim participation, innocent or not, in the plot against Gregory XVII and the Jesuit priest-librarian had given him a primer on integrism and its ramifications in France. Now Tim had to turn into an expert on Archbishop Leduc, the Fraternity, and all its connections. And his instinct told him that he had precious little time to acquire this expertise—before he was equipped to act to defuse new tragedies.

Again, the library of the Jesuit Residence provided Tim with basic information, this time in written form. There were biographies of Archbishop Leduc, some hagiographies and some savage denunciations, a slim autobiography, Leduc's own broadside against the Vatican Council, and several reasonably levelheaded discussions of "L'affaire Leduc."

A photograph of a youthful-looking, smiling, blue-eyed priest, a picture obviously taken decades ago, graced the cover of one of the biographies. The face was somewhat familiar to Tim as he looked at the photograph, but he could not place it, and made no effort to search his memory. As life stories of bishops went, Leduc's career had been rather interesting, Tim thought, as he plunged into his latest research project, an undertaking requiring quite a few days of reading, note taking, and analyzing.

Jules Leduc was born in 1905 in Ajaccio on Corsica, the island that had been Napoleon's birthplace, the year when the French Parliament had approved the law on the separation of church and state, and the expulsion of religious orders. That was the latest milestone in the battle between the two great entities, dating back to the 1789 revolution, an event the French Church had neither forgotten nor forgiven to this day. As it happened, an amazing ironic coincidence, the separation law, born the same year as the archbishop, would become a lifelong obsession for him. He saw it as high crime and treason.

One of eight children—five of whom took religious vows—Leduc was ordained as priest at the age of twenty-four. Because he was spotted by the Church as a man of great promise, Leduc was sent to Rome to study for doctorates in theology and philosophy at the Jesuits' Gregorian University, another irony for this priest who hated Church "liberals" from the bottom of his heart. A bishop assigned to a diocese in southern France—in Languedoc— at forty-five, Leduc was named archbishop of Casablanca at fifty. It was 1950, and Morocco was still part of metropolitan France as were Algeria and Tunisia. Leduc believed that North Africa should remain French forever, not only because of his patriotism, but, principally, his fear that otherwise Islam would engulf that vast region. Islam was the object of one of Leduc's many profound hatreds.

It took Vatican Council II, which he attended in the mid-1960s, to unleash fully the furies that possessed Leduc. In a flood of articles, lectures, and books—among them *I Accuse the Council* and *They Uncrowned Him,* meaning Jesus Christ—Leduc declared that the Council was a criminal conspiracy against the Church and the past popes. He spoke darkly of the Council and its modernizing decisions verging on "satanism" and being "AIDS of the Church," the second epithet hurled some years later, when AIDS was actually isolated and identified.

Leduc despised and condemned everything about the post-conciliar new Church: the Declaration on Religious Liberty, which he described as a "fundamental vice" and the "death of the social reign of our Lord Jesus Christ"; the policy of ecumenism aimed at reuniting Christian churches after the Great Schism of 1054, because, the archbishop felt, Catholicism was the only "true religion"; and the approval of the new Latin Mass by Pope Paul VI, replacing the ancient Tridentine Mass, and, horror of horrors, the legitimizing of Mass in vernacular. Leduc similarly denounced the new liturgy, with the priest at Mass facing the worshipers rather than the altar, shocking him as an affront to Jesus Christ.

Given his odium toward the Council and the "liberal" Holy See, Leduc resigned his archbishopric in 1968, presumably before being fired for his runaway rebellion. Two years later, he founded his Pius V Fraternity, and within four years he ordained his first priests, an illegal act in the eyes of the Church that led Paul VI to suspend him in his spiritual prerogatives. By then, however,

Leduc's "parallel church" was progressing with astounding speed. The archbishop, for one thing, was a highly likable personality and a fine and convincing speaker, particularly to the ears of Catholic conservatives. Young priests swarmed to the seminary he had established at the lovely old town of Mirepoix in Languedoc to spread the Leduc doctrine. Integrism was strong in France.

Leduc, as Tim discovered, had a high opinion of himself. He had designed his own coat of arms in which a bishop's wide-brimmed black hat reposes atop a cross that tapers off as the tip of a sword. The motto, in Latin: "We Believe in Charity." The arch-bishop often explained, in all seriousness, "I cannot help it if I am always right!"

"You know, Tim," the priest-librarian told him, "Leduc is, in effect, a papist against the pope, and he literally believes that he is *plus catholique que le pape.* You may think he is crazy, but don't sell him short."

Leduc, in fact, had a following not only in France but in a half-dozen countries with Catholic majorities. In Spain, for example, Tim read, a young Catalan priest linked to the Fraternity had become a media star with his "Moors versus Christians" nation-wide television program.

Hoping to quell Leduc's rebellion, Gregory XVII received him on November 18, 1978, within a week of his election, but these two strong-minded Frenchmen could not accept a compromise. Negotiations between their representatives trailed inconclusively for nearly three years, then broke down when Leduc refused to budge from his extreme positions. He also described the Vatican Council as a "heresy" and the Church's "self-destruction." And he compared Gregory XVII to Pilate, rendering further conversa-tions rather difficult to keep alive.

Studying the Leduc dossier, Tim noticed with curiosity that in consecrating his own bishops, the archbishop was in violation of Canon Law promulgated by Pius V and proclaiming that "all bish-ops" must be nominated by the Holy See. But it was obviously too late for theological and legalistic niceties and technicalities. Leduc was on the offensive, a *blitzkrieg.* And soon after Pope John Paul I died in 1978 after his month-long reign, *Civilita Cristiana,* a pro-Leduc publication in Rome, charged that Church "liberals" had planned to kill him because they "feared" that he would reverse the reforms mandated by the Vatican Council. Yes, Tim reminded himself, offense is the best defense. Was it part of careful, patient advance planning?

Tim also noticed that the collapse of the negotiations between the Holy See and Leduc's representatives occurred in February 1981. The attack against Gregory XVII occurred exactly three months later, on May thirteenth.

Chapter Twenty

JAKE KURTSKI WAS stretched on the narrow bed in his cell-like Rome hotel room, furiously chewing on a dead cigar and swearing softly to himself in Polish and in English. He had just left the young Frenchman, his conspiracy contact—he still did not know his name—who had given him startling new marching orders, consisting of a command to turn himself into a cheap hired gun.

This angered Kurtski more than anything in years, certainly since Vietnam. In Kurtski's mind, there was a world of difference between strategic political assassinations—as, for example, Phoenix had been in Vietnam—or supervising strategic international terrorism and participating in coups d'état in shitty little countries in Africa or Asia—and just plain individual murder. "For Chrissakes," Kurtski had told the Frenchman, he had been "a U.S. Army intelligence officer and a senior CIA officer, and not a *focking* shooter." Kurtski, after all, had a solid reputation, commanding very high prices for his work and advice, and was treated with professional courtesy by most of the important intelligence services in the world. People understood and appreciated one another in their murky universe.

After the Vietnam War ended in 1975, and Kurtski was among the last to be evacuated by helicopter from the roof of the American Embassy in Saigon, he concluded that he had no further profitable future with the CIA. The whole climate and culture of U.S. intelligence work was changing after the Vietnam disaster, with the Agency's good name being blackened for all the covert activities, both good and bad, it had undertaken. The best Kurtski could expect at that point was to be put in charge of training recruits at The Farm or something equally demeaning. He knew they would not trust him as a Station Chief anywhere, his patronizing in-house CIA image defined by the nickname he had acquired in Phoenix: "K.K.," or "Killer Kurtski." He was not cut out to be a CIA diplomat.

Kurtski therefore resigned, collected his severance pay, and turned to new pursuits in the very active private sector, as he called it, of the intelligence craft and associated endeavors. He spent several years in the employ of an officially recognized, registered, and respected—though sometimes shady—corporation of international arms dealers in Alexandria, Virginia, just past Washington's National Airport.

The corporation, a billion-dollar business, specialized in global legal and illegal weapons transactions, some of the latter quietly blessed by the U.S. government. Kurtski, not surprisingly, devoted himself to the illegal side of the enterprise, earning more money than he ever had in his life. He lived comfortably in an expensive apartment in a Foggy Bottom deluxe condo in Washington, allowed himself unlimited sex and booze binges when he was in town. He flew around the world first class, stayed at five-star hotels, his peasant physique and body language incongruous in the thousand-or-more-dollar suits from Armani or Savile Row, his sartorial tastes being incongruous as well. But in the frantic life of masses of people jetting across oceans, staying at the best hotels, and eating at the most fashionable restaurants, Kurtski did not stand out any more than any other improbably dressed, free-spending, expense account businessman, which was fine as far as he was concerned. He saw nobody outside of business meetings: He disliked people in general and was disliked in turn—he had always been a self-sufficient loner.

After a time, Kurtski became bored with selling and delivering and buying and transfering used jet fighters, armored cars, mortars, grenade launchers, M-16 and AK-47 assault rifles and whatnot. It was too routine for him. Through his arms salesmanship, however, Kurtski became acquainted with the Fraternity of international mercenaries who were mainly French, Belgian, English, and South African, and easily allowed himself to be talked into contributing his expertise—that was where his Phoenix reputation had proved most valuable—to their various violent undertakings. Knocking over regimes from Guinea-Bissau to Lesotho, the Seychelles, assorted Arab Emirates on the Persian Gulf, and Brunei—though that one had failed and the super-billionaire sultan had preserved his power—was the outfit's principal line of business.

Kurtski, often the main military brain behind the coups, continued to prosper. He also diversified, more from his twisted sense of aesthetics than merely for added profit, into global prostitution rings, facilitating transfers of gorgeous, impoverished adolescent girls from Southeast Asia, and sometimes from North Africa, to classy brothels in Europe. He was not averse to taste the fruit himself, but he would not touch drugs. He had enough sense not to become involved in international drug transactions; he remembered the CIA foolishness in running narcotics from the "Golden Triangle" in Indochina.

In the early 1980s, Kurtski gave up the mercenary life, enthusiastically accepting a fantastic financial offer from his old CIA associates—now Agency bosses—to help oversee the contras' campaign against the Sandinistas in Nicaragua. That was great, he thought. Not only did he owe it to his adopted country, the United States of America, but he could get his revenge for Vietnam against the God-damned communists. Kurtski devoted a year or so to the cause of the contras, acting as the chief of staff of the field forces. Every once in a while, he swooped down in a chopper on an advance contras command post to take over interrogations of captured Sandinista prisoners. He enjoyed every moment of it, bringing back memories of Vietnam and of youth. Not infrequently, he crowned an interrogation with a ritualistic point-blank shot to the prisoner's head, an old habit. This, of course, was not murder: it was the continuation of politics by other means.

But soon the contra war had run its course, and Kurtski began to look for a real big score, something that would keep him in luxury for the rest of his life without working—just fucking and drinking to his heart's content. After all, he was now over sixty, and there was not too much time to waste.

As luck would have it, the telephone rang one night at Kurtski's Washington apartment, where he was resting for a week from the jungles of Honduras and Nicaragua. On answering, he heard a voice from his recent past. It was Bob Dennard, the French patriarch of the great mercenaries, who invited Kurtski to come to Paris for a weekend—all expenses paid—to meet "a new friend." Kurtski was ready for a change in his life; he no longer really gave a shit about the contras, and he was intrigued by the call. Dennard was a trusted companion who never acted without a precise purpose.

In Paris, at the Left Bank apartment of a woman Dennard knew well, Kurtski was introduced to a young Frenchman in a gray suit who said in his accented English, "Mr. Kurtski, we know all about you and we wish to offer you some very interesting and well-paid work."

Kurtski sized him up quickly, concluded the Frenchman was businesslike and for real, and replied that he would like to hear more about this "work."

"But," he added, "what did you say your name is?"

"I didn't because you don't need to know it," the man explained. "I could lie and say that my name is Duclos or Lelong or De Gaulle, but why bother? If we decide to cooperate, it is I who shall be contacting you, not the other way around. So my name doesn't matter."

Kurtski shrugged, saying coldly, "Suit yourself . . . so what do you have in mind?"

The Frenchman outlined briefly, and Kurtski thought with astounding frankness, his superiors' desire to have him set in motion the assassination of Pope Gregory XVII.

"I assume this isn't a joke," Kurtski said. "But I have to know quite a bit more about it. How do you visualize it, what do you propose to pay me, and like that . . . And, of course, I'd like to think about it. It's rather sudden, don't you think?"

"That's fine," the Frenchman replied. "For today, I just wanted to meet you. You were highly recommended by Monsieur Dennard and a few other friends. Yes, do think about it. And I have to report back to my superiors what impression I have gained of you. I suggest that we meet in Rome in exactly one month—and take it from there if we decide to proceed . . . I'll call you a few days ahead of time so that you can make it easily on the appointed day."

Kurtski and the Frenchman met twice in Rome to go over the

emerging plan. At their last meeting they agreed that the best opportunity to kill the pope would be when he flew to the United States in the fall. Meanwhile Kurtski moved to Rome for the duration to start the actual preparations. He picked as his temporary home a small room at Hotel Columbus, the huge gray pile of a building on Via della Conciliazione, a block from St. Peter's Square, where package tours of pilgrims succeeded one another the year round, creating maximal anonymity for its patrons. Kurtski had picked the Columbus in part because of that environment—and in part because he enjoyed waking every morning to see St. Peter's Basilica and the Apostolic Palace when he craned his neck to the left. It gave him a strange sense of identity with the Holy See and the pope he had been retained to help assassinate. He occasionally wondered what Gregory XVII was doing at that moment.

On this particular morning, as his preparatory work to blow up the airborne papal plane had been proceeding smoothly, Kurtski received a telephone call in his room from the young Frenchman. The man sounded gravely preoccupied and there was urgency in his voice. He told Kurtski he needed to see him immediately, proposing that they meet at the sidewalk café below, directly across from the Columbus.

"Our plans have changed drastically," the Frenchman said as soon as he sat down at the little round table, without greetings and the usual pleasantries.

"There is a new priority," he continued almost breathlessly, not his normal businesslike self. "We may have been penetrated. We think we know the identity of the penetrator. He must be killed before we can go ahead with our plans concerning the pope. Unless he is liquidated, as soon as possible, our entire project will be exposed and it will collapse. And my superiors believe that you, Mr. Kurtski, are the man to perform the killing. Nobody else can do it for us. Nobody knows you, nobody knows about our arrangements, nobody can tie you to us. Moreover you are not French. You're perfect for the job."

"Now, wait just a goddamned minute," Kurtski told him, his temper rising. "What do you take me for? I'm not a professional gunman. This isn't what I do. Just forget this whole *focking* idea. There's no way I'm going to go and kill somebody on your say-so, do you understand?"

"You have no choice, Kurtski," the Frenchman said. "You have to cease all your planning for the assassination of the pope until you dispose of the penetrator. It's that simple. And if there is no plan to kill the pope, there'll be no more payments to you. But, on the other hand, you will be paid extra for killing this man . . ."

"I don't care," Kurtski barked. "I won't do it, okay?"

"No, not okay," the Frenchman hissed. "If you refuse, we'll denounce you to the authorities both in France and Italy as the chief plotter against the pope. You see, I've taped our conversations, and we can edit them selectively. And you have no idea who we are! You can't accuse anybody because there's nobody for you to accuse."

Kurtski turned red, his heart beating fast, his breath dangerously shallow.

"You cocksucker," he roared back in rage, defeated and helpless for the first time in his adult life. "So who's the man you want killed?"

"He is a compatriot of yours," the Frenchman said. "He's a Jesuit priest named Timothy Savage. He's in France right now. In the South. We'll meet again tomorrow—I'll tell you later where—and I'll have all the details for you . . ."

Back in his room at the Columbus, Kurtski threw himself on his bed, panting in fury, fearing a heart attack. He felt his normally high blood pressure skyrocketing, his bloated belly pumping inside like a bellow. He grabbed a dead cigar from an ashtray on the bedside table, chewing on it hard to steady his nerves.

"I can't believe it, I can't believe it," he kept repeating to himself. "And it's that *focking* Savage, of all the people in the world."

In Toulouse, Tim Savage was pendering his next step. Having heard and read so much by now in general terms about the Cathar "heresy" and the murderous papal crusade nearly seven centuries ago to eradicate it, he decided that he needed to know considerably more about the Cathars. He had to understand, for example, whether Leduc's own heresy had in any way been inspired by the

Cathars or whether the archbishop had deftly appropriated for his own ends, and accordingly twisted, the Cathar legend, still so powerfully alive and greatly admired in the Languedoc. After all, Cathar leaders had always been know as "the Perfect"—the word *Cathar* being Greek for *perfect*. And it also seemed quite relevant, Tim thought, to determine whether the surge of Protestantism there in the aftermath of the Reform—another historical gem he had unearthed—had formed some sort of antipapist bridge of protest between the Cathars and the modern "integrists." Rome, in any event, had never been very popular in the Languedoc.

To concentrate on his homework on the Cathars, back to the tedium of academic research, Tim had selected—on the recommendation of his friend, the Toulouse priest-librarian—an extraordinary bookstore in the village of Le Somail on the southern bank of the Canal du Midi. The canal is the seventeenth-century hand-dug waterway linking the Atlantic and the Mediterranean along the Pyrénées, one of the most spectacular engineering feats in Europe, sponsored by Louis XIV. The bookstore, Tim had been informed, was not only the Languedoc's, but possibly the world's, greatest depository of Cathar literature and Troubadour lore, and the abode of perhaps the leading living scholar of the Cathar experience.

To reach Le Somail, Tim drove in his rental car from Toulouse to Carcassonne, the ancient walled city, along the Autostrade des Deux-Mers, the Route of the Two Seas, which parallels the great canal. He discovered in the process French drivers' unshakable devotion to tailgating at speeds in excess of eighty miles per hour. From the autostrade, Tim veered to the southeast over secondary highways en route to the bookstore village. For this expedition, Tim had chosen to travel as a "civilian," in sports attire the French call *très cool,* their phrase for casual chic, which also means elegant footwear, but no socks.

Le Somail is so tiny that its two main structures are the barn-like bookstore and a small hotel and restaurant on the other side of the canal. Past the bookstore, Tim found only the Hat Museum, a mysterious institution, closed the entire time of his stay in the village, and a few modest houses. He checked in at the hotel, being the only guest there, and climbed the stairs to the first floor and his minuscule room. From his window, Tim watched the slow passage of a huge barge down the canal toward the Mediterranean. Once a carrier of wheat and wine up and down the waterway, part of a fleet upon which much of the commerce between the two French seacoasts once depended, the barge now carried tourists, a half-dozen of them sitting topside on deck chairs, sipping cocktails. They waved at Tim. Tall plane trees, bordering the length of the canal on both sides, he could see, reflected in the smooth water.

Late in the afternoon, Tim crossed the stone bridge over the canal to visit the bookstore. Monsieur Raymond, the owner, was behind a small desk just inside the entrance, going over credit card slips. His majestic shape—obese would be an understatement—matched perfectly the immensity of the bookstore with its rows of display cases and shelves and stacks of books on the ground floor and along a first-floor galley above.

Monsieur Raymond greeted Tim politely in French, still concentrating on his paperwork. Then he looked up, smiled, and switched into fluent English.

"Oh," he said, "you must be English. Or perhaps American . . . How can I help you?"

"I am American," Tim replied with a smile of his own. "And I am interested in Cathar history. I was told by friends in Toulouse that your bookstore here is a treasure trove on the subject. So here I am."

The bookseller's eyebrows shot up in absolute amazement. With massive effort, he rose from the armchair behind his desk.

"Cathar history?" he asked incredulously. "My God, you are the first American, in fact the first foreigner, to be interested in the Cathars. It's incredible! But, please, tell me why you would care about an obscure heresy seven centuries old?"

"Well," Tim said, "I am a professor of history of religion at Georgetown University back in Washington where I live, and I'm spending several months in France to see what I can learn, even superficially, about medieval heresies. I think they are relevant to the great religious upheavals of our time. I was also told that you personally, *monsieur*, are enormously knowledgeable about the Cathars. If you can spare the time, I would love to ask you a few things."

Tim had been on the verge of saying that he was a Jesuit specializing in Islam, but something in the back of his mind had warned him to conceal his real identity. Perhaps Monsieur Raymond was anticlerical, still a powerful strain in France.

"Why, it will be a pleasure talking to you, sir," Raymond said. "Come to dinner tonight. It's very rare for us to have guests . . ."

"I must warn you that I'm not impartial when it comes to Cathar history," René Raymond, the bookseller told Tim as he poured them wine before the meal. "You see, I'm a direct descendant of Viscount Raimond Roger Trencavel, who was hurled down a pit and left to die as a Cathar leader after the pope's barons conquered Carcassonne in 1209. In those days, the name Raymond, my name, was spelled with an 'i,' making it *Raimond*. The Viscount was a nephew of the ruler of Toulouse, Count Raimond VI. So I'm really part not only of a royal Languedoc family, but Cathar history as well."

"Well," Tim said, "this is quite an honor to be with you. And I'm so lucky to have found you. I've been reading, of course, about the Cathars, their doctrine of dualism, their rejection of the orthodox doctrines of the Church in Rome, and so forth. But I must confess that I am completely confused by all that I've read . . . And as I hear you say, as you did a moment ago, that you can't be impartial about Cathar history, I frankly have the impression that you are speaking of the past as well as of the present, that it's all still very much alive. Am I wrong?"

"No, you are not wrong, my friend," Raymond answered, shifting his huge body on the sofa where he sat in the living room of the house behind the bookstore. Tim was in an ample armchair facing his host. The living room, too, was overflowing with books.

"You are very perceptive and you are quite right in observing that Catharism—let's call it that—is quite alive in a whole variety of ways," he went on. "People in the Languedoc and elsewhere are very much aware that Catharism and Cathar history remain a reality, and are not merely some heresy from early in the millennium that had been extirpated and basically forgotten. When I say that I'm not impartial about Catharism, I mean that I firmly believe that the Cathars were right in their interpretation of the Christian religion, that they continue to be right today, and that this whole matter has not been resolved by the crusades, massacres, and burnings at the stake of uncounted thousands of Cathar families in the thirteenth and fourteenth centuries. In fact, I regard myself as a militant Cathar. I am not a *perfect,* but I'm a *believer.*"

"This is most extraordinary," Tim said, not quite sure what else to say. He knew that the Cathars had been the most extreme of all heretic sects to oppose the Roman Church, considered by the Church its greatest enemy, but he had not been prepared to run into a fiery, present-day spokesman for Catharism, preaching the doctrine as if the battle were still actively being waged. And perhaps it was. Tim felt he was in a blur of today's realities and the imagined and remembered past of many centuries ago. And Raymond was deepening this impression as he held forth on the unchanging relevance of Catharism.

"We shall never forgive Rome and the popes for the enormity of the crime they had committed against us, the Cathars, with the crusade of Pope Innocent III, the Inquisition, and the killings that went on and on," he told Tim. "That was the first act of genocide, the first Holocaust, as we would now call it, in history. It was religious cleansing. And Rome, even with the supposedly progressive popes like Leo XIII, John XXIII, and even Gregory XVII today, has not admitted her error, apologized in a Christian spirit, and extended to us the hand of reconciliation. So Rome remains the enemy."

"What I haven't quite grasped," Tim said, "is the reason the Church attacked the Cathars with such fury. Weren't they the kindest, gentlest, most moral of all Christians? Shouldn't Rome have applauded their piety and rigorous morality? If I understand it correctly, they weren't challenging Rome over power or leadership."

"No, of course, not," Raymond answered. "The Cathars were not out to grab power in southern France any more than in Lombardy or in Bulgaria or Bosnia where, as you know, the Bogomils are said to have launched what is now known as our Cathar 'heresy.' You mentioned piety, but even I must admit that piety produces heretics as well as saints—and this was probably what happened with the Cathars, if you insist that they truly were heretics."

They moved to the table in the adjoining room where a maid awaited them with a huge pot of *cassoulet,* and Tim picked up the thread of their discussion before dinner.

"I understand that the 'heresy' wasn't a power grab by the Cathars in the normal sense of the word," he said, "but, at the same time, they seemed to turn into spiritual rivals of the Roman Church, and I assume that if successful, they would deprive the popes, such as Innocent III, of influence and therefore of secular, political power. Would you agree with that, I mean as a process of political dynamics?"

Raymond laughed with appreciation, patting Tim on the shoulder with his left hand while pouring them with the right hand Clos Centeilles, a fine wine from Minerve in northern Languedoc.

"This wine comes from Pouzols-Minervois vineyards," he said. "I don't want to spoil your dinner, but Minerve, the very old fortress town on a bluff not far from here, on the other side of the Canal, was the site of one of the most savage ravages of the Cathars by the armies of the pope and of the King of France, our other sworn enemy. At least 140 Cathars, men and women, were burned at the stake when Minerve was captured in 1210; it was one of the first massacres of the crusade. Anyway, let us drink a toast of Minervois wine to the memory of the martyrs of Minerve."

They drank the toast, and Raymond returned to Cathar history.

"Yes, you have a point about the interpretation of religions and political dynamics," he said. "And you must bear in mind that the Cathars had their own, different ideas about religion and the Church. They did regard themselves as the true Church of God, which naturally rankled Rome. They believed that, like Christ's, their destiny were persecution and martyrdom, and were convinced that, under the doctrine of dualism, the organized Catholic structure represented the devil. And because the Cathar message was very widely accepted in this part of the world in those days, the Cathars, whether they realized it or not, were inviting the reprisals by Rome, which, of course, did understand the political process. When attacked, as they were during that Albigensian crusade that lasted twenty years beginning at the start of the thirteenth century, they fought back like mountain lions. But even if Innocent III resorted to force to protect his power structure, there was no excuse for the wave of inhumane, never mind anti-Christian, destruction of people wrought by such commanders as Simon de Monfort and their armies. Hitler could have learned from them . . .

"The established Church in Rome believes in continuity," Raymond went on, "and so do we. This means, as I told you before, that the Cathars will regard it as its greatest enemy forever—unless it repents. The Albi Crusade—it's called that because the movement was born in the Languedoc around the town of Albi in the twelfth century—will never be forgotten or forgiven. And, mind you, Professor, that to this day, even as we speak, there are masses of people here, in the south of France, who feel very strongly about it. It is a powerful spiritual force."

"Still," Tim insisted, "how do we reconcile this spirit of vengefulness, if I understand you correctly, with the goodness and sweetness of the Cathars, the merciful behavior of the 'Perfects' as leaders, the chaste life they prescribed, and all their other attributes?"

"We reconcile it," Raymond answered, "in the same way as the 'Perfects' and their followers thought it was natural to fight to the death, killing as many enemies as possible to defend their faith. That's why they willingly died and enthusiastically killed in the defense of Béziers, Minerve, Montségur, and all their other towns and fortresses . . . You know, eye for an eye, and so forth . . . And we have very long memories . . ."

"I have one more question before I go back to my hotel," Tim said with extreme care, articulating an idea that had begun to form in his mind as he listened to Raymond.

"Please, go ahead and ask," the bookseller encouraged him. "Our stories and our lives are open books."

"How, in your opinion, would people who think of themselves as Cathars respond if other French Catholics, who hate Rome for other reasons, were to propose the ultimate vengeance—the assassination of the pope?"

Raymond stiffened, his eyes narrowed, and he rose from the table.

"This is one question to which I have no answer and do not wish to contemplate," he said slowly. "It was a pleasure to have you at my home . . ."

"My next stop is the seminary in Mirepoix," Tim said, mainly to have the last word. "I'll ask the same question there. . . ."

Chapter Twenty-one

IF AN ALLIANCE EXISTED between the Cathars and the Pius V Fraternity, sharing their hatred of Rome, potentially it could be quite an explosive one, Tim Savage thought as he drove from Le Somail toward Carcassonne over empty Languedoc roads.

The Cathars, if Raymond the bookseller was to be believed, never forgave the papacy for the massacres of the crusade in the thirteenth century and the continued killings well into the next century. Did Raymond's resentful, brusque reaction to Tim's question about likely Cathar sentiments toward conspiracies to assassinate the pope mean that he had hit a nerve and touched upon a reality? Or was he simply insulted, as a "militant Cathar," over Tim's insinuation?

At the same time, there was no doubt about the Fraternity's hatred of the papal institution over the modernization of the Church by Vatican Council II, hatred that extended to Gregory XVII for moving ahead with the reforms. Conversely, Rome today could not tolerate the Fraternity's rebellion any more than Innocent III tolerated the Cathar heresy.

It was astounding, Tim thought, how differences in the interpretation of faith and liturgy within the same religion could arouse murderous passions, often lasting for centuries. It was true of Christianity, as it was true, among other examples, with Islam, squaring off the Sunis versus the Shiites and the Sufis. Internecine religious hatreds were often deeper than those *between* rival religions; there is nothing worse than feuds within a family, for they have a way of turning into blood feuds, if not stopped early.

There was, however, the danger of jumping to exaggerated conclusions about any alliances. The Cathars were not a structured clandestine organization—they had a scholarly Center of Cathar studies on a busy shopping street in downtown Carcassonne, and they published a learned quarterly of Cathar Studies in the little town of Fanjeaux where Saint Dominic once preached *against* the Cathars. The *Pays Cathare,* the land of Cathars, was indeed a tourist attraction in the Languedoc, with pamphlets portraying in color the ruins of Montségur, Béziers, Minerve, Montaillou, and other ancient Cathar settlements and fortresses where the "Good Men" and "Good Women," as the heretics called themselves, were burned at the stake, decapitated, defenestrated, and massacred by papal crusaders. It was medieval folklore, and none of it was even remotely sinister in the modern context.

This fact naturally ruled out any formal alliances, Tim concluded as he reached the outskirts of Carcassonne and its industrial suburbs. But, he decided, the basic idea ought not be discarded altogether. A right-wing, if not downright reactionary, brand of Catholicism was remarkably strong in southern France—as were right-wing politics—and it was quite plausible that those still faithful to Cathar ideals and traditions would be active supporters of the Fraternity and its fight against Rome. They would be likely to favor the ancient church rules and rites that Vatican II had buried. The Fraternity, of course, was a public religious institution though it did not follow that everything it did in its endeavors was public or publicized. Thus, involvement on the part of individual Cathars would add to its strength and reputation. Cathars and Catharism were highly popular and respected in the *Pays Cathare.* Besides, Archbishop Leduc was anxious to expand his following, and the Fraternity proselytized in a discreet manner. It cost a lot of money to run his organization's far-flung activities.

What intrigued Tim the most was whether people of Cathar persuasion, however it could be defined nowadays, were being manipulated by the Fraternity of St. Pius V for very specific purposes. For reasons of Cathar history, still thinking of their region as a giant battlefield, they might be fertile ground for anti-papal sentiment leading to decisive action. Why, for example, had Raymond, the bookseller, reacted so angrily to Tim's question about the Cathars and the pope? Was he sympathetic to the Fraternity because his hatred of Rome over the anti-Cathar crusade dovetailed so neatly with Leduc's contemporary ire?

*   *   *

Action was very much on the minds of four men gathered in the late afternoon later that week in the elegant ground-floor library of a large eighteenth-century mansion on a rural estate known as "Les Homs" below the hilltop town of Fanjeaux and a quarter-mile over a sandy lane from the highway running southwest from Carcassonne to Mirepoix. It was a walled estate, sitting alone in an empty field with cyprus trees hiding it from view. Stone towers at the four rounded corners on the roof of the four-story structure afforded its inhabitants protection. The iron gates guarding the courtyard were padlocked, and there were black iron shutters over the mansion's windows. Two cars were parked in the courtyard. On the wide terrace leading to the main entrance, three athletic young men in dark suits stood silently, arms akimbo.

In the library, its walls covered with precious Gobelin tapestries above the bookcases, the four men sat around a beautifully polished oak table, conversing intensely in low voices. Three of them had come to "Les Homs" urgently summoned by Bishop Charles Laval, who had been informed about Tim Savage and the imam. The youthful-looking bishop, who resided at the mansion, was one of Leduc's deputies. Rotund and hard-eyed, Laval had worked for him in Casablanca as private secretary, and was the first to be consecrated by Leduc after the founding of the Fraternity, a major act of defiance of Rome that Gregory XVII had chosen to tolerate that one time. Laval's own private secretary, a mousy middle-aged priest blessed with an infinitely inventive mind, sat next to him. The young Frenchman in a gray suit, who served as the Fraternity's chief of security and liaison for foreign operations, was at the other side of the table. And next to him the chair was occupied by Jake Kurtski, who had arrived from Rome, via Toulouse, that morning with the security chief, who had finally admitted that his first name was Jean-Pierre. Kurtski was not concealing his annoyance, staring at the ceiling decorated with frescoes of a posse of flying angels in pastel colors, and chewing on his usual dead cigar.

For one thing, Kurtski did not understand a word of the conversation conducted in French among the three Fraternity of St. Pius V men. Jean-Pierre addressed him in English only as required—to ask quick questions and relay instructions—and Kurtski was furious at being treated dismissively as a servant.

"Do we have any idea where this American Jesuit is to be found at this point and what he is doing?" Bishop Laval asked the security chief, sounding highly impatient.

"Well, Excellency," Jean-Pierre replied, "we are not certain. We know, of course, that he was in Toulouse last week, when he met with the Muslims and you had the call from the prelate at St. Adalbert's telling you about it. As soon as you informed me, I phoned the imam on the off chance that the Jesuit had given some indication concerning his plans, but he had not . . . It also occurred to me to inquire at the Jesuit Residence in Toulouse, but they didn't know where he went. He was not returning there. But we did have some luck this morning, Excellency . . ."

"What happened?" the bishop inquired, leaning forward.

"Our old friend Raymond, that bookseller in Le Somail, called my office to report that an American professor of religion had come to see him yesterday," Jean-Pierre said. "He wasn't dressed like a Jesuit and didn't tell Raymond that he was a Jesuit. But it must be the same person . . . Raymond became very suspicious when, at the end of the evening, the American asked how Cathars would feel about an assassination of the pope. He thought that he should call our attention to it immediately . . . The American spent the night at the local hotel, but, of course, he has already left . . . And, yes, he told Raymond that he planned to visit our seminary at Mirepoix. That's all we know so far, Excellency."

"Yes, it all makes sense, but, unfortunately . . ." The Bishop thought for a moment. "I suspect that Raymond's call confirms that the Jesuit is busy tracking the matter of Gregory XVII. His question about the Cathars obviously was not accidental. I can't imagine why and how he located the imam in Toulouse, but now the fact is that the secret is no longer a secret—and we may be facing a terrible crisis . . . I've already mentioned to the Archbishop the priest's call from Toulouse, and he is very disturbed . . ."

Jean-Pierre and the private secretary nodded, and Bishop Laval went on, analyzing the situation.

"But we must be rational about it," he said. "First things first . . . To begin with, we must assume that the Jesuit already has, or will very soon, communicated his findings about the 1981 attempt to the persons on whose behalf he is acting. I can't believe that he is doing it on his own. It could be on behalf of Rome, but the Jesuits aren't getting along so well with the pope. Still, we know nothing about him. In fact, our top priority must be to learn exactly who he is. We have friends in Rome who could help . . ."

"Absolutely," the security chief agreed, making a note.

"If Rome has been informed about 1981," the bishop continued, "the consequences could be devastating. It is, of course, possible that Gregory XVII will keep silent about this whole subject. I'm not convinced that the pope has much to gain at this point from going public. After all, he is a rational Frenchman. Yet, we cannot take chances."

"That's a good point, Excellency," his private secretary commented. "We can cut our losses up to a point if the Holy See keeps its mouth shut, and I'm inclined to think that it will. The pope needs no new scandals and problems in the Church. I fear, however, that we have to suspend our planning for the new action—at least until the situation is clarified. And buy ourselves some protection . . ."

He cleared his throat and signaled that he had more to say.

"The whole thing has become incredibly complicated," he went on. "We cannot rule out the danger that, no matter what, the facts behind the assassination attempts will surface in some fashion . . . and then a revolt could develop within the Fraternity itself. Obviously, only very few of us are aware of the truth and of the Archbishop's thinking. An awful lot of our brothers and sisters, who haven't quite reached *our* level of analyzing and correctly interpreting the Archbishop's commands, may be appalled and shocked by our actions. We could lose followers on a vast scale. Whatever we do, we must remain watchful, alert, and extremely careful. Therefore no new efforts to achieve our objectives.

"Naturally," the bishop said harshly. "All preparations must be put on hold. In the meantime, we cannot afford to let the American Jesuit run around loose. Even if he doesn't say a word of what he knows, he remains an enormous danger to us. If nothing else, we cannot proceed with any of our plans so long as he remains alive. His death is a fundamental necessity. In sentencing him, I feel that we are acting as if we were an ecclesiastic tribunal in the old days. So he must be located and the sentence carried out. But, in God's name, find him quickly."

Jean-Pierre turned to Kurtski, speaking to him in English.

"The orders I gave you in Rome have been reconfirmed," he said. "You are to track down this Father Timothy Savage and execute him on the spot. Of course, we shall help you to find him. He cannot be very far from here. In fact, we have an idea where he might be."

"*Fock* you," Kurtski replied evenly. "It will be done, one way or another. And I'll do it but just make sure I get paid . . ."

Bishop Laval rose to signal the end of the meeting. Taking Jean-Pierre aside, he whispered, "Why don't you coordinate with our friends at SDECE in Paris? Perhaps you should talk with your pal Sainte-Ange there, and tell him what's happening. Remember how helpful they were to us with de Marenches?"

One of the things the Jesuit librarian had told him in passing, Tim remembered, was that the Pius V Fraternity had a seminary for its priests in the town of Mirepoix, not far from Carcassonne. It was run as openly as any other Catholic seminary. Interestingly, Mirepoix had been the site of a synod of "Good Christians"—the Cathars—in 1206. The first fact was most relevant to Tim as he pondered where to turn next. A visit to the Fraternity's seminary, he decided, would be the logical step at this juncture. He was unaware of the existence of any other public Fraternity institutions, and therefore he had no choice, regardless of risk. The second fact, that a Cathar synod had been held in Mirepoix over 780 years ago with 600 heretic knights in attendance, was totally irrelevant, except in the symbolic sense of interactions and overlapping currents in the religious history of southern France. However, he thought, it served as a good explanation to Raymond, the bookseller, of his announced plan to visit Mirepoix.

In Carcassonne, Tim picked up an armful of pamphlets at the Center of Cathar Studies. The next day, he set out in his rented car for Mirepoix. About halfway, he passed Fanjeaux, lording over the landscape from its steep hill, another monument to the religious past that refused to go away. A sign along the highway identified Fanjeaux with St. Dominic.

Mirepoix, as he saw upon entering it from the highway in midafternoon, was a jewel of a medieval town tucked away off the beaten path of modern tourist travel in the gently undulating foothills of the central Pyrénées. The five or six thousand people to whom Mirepoix is home and the farmers from the surrounding countryside do not at all mind this privacy of isolation, though they are content to welcome occasional tourists driving to Carcassonne or the Principality of Andorra in the high mountain passes to the south.

The Mirepoix people are well-off and pleased with their lives, and on warm-weather afternoons, once or twice a week, they gather to dance old-fashioned dances to the exhilarating music of accordions, guitars, trumpets, and violins on the concrete floor of the municipal open market, cleared of its stalls for the occasion, next to the arcades of Mirepoix's rectangular main square. They really have fun, these middle-aged farm couples and the young and elderly town dwellers. And, of course, everybody knows everybody. Tim, having registered at the little hotel behind the square, strolled over to sit in a sidewalk café and watch them enjoy themselves, a vanishing art, even in rural France.

Settled a millennium or so ago, Mirepoix has a rich history, what with the endless power rivalries and, as everywhere else in the Languedoc, religious feuds and wars. At one point, the whole region was ruled by both the king of France and the king of England. As far back as 1143, when records began to be scribbled in monks' calligraphy, Mirepoix had declared its fealty to Raimon Roger, the Count of Foix, who reigned over his independent mountain fief. He must have been an ancestor of Monsieur Raymond, the bookseller, Tim thought as he scanned the local tourist pamphlet with its smattering of history. The count and Mirepoix were firmly anticlerical, battling the bishops of the established Roman Catholic Church for sway over the Pyrénées area. It was nearly a century *before* the Cathar wars, but it solidified the climate in which the count's descendants would later welcome to Mirepoix men and women whom the Holy See already regarded as heretics. This had been solid Cathar country, starting with the aristocracy.

Having resolved to pay a visit to the seminary, Tim was uncertain whether, if it worked well, he should try to obtain through its Father Superior an appointment with Archbishop Leduc. All the signs, he believed, now pointed in the archbishop's direction and, sooner or later, he would have to meet him. Otherwise, Tim would have to report to Monsignor Sainte-Ange that his inquiry would come to a halt. Actually, he was not sure whether he in fact had the authority to set in motion what might well become a confrontation with the archbishop; this might not be proper in terms of protocol for an obscure Jesuit; Tim, of course, planned to appear at the seminary in clerical garb. He would sleep on the Leduc quandary, then see how matters developed at the seminary. His instinct warned him against contacting Sainte-Ange. He would have loved, however, to hear Sister Angela's voice, along with her advice. Since Paris, Tim kept thinking about her much of the time—during his long drives, trying to fall asleep at night.

The following morning, Tim went unannounced to the Fraternity seminary. Guided by directions from the hotel clerk, he drove southwest for about three miles to the unmarked entrance to a large estate, a wide open gate in an enclosure of fences covered with greenery. Turning left past the gate on to a long tree-shaded driveway, Tim saw ahead a Provençal-style three-story mansion, gleaming white in the morning sun, and lesser structures surrounding it. There was a touch of an American college campus about the estate, Tim thought. As he neared the main building, he noticed priests in cassocks and younger men in less formal clerical attire coming and going relaxedly over well tended lawns, skirting spectacular flower beds. Tim was reminded of his Jesuit seminary back in Pennsylvania. The Mirepoix campus was so pleasantly peaceful, so removed from the tensions and conflicts of the outside world.

Tim parked his car against the mansion's western wall, among a dozen or more shiny Citroëns and Renaults, and walked over to the main door. The reception hall was roomy and cool, and a pale young priest sat behind the front desk. An oversize color photograph of a stern archbishop in full regalia, wearing the miter, reigned over the room from the white wall behind the reception desk. It had to be Archbishop Leduc, and Tim again had the impression that the face looked vaguely familiar and, again, he could not place it. Perhaps he just remembered it from newspaper photographs accompanying stories about the Fraternity of St. Pius V's activities. A small painting of the Lourdes Virgin, an amateurish effort, hung on the right of Leduc's photo portrait, along with a crucified Christ sculpted in what looked like ivory. The archbishop must have brought it back from Africa. Next to Christ, Pius V stared into the distance from another amateurish painting—he was not as large as Leduc. Pope Gregory XVII was nowhere to be seen.

"Good morning, Father." The priest-receptionist surprised Tim with the greeting in American English. "Welcome to our seminary. And what can we do for you?"

"Well, I was hoping to take a quick look around, if it's not too inconvenient," he replied, without showing his surprise. To remain stone-faced in every imaginable situation, no matter how sudden and unexpected, was one of the many useful things the CIA had taught Tim. "But how did you know to address me in English? Don't I just look like any other Jesuit?"

"I guess not," the priest said with a patient smile. "You look like an *American* Jesuit, Father . . . Ah, I could tell it right away. You see, I'm from California, from Sausalito, and we American priests can sense one another instantly, even in the Languedoc. Yes, sir . . . And, of course, we would be delighted to show you around the seminary. It's a relatively new one, but we're very proud of it. Actually, Abbé Loïc, our equivalent of General Superior, will be happy to give you a personal guided tour, Father Savage . . ."

This time, Tim had to try even harder to dissemble how taken aback he was. He had a sinking feeling, sensing that his carefully prepared act had been betrayed. Tim was determined not to ask how the priest, and indeed the seminary, knew his name—and that he was coming this very morning. He may have been discovered, but he had to go on playing the game. He could not let his mission unravel at the first obstacle.

"That is too generous on the abbé's part," he said. "He must be very busy and I'd hate to disturb him . . ."

"Not to worry, Father," the Californian told him. "The abbé is awaiting you in his study . . . and with great coffee! Please follow me."

Abbé Loïc was a big, beefy man in his fifties, exuding enthusiasm and good cheer. Standing at the door just inside his study, he opened his arms to embrace Tim, giving him no opportunity to resist the rapid gesture. The Abbé smelled of garlic, not an uncommon phenomenon in southern France.

"It's an honor and a pleasure to receive you, Father Savage," the Abbé said in English, releasing Tim from his steel embrace. "We've heard so much about you."

"And I've heard so much about the Fraternity and the seminary," Tim answered, wondering just *what* the abbé knew about him—surely not about his Islam expertise. "So I took advantage of touring this part of France on my vacation to drop in on the seminary as an uninvited guest. I thought I'd just take a quick look without being a nuisance . . ."

Now he knew he had to be extremely careful—and creative. He was in a dangerous—possibly lethal—game over which he had very little control. Tim knew he was trapped, not quite understanding how it had happened. Where had he slipped, given himself away? Had he been betrayed and, if so, by whom? Had the Fraternity been on his scent all the while he believed he was on *its* scent? For the first time since Vietnam, he feared for his life.

The moves on the chessboard were suddenly being played in reverse, and the Fraternity could checkmate him at any moment. The idea entered his mind that his adversaries could simply liquidate him in a mountain highway "accident," or something similar. If, indeed, they did try to kill the pope, they certainly would not hesitate to do away with an unknown Jesuit.

Among survival skills, physical and psychological, in the event they were captured, the CIA taught its officers—most fundamentally—to exercise maximal self-control in order to remain calm, regardless of provocation, and be able to plan countermoves and escape routes. This was what Tim was hoping to do in response to the Fraternity's next moves. Beyond that, his destiny was in God's hands, an ironic state of affairs considering it was a face-off among priests of the same faith. In any case, Tim could no longer lead insouciantly his double life: an arms dealer or a professor of religion one day, a Jesuit priest the next. Henceforth it would be the Society of Jesus for him, full time and no disguises.

"I understand that you studied and taught at Georgetown University," Abbé Loïc said. "A very famous Jesuit center . . . But I, too, had a bit of experience with the American education system. Way back, in the late 1960s, I spent a semester on a fellowship at the Divinity School at Harvard, and, my God, how I did love it and how I loved Cambridge. The Charles River . . . We must chat about it at dinner tonight . . . Yes, of course, you are our guest here, and I want you to spend at least one night with us to get to know how we live and function in provincial France. Nothing as inspiring as your Jesuit seminary at Warnersville, but we hope you will like it."

"It's so kind of you to be so hospitable to a guest who descended on you out of the blue," he said, aware of how stilted it sounded. They were like two actors reading lines from a script.

"Shall we take a look at the seminary?" Abbé Loïc proposed, getting up. They had been sitting at a low table in the corner of the study, sipping the abbé's coffee. It *was* excellent, Tim acknowledged to himself. Was it like the last cup of coffee before the prisoner is executed on death row?

The abbé conducted Tim through airy classrooms in three academic buildings on the campus, each room decorated with portraits of Pope Pius V and Archbishop Leduc who seemed to watch over the seminarians' progress. He introduced Tim to the professors: philosophy, theology, history of the Church with emphasis on the Council of Trent in the sixteenth century, lives of great Saints and Fathers and Doctors of the Church, life stories of Pius V and Pius X, liturgy, ethics, sociology, and advanced Latin, Greek and Hebrew. A most impressive curriculum, Tim had to admit. There must have been sixty or seventy students attending the seminary, vastly more than at any other seminary with which Tim was familiar, and an unusual number of middle-aged men. What, he wondered, prompted so many late vocations? Most of the students were French, it appeared, but as the abbé pointed out, there were Swiss, Belgian, German, Austrian, and even a few American pupils among them.

"Our teachings, you know, have a very wide appeal in this savage world," he said. "You see here our Church being reborn."

Tim and his host lunched, abundant Languedoc style, in a refectory that resembled an American college cafeteria, confining their conversation to comments about the religious education in seminaries in France and the United States. Tim had resolved not to plunge into dangerous waters, to remain passive. Abbé Loïc also seemed content with pleasantries and platitudes. Tim spent the afternoon napping in his room in the seminary's guest cottage, faithful to another CIA training admonition: in difficult situations, get all the rest you can so that you may be relaxed, on your guard, and ready for everything.

In the early evening, soon after Angelus prayers, the abbé came to escort Tim to his house for dinner. It was a comfortable home, with Provençal furnishings, bookcases in all the downstairs rooms, a small altar in the corner of the living room, with large paintings of Pius V and Pius X—none of Gregory XVII—and an autographed color photograph of Archbishop Leduc in a place of honor on the wall.

After they prayed, the abbé opened a bottle of red Fitou, and signaled to the nun across the room to begin serving. As soon as Tim tasted the first tablespoon of fish soup, his host turned to him without a trace of the bonhomie he had displayed all day.

"Our friend the bookseller, Monsieur Raymond, tells us of your interest in medieval heresies," he said accusingly. "He also tells us that you had presented yourself as a professor, concealing your identity as a priest without a valid reason, which, by the way, is a sin. Would you care to explain your behavior?"

"As it happens," Tim replied carefully, "I am, as a scholar, quite interested in heresies. And since you seem to know so much about me, you must be aware of my scholarly work at the Vatican. Furthermore, it's been drilled into me from my first day in France that so many of you are still so anticlerical that it's often easier to do religious research without identifying oneself as a priest. Hasn't that crossed your mind, Father?"

"Well," the abbé said, sounding more conciliatory, "the thing is that we must be very protective of our sacred work, and perhaps we overreact in unexpected situations. And you *were* unexpected when you turned up at the bookshop on the canal. And, yes, we also know about your meetings with Muslims in Toulouse . . ."

Tim ate his soup in silence. How *did* they know? There are no miracles in intelligence work, even when it deals with God's religion. But there are double-dealings, double agents, double betrayals on every conceivable level. The craft of intelligence must have been invented by the Church at the dawn of Christendom to survive as an institution. Was that why so many key CIA career people were Catholics? Abbé Loïc had made the next move after the obvious attempt to unnerve him by revealing, a bit smugly, that his cover had been blown and that the Fraternity was aware of his dealings with the Muslims. But it was unclear how much he knew about his basic mission, so Tim had to go on being patient, awaiting the endgame.

Roast fowl was brought to the table and the abbé picked up his train of thought, now looking at Tim with a slight smile.

"All right," he said. "I understand that, as a scholar, you are interested in heresies. After all, they are part of the history of the Church. But from what you know about us, do you believe that the Fraternity is a heresy? You know, something tells me that you are more interested in us, as hypothetical heretics, than in the Cathars . . ."

"I cannot answer that," Tim told him. "I am not a theologian and it is way beyond my competence to render judgments of such significance. All I know, in broad outlines, is what the Holy See has expressed publicly on the subject."

"Would you like to learn more about us?" the abbé asked.

"Well, yes, of course I would," Tim said. "You mean here at the seminary?"

"No," Abbé Loïc answered. "There is a better way. The Archbishop would be pleased to talk to you about the Fraternity, to acquaint you with it. In fact, I've been told that he will be free to receive you early tomorrow afternoon at his place."

Somehow they never got around to chatting over dinner about Harvard, Cambridge, divinity schools, and seminaries.

*   *   *

At "Les Homs" mansion, Jean-Pierre, having just received a call from Abbé Loïc, knocked on the door of Jake Kurtski's fourth-floor room a few minutes after midnight, awakening him from a deep sleep. Kurtski had downed a half-bottle of Absolut vodka before passing out.

"Kurtski," he said, "Be ready to hit the road the first thing in the morning. Your work awaits you . . . I'll tell you more before departure. Be downstairs at seven o'clock."

Then, Jean-Pierre placed a call to Paris, to Georges de Sainte-Ange, the head of the French secret service.

"Sorry to disturb you so late at home," he said, "but I thought you'd like to know that we've found our man. Tomorrow is the big day. We're counting on your guys. . . ."

Chapter Twenty-two

IT WAS JUST too damned easy, Tim worried as he lay in bed in his guest cottage room reviewing the day's alarming events. Whereas he had had doubts and reservations when he went to the seminary about requesting a meeting with Archbishop Leduc, it was now being offered to him on a silver plate. It was literally too good to be true. Tim knew he was not being invited to see the archbishop: he was commanded, no, *ordered,* to appear before the old man with no time being wasted. Why?

In fact he was the Fraternity's prisoner at the seminary and about to be offered sacrificially to the archbishop. They clearly regarded *him* as enemy, and the question was whether the St. Pius V Fraternity hoped to co-opt him, bring him over to its side by convincing him of the validity of its beliefs, or neutralize him, one way or another. His realistic inclination was to think that the latter was probably the case.

Tossing and turning in his bed, Tim wondered at the same time about how much the Fraternity, or its top men, actually knew about his mission. Yes, they were aware in some fashion of his session with the Muslim council in Toulouse, but he could not be certain how much they actually knew of what he had been told. By the same token, it did not follow that they had also heard of his meeting with the Stalingrad imam in Paris, let alone his trip to Istambul. They had heard from Monsieur Raymond that Tim had asked him how the Cathars might react to the notion of killing Gregory XVII, but all this did not necessarily suggest that he had actually discovered the conspiracy and its origins.

It was like playing blind man's buff, along with chess, with each party unsure of what the other knew. All things considered, Tim reasoned, this fact gave him a relative advantage—for the time being. Thus Archbishop Leduc was suddenly so anxious to meet him, Tim deduced, to discover his mission, just as he was anxious to ask questions of the archbishop. Presumably, Leduc would decide afterward what ultimately was to be done with Tim. He felt his professional juices rising as he mentally blessed his CIA mentors and prepared for combat.

In the morning, the abbé joined Tim at breakfast in the cafeteria.

"I trust you slept well," he said engagingly, "and that your morning prayers—I think I can guess what they were—will be answered. You have a most interesting day ahead of you."

"Yes, Father, I know," Tim responded with equal joviality. "I'm really looking forward to my meeting with the archbishop."

"Indeed, you will find it fascinating," the abbé went on. "And you won't have to go very far from here. The archbishop's residence is the Cisterian abbey of Villelongue in a little valley just below the old Saissac castle on the slope of the *Montagne Noire,* the Black Mountain. It faces Fanjeaux, the little hilltop town you must have passed on your way here to Mirepoix. It's less than an hour away . . . At the entrance to Fanjeaux, on a little square just off the highway, there is a café, and somebody from the abbey will meet you there to show you the way to the archbishop's residence."

The abbé embraced Tim in warm farewell, and watched him get into his green rental Peugeot in the parking lot and drive away toward the exit from the seminary campus and the highway. Once Tim had turned right toward Mirepoix, a black Citroën pulled out of the lot and proceeded at a considerable distance in the same direction. It was driven by a young man wearing a dark suit, and his companion was similiarly attired. Their car had a tall antenna for the two-way radio.

In the courtyard at "Les Homs," Jean-Pierre led Jake Kurtski to a black Citroën with a radio antenna. The Fraternity received a discount on Citroëns.

"Get in," the Frenchman said. "I'll drive you to work."

"And here's your piece," he added, handing Kurtski a heavy 9-mm caliber automatic pistol with a silencer, "and two extra clips, just in case."

Kurtski stuck the weapon in the waistband of his trousers, his checkered sports jacket helping to conceal it. He had a splitting headache from the previous evening's vodka, but his hand never trembled when he held a weapon, even with the worst hangover.

Traveling the short distance from "Les Homs" to Fanjeaux in Jean-Pierre's car, Kurtski closed his eyes and let his mind wander over the past and present in eager anticipation of the encounter with Tim Savage. How weird and extraordinary, he mused, that the final chapter in the Vietnam Phoenix battles would be played out—to the death—between two CIA counterinsurgency veterans in the serene beauty of the foothills of the Pyrénées, literally a world away from their last clash in the Mekong Delta.

Much as he detested today's role of gunman, Kurtski was pleased that Tim Savage was the designated target: it was some kind of justice, though he never thought in poetic or divine terms. In fact, it was settling old scores after Savage's cowardly insubordination in that village. He had always regarded Savage as chicken, pussy, a wuss who probably was a queer for good measure. That must have been why Savage had become a priest—to have some of that tasty fucking of young boys. Yeah, if Kurtski was to kill anybody, it might as well be Savage—with pleasure.

The late September sun was already high in the Languedoc sky when Tim reached Fanjeaux atop its steep hill. It had stood there forever, at least since Roman days when it served as a center of trade and communications in the region. The Romans had erected there a temple dedicated to Jupiter, calling it Fanum Jovis, after their chief deity; in time, Fanum Jovis became Fanjeaux. Later, it turned into a great Cathar center and St. Dominic's favorite site to preach against Catharism early in the thirteenth century. From its height of 1,100 feet, Fanjeaux, the ancient fortress town, dominated the countryside as far as the eye could see.

Tim left the highway before it began its descent toward the central Languedoc plain, pulling up at the café on the square at the entrance to the town. He walked inside, looking around for whomever was supposed to meet him there, but the place was empty, except for the owner in a baseball cap busy behind the zinc counter. Tim went tense as he had in the Mekong Delta when action was about to start. But something was wrong. Just then, the black Citroën from the seminary halted at the edge of the highway, below the square.

"Okay," the driver said into the radio handset, "he's arrived at the café. Now he is entering it . . ."

"Good," came the answer. "Stay there for now and keep your eyes open. Report immediately anything you see that is out of the ordinary."

"Roger," said the driver, who was addicted to American police television shows and movies. "And here are the other guys . . ."

An identical black Citroën had driven up the incline of the highway from the plain in the northeast, turned right, gained the square, and came up to a stop in front of the café, next to Tim's green rental car. The timing was perfectly synchronized, down to the second.

"All right," Jean-Pierre told Kurtski. "This is the place. That's where he is. Now go and do it . . ."

Kurtski grunted, producing the pistol, lengthened by the silencer, from his waistband, and pushed open the door of the café. Tim's back was turned to him, and Kurtski raised the gun in his right hand for a bull's-eye single shot in the head. But Tim, all his senses sharpened, heard the door and the soft steps, wheeled around, and crouched. The bullet whistled harmlessly over his left shoulder, and Tim hurled himself at Kurtski, knocking him down. The pistol fell out of Kurtski's hand onto the floor.

Tim looked down at the prostrate man. It took him a moment of utter disbelief to recognize Kurtski. What on earth was Kurtski doing there in the Languedoc town trying to kill him? Why was he interfering with Tim's mission? On whose behalf was he acting? Kurtski, to be sure, had hated his guts in Vietnam, but it could not have anything to do with this attack in France so many years later, could it? All these questions rushed through Tim's mind as he recalled that Paul Martinius, his CIA friend in Rome, had mentioned in passing that Jake Kurtski was in town for some unknown reason. They did not pursue the subject, and Tim had dismissed it. But now he had to fight for his life with him, and Kurtski's motives mattered not. What mattered was Tim's survival.

Kurtski was fifteen years or so older than Tim, out of shape, and this made the difference. With Kurtski attempting to get up while simultaneously reaching for the pistol, Tim kicked him full in the face. Kurtski was too slow and uncoordinated to escape the vicious karate kick. Now his face was oozing blood, his front false teeth smashed and filling his mouth; he was suffocating on the shards of the dentures, trying to spit them out, and emitting horrible guttural sounds. But he got up to his feet, dragging himself to the door. It was Tim who picked up the pistol, aiming at Kurtski, his finger almost squeezing the trigger.

"Sonofabitch," he said aloud, "I cannot shoot this bastard when I look into his eyes . . . But get the fuck out of here before I change my mind and kill you . . ."

Tim heard the owner frantically telephoning the *gendarmerie* from his office behind the zinc bar as he watched Kurtski stumble outside. No, he could not kill the disarmed and suddenly defenseless Kurtski, even if he were not a priest. That was what Vietnam had been all about for Tim, his refusal to murder defenseless people. No, he could not do it even though Kurtski had set out to assassinate him. But Tim also comprehended in seconds that Kurtski had acted as a gunman—an executioner?—on behalf of the archbishop's Fraternity. There was no other explanation, but he had to analyze this later. The incident at the café was not yet quite finished.

Standing by the driver's side door of the black Citroën, Jean-Pierre was in a state of tense anticipation—he had heard the pistol shot as well as the thud of the collapsing body and the gunman's horrifying grunts. Then he saw Kurtski, blood covering his face like red paint, tumbling out of the café, gasping for air, and crying, "I need another gun . . . Get me a gun . . . I lost my gun . . ."

Shocked, Jean-Pierre quickly regained his composure—he was a veteran secret service operative despite his young age—and pulled a powerful Luger automatic from the holster under his black suit jacket. He threw it at Kurtski, yelling, "You're on your own now and keep your mouth shut if you want to live!" Jumping behind the steering wheel of the Citroën, Jean-Pierre yanked the car into reverse and backed out of the square, tires squealing wildly. He turned left and hit the highway downhill toward Carcassonne; "Les Homs" was on the way, but Jean-Pierre had no intention of stopping there. He radioed the driver of the other

Citroën, shouting, "Out, out! Go to Carcassonne, the usual place there, but don't attract attention to yourself!" Then he radioed the bishop at "Les Homs" that "we've got a crisis: it's all getting out of hand!"

Tim Savage walked out of the café at that precise moment, clutching the pistol in his hand. Kurtski, ghostlike and unsteady on his feet, stood in front of him, waving crazily the Luger the security chief had tossed to him.

"Okay, so let's see who is the real man here, you *focking* faggot priest," Kurtski screamed through his smashed dentures, slurring the words sickeningly.

Both men were trapped. After Jean-Pierre had abandoned him to his fate, Kurtski had no way to escape without a car. Tim's green Peugeot sat in front of the café, but he knew that, should he try to leap into it, he would be unable to keep Kurtski in check with his gun. Kurtski could then bring him down with a single shot: they were so near each other.

Combat could not be avoided if Tim hoped to survive—otherwise he would be executed by Kurtski then and there. He also realized that they could not simply continue standing in front of the café, guns pointed; the police were certain to reach Fanjeaux any moment now. He began to move slowly along the inner edge of the square, his pistol aimed, placing himself on Kurtski's left side and backing in the direction of the town's portal. This gave him the advantage of open space behind him, leaving Kurtski caught between the Jesuit and the door of the café, effectively hemmed in. It had occurred to him—and obviously to Kurtski—that neither of them would fire first so long as they faced each other because neither could guess the result. If a shot missed, the instantaneous return from the adversary would almost certainly hit the first shooter. Besides, if they both were captured by the *gendarmes* on the square, neither of them could explain credibly or even plausibly their armed presence there. For Tim—and the Church in Rome—it could have devastating consequences.

Tim's idea therefore was to lead Kurtski, who began to follow him, into the narrow streets and byways of Fanjeaux where, with his greater agility, he could, sooner or later, corner him. And Kurtski would have no choice but to be drawn into the town unless he chose to break away and flee. Tim assumed, however, that the man was like a wounded animal, determined to fight until the end. He was grateful for the CIA's instruction in urban guerrilla warfare.

Tim moved slowly backward through the deserted little streets, pointing a pistol at Kurtski, who was advancing just as slowly, dripping blood on the cobblestones, fifty feet separating them. Tim was lucky that in the sparsely inhabited Fanjeaux, no more than a thousand people, the streets were almost always empty, except for an occasional car or passerby. He had the town to himself as he attempted to reel in Kurtski.

Continuing to walk backward, with an occasional quick look over his shoulder, Tim moved deeper and deeper into the town, past old churches and private houses dating back to the early centuries of the millennium, until he suddenly found himself in front of what had been the home of St. Dominic in his anti-Cathar preaching days. A plaque on the wall identified the house as Dominic's abode, and Tim noticed it out of the corner of his left eye. Would the spirit of St. Dominic save Tim from the new heretics?

Past Dominic's house, Tim, still aiming his pistol at Kurtski—advancing at the same rate of speed—disappearing and reappearing around Fanjeaux street corners, veered backward to the right, moving northeast toward the outer limit of the fortress town. Presently, Tim reached a wide graveled esplanade known as Le Seignadou towering over the nearly vertical drop into the valley below. It offered a clear view of the Pyrénées in the south, the Black Mountain in the north, and Carcassonne on the horizon, at the end of the great Languedoc plain. Legend had it that it was on Le Seignadou that St. Dominic, who often preached there, had one night the vision of a huge ball of fire falling three times in a row from the sky on the fortified village of Prouilhe below. Was it an omen?

Tim backed up to the low wall on the edge of the esplanade, ready to fire the instant Kurtski rounded the corner from the narrow street leading from St. Dominic's house and came into plain view. But Kurtski emerged faster than Tim had expected, spotted him by the wall, and fired three times. With the bright sun in his eyes, Kurtski missed the first two times, but the third bullet grazed

Tim's shoulder as he was diving for the ground. Kurtski rushed toward Tim, his gun blazing, but he missed again. Now Kurtski was the easy target, and Tim, a CIA-trained sharpshooter, fired from the ground, hitting him squarely in the heart. Kurtski stopped for a split second, enormous surprise on his face, and fell forward, dead.

Crossing himself, Tim walked slowly to the spot where Kurtski lay, a thin trickle of crimson wetting the dry gravel; Tim could not look at the bloodied face on the street. Standing over the body, Tim shook with stifled sobs of vanishing tension, made the sign of the cross, and silently said the words of absolution. A flock of black birds soared over the esplanade, scared by the shots, cackling hysterically.

Now staring at the cadaver, Tim told himself bitterly, "My God, I became the killer of the man who once demanded that I should kill and be a killer . . . God, forgive me for I have sinned! . . ." His next thought was that Monsignor Sainte-Ange had made the right choice in recruiting him: a killer to track down killers!

Tim Savage dragged himself from the empty esplanade, leaving Kurtski's body behind, back into the narrow streets of Fanjeaux. He walked again past the house of St. Dominic toward a church he saw ahead. It was the thirteenth-century Church of Notre-Dame de l'Assomption, erected on the vestiges of Fanum Jovis, the temple of Jupiter. The church was dark and cool; it belonged to another time.

Tim needed the peace of the church to pray and collect his thoughts. He sat in the front pew, facing the altar. What was he to do next? Under the circumstances, should he keep his appointment with Archbishop Leduc? There was no doubt that someone really wished Tim dead—evidently in connection with his pursuit of the truth, for there could be no other reason—and, through a strange and sinister coincidence, had hired Kurtski to do the job. Should that prevent him from continuing and perhaps even completing his mission? Should he abandon it to save his life because his invisible enemies would surely try again? Tim felt so close to the end of the investigation that he must take the ultimate step. And, inevitably, that step had to be the meeting with the archbishop. Tim had already learned enough to be absolutely convinced that Leduc, and only Leduc, could provide him with the final answer. But how would get to the abbey?

"You are bleeding, Father! Are you hurt?" a feminine voice said behind him. Tim turned around and saw an elderly—and motherly—woman, a scarf on her head, looking at him with concern. He now felt the sting in the shoulder where Kurtski's third bullet had grazed him. Touching it, Tim felt on his fingers the wetness of his own blood.

"Oh, it's nothing, Madame," he said lightly. "Nothing serious . . ."

"Well, Father, you don't *want* it to become serious," she said with severity. "We have no hospital or clinic here so you will come to my house to have it bandaged."

The house was across the street from the church, and the woman expertly cleaned the bullet scratch and applied a dressing to it after Tim had removed his jacket and his shirt. She fed him lunch of a thick soup and bread, never asking what had happened, how Tim had been hurt. But Tim had a question of his own after finishing the meal.

"How does one get to that Cisterian abbey of Villelongue, there by Saissac? he asked.

Chapter Twenty-three

Tɪᴍ ʜᴀᴅ ʟᴇꜰᴛ his green rental Peugeot at the door of the café at the entrance to Fanjeaux, but the small square swarmed with *gendarmes* from Mirepoix. Tim could see them, their cruisers' blue lights flashing furiously, when he walked to the town's arched gate overlooking the square.

It would not do for an American Jesuit in clerical garb and armed with a Luger to be detained and interrogated by the French police, particularly when Kurtski's body, his pistol still in his death-stiffened hand, were found at the edge of the esplanade. Obviously, Tim could not risk it, being now in effect a fugitive from French justice—a criminal—and realizing that it would not take a Poirot's investigative genius to link him and Kurtski. Explanations would be impossible, and even the full truth would not seem credible to French law enforcement.

Therefore Tim resolved to lie. The elderly woman who had taken care of him was unaware of the fracas on the square and the gun duel on the esplanade, Tim's shoulder wound notwithstanding, and she proceeded to give him directions on how to reach the abbey.

"But," he said, "the problem is that I don't have a car."

"Then, how did you get here?" the woman asked.

"I came by bus from Carcassonne, getting off at Fanjeaux and hoping to run into somebody driving to the abbey who would give me a ride," Tim answered, the image of the innocent American priest-tourist. "I've read a lot about the Cisterian abbey and I understand that it is quite beautiful."

"Oh, yes, it is very beautiful and you shouldn't miss it," the woman said, glancing sideways at her husband. He was a stout Languedocian, a retired farmer, relaxed and comfortable in his blue coveralls, puffing on his pipe in his armchair by the window. He caught his wife's look.

"If you have no car, Father, I'd be happy to drive you to the abbey," he said, getting up. "I have to go in that direction any-way . . ."

It took the man's pale blue *Deux-Chevaux* Renault clanking wreck of a car no more than twenty minutes to get down to the square— it was still crawling with police, but no attention was paid to them—and drive three or four miles north on the highway to the turnoff for the abbey. The splendidly preserved structure sat in a thicket of trees, surrounded by yew hedges, at the end of an elon-gated, shady valley.

Tim thought that the Cisterian abbey was perfectly chosen as the venue for the archbishop's residence. It was built in 1150 by the "gray" or "white" monks, as the Cisterians were variously called, to serve as a monastery for what was one of the oldest religious orders in Europe, founded by St. Robert in 1098. Their name came from the Latin *cisterna,* meaning cave or cavern, and, accord-ingly, their philosophy and theology called for a return to simplic-ity, the rigorous life, and the self-denial of primitive monachism. For a time, up to the mid-fourteenth century, the Cisterians were the most powerful order in Western Europe. Small wonder, thought Tim, that Archbishop Leduc felt safely at home in the *cis-terna,* the symbol of extreme conservatism.

Thanking the old farmer for the ride, Tim walked up to the abbey's garden gate. He was greeted by two young athletic men in black suits, guns bulging under their jackets, with earpieces and wires disappearing under their shirt collars. They seemed to be clones of the guards at the Fraternity's seminary.

"Father Savage, I presume?" the slightly older of the two guards asked Tim gravely in English. He must have learned it from reading up on Stanley and Livingstone, Tim decided. The formal, respectful reception at the abbey struck him as faintly amusing after his shoot-out with Kurtski.

"Yes, I am," he said. "I have an appointment with Archbishop Leduc and I trust I am not too late. I was unavoidably delayed on my way here."

"Of course," the guard told Tim, indicating with a wide, inviting gesture of his arm the entrance to the abbey. "His Grace is expecting you."

He escorted him inside, passing two other tough-looking young men stationed in the spacious vestibule. Tim noticed surveillance television cameras high on the wall, pointed at the entrance door. The guard opened a heavy oak door on the right, holding it for Tim.

"Please, go ahead," he said.

Archbishop Leduc was standing in the center of an elegantly appointed library: bookcases along the walls, a deep fireplace topped by a marble mantelpiece between windows looking out on the garden, and a Louis XV desk with ormolu mountings in a corner under a portrait of Pius V. The archbishop's tall frame was emaciated and stooped, giving him the appearance of total exhaustion, but when he stepped forward Tim saw his deeply set blue eyes, hard, unforgiving, and cold as ice, under thick dark eyebrows. Tim realized in a flash why Leduc's photographs had seemed so familiar to him.

"Good day, Your Grace," Tim said in French. He paused and added, choosing his words with care, "It is an honor to see you again . . ."

The archbishop extended his right hand as if to have his ring kissed, an old habit, but withdrew it immediately. He nodded slowly at Tim.

"Yes, of course, we *have* met before, and it is good of you to remember," he replied in a deep, hoarse voice. "And I'm sorry about your problems this morning." Tim could not determine whether the old man was being sarcastic or simply polite in an old-fashioned way.

"And I remember you very well, too," the archbishop went on. "You are the highly respected Islam scholar, and we were together in your office in Rome the day the Holy Father was shot, five years ago or so, wasn't it?"

"Yes, Your Grace," Tim told him. "You were at my office and we talked for a long time that afternoon about Islam fundamentalism. I recall that your experience with Muslims during your years in Casablanca had you very concerned with subversive Islamic movements and terrorism developing these days in Africa and the Middle East. I also recall wondering at the time why, given your own knowledge and expertise on Islam, you were wasting so many hours with me."

Leduc looked into Tim's eyes with his hard stare, holding it steadily for a long moment.

"It seemed like a good idea at the time," he said thoughtfully. "But, I must say, it was a strange coincidence that we were there, at your office, discussing Islam fundamentalism and terrorism at the very moment when that Turk—a Muslim—nearly succeeded in murdering the Holy Father. I guess that was the 'Muslim Connection' people were talking about after the shooting . . . It was a miracle that the pope survived the attempt."

"If I may repeat your words, Your Grace—when we heard on the radio that he would live—that it was 'God's Will,' " Tim said. "I can still hear you saying it . . . And I, too, think it is an astounding coincidence that we now meet here."

Leduc contemplated Tim for another long instant. Then he gestured toward a corner, across the library from his desk, and deep armchairs upholstered in red leather.

"Do sit down, Father Savage," he said. "I understand that your new scholarly pursuit is French heretics of the past and the present. And that you have questions about our Fraternity. I shall be happy to be of help, if I can. . . ."

"The abbé over at the seminary in Mirepoix had the impression that you regard our Fraternity as heretics and our beliefs as heresy," Archbishop Leduc declared. "And I am curious how you reached your conclusion. Is that the result of your own deep studies over the last weeks or months or have you simply accepted the official view of your bosses at the Holy See?"

Tim stirred uneasily in his armchair. Leduc had smoothly thrown him on the defensive with his sarcasm, after only a few minutes of conversation about his "own deep studies" over such a ridiculously short period. Even more, however, Tim was disturbed that the archbishop knew so much about his activities— and so quickly about his *contretempt* with Kurtski.

How did he know that Tim had been trying to find out the nature of the Fraternity of St. Pius V's involvements? How did he know about his inquiries? How had the abbé in Mirepoix discovered his identity, and why had he gone through all the motions of friendly hospitality, including the invitation to Tim to meet the archbishop? And was the archbishop aware of his mission for Monsignor Sainte-Ange? Had he learned about Tim's meetings with the imams in Paris and Toulouse—and about Istambul? How did Kurtski fit into the picture? Why did someone wish him dead? It was all too neat, too well orchestrated!

"Well," he replied truthfully, "I cannot say that I've actually reached any conclusions as to whether the Fraternity constitutes a heresy because it's not my function to do so. That's what I told the abbé. It is the business of the Congregation for the Doctrine of the Faith back in Rome. But the reason I am trying to study French Catholic heresies, like the Cathars and the new movements like the Fraternity, is that I am basically interested in fundamentalisms—including Islam fundamentalism that you and I discussed at my office over five years ago. You might say that I am concentrating on comparative fundamentalisms."

"Comparative fundamentalisms?" Leduc repeated, sounding incredulous. "Is that a new discipline under the teachings of those liberal fools of the Second Vatican Council or is that an invention of the Jesuits who, in my opinion, *are* liberal fools as they have always been? I must say that I'm not surprised that the Marquis de Sade was a pupil of the Jesuits in Paris for four years, something I've been told by our scholars just the other day! And so was Fidel Castro in Cuba!"

"It's not a discipline, but a reality," Tim said, having just invented "comparative fundamentalist studies." He went on: "In today's world fundamentalism is a powerful phenomenon, whether it is Islamic, Christian, or Jewish. I sometimes wonder whether it might become the religious hallmark in the approaching new century and millennium. Therefore I believe it is appropriate for me, as an Islam scholar, to look at contemporary Christian fundamentalism. After all, our three monotheistic faiths descend from Abraham, and parallels do exist . . . And, you know, in my country we have important Christian fundamentalist denominations, especially among Protestants—like some Baptists, Pentacostals, and so forth—and some fundamentalist movements that overlap with politics, like our new Christian Right . . . So the French experience is very relevant to my work. Anyway, my superiors approve of it."

"I am afraid that you are confusing doctrines, faiths, and heresies in the Catholic Church, Father Savage," the archbishop remarked. "But so are your superiors, including Pope Gregory XVII, who claims that I have led the Fraternity into schism, but who, as a Frenchman, should know better . . . Would you like for me to explain what we are and what we stand for?"

"Yes, please, Your Grace," Tim answered. "I'm sure I shall never find a better source."

"To begin with, forget fundamentalism," Leduc said. "It's pure nonsense as far as we are concerned. But you must have heard the description of 'Integrism' applied to us, and this is more precise. We are proud to be Integrists. And 'Integrism' comes from the Latin adjective *integer,* meaning 'untouched, entire.' To the Fraternity, it stands for the untouchability of the Church's eternal doctrine, the doctrine of the Council of Trent defined forever in the sixteenth century and beautifully reaffirmed by St. Pius X in 1903—not such a long time ago—who asserted that his principal objective was 'to restore all things in Christ, in order that Christ may be all and in all' and 'to teach and defend Christian truth and law.' That is exactly what the Fraternity does. That is why I founded the Fraternity in the first place—to defend the true Church from the baboons of the Second Vatican Council. And I was right."

"But what is there to 'restore'?" Tim inquired with deep respect, anxious to keep the archbishop talking about his beliefs and the Fraternity. It would be absurd to argue with him. And, with luck, the old man might reveal in his extraordinary vanity what Tim Savage had set out to discover. Tim knew this was his only and last chance to pull together all the strands of the conspiracy.

Leduc, flatly informing Tim that there was plenty to "restore" in the Church after the Second Vatican Council's "vandalisms," as he called them, his basso voice rising to the rafters, proceeded to expound in the most minute detail, with long Latin quotations, on the doctrines of Trent and Pius V and Pius X. He seemed to enjoy hugely holding this tutorial for Tim, unmindful of the passage of the hours and the darkness descending on the garden outside. He was not, however, aiding Tim's cause with great revelations.

When the archbishop finally stopped, his narrow lips in a thin, triumphal smile, Tim frantically tried another approach to save the day.

"You are an amazing teacher," he told the archbishop. "But there is one more thing I would beg you to do, Your Grace. Could you summarize for me the key points of your rejection of the Vatican Council?"

"It's all in my book—the title is *They Have Uncrowned Him: From Liberalism to Apostasy—the Conciliar Tragedy*—and you should have read it, if you are serious about your studies," Leduc said with a touch of petulance. "Especially the chapter on Brigandage of Vatican II. Brigandage, of course, means depredation by brigands. The word goes back to the Council of Ephesus in 449 A.D. . . . But I shall give you a summary. Pay attention!"

"Yes, Your Grace," Tim responded humbly.

"In the first place, there is the question of the Decree on Religious Freedom," the archbishop announced. "It was an incitation to equate error with truth and an assault on the social kingdom of Christ. The Church must safeguard the religious unity in the true religion and protect Catholic souls against scandal and dissemination of religious error, and limit and prohibit, if required, the freedom of false cults. Is that clear?"

"Yes, Your Grace," Tim said. "Very clear. Please continue."

"And that maniac in Rome, that Gregory XVII, keeps agitating in favor of ecumenism, of the unity of Christian churches," Leduc spat in disgust. "*He* is in defiance of the Church, not I! He is destroying the Church! He is violating the Second Commandment: 'Though Shalt Not Have Other Gods Besides Me . . .' Who is *His* God, the god he has placed ahead of the Lord and ahead of Christ? You shall see: this pope will pay for it one day . . . It breaks my heart! And, as you know, I am always right!"

Tim held his breath. What was the infuriated archbishop telling him?

"Pay for it?" he asked, trying to control his voice, keep it normal. "You mean literally? Like with his life?"

"There are many ways of redeeming sins." Leduc shrugged. "It is always God's will."

"I understand," Tim said. "And the other points?"

"*Vocem Iucunditatis Annuntiate!*" the archbishop sang out in his rich, deep voice with a French inflection in Latin. "Do you know what it is, Father Savage?"

"Yes, *Declare It with a Voice of Joy!*" Tim answered, smiling despite himself. The old prelate's sense of theater and drama remained intact. "It's the beginning of the Solemn High Pontifical Mass in the Tridentine Rite. The line is from the prophet Isaiah . . . I first heard it when I was a brand new priest in Rome. There was only one church where you could hear a Tridentine Mass, and I was curious. Besides, I love Gregorian chant . . ."

"Exactly!" Leduc cried triumphantly. "It's the Mass! It's liturgy! The Council and the conciliary popes, from Paul VI to Gregory XVII, have betrayed the Church and the religion when they abandoned the great and true Tridentine Mass, recited and sung in Latin—with the Gregorian chant—and proclaimed that Mass would henceforth be said in vernacular, the local language. I say 'betrayed' because that is precisely what they did: they destroyed the unity of Catholicism that the Latin Mass had provided and replaced it with a Babel Tower of tongues, with no certainty that the prayers were adequately translated. You do *not* translate Mass! You declare it, in Latin, a universal language, with a voice of joy as the Fathers of the Church did . . . Can you imagine the Liturgy of the Word in the vernacular? It's a travesty! The betrayal of the Tridentine Mass symbolizes the subversion of the Church by the Vatican Council . . . Today, eternal Rome is reduced to silence, paralyzed by that other Rome, the liberal Rome, that is occupying it . . ."

Leduc stopped to catch his breath, having failed to point out to Tim that he favored Latin as a dead language, ruling out all risk of liturgical evolution.

"And the liturgy!" he resumed, "Liturgy and the priest! What they've given us is the Mass of Luther! The sense of mystery of liturgy has been shattered. In the past, the priest faced the altar and Christ and the Virgin Mary—and the faithful could not observe his ritual gestures because they only saw his back. That was part of the mystery, the reenactment of Christ's sacrificial death on the cross, and the priest's prayers were whispered respectfully, not shouted. Now he faces the congregation, and the fervent faith is gone. It is like theater, sometimes with guitars, not a Solemn Mass . . . And the Council has authorized the use of ordinary bread instead of blessed wafers as the Body of Christ at Holy Communion . . . It is pure blasphemy that must be stopped . . ."

"How, Your Grace?" Tim asked.

"I am personally prepared to lead a crusade to remake Christianity as it is desired by the Church," the archbishop said, crossing himself. Tim did not.

"And do not forget that we have a half-million members and followers," he added threateningly.

Night had fallen, but Archbishop Leduc seemed most anxious to pursue the conversation, inviting Tim to join him for dinner. It was like the previous evening with the abbé at the seminary. It occurred to Tim that perhaps both prelates experienced a deep need to explain their faith and actions at enormous lengths to outsiders likely to understand them and ready to listen. Perhaps they had very few such private opportunities and listeners as avid as Tim. But Leduc having volunteered to lead a crusade to save Christendom, Tim saw an opening.

"You have mentioned a crusade, Your Grace," he said after they sat down at the table in the rectangular, high-ceilinged dining room decorated with Flemish tapestries, "and this made me think of the Albi crusades here in the Languedoc back in the thirteenth century. With my scholarly interest in heresies, I'd be most intrigued to hear how you judge the Cathar heresy and all that surrounded it."

Leduc was clearly pleased with Tim's question. Even his icy blue eyes grew warmer.

"Well," he said, "I am so glad you asked. You see, the Cathars are our inspiration in every way. They led saintly lives. We are very much alike, we share the same objectives—you may wish to call them heresies—and we share the same enemy. The Cathars, too, were in schism. They called Rome the 'Wolves' Church' and this is what Rome is today. The pope, Innocent III, was determined to eradicate them with the sword and fire of *his* crusade in the early

1200s—he even authorized secular power to burn convicted heretics—and Gregory XVII is determined to do away with me and the Fraternity through more subtle and sophisticated warfare.

"As you probably know," the archbishop continued, "the pope has resolved to excommunicate me because I propose to consecrate our own bishops—bishops of the Pius V Fraternity—just as I've already ordained a number of priests on my own authority. The Cathars who, by the way, were very much of an elite, aristocratic religion, had their own bishops, too. They took the view that they were a separate church, which obviously is *not* what the Fraternity has in mind, but we are *reshaping* the Church, and that is not so different, in my opinion. The Cathars fought and died—and killed to defend themselves—for twenty, thirty, or more years. Perhaps the only difference between us is that they battled to resist the Albi crusade while we are the ones who are launching a crusade against the common foe. But it was Divine Providence that, almost eight centuries later, blessed us with the Cathar example, the example of the pure and Perfect Ones . . .

"Naturally," Leduc added, "we do not share the Cathar theology: we do not accept their Manichaean notion of dualism between the good Lord and Satan with equal powers struggling for the control of the world. And we do not believe that even the most perfect secular Catholics—like their 'Perfects'—abstain from sex, even for procreation, or that it is a sin to consume foods from animals that engage in sex. Yes, we eat meat, drink milk, and savor cheese, unlike Cathar 'Good Men' and 'Good Women.' Every sect is entitled to its practices so long as it does not undermine the fundamental precepts of the Church and religion. For our part, we act—like launching a crusade—when the faith is betrayed, like now."

"In your crusade, Your Grace, would you countenance killing and death?" Tim asked, looking into the archbishop's hard eyes—thinking as much of his experience with Kurtski this morning as of Gregory XVII's experience with Circlic, the Turk, over five years later.

"That would depend," the archbishop replied. "You know, a crusade is a war, and in our religion there is such a thing as a just war, *ius bellum,* sanctified by St. Augustine and St. Thomas

Aquinas . . . And there is the old tradition of *Sic Semper Tyrannis*—
'Thus Ever to Tyrants!' "

"But, then, there also exists in our religion the Sixth Commandment, Thou Shalt Not Murder," Tim ventured. "How does
one reconcile all these concepts?"

"I believe it is a matter of absolutely honest judgment—
absolute honesty in the eyes of the Lord—that in the end must be
trusted by all Christians," Leduc said. "It's not a question of theological semantics. Popes, too, have killed and killed, even in the
absence of an overarching moral judgment."

"Well, Your Grace, would you countenance, for example, the
killing of the papal legate by the Cathars, which Innocent III used
to justify the Albi crusade?" Tim pushed the argument, the archbishop visibly enjoying the intellectual skirmish with him.

"Probably not, but for commonsense reasons," Leduc told
him. "The Cathars gained nothing by murdering the papal legate.
Remember the Cathars were the nobility elite. All it did was open
the way for the pope to demand that the French king, Philippe
Auguste, lead the following year with his armies the crusade
against the Cathars in the Languedoc. I'm sure you know your
history . . . My answer to your question is not that the end justifies
the means—that is another school of power philosophy—but that
a correct judgment of the circumstances, benefiting the Church
and most people, must be made by those of us who are in charge.
Do you see what I mean?"

"Why, would you say, Your Grace, the Fraternity enjoys such support in the Languedoc and elsewhere in the South?" Tim asked.

"It's the Cathar tradition," the archbishop answered. "It is still
so much alive here that the people see in our work the preserva-
tion of the Cathar spirit. They accept our moral judgments and
decisions, and I know that we can count on this support in every
instance. The weight of history is with us."

"But would other Catholics, French Catholics, at least, go
along with your crusade, even if pushed to the extreme—like
killing in the name of the faith?"

"You seem obsessed with killings," Leduc said gently to Tim.
They were back in the library, over coffee and cognac, the arch-

bishop having invited him to spend the night at the abbey, given the late hour. Tim, of course, had no place to go—and no means.

"You will be safe here with me," the archbishop assured Tim with what the Jesuit could have sworn was a twinkle, slightly malicious, in his eyes. "I knew you had a *contretemps* this morning, but we must not dwell on it."

"Sure," Tim said, wondering uneasily how Ledoc already knew about it, "but why did somebody wish me dead? And using a gun-man I happened to know from my past? I am not obsessed with killings, Your Grace, but I take a dim view when they come so close to me, personally or institutionally."

My God, Tim thought, I am smack in the middle of a conspir-acy. He shuddered.

Leduc sniffed his cognac appreciatively and turned to Tim.

"Yes, I admit that what happened this morning with you was not the best idea," he said. "Someone had lost the sense of perspective. It was a wrong moral and strategic judgement. Besides, I did not know you as I think I know you now."

"Then you must know, Your Grace, that I killed the man who had attacked me—in self-defense and without making any moral judgments," Tim told him. "Indeed, I was forced to become a killer, something I had always resisted, and therefore I cannot for-give what occurred today."

"Yes, I am aware of it," the archbishop acknowledged. "The message was radioed to me here from our people in Fanjeaux. And I must also confess that I had accepted the recommendation from Bishop Laval—he is my good right hand—to have you killed because, as they say in detective novels, you knew too much or you were getting to know too much. As I said, it was a wrong moral judgment and a strategic stupidity, but I take full responsi-bility for it."

"Getting to know too much about *what?*" Tim asked, hoping he sounded perplexed. Now he had the scent of blood.

"Oh, come on, Father Savage! You know what I'm talking about . . ."

"I do? What is it?"

"It is the fact that, for reasons that remain unclear to me, you have been striving to trace to the Fraternity, or even to me personally, the attempt to assassinate Pope Gregory XVII. I have no idea whether this is something you are doing on your own, and if so, why, or on orders from Rome, though it strikes me as odd that an American Jesuit who specializes in Islam would be given the job. I was informed that you had a meeting with the imam in Toulouse and that he had told you about supposedly procuring an assassin for Roman Catholic fundamentalists to kill the pope for them, but I fail to see why an Islam scholar would be required for such a task. This would be police work, no more. Anyone could have been sent to talk to the imam, don't you think, Father Savage?"

"That is true," Tim agreed, choosing his words with extreme care. As he listened to Leduc, it seemed quite possible that the archbishop was ignorant of Tim's Istanbul foray and his Paris connections and conversations. That was encouraging. Leduc seemed to be familiar with only one aspect of his investigation, which gave Tim at least a temporary advantage in their confrontation.

"And is it also true that it was you who actually did meet with that imam in Toulouse?" the archbishop asked in a prosecutorial tone.

"Yes, Your Grace, it is true," Tim said. There was no point in denying it at this stage.

"What did he tell you?"

"That, in effect, his Muslim council had been asked by Catholic fundamentalists in Toulouse, with whom they have some kind of contact, to make arrangements to hire a Muslim assassin to shoot the pope. What you heard, Your Grace, is essentially accurate."

"How, then, did you link these 'Catholic fundamentalists' with the Fraternity?" Leduc asked. "What about your questions to the bookseller in Le Somail where you concealed being a priest? What made you go to the seminary in Mirepoix?"

"Well, it's a long story," Tim replied, "but when the imam mentioned Catholic fundamentalists, suggesting it was an organization and not just a bunch of free-lance fanatics, it was a fairly simple deduction that what he had in mind was your Fraternity— even if he knew nothing about it. I could have been wrong, but I had to pursue it. Nothing else made sense."

"You sound like a professional investigator, like a CIA agent or something," Leduc said. "But did you believe the imam?"

Tim assumed, from the archbishop's passing comment, that the Pius V Fraternity was unaware of his CIA past, which was not particularly surprising. It had checked his Rome background, but it would have been most unlikely to trace him back to the agency where, like so many operatives, he had worked under deep cover.

"To be honest with you," he said, "I had no reason *not* to believe the imam. I can't think why he would make it up. There was nothing in it for him."

"Then, Father Savage, if you really think that we are the Catholics in question, I must assume that you also believe that the Pius V Fraternity—and I—were behind the assassination attempt against Gregory XVII. This is my deductive French Cartesian logic. Am I right?"

The conversation had now escalated to a dangerous level, and Tim sensed that every single word counted heavily. And his life could still be at stake. He was convinced at this stage that the archbishop was not aware of all his activities and their origin, let alone his personal background. But, by the same token, Tim lacked precise knowledge about much of what Leduc and the Fraternity had actually done—and how. Somewhere in the abbey, the clock struck midnight.

"Your Grace," Tim said very slowly, "I cannot jump to conclusions on the basis of what I was told by a Muslim imam in France whom I had never met before and whose motivations may be vague. I am not sure—so far—what to believe."

The archbishop rose from his chair and paced up and down the library for several minutes, his hands clasped behind his back. Tim thought that he heard him murmuring prayers. He, too, could use divine guidance.

"I shall be honest with you—up to a point," Leduc said, easing himself back into his leather chair. "But we both must be realistic about this situation. I shall not deny that, yes, we had sought the help of our Muslim brethren in finding an assassin. However, I shall not confirm it to you, either. You are free to interpret any way you wish my earlier statements about my crusade, about just wars and the moral right to kill in the name of the faith. Yet, I do not believe, Father, that I am ready to ask you for absolution."

Tim nodded silently.

"Concerning the attempt to kill *you* today," the archbishop continued, "I've already indicated that it had not been the best idea. When Bishop Laval and our security chief had learned of your meeting with the imam—it doesn't matter how they learned it—as well as of your visit to the bookseller, they concluded that you already knew too much and that you represented consider-able peril to us and our plans for the future. They suspected that you had other sources and connections as well. Next, the book-seller informed them that you had mentioned plans to visit the seminary. So we were ready for you when you arrived in Mire-poix. Their recommendation, as I told you, was to have you killed. Our people reasoned that nobody would ever reconstruct what exactly had happened in Fanjeaux, and the crime would soon be forgotten, if it were noticed in the first place. You see, you are nobody as far as the world is concerned . . ."

"Thank you for the compliment, Your Grace," Tim said with a feeble attempt at ironic humor. "But you have a point: nobody would miss me if I vanished in a godforsaken French village."

But he immediately corrected himself—mentally. Angela would not only miss him personally, but she would have an idea of what might have happened and act accordingly through Vatican chan-nels. And his family in Washington knew everything about those missing in action: his father's death in World War Two and Tim's risk taking with the CIA in Vietnam and elsewhere.

"Now I'm glad that the attack on you failed," the archbishop said matter-of-factly. "Having met you, which I didn't really expect, I can see that your knowledge about this nasty affair is confined to what the imam had told you. He could not prove it and you could not prove it—if it was your intention to pass the information on to your superiors, whoever they are. I imagine it is Rome, but I don't care. And I don't believe you are doing all this to amuse yourself intellectually . . . In other words, you are not the danger my people feared you were, and it would have been an unnecessary and morally indefensible murder. I should not have sanctioned it. This was the only time, I think, when I was not right . . . So all I can offer you is, *Mea culpa, mea maxima culpa*—you know, it's from the Tridentine Mass."

"I'm relieved to hear, Your Grace, that it would have been wasteful to kill me," Tim answered in his most professional manner. "But where do we go from here, if anywhere? Do I just go back to tend my flock of sheep at the Islam office in Rome? Do I suffer an accident somewhere? Do I just forget everything, or what?"

"I said that we must be realistic," Leduc replied. "Realistic means we both forget everything about this whole business and go our separate ways. I have nothing against you personally, Father Savage, and I doubt that you can really harm me or the Fraternity, no matter what you tell them in Rome. With no actual proof, it would be at best just another rumor, just another accusation against that demented old archbishop in the south of France, more inconclusive speculation about the assassination attempt . . . Meanwhile, get some sleep. A security man will show you to your room."

Tim said nothing, just bowed his head as he left the library.

He awoke in midmorning in a huge double bed in an enormous bedroom with a vaulted ceiling. Looking out of the window, he saw a shepherd behind his flock of sheep. The surveillance television camera in a corner just under the ceiling observed Tim rise, and five minutes later a young security man in a black suit brought him a tray with coffee and croissants.

Downstairs, in the driveway, his green rental Peugeot gleamed washed and clean in the morning sun. Leduc's talented young men had evidently hot-wired the car that sat in front of the Fanjeaux square café and driven it over to the abbey for him. This is efficiency, Tim thought admiringly as he pulled his keys out of his pocket to unlock the vehicle. In a crazy sort of way, it was stimulating to be dealing with first-rate professionals. If he could only figure out how and where Leduc's men had procured Jake Kurtski to be his designated shooter: it was just professional curiosity.

As Tim drove out of the abbey's courtyard, Archbishop Leduc made two telephone calls over his secure line from his regal bedroom on the second floor. The first call was to Jean-Pierre at "Les Homs," just a few miles away.

"The American has just left the premises," he said. "Let's be sure we don't lose him. I want a report on his movements every day—and more often if warranted."

The second call was to a residential number in Paris in an apartment likewise equipped with a secure telephone line. The man he wanted to reach answered on the first ring.

"Let me tell you," Leduc said angrily, "that you're not doing your job properly. We almost had a disaster here yesterday with the American Jesuit . . . Yes, he's very much alive and he is much smarter than we thought. He managed to kill your killer. Your guys better get their act together before we have a real catastrophe. You managed to blow up poor Greenpeace's *Rainbow Warrior* way out in the Pacific, but you can't catch a wandering American Jesuit in France. God, I almost wish de Marenches were still in this world. At least, he understood the *métier*. . . ."

Chapter Twenty-four

THE MORNING AFTER his return to Rome from France—there was nothing further to accomplish there after the encounter at the Cisterian abbey—Tim Savage read in *L'Osservatore Romano* that Archbishop Jules Leduc, former head of the Archdiocesis of Casablanca and the founder of the Pius V Fraternity, had been excommunicated by Pope Gregory XVII for consecrating four bishops on his own authority. A lengthy editorial on the Vatican newspaper's third page, usually devoted to matters of theology and philosophy, explained that Leduc was penalized for this "irregular" act inasmuch as, under canon law, only the pontiff can name bishops. The article pointed out that the archbishop had been suspended from the exercise of holy orders ten years earlier after ordaining fourteen Fraternity priests without permission from the Holy See and remained "recalcitrant" thereafter. It also emphasized helpfully that "heresy" and "schism" were among other reasons for excommunications.

Tim calculated that Leduc must have held the consecration the day after their marathon session in the abbey. The private, unpublicized ceremony had taken place at the seminary in Mirepoix. Reading *L'Osservatore,*, Tim told himself that the archbishop had now launched the latest phase of his crusade against Rome. His immediate task was to prepare the report on his mission for Monsignor Sainte-Ange: It had to be a very careful and creative effort for Tim was experiencing strangely mixed emotions about Gregory XVII's powerful private secretary. Again, it was pure instinct.

His first call in Rome was to Sister Angela to say that he was back and to ask her to set up an appointment with the monsignor.

"I have returned!" Tim announced over the telephone, sounding a bit more dramatic than he had intended. "How are you and how's everything there?"

"Hi! Welcome home!" Angela responded merrily. "We've missed you around here. At least I did."

"And I've missed you and I've thought a lot about you, especially about our Paris chats," he said. "I hope to see you very soon—perhaps still this week if I complete my report and the Monsignor can receive me right away."

"How did it go?" she asked. "Did you find what you were looking for?"

"Probably not everything, but an awful lot—enough to make a difference," Tim told her.

Angela telephoned Tim at Villa Malta the next day.

"The Monsignor doesn't want anything on paper," she reported. "He wants an oral presentation, and he can see you tomorrow at ten o'clock in the morning. I'll see you then."

That *is* curious, Tim thought. Nothing on paper? Is he worried about a paper trail? It would be like a top-secret military or CIA debriefing, a performance for an audience of one, but he believed he could handle it well. The next question in his mind was how Leduc's provocative move with the bishops and the Vatican's swift reprisals would affect the broader state of affairs. Leduc and Gregory XVII were now officially and openly at war. Did the pope realize what a lethally dangerous adversary he had in the old archbishop? And did Sainte-Ange?

It was raining on that October Saturday morning when Tim crossed St. Peter's Square on his way to his meeting with Monsignor Sainte-Ange in the Apostolic Palace. The square was deserted, except for a half-dozen bored *carabinieri* huddled under the Bernini Colonnade, next to the wide stairs leading to the Bronze Doors. The Swiss Guard noncommissioned officer on duty at the doors along with a younger guardsman inquired about Tim's business and waved him on with a quick salute.

Tim reached the second *loggia* of the Palace by elevator after walking across the wide inner central courtyard, the Cortile S. Damiano, the way most official visitors to the Papal Household come and go. The pope, descending from his third *loggia* domain, uses a small private elevator to which only he and the monsignor have keys: it takes him to another courtyard where his limousine or the Popemobile await to whisk him out of the Vatican through the Sant'Anna Gate. On the second *loggia,* Tim was met by an usher in white tie and tails who escorted him to Sainte-Ange's office ante-room along the gallery forming the outer side of the Palace.

The monsignor, however, was not in the tiny, square room when Tim arrived. The usher waved him to a straight chair at a small table in the center, asking him to wait a minute or so. Sainte-Ange materialized from a side door fifteen minutes later, plopping himself down on the other chair and explaining breath-lessly that he had been delayed by urgent business with the Holy Father. Tim smiled politely.

"So, Father Savage, please tell me, in as much detail as possible, about your travels, investigations, and accomplishments," the monsignor asked in his accented English. "Skip nothing. But, first and foremost, have you brought us the truth the Holy Father so fervently desires?"

The monsignor cultivated the gift of sounding patronizing to everybody below the rank of pope. That it antagonized Curial cardinals and archbishops, prefects of congregations and presidents of pontifical councils and commissions troubled him not at all. He had the power. Now he was addressing Tim in his accustomed way, though at their original meeting he had made an effort at friendly warmth.

"I cannot claim, Monsignor, to have the full and complete truth, certainly not in a documented fashion," Tim said, having rehearsed his presentation over and over since Angela's call the day before. He paused briefly, for effect, and continued:

"To sum it up, my professional conclusion is that the conspiracy to assassinate the Holy Father on May 13, 1981, was conceived and directed by Archbishop Jules Leduc and his senior associates in the Pius V Fraternity in the south of France. I met with the archbishop and he doesn't deny—nor does he formally confirm—this fact. He is conducting a crusade—it is his word—against the Holy See and its present head, and believes that it is a just war—*ius bellum*—in which killing is permissible.

"To execute the plot and conceal its authorship, the archbishop and his associates turned to Muslim fundamentalists in Toulouse with whom the Pius V Fraternity maintains close contacts—as fellow fundamentalists—to procure and hire an assassin. The Muslims, as I understand it, agreed to do so on the grounds of religious fundamentalist solidarity. They were not told by the Fraternity at the time that His Holiness would be the target. The Toulouse Muslims, working through their European channels, entered in communication with a terrorist organization in Turkey, requesting that a first-rate gunman be selected and hired for the job—with a guarantee of substantial payments, before and after the attack. The assassin, of course, was Agca Circlic. But it was only in Rome, a few days prior to the shooting, that Agca Circlic was instructed by an emissary of the Fraternity, who had been sent from Toulouse with the final orders, that Pope Gregory XVII was to be his victim. Circlic doesn't know to this day who had actually ordered and financed the conspiracy and had hired him. This is why he was so totally useless to Italian investigators. The archbishop and the Fraternity had assumed that with an unwitting Circlic in prison or dead—they realized that he might have been killed on the spot, which would have been just fine with them—their secret would never surface and the world would accept the 'Muslim Connection' or Soviet theories, and let the matter lapse and be forgotten. They were basically right. The Muslims in Toulouse have subsequently learned that they had been used; they were shocked, but not about to disclose their role. My impression, however, is that the archbishop and his people have not given up and that the Holy Father remains in great danger. You are facing extreme theological fanatics with total determination, vast resources, a highly professional organization, and a very considerable following . . . I have no idea how they might react to the excommunication of the archbishop . . ."

Deep silence fell over the confining, small room. Monsignor Sainte-Ange shifted his weight in his chair. Tim stared at the ceiling.

"This is most interesting," he said at length. "But can you estimate how widely this knowledge is disseminated, if at all? Who else knows about it?"

"It's very difficult to say," Tim replied. "Different people are aware of different aspects of the conspiracy. The Muslims, for example, know what they actually did in this affair while lacking most of the background of what led the Catholics to solicit their help. Archbishop Leduc and some of his top people in the Pius V Fraternity naturally know what they had planned and set in motion. But they, too, have gaps concerning how the Muslims in France and elsewhere had handled the planning. The Catholics, it seems, trusted the Muslims completely. So what I've done to the best of my ability is to pull together as much knowledge as possible. But there could be some useful information for you with the French Secret Service. I thought it would be prudent for me to stay away from them."

"I see," the monsignor said, ignoring Tim's remark about the SDECE. "But is there any proof of anything that you've told me? Any proof at all? I heard you say that you could not document your findings, which is understandable, but does it mean that we must rely on nothing more than what various persons wished to plant with you—which could be the case?"

Tim refrained from telling Sainte-Ange much of his conversation with Leduc, as well as details of his meetings in Istambul and Paris. Likewise, he omitted Jake Kurtski's attack on him in Fanjeaux on the Fraternity's orders. He felt increasingly uneasy with the private secretary, an unease that grew because of the manner in which he formulated his questions. It was as if the monsignor was attempting to rebut or undermine the conclusions that Tim had presented to him; he was almost hostile.

"Well," Tim said, "I am going on what I was able to learn from different individuals—I don't know how else to conduct an investigation—and making a judgment of whether it is credible. I also engaged in considerable reading—history, religion, heresies, biographies, and so forth, so that I could better understand the context into which new information fits. Patterns then emerge to make some or all of the pieces fall into place. This is how intelligence work is done. And, as you know, proof is like evidence in a criminal case, and this, of course, is one. Not having hard proof or evidence in hand immediately, does not mean that it will not materialize subsequently. There rarely exists instant public confessions. So one goes on working . . . And, yes, there always are loose ends. Finally, it depends on what you plan to do with all this material. If you do not propose to go public with it and, instead, keep it secret, then formal proof isn't necessary anyway—so long as you believe the conclusions. But it's none of my business what you wish to do with it."

"No, it's none of your business," Sainte-Ange agreed pointedly. "In any event, you are not to discuss this matter with anybody— probably forever. This is a direct order from the Holy Father. In the meantime, please remain available at all times. I may have additional questions after I've digested what you brought me today and have discussed it with His Holiness."

"Will I have a chance to present my findings personally to the Holy Father?" Tim asked.

"I doubt it," the monsignor answered. "He's extremely busy these days. But I promise you that the Holy Father will hear every word of it from me."

Sainte-Ange knocked lightly on the door before entering the papal study. Gregory XVII was at his desk, writing by hand in French the first draft of an encyclical on social justice versus capitalism. Now that Marxism was in retreat everywhere, he hoped to issue it early the following year. The final text would be translated into Latin for publication. He looked up questioningly.

"Holy Father," the private secretary said, "the American Jesuit has completed his mission and he has just left me after presenting his conclusions. Is this is a good time to acquaint you with his findings?"

"Yes, by all means, go ahead," the pope told him. "Is It as bad as we feared, better, or worse?"

"Actually, it is all of these things and a great many elements remain unclear," the monsignor said. "But this is the best we can ever hope to obtain as the trail grows cold. You were absolutely right, Holy Father, to decide to undertake our own secret investigation after the Italian government formally ended their inquiries. Had we waited longer, we might have lost the thread of events altogether. In any case, we have agreed—as you will recall—never to make the findings public, whatever they might be. Since nobody knows about the existence of our investigation—except the two of us, Sister Angela, and the American—there will be no pressure to disclose anything. Sister Angela, who naturally will not be apprised of the conclusions, will be in no position to reveal any materials. Besides, I trust her implicitly: I hired her because she is the daughter of close friends in Paris. The American, who is a totally obscure personage, has no reason or incentive to break the secrecy. I am sure that he realizes that whatever he might say on the subject would be instantly denied by the Holy See on the highest level. And he has no written proof of what he claims to have learned. So, in this sense, we need not be concerned."

"If the Vatican Secret Archives were still secret, I suppose we could store all that information there," Gregory XVII said with light sarcasm. "So we'll keep it in our heads. But do get to the point, please."

"First and most important of all," the monsignor related, "it did not come from inside the Vatican. That would have been what we had feared the most. And Savage, the American, confirms what we thought all along, that you were the victim of the 'Muslim Connection.' The Turk had been recruited by a Muslim terrorist organization without being told, until the last moment in Rome, that you were the person he was to assassinate. That is the good part, meaning that we now know that Circlic was not a madman acting on his own, as many investigators had suspected at the outset. And, as you remember, Holy Father, Circlic never revealed to the Italian investigators nor to the tribunal that tried him the identity of those who had hired and paid him. Savage says that he was able to establish clearly the link between him and the Turkish terrorist organization. He seems to have no indications that an Islamic government might have been behind it—at least, he made no mention of it to me. This, of course, is very important to us because it removes possible clouds over your efforts to strengthen the dialogue between the Church and Islam. So our Islam and Middle East policies are safe."

"What about the theory that the Soviet Union and the Bulgarian secret service, acting for the KGB, were the authors and executors of the conspiracy?" the pope asked. "I am assuming that we are dealing with a conspiracy, whatever its origins."

"It doesn't appear plausible, either," the monsignor answered.

"The American made no references to it, and I suspect that he shares the CIA's conclusions, with which he is surely familiar, that Moscow had no part in it. And it makes good sense: From everything we've seen in recent years, the Soviets are interested in good relations with the Vatican, and killing you would not have advanced their cause in the world, particularly since that fellow Gorbachev took over."

"I'm glad to hear that," Gregory XVII remarked with a smile. "At least I don't have to go to war against him with all of the 'Pope's Divisions,' as Stalin once put it. But, seriously, it *is* a good thing to know. Remember the effort by the Americans and everybody else at the time to discredit the Soviet theory so that they wouldn't be forced to break relations, or worse, with the Russians? I imagine this is why the CIA chose to shoot down that theory, just in case . . . But if not an Islamic government or the Soviets, *who* did organize the conspiracy against me? Any suggestions from your Jesuit?"

"This, I'm afraid, is the bad part of his conclusions, and I think that he came quite close to the whole truth," Sainte-Ange told the pope, his forehead wrinkled in concern. "The American insists that he has obtained information during the several weeks he spent in the south of France that the conspiracy had been originally hatched there by what he calls 'Catholic fundamentalists' who used their contacts with Muslim fundamentalists in Toulouse to have them arrange to recruit Circlic through their connections in Turkey. Apparently, Catholic fundamentalists and Muslim fundamentalists feel solidarity with each other."

"You mean, 'Fundamentalists of the World, Unite!'?" the pope commented with a smile. "But actually your man may be on to something. Such ties, if not actual alliances, do exist among religious extremists around the world. Do you think that what he had in mind was our friend Archbishop Leduc and his Pius V Fraternity? Right in our backyard in the South?"

"Savage did not mention specifically Leduc or the Fraternity," the monsignor replied in the soothing voice he always adopted with his old friend the pope, especially when he was dissembling. "And I doubt that, despite, his professional talents and his excellent command of the French language, he would have been able to penetrate their organization to such an extent. The Muslims there probably never heard of Leduc and his Fraternity. Also, I don't believe that Savage understands enough about all the fights and intrigues in the French Church to make any sense of it. He did say, however, that some people in a position to know refused to confirm or deny that any of our fellow French Catholics were out to murder you. The American also fears that you still are in danger . . . My own impression is that he is right about Catholic fundamentalists, but that they are a handful of individual fanatics and not an organization like the Pius V Fraternity."

Gregory XVII leaned forward over his desk, running the fingers of his right hand up and down over his lips as he always did when he was in deep thought.

"I hope and pray that you are correct in your assumptions," he said after a while. "I realize that Leduc hates and despises me, that he personally is a fanatic, and that he has much support in the French Church. He has led his people into schism despite my efforts to negotiate at least a truce with him, but this is very far from planning to murder the pope. Much as he annoys and frustrates me—as he did by forcing me finally to excommunicate him—I cannot conceive of Leduc having recourse to assassination to settle theological or liturgic differences with Rome and with me. Besides, he is a priest, respectful of life, and I must reject the notion that he could, in effect, be a murderer. "It's absurd . . . I wonder, however, why even certified fanatics, acting as individuals, would want me dead?"

"I would imagine that even Catholic fundamentalists could be paranoid," Saint-Ange answered. "It doesn't take many people to engage in a conspiracy, and paranoia, even in the case of individuals, is a terrible danger that cannot be foreseen. Look at the killing of the Austrian Archduke in Sarajevo that led to the Great War, the assassination of Kennedy, and so on throughout the history of this century . . ."

"Speaking of foresight," the pope remarked, "what about the warning from de Marenches in Paris prior to the assassination attempt? It might be quite relevant in light of what the American has discovered about French Catholics who do not like me. Perhaps de Marenches had some clue or insight about paranoid

Catholics. As I recall, I accepted your advice not to heed his warning because it was too vague in simply saying, as you had told me, that I faced danger from France—and therefore we took no special precautions. We didn't even inform our own *corpo di vigilanza* plainclothesmen. I think that you argued that there was a risk of the warning being leaked to the press in some way and precautions, if we took them, might suggest that the French pope doesn't trust his compatriots. De Marenches did not identify more precisely the provenance of the danger, like a name or something, did he? You did read that warning message, right?"

"Yes, I read the message, and, no, he went into no detail," the monsignor answered smoothly. He was always prepared to lie to Gregory XVII for what he considered his boss's own good.

"And one more thing," the pope said. "You did tell me some time ago that the American was aware of the warning, but he didn't quite know what to make of it. Is it possible that he may now link the warning to what he found out in France?"

"It is possible and *that* would be a problem, Holy Father," Sainte-Ange replied. "This is why I told you at the outset, Holy Father, that some of the material collected by Savage could be damaging to us."

From his own office, the monsignor made a quick telephone call to Paris over his secure line.

"I believe that a family reunion is really overdue," he said to the person who answered. "Would dinner tomorrow be convenient? I'll arrive on a late afternoon flight from Rome and I'll plan on spending the night with my sister. I won't be missed too much here on a Sunday."

De Marenches' warning was very much on Tim Savage's mind when he left Sainte-Ange late that Saturday morning. He had been thinking about it ever since his conversation with Archbishop Leduc at the Cisterian abbey, remembering what the old Jesuit had told him in Rome months earlier and what he had read in the newspaper clips Angela had located for him. Leduc having, in effect, confirmed the conspiracy he had spawned, the unheeded warning from the French secret service chief clearly was a big piece of the whole puzzle, perhaps a vital one, but Tim could not quite fit it into the picture. There had to be more to this affair than what he had learned in his travels, but it kept eluding him. There still was a missing link.

Why, for example, had Sainte-Ange not mentioned the warning when Tim was being entrusted with the mission of investigating the shooting on St. Peter's Square? It had been by sheer happenstance that he had learned of it at all, curiously coinciding with the advice from his friend, the Rome CIA Station Chief, that he should familiarize himself with the figure of de Marenches. He also continued to wonder about the private secretary's attitude toward him as he expressed doubts about Tim's discoveries and conclusions. Why did he forbid a written report? It was worse than the CIA's obsessive "Eyes Only" stuff. Moreover, Tim was intrigued by Sainte-Ange's brusque rejection of his suggestion that he be allowed to make a presentation personally to Gregory XVII.

Increasingly disturbed, Tim called Angela in the afternoon, ostensibly to thank her for arranging the meeting with the monsignor. He then asked whether it would be possible for her to join him for dinner that evening. Angela hesitated only briefly and they agreed to meet at a small, hole-in-the-wall fish restaurant on a street off Borgo Pio, a five-minute walk from the Vatican through Sant'Anna Gate.

"It looks like this is our farewell," Angela told Tim as they sat down at the tiny table in a corner of the noisy restaurant. It was a favorite spot this year for Rome's *jeunesse dorée* whose cars and scooters were parked outside, forming a wall around the entrance. The menu was inscribed with white and colored chalk on a big blackboard standing on the bar counter, and diners shouted their orders to the three or four waiters fighting their way back and forth through the throng. It was an excellent spot not to be noticed. Angela wore a plain, gray dress, almost a nun's habit, under a raincoat. Her face was pale. Tim was reminded of a Botticelli painting, not an unusual reaction among those who knew Angela.

"Why a farewell?" Tim asked, surprised.

"Monsignor Sainte-Ange told me that you have completed your assignment and that there would be no further need for communication between you and me," Angela said.

"Well, assignment is one thing and communication between us is something else," Tim said. He was extremely annoyed with the monsignor, and now not only over their morning conversation. "You don't mean that he actually forbade you to see me? So we wouldn't have a friendship outside of work?"

"He didn't say it in so many words," Angela replied, "but that is what he had in mind. He likes to control everything and everybody, and I imagine I'm in violation of his instructions by seeing you tonight. After all, I do belong to his Papal Household staff. Still, I couldn't simply hang up on you—forever. So this *is* a farewell . . . I believe, however, that his main reason for ending our contact is to make all traces of your mission vanish."

"Would you risk violating his instructions to meet again, if we wished to meet?" he asked her gently.

Angela looked down in silence at her plate, toying with her fork and her *scampi*. Then she raised her head to meet Tim's eyes.

"Why don't we take things a day at a time, as they happen," she said, delicately placing her hand on his. "We don't have to make final decisions tonight. I certainly do not . . . Do you feel like talking about the rest of your stay in France, after we parted in Paris? When I saw him after your visit this morning I had the impression that for some reason the Monsignor seemed disappointed with your work . . . Should he be? It all seems so mysterious."

"It is," Tim answered. "In fact, it gets curiouser and curiouser, if I may quote from *Alice in Wonderland*. It was normal to encounter resistance, even hostility, when I was investigating in the field. That's what you expect. But I found the Monsignor to be nearly as hostile and incredibly suspicious of what I was reporting to him. He treated me as if I were trying to sell him a bill of goods. If he was disappointed, I have no idea what he had expected of me. To validate some pet theory of his, or what? I have no agenda of my own."

Tim then gave Angela a fairly full account of his investigations in France, including his meeting with the imam in Toulouse and the conversations with the abbé at the Pius V Fraternity's seminary and with Archbishop Leduc at the abbey. He told her about his shoot-out with Kurtski, going back briefly to their Vietnam past, as well as about the archbishop's explanation for the attack on him in Fanjeaux.

"So my conclusion is that Leduc was the man who conceived and engineered the attempt on the pope's life," Tim told her. "This is the conclusion I presented this morning to the Monsignor—although I chose to omit quite a few things, like Kurtski's attack on me and my actual encounter with Leduc. I had the weird feeling that I shouldn't tell him all I know and all I did. But I would've told the pope if I had been permitted to see him, which Sainte-Ange vetoed. Very strange! You know, I now feel caught between two hostile sides: Leduc there and Sainte-Ange here."

"The Monsignor obviously wishes to be in full command of this operation," Angela remarked. "If he isn't happy with the outcome, which, for whatever reason, seems to be the case, he prefers to obliterate your investigation altogether. This is why, I think, he didn't want anything from you on paper."

"That's fine with me," Tim said, "except that, as I warned Sainte-Ange, the Holy Father remains in great danger. By the way, Angela, do you remember this business of warnings from de Marenches of the French secret service? You sent me some clippings, and then I asked you to find out if Sainte-Ange knew more about it—and he said he didn't, right?"

"Yes, of course, I remember," she answered. "And you know, when I returned from Paris the Monsignor asked me whether I had seen you. He also asked, rather casually, whether you had referred in any way to de Marenches."

"Yeah, it gets curiouser by the minute," Tim mused. "But, all things considered, I cannot understand why Sainte-Ange wanted an investigation in the first place, and then why he recruited me for it."

"Oh, that's very simple," Angela said. "My very educated guess is that it was the pope who had demanded an investigation after the Italians had given up on it, and Saint-Ange had to obey. He likes to tie up loose ends, especially concerning his survival. It was never the Monsignor's idea: he believes in letting sleeping dogs lie. The pope did develop some doubts after you were recruited, but dropped them in the end . . ."

"How do you know?"

"When you work there for a while, as I have, you learn to listen and remember. It is, after all, a tight little place. I've seen this sort of thing, involving the Holy Father and the Monsignor, happen before. They always work it out."

Monsignor Sainte-Ange, wearing a plain gray flannel suit by Adolfo, was met at the bottom of the Air France plane's ramp in midfield at the Charles de Gaulle Airport in Paris by a polite young man who led him to a waiting car. Forty-five minutes later, the monsignor entered a luxurious apartment in a building off Avenue Foch in the fashionable sixteenth *arrondissement*. He had left the Apostolic Palace shortly before noon, prior to Gregory XVII's regular Sunday appearance in his window, having informed the pope that he had a family emergency in Paris involving his older sister and would return the next day. The pope wished Sainte-Ange a safe trip and blessed him. Sainte-Ange also left routine instructions with the assistant private secretary, a Brazilian monsignor.

His cousin, Georges de Sainte-Ange, the head of SDECE, the French CIA-like secret service, was awaiting him in the living room. He had played golf in the morning, probably the last decent-weather Sunday of the year, and was still in his sports clothes.

"Greetings, dear cousin Georges," the monsignor said. "I hate to spoil your weekend, but we have a bit of a problem on our hands."

"So I gather," Georges responded. "I've already heard from the abbey early last week. And a furious call it was! I'm curious as to what you can add to it. And may I offer you a glass of champagne? Is Veuve Clicquot okay?"

The private secretary looked puzzled.

"But I cannot see the connection between what I came to discuss with you and that call from the abbey," he said. "Tell me about the call and I'll fill you in on what I learned yesterday morning in my own office."

"It was about that fellow Savage, the American Jesuit," Georges de Sainte-Ange said. "This reminds me, dear cousin, that you never informed me that you had him working for you."

"I meant to do it once I heard his report," the monsignor explained. "I'm really sorry. But what about Savage?"

"Well, to put it briefly, our friend was very upset that my people screwed up, which they did, and failed to liquidate the American."

"What, in God's name, are you talking about?" the monsignor exploded.

"Actually, there was no operational reason for you to be aware of it beforehand, particularly since I had no idea that Savage worked for you," Georges told him. "But Archbishop Leduc had discovered very recently that Savage had learned plenty about the plan to assassinate your pope, including the rather disconcerting fact that he, personally, and his Fraternity had arranged to hire the Turkish gunman. Savage told Leduc when they met the other day that he had come up with it in the course of his investigation. This had led Leduc, with impeccable logic, to the conclusion that it wouldn't be wise to let the American go home to Rome and babble about it in front of Gregory XVII. That's why he had ordered him killed in Fanjeaux. You, of course, knew the background, but Leduc was afraid that the pope would want to hear Savage's report himself. It was fortunate that you were able to to keep that part of de Marenches' warning—about Leduc—from Gregory XVII the first time around. The archbishop, however, could not take chances that Savage would break the news to the pope five years after the fact—and after the death of de Marenches and his colonel. So, he wanted Savage dead, you see."

"That is extraordinary," the monsignor commented, feeling completely off balance for the first time in his career. "Savage never said a word to me about any attempt to kill him. In fact, the son of a whore didn't even mention that he had actually spoken with Leduc . . . But how did your people figure in the plan to murder Savage?"

"I'm afraid that I forgot to let you know, way back, that my Service provides security for Leduc and the Fraternity," his cousin said. "It's one of those complicated French political situations I wouldn't have wanted to bother you with, anyway. You know, the rightist premier under a socialist president, a rightist religious movement, my minister and that sort of thing . . . The guards at the abbey, at the residence of Leduc's deputy, a bishop named Laval, and at the Fraternity's seminary in Mirepoix are SDECE personnel who report directly—and only—to me. So are the drivers and support elements. We have a special office for it in Carcassonne . . . So when Leduc and Laval decided to have Savage eliminated, the archbishop asked me to orchestrate it. Leduc's personal security chief, one of my guys, already had on the payroll an American mercenary who once worked for the CIA in Vietnam and whom I had found, and he was to do the killing. My people were to organize the logistics, but it all went wrong and, instead, Savage killed the other American. So, naturally, Leduc went ballistic . . ."

"Incredible," the monsignor said. "So, not only does Savage know almost everything about the conspiracy, but he is playing some kind of a game with me—not informing me about meeting Leduc or about the attempt to kill him . . . And he knows something, though probably not everything, about de Marenches' warning. Can you imagine what this goddamned Jesuit can do with this information? It's pure dynamite! How do we control him? Do we have to get rid of him at all costs? And, by the way, Georges, how did you know that Savage works for me?"

"Ah, that's an easy one, dear cousin," the intelligence chief replied. "The moment I heard from Leduc that an American Jesuit was investigating the 1981 shooting, I had to assume that he was working for *somebody*. Savage wouldn't be doing it on his own because there was no reason for an Islamic scholar from the Vatican to embark suddenly on investigating conspiracies to kill the pope. And, of course, I ran a quick check on him and, surprise of surprises, it turned out that he was a CIA veteran as well, which I'm sure you knew from the outset . . . You know, Romain, it is a shame that, as family, we don't stay in better touch. We could both learn a lot . . ."

"Unquestionably," the monsignor replied, "but the reality is that Savage is now a problem and a liability for both of us, a much greater problem than I thought when I called you yesterday. We better find a solution before it is too late."

"Yes. I just hope and pray that Pope Gregory XVII never loses his faith in you. Our family could never afford it."

"I killed Jake Kurtski," Tim said quietly to Paul Martinius.

They were having lunch at the penthouse restaurant of the Hotel Eden, across the street from Villa Malta. It commanded the most magnificent view of Rome, across the Tiber and the Aventine hills, with St. Peter's Basilica looming majestically in the distance. Tim had called Paul on Monday, two days after his meeting with Sainte-Ange and his dinner with Angela. He needed to share his new knowledge with the CIA Station Chief. They agreed to get together the following day, selecting the Eden as the most convenient spot in the neighborhood.

"You did *what?*" Martinius gasped, choking on his beer. "What the fuck are you talking about?"

"I shot Kurtski dead because he was trying to shoot *me* dead," Tim told him. "In a little town on a hill named Fanjeaux in the Languedoc in France . . . I guess that what goes around, comes around. Maybe it was the final chapter of Vietnam for both of us. You remember what happened there, when I refused to kill on Kurtski's orders, resigned from the Agency, and all that . . ."

"Holy shit!" Martinius exclaimed. "How did it happen? Why was that bastard out to kill you? I know that he was in Rome earlier in the year—I think I mentioned it to you at the time—but I had no idea he was involved in your kind of stuff."

"Let me tell you the whole story as I understand it," Tim said. "The big headline is that the conspiracy against Gregory XVII, part of a secret 'crusade' against Rome, was planned and carried out by old Archbishop Jules Leduc and his fanatic Pius V Fraternity. They worked through their contacts in the Muslim fundamentalist community in Toulouse who, in turn, helped to recruit Agca Circlic through *their* contacts in Istambul. I was able, much of it through sheer luck, to reconstruct the main outlines of how it was done—until the conspiracy collapsed when Circlic failed to kill the pope that day on St. Peter's Square. At one point, however, Leduc and his people found out how much I had learned—which, presumably, made me dangerous to all concerned—and Kurtski became the designated hitter. But I don't think they had the slightest idea of Kurtski's and my history in Vietnam. It was just the weirdest coincidence in the world."

For a full hour, Tim recounted for Martinius every step of his investigation, culminating with his late-night session with Archbishop Leduc.

"But this thing still remains very odd," he said. "When I went to see Sainte-Ange on Saturday morning to make my presentation orally—I was forbidden to put anything down in writing, which I thought was strange—the Monsignor spent almost the entire time trying to knock down my story, to challenge me over my lack of proof or evidence. It was like telling me, 'You're full of shit and nobody will believe you, anyway, if you come out with your revelations.' He made a point of informing me that I was a nobody, which suits me fine, but it doesn't explain his demeanor. I had the very distinct impression that Sainte-Ange, having recruited me, now wanted to sweep that whole business under the carpet, forget about it, and make me forget about it, if I know what's good for me . . . And, by the way, he wouldn't let me make my presentation directly to the pope, who he said was too busy . . . What do you make of it?"

"Maybe he didn't like your conclusions," Martinius offered, "and I mean it. This isn't a simple affair of just trying to knock off the pope. There's more to it . . . But how did Saint-Ange react to your shoot-out with Kurtski and your conversation with Leduc?"

"Well, I must confess that I didn't mention either to Sainte-Ange," Tim replied. "My instinct warned me against telling him everything. And the way he treated me the other day sort of vindicated my caution. I really distrust him."

"Then I had better clue *you* in on a couple of things you should know at this stage that I didn't feel free to tell you the last time we met," Martinius said. "But I did tell you to look into some activities of the late Alexandre de Marenches of the French SDECE. Remember?"

"Yes, I do, and I know that he had sent a warning to the Vatican that a plot against the pope was in the works, but they paid no attention to him here," Tim answered. "That warning story and what's behind it is a big gap in my research."

"Let me see if I can help you a bit," Martinius interjected. "De Marenches had sent Monsignor Sainte-Ange a fairly detailed report on the preparations to kill the pope, including—specifically—Archbishop Leduc's and the Fraternity's leading role in the plot. As you realize, the Holy See chose to ignore this warning—or, more to the point, Sainte-Ange decided to ignore it. I have no way of knowing what he had, or had not, told Gregory XVII, although I have my suspicions . . ."

"I, of course, had no idea that Sainte-Ange had been aware from the very beginning that it was Leduc who was gunning for his boss," Tim said. "But how do you know about it?"

"It's very interesting, Tim," his friend told him. "De Marenches shared his information about the plot both with us—the Paris Station—and with Interpol in Lyons. I imagine that he didn't trust Sainte-Ange, either, for whatever reasons, and wanted to make sure that others were informed as well in great secrecy. The Agency and the White House naturally did nothing about it— there was nothing to be done—and when the assassination attempt actually occurred, the top-level Administration policy decision in Washington was to stay out of it completely. This is why, Tim, the CIA rejected the Soviet KGB theory from the very beginning. It was incredibly frustrating, but that's the way life is in this line of work."

"Do you know why Sainte-Ange resolved to ignore the warning?" Tim asked.

"No," Martinius said, "that's *my* gap in the story . . . But I have to assume that it's a matter involving the Vatican, the French Church, and French politics. That's an anthill I don't propose to stir, certainly not from Rome. And especially because there have been other mysterious events involving some of the principals, none of which is in my jurisdiction."

"For example?" Tim inquired.

"For example that de Marenches died not too long ago," Martinius said. "The official story was that the cause of death was a heart attack. My British pal, the Interpol chief, told me at the time that de Marenches had no heart disease history and that his cadaver was cremated before an autopsy could be conducted. His family were terribly angry. In any case, the real circumstances of de Marenches' death remain a closely held secret at the highest levels of the French government. But, as I listen to you, I begin to wonder whether there was a connection between it and the plot to assassinate the pope. You know, Colonel Bernard Nut, who was de Marenches' most trusted aide, who had hand-delivered the warning to Sainte-Ange, was shot to death in Nice shortly after his chief died. I'm afraid we'll never find out what happened and how all these intrigues are linked."

"My God !" Tim whispered.

"And one more fact for you," Martinius continued. "Immediately after he died, de Marenches was replaced as head of the SDECE by Georges de Sainte-Ange, who had been the head of their Soviet Division, a career spook. As it happens, he and Romain de Sainte-Ange, yes, the pope's private secretary, are first cousins. It's a family back channel. This may be why, I suspect, the Italian investigating magistrate never received a reply to his request for additional information concerning de Marenches' warning about which he had heard in very general terms. So, there you are."

"But do we know why Sainte-Ange had blocked de Marenches' warning?" Tim persisted. "This could be the principal piece in the whole puzzle. Besides, I think that the pope's enemies haven't given up."

"No, we do not," the Station Chief said. "And I wish we could find out before somebody takes another potshot at Gregory XVII— or at you, old buddy. . . ."

Chapter Twenty-five

1987

TIM SAVAGE NEVER SAW Monsignor Sainte-Ange again. Autumn had turned into winter and into spring anew, and, as far as the Apostolic Palace was concerned, it seemed as if Tim simply did not exist. He had resumed work at his office, reassuring colleagues that he had recovered from ill health, and plunged back into matters affecting the Vatican's interests in Iran, Iraq, Sudan, and other Islamic countries. In papal Rome, both the unwritten protocol and unspoken political rules sheltered Tim from curiosity and questions. Everything was normal—as if he had never left his desk at Via dell'Erba 1.

At first, following his conversation with Paul Martinius, Tim thought that Sainte-Ange might recall him for a more detailed—and calmer—debriefing. But, perhaps, as Angela had told him, the private secretary, disappointed with Tim's report and conclusions, had decided that the American had, so to speak, outlived his usefulness and no further contacts were desired.

Tim was certain that the monsignor had no concerns about his discretion, not only as a matter of his integrity as a man and a priest, but because he would not disobey Gregory XVII's orders, relayed by Sainte-Ange, to maintain eternal public silence about his mission. In any case, Tim had no intention of divulging the investigation he had pursued. That had been his CIA training, the Agency also requiring a written pledge of secrecy from its employees. He did not regard Kurtski's attack on him as an excuse for breaking his silence: For an intelligence professional, the Fanjeaux incident was merely part of a day's work. Romeo team's raids in Vietnam, with all their perils, had also been part of a

302

working day. Nor did he consider that his conversations with Angela and Martinius violated the canon of discretion: He had discussed the subject with each of them in the past in the context of the investigation. Back at Villa Malta, Tim had burned in the furnace his investigative ledger with all his notes and other written materials he had accumulated.

And Tim did not believe that, under the circumstances, he faced further physical danger. The assignment was over, his involvement in the assassination affair had ended, and he was back in the safe mantle of Vatican anonymity. He doubted that Leduc would again go after him. As Sainte-Ange had stated correctly, the assassination conspiracy was no longer any of Tim's business. He had done his duty in cautioning the private secretary that, in his opinion, the pope was still in danger, but it was up to the Holy See to protect Gregory XVII.

Angela, however, was very much Tim's business and very much on his mind. Without the urgency of the investigation, he had the leisure—and definitely the inclination—to meditate about his own life, and not in a theological mode. He realized, among other realities, that he had never been seriously in love, though it would not be very long before he reached his half-century mark—he had just passed his forty-fifth birthday. And there was no question that his meditation had a lot to do with Angela. It was no more unchaste thoughts, not just unavowed lust: it went much deeper. So now what? Tim asked himself as he stared at the springtime greenery of Rome extending almost endlessly from his window high up at Villa Malta. He could not forget the touch of her hand on his own that Saturday evening at the fish restaurant.

Priests falling in love with nuns, as Tim knew, was not at all that uncommon. Nor was it uncommon for nuns to reciprocate. Since the marriage of a priest to any woman was prohibited in the universal Church, certainly since Christianity's early centuries, it would be idle for him to contemplate it even in his wildest dreams—and he was having the wildest dreams these nights. He was reminded of St. Augustine's comment in *The City of God:* "At times, without intention, the body stirs on its own insistence . . . At other times, it leaves a straining lover in the lurch." Maybe the

Protestants were right in letting their clergy marry. But this, too, was irrelevant. The obvious solution, should he wish to marry and there was a reciprocating partner, would be to recant his vows and leave the Church. This was occurring increasingly, for reasons of principle as for other reasons, as the Roman Catholic Church was losing its appeal and a number of its members. And, quite aside from Angela, Tim had felt in recent years his faith weakening and doubts emerging as to whether his priestly vocation was really total and absolute—and not a psychological and spiritual reaction to his Vietnam trauma. He did not want to admit it fully even to himself—he had not been to confession since he had embarked on the papal investigation—but the doubts and discouragement were mounting.

Living as he had for years in the center of the Holy See's policy making, watching at close quarters Vatican intrigues and promotion-driven political corruption, the arrogance of power, ruthlessness, and hypocrisy, Tim had begun to wonder whether *believing* in the Church and *belonging* to the Church as part of the pious priestly bureaucracy were one and the same. And his exposure to Archbishop Leduc's deadly maneuvers and conspiracies as well as his startling experience with Monsignor Saint-Ange, topped by what he had learned from Paul Martinius, had further undermined his priestly faith and commitment to rigorous, blind submission.

Mysteriously, Tim thought, his fundamental doubts had converged with his attraction to Angela, creating a whole new dilemma. He was anxious not to confuse the two sets of situations: not to justify his love for Angela—he was now convinced it was love, a new emotion for him—with his disappointment in the Church. It would be wrong to allow himself the luxury of rationalization. Finally, Tim had no clear idea how Angela felt about him and *her* Church vows. Her warmth in Paris and touching his hand at a Rome restaurant were hardly declarations of love.

The most rational thing to do would be to see Angela again, to try to gauge her feelings toward him, if any. He could be dead wrong about reciprocity. Tim faced, however, the practical problem of getting in touch with her. Since Sainte-Ange had terminated his ties to the Apostolic Palace and had so informed Angela, he could no longer call her directly. He had to take it for granted that all calls to the Papal Household, of which Angela was part, were monitored, and he could not risk embarrassing her.

Finding elusive people was supposedly one of the most elementary skills of intelligence officers. As Tim began to work out a plan, he was put to shame a few days later when Angela called and asked him quite plainly to have dinner at the midtown apartment of a French woman friend.

"She's away this week so we'll be undisturbed," she said gaily. "And I'll cook . . . yes, I know how . . ."

Angela looked beautiful in Tim's hungry eyes, the dinner was prepared to perfection, the wine was fine, and she came to the point quickly.

"There are two things I want to say to you, Tim," Angela told him as soon as they sat down at the table and she had served him. "The first thing is that you should waste no time getting out of Rome—for good. They are out to get rid of you. I don't mean physically, of course, but you have absolutely no future in the Vatican. My impression is that Sainte-Ange is not only disappointed and furious as a result of your mission, but he believes that your presence should no longer be tolerated in the Curia. That you must be punished in some way . . . I've heard enough around the office to know how you are regarded by the Monsignor. And, naturally, he has the power to have the punishment inflicted. My best guess is that you will be dismissed from the Council and the Commission—with no formal reason given—and that you will not be given any other post in the Vatican. Not even at a pontifical university, like the Gregorian."

"I guess I shouldn't be surprised," Tim said. "I'm the last person he would want around Rome. He's probably worried that staying here and being around Church people in the normal course of events, I might inadvertently betray something of what I know, and that it would be instantly all over Rome. I imagine that it's safer and more convenient for the Monsignor if I'm sent away as a missionary or something somewhere far in the world, like East Timor or Patagonia, where nobody would know what I'm talking about—even if I do talk, which I don't intend to do, anyway."

"It's not for me to offer you advice on how to manage your life, but perhaps you should resign before you're fired," Angela remarked. "But that's for you to decide. The other thing I wanted to bring up tonight is—us . . ."

"Us?" Tim asked with overwhelming incredulity, his heart beating faster. "What about us?"

"Look, I believe in being open and honest," Angela told him. "For reasons I won't go into at this point, I have resolved to renounce my nun's vows. I no longer wish to live this kind of life. Suffice it to say that the Monsignor's behavior toward you was the last straw for me. I've seen too much of that sort of thing . . . Nor do I wish to cloister myself in a convent and pray and hope to become Mother Superior someday."

"It's miraculous," Tim broke in, unable to keep silent as she spoke, "to hear you tell me about resigning your vows because giving up priesthood is exactly what has been going through my mind and, I guess, my soul . . . And not only because of my recent experiences as a Vatican detective . . ."

"Well, perhaps it isn't so miraculous," Angela answered. "We haven't known each other long or well, but I have the impression that we think very much alike. And I trust you . . ."

"Yes, we do, and I trust you, too," Tim said, not quite believing what was happening. "What do you suppose would happen if we both left the Church?"

"For one thing, we might give some thought to life together," she said firmly. "I told you that I'm open and honest. I am attracted to you. I think that you are attracted to me . . ."

"My God, yes!" Tim exclaimed, so full of joy that he could not articulate another coherent sentence. "You will never believe how much I've thought about you since the day we met!"

"But we don't want to do anything rash, Tim," Angela said. "Why don't we think about all our ideas and talk about them, and, God willing, we shall find the way."

They parted kissing chastely on the cheek.

May 13, 1987, the feast of Our Lady of Fátima, fell on a Wednesday. Archbishop Leduc had planned to deliver a homily at a solemn Mass at noon in the chapel of the Pius V Fraternity seminary in

Mirepoix. He left his residence at the Cisterian abbey mid-morning, going over his prepared text in the right-hand side seat of his powerful armor-plated black Mercedes limousine. Jean-Pierre, his security chief, was next to him, an automatic assault rifle at his feet. The black-suited driver and the security agent in the front seat with him had their weapons within easy reach. A lead black Cit-roën with four armed agents and a chase Citroën with its security complement brought up the rear. This was the routine mode of Leduc's travel.

The motorcade made a right turn at the Carcassonne–Mirepoix highway, then began the three-mile climb toward Fanjeaux. At its highest point, the Fanjeaux square where the café was located, the highway veered sharply to the left to descend to the southwest plain. As Leduc's limousine passed the café, moving at about thirty miles per hour, a heavy white semi twelve-wheeler, of the variety used for transporting tons of merchandise, that had been parked for an hour at the edge of the square, suddenly lurched onto the highway at the curve. It was precisely 10:23 A.M. that sunny morning.

The truck's front end smashed into the Mercedes, hitting it with such force that the car's right-hand side, with its armor plates, was impelled into the middle, flattening it like a tin can and sending it hurling down a ravine on the far border of the highway. Within seconds, the vehicle exploded in an orange ball of fire, incinerating its occupants. The truck went into reverse, regained the road, turned left, and raced downhill toward Carcassonne. Exactly thirty seconds had elapsed, which was the time specified in the detailed timetable for the crash to occur. The white semi was already out of sight when the chase car had reached the top of the Fanjeaux hill and the security agents saw the burning remains of Archbishop Leduc's limousine.

At the precise moment the archbishop's Mercedes was exploding below the Fanjeaux square, three high-velocity bullets were fired in succession at the altar from the inside of the door of the little church at the foot of Via di Porta Ponciana in Rome, three blocks down the street from the Jesuit residence at Villa Malta. It was the church where Tim Savage usually celebrated the early morning

Mass on Sundays and the ten o'clock Mass on Wednesdays, when he was in Rome. On this particular Wednesday, Tim was celebrating his first Mass at the little church since his return from France.

Standing behind the altar, Tim was facing the congregation of ten or so elderly women when the shots were fired. What had probably saved Tim's life was the fact that the church was penumbral and he had begun to turn to kneel before the altar, making him a moving target. All three bullets missed, becoming embedded in the wall just below the sculpture of the crucified Christ. Tim never saw the assailant, but the police later found the discarded Walther automatic on the stone floor by the door; not surprisingly, there were no fingerprints on the weapon. The shooter had probably fled on his *motorino,* becoming an untraceable part of the Roman traffic gridlock.

Back at his Villa Malta room, still shaken from the church shooting, Tim turned on his television set for the RAI UNO noon newscast. The lead story was a report from Toulouse that Archbishop Leduc, the controversial leader of a traditionalist Roman Catholic faction in France, had died that morning in a fiery accident at the small town of Fanjeaux in the foothills of the Pyrénées. Leduc's face appeared on the screen along with some footage from church-occupying marches by Pius V Fraternity militants and a sound bite of the original Vatican announcement of Leduc's excommunication.

The date—May thirteenth—also flashed on the screen at the end of the broadcast, and Tim abruptly realized that this was the Feast of Our Lady of Fátima, the anniversary of the day on which Agca Circlic had attempted to assassinate Gregory XVII. This could not be a coincidence—simultaneous lethal acts against two persons directly involved in the matter of the attack on St. Peter's Square. It was diabolical symbolism, but, Tim wondered, was it also a fresh threat against the pope and those who knew too much? In any case, these acts had to have been perpetrated by someone who knew absolutely *everything.*

All in all, it made no sense. If these events on the anniversary of the 1981 attempt were meant as a menace to the pope by Leduc's Fraternity, why was the archbishop himself killed this morning? Tim did not believe for a moment that Leduc's death in Fanjeaux was an accident—it simply was not credible—so it could be ruled out as a warning to Gregory XVII. In that case, who would wish the old archbishop dead? Some rogue elements in the Pius V Fraternity? Not likely, either.

The attack on Tim in the church that same morning was obviously related to the conspiracy and synchronized with the Leduc "accident." However, if it stemmed from fear that he would reveal his knowledge, it could have harmed nobody but Leduc and the Fraternity. Yet, Leduc had been executed at the same moment more than a thousand miles away, and why choose the Fátima anniversary for the attacks? What kind of a message was being sent by whom—and to whom?

Tim and Paul Martinius met early in the evening at the Excelsior Hotel bar on Via Veneto, a tourist-infested oasis of wealth where cocktail-time crowds provided suitable cover for discreet meetings. Martinius had called Tim just as the Jesuit was about to phone him. Events were now moving rapidly, and both were anxious to compare notes.

"My Interpol friend tells me that Leduc's death was no accident," the CIA man said. "The French police, who have been investigating it all day, say that it was murder pure and simple. That truck had been waiting for the archbishop's limousine much of the morning, its engine running and ready to go. When Leduc appeared on the highway curve, the truck just smashed into his car, broadside, like a tank . . . And the next thing anybody knew, the truck had disappeared. So, who do you think wanted to kill him?"

"I really don't know, Paul," Tim answered. "And what's more, I cannot make any sense out of it, especially because of the date and what happened to me today."

"Meaning what?"

"Do you realize that today is the Feast of Our Lady of Fátima and the anniversary of the attempt on the pope?"

"Christ, no . . . I didn't make the connection!" Martinius said, a bit too loudly. "And what happened to you?"

"Well, someone fired at me three times with an automatic weapon when I was at the altar celebrating Mass at the little church at the bottom of Porta Ponciana. As you can see, he missed. But the best I can reconstruct it, the shooting was at exactly the same time Leduc was killed up in Fanjeaux."

"At least you're in good company, getting shot at while saying Mass," Martinius said, regaining aplomb. "There was the Polish bishop in the eleventh century, Becket in the twelfth century, and Romero a couple of years ago . . . *'Oh, rid me of that meddlesome priest!'* Remember?"

"Thank you," Tim said, "that's very uplifting. But where does it go from here? Clearly, conspiracies around Gregory XVII aren't quite over. The place is redolent with hatreds, revenges, and Roman vendettas . . . And, by the way, did your people also check with the SDECE to see whether they thought it was an accident that killed Leduc?"

"No," Martinius replied. "We stopped sharing intelligence with the French after de Marenches died . . . We don't like the new fellow."

Late in the evening, Monsignor Sainte-Ange called the Paris apartment over his secure line.

"Was it necessary to go quite that far this morning, Georges?" he asked. "It really looked horrible on television, the wreck and so on. And are you quite sure that you'll get away with the 'accident' version?"

"The answer is 'yes' to both questions," his cousin replied. "You cannot perform autopsies on incinerated bodies. And the problem with shooting at people is that you never know whether it will succeed—as Leduc found out with Circlic and your guys in Rome found out when they missed Savage in the church . . . Anyway, we removed today one cancer that was beginning to spread all over the body. My boss, the president, thinks so—and I, a civil servant, of course agree with him. But we must extirpate this other cancer as soon as possible. He is quite resistant, or lucky, as we have now seen twice. He's a pro, too, and he'll figure out all the connections, sooner or later. Although nobody would believe him if he chose to speak out, we can't afford to let him be a loose cannon. It would be bad for France and it could hurt us with the politicians here who know that Leduc was close to the *Front National* and my other conservative friends, and that probably I, too, had ties with the arch-bishop."

"Why, then, don't I leave this to you," the monsignor said. "You are *the* pro . . ."

"You can count on it, dear cousin," Georges promised him.

Late in the afternoon on Thursday, Gregory XVII called Sainte-Ange over their private line to ask him to come to his study.

"Romain," the pope said in a tired, sad voice, "I am very disturbed by a series of recent events and I hope you can help me with some explanations."

"Of course, Holy Father," the monsignor replied with a sense of doom.

"I was very shocked by the death of Archbishop Leduc," Gregory XVII told him. "He sinned by leading his people into schism. He caused a lot of damage. But I always had a certain respect for him because he had his own sense of integrity, I thought, even while performing or ordering evil deeds. Like trying to kill me . . ."

Sainte-Ange froze.

"Kill you, Holy Father? Leduc? I don't understand . . ."

"You see, my dear Romain, a secret letter from Archbishop Leduc was delivered to me—I prefer not to say by whom—yesterday morning, just about the time he was being murdered in Fanjeaux. It was a stunning letter. He wrote that since I was to learn the truth anyway, very soon, from the American Jesuit, including the fact that he had tried to have him killed because the American had discovered everything about the conspiracy, he wished to tell me that truth himself . . . And now I must wonder whether his death really was an accident . . ."

The monsignor was silent, breathing heavily.

"Leduc wrote that he had organized the conspiracy against me," Gregory XVII went on, "because, in his opinion, I was destroying the Church by implementing the reforms of the Vatican Council and therefore he believed he had a divine mandate to conduct a crusade, a war, against me. Because it was a 'just war,' he wrote, this justified assassinating me. He added, rather curiously, that theology and politics often blend."

"He was a madman, a criminal madman!" Saint-Ange cried.

311

"Perhaps, perhaps," the pope said. "Maybe he was a holy fool, as one used to say, maybe a heretic. But he begged my forgiveness and, I, of course, was prepared to forgive him—as I've foregiven Agca Circlic. But there is one thing I fail to comprehend."

"Which thing, Holy Father?" Sainte-Ange asked. He was feeling weak.

"When you received the warning from de Marenches that a plot against me was being hatched in France," the pope said, "you informed me about it. On your recommendation, we decided to ignore it. The reason you gave and I accepted was that any extravagant precautions might suggest that the pope is afraid of his own flock. You thought that de Marenches' warning might be leaked to the press—we've already discussed some of it the other day."

"That is correct, Holy Father," the private secretary agreed. "I was doing what I always do—trying to protect you in every way."

"But, Romain, you did not tell me that the Archbishop was the head of the conspiracy," Gregory XVII continued. "Leduc wrote me he had subsequently learned of de Marenches' warning from friends in the SDECE—you have a cousin running it, don't you?—and he wrote that it had identified him as the inspiration behind the conspiracy. Why did you keep this from me?"

Sainte-Ange looked away from the pope, staring at a painting of Our Lady of Fátima on the far wall of the study. He coughed, began to speak, halted, and started again.

"There was only one reason," he said very quietly, "and the reason was that I was determined to prevent a complete and final split within the Church of France. I know how kind and understanding you are, Holy Father, but I felt we couldn't risk a violent reaction from you against Leduc if I had told you everything about de Marenches' warning. I feared, for example, that you would denounce him publicly before I could dissuade you . . ."

"Romain, you are my friend and helper, but you are not my brother's keeper," Gregory XVII told him severely. "It was not for you to make judgments in my place. You seem to have developed such a proclivity . . . as, for example, you convinced me last week not to receive the American Jesuit and hear his report on the investigation that I had demanded in the first place. Now I see that if I had heard the truth from the American, Leduc might be alive today and the scandal over his assassination would not be spreading across France. You surely realize that nobody believes it was an accident. You have caused the Church—and France and me—grievous damage, Romain . . ."

"But I tried to do everything right," Sainte-Ange said pleadingly. "To protect you. I went to see Leduc—yes, behind your back—after the shooting on May thirteenth to beg him not to attempt another attack against you. He wouldn't promise me . . . So I had to engage in damage control, to make sure that nobody knew about the conspiracy. With the help of my SDECE cousin, we caused de Marenches' 'mysterious death' and the shooting of his top aide, a colonel. The secret had to be protected, I thought, at all costs. When you demanded the investigation, I carefully chose someone who appeared to be highly qualified in intelligence and Islam—I was pushing the 'Muslim Connection' to conceal Leduc's role—but who, not knowing France, was unlikely to come up with much. In short, I had hoped that the 'Muslim Connection' track would be accepted once and for all and bury forever the Leduc secret . . . Oh, God, I was so frightfully wrong! I wish I were dead! . . ."

Gregory XVII rose from behind his desk.

"I wish to celebrate at the Basilica tomorrow a Solemn High Pontifical Mass in memory of Archbishop Leduc," he said. "It will, of course, be Mass according to the Tridentine Rite—in Latin."

"Monsignor Sainte-Ange died suddenly this morning, right after the pope celebrated a solemn Mass—a Tridentine Mass—in memory of Archbishop Leduc," Angela told Tim Savage. "It was a heart attack or, at least, that's what the pope's personal physician said to us. He is such a loyal man and would not countenance even the thought of mortal sin on the Monsignor's part. Sainte-Ange was found in his chair behind his desk in his office. There will be no autopsy, on orders from the Holy Father, and the burial in hallowed ground is tomorrow. I guess it was God's will to wind up matters in this fashion."

Angela had telephoned Tim at Villa Malta from the Vatican, and they talked briefly about the monsignor.

"Yes," he said, "and I think that the Holy Father is no longer in danger. The conspiracy, too, is dead now that Leduc is gone—and

I hope the pope's next private secretary is wiser when it comes to protecting him."

"So, I guess all that's left is us," Angela told Tim. "I've lost my employer and my job. The new private secretary will select his own staff, and I no longer wish to be part of it. Now I have to think about my future. And I was hoping that we might think together. Does that appeal to you?"

"I think it's the greatest idea I've heard in all my life," Tim announced with boundless enthusiasm. "It's *our* future we must think about. And, you know, I realized that this phase of life had ended for me when my mother telephoned me from Washington yesterday with the news that Father Hugh Morgan, my great friend and mentor, had died from cancer; he had been ill for a long time . . . I guess it was a sign from above."

Tim's next caller was Paul Martinius.

"I thought you'd like to know that Georges de Sainte-Ange has just resigned in Paris as the head of the French intelligence service and has vanished from sight," he said. "Nobody knows where he is. . . ."

At the Holy See, Pope Gregory XVII chose to maintain public silence about the "full truth" and its aftermath. He began exchanging letters with the mother of Agca Circlic in Turkey, and the Vatican announced its official support for Circlic's petition to the Italian tribunal for clemency and immediate release from prison. It said the pope was praying for the gunman who had nearly killed him.

The Pius V Fraternity named young bishop Charles Laval, who was Leduc's right-hand man, to replace him as its new head, proclaiming that it now had nearly a million members and was determined to carry on the battle to "save" the Church.

"*Sic transit gloria mundi*—Thus passes away the glory of this world," Father Tim Savage, the obscure American Jesuit, said sadly to Sister Angela. "It is time for us to go . . . it is time for a new beginning."

Afterword

TO KILL THE POPE is a work of fiction.

It is based, however, on real events, facts, and persons: the attempt to assassinate Pope John Paul II on May 13, 1981, its aftermath, and the secret investigation of the conspiracy conducted subsequently at the behest of the Holy See.

The secret investigation was launched after the Italian government and intelligence and law enforcement agencies worldwide had decided not to pursue the matter any further—for complex political reasons. Officially, although the case is closed, the crime remains unsolved nearly twenty years later, and the Turkish terrorist who shot the pope is serving a life prison sentence in Italy.

The Vatican has chosen not to reveal publicly the results of its own secret investigations, which is the main theme of this book. But the truth about the investigation and the assassination attempt against John Paul II is disclosed here for the first time.

The fictional form was adopted for *To Kill the Pope* in order to honor commitments of discretion to my principal sources. Most of the crucial knowledge was acquired in the course of my years of research, in and out of Rome, for my biography of John Paul II, published in 1995. This story could not have been written without the guidance, advice, and encouragement of key individuals I had come to know during that period.

The characters in this novel are often, of necessity, composites of existing persons, although many are pure invention. Certain peripheral facts, including dates and specific events, have been altered, to a greater or lesser extent, for storytelling purposes. All the *dramatis personae* prior to 1950 represent themselves and is faithful to history, as are the events before that date and in the remote past as described herein.

Pope Gregory XVII, of course, does not exist.

Monsignor Romain de Sainte-Ange, the papal private secretary, was wholly created for story plot requirements. No papal secretary in memory has ever behaved in the manner presented in this novel nor has he died in office from a heart attack—nor has he committed suicide. Naturally, all popes have powerful private secretaries.

Father Timothy Savage, the American Jesuit and the central personage in this tale, is a composite figure: he is patterned after the man who conducted the actual secret investigation, though liberties were taken concerning Tim's background. Any similarity between this fictional character and the former Head of the Office for Islam in the Vatican's Council for Interreligious Dialogue, an American Jesuit, Father Thomas Michel, S.J., is entirely coincidental. Placing Savage's office at Via dell'Erba was my invention for storytelling purposes only.

Archbishop Leduc is modeled after a now deceased retired French archbishop. The latter died in 1991, four years after the fictional Archbishop Leduc, apparently from natural causes—not in a highway "accident." However, all the quotations attributed to Leduc come from the published writings by the role model.

John Paul II was actually attacked by a bayonet-wielding Spanish priest, Juan Fernando Krohn, a member of the real archbishop's Fraternity, at the sanctuary of Our Lady of Fátima, in Portugal, on the first anniversary of the 1981 Vatican assassination attempt. At the same time, all other characters mentioned in the book as members or followers of the Fraternity are imaginary.

Alexandre de Marenches, the late chief of the Service de Documentation Extérieure et Contre-espionage (SDECE), the French equivalent of the CIA, was a real-life figure and the bearer of the warning about the impending assassination attempt against John Paul II. Controversy about the circumstances of his death—heart attack, suicide, or murder—persists in France to this day as a sensitive "cause célèbre."

Jake Kurtski has never existed: That is why he had to be invented.

The actual secret investigation by the real Tim Savage character was conducted in the early 1990s—for narrative reasons, it occurs in the novel five years earlier. The Vatican had announced as late as 1999 its official support for clemency and immediate release from Ancona Prison for the Turk who had shot John Paul II on St. Peter's Square. This act follows the Holy See's acceptance of the findings of its own secret inquiry, in effect exonerating the gunman. Shortly afterward, John Paul II announced that he would travel to Fátima on May 13, 2000—the first time in eighteen years. All loose ends now appear to have been tied up.

Much of the basic material in the book is factual. Some of it remains highly classified by the Italian, U.S., and other governments. Most of my substantive knowledge has originated in interviews and conversations at the high Vatican and Rome levels—and sources elsewhere in Europe and the Middle East.

Finally, original textual materials include actual CIA testimony before Senate committees in Washington, the Central Intelligence Agency's internal reports on the 1981 attack on John Paul II, reports by Italian government investigators, findings by Italian investigating magistrates and courts, and by Interpol, and quotations from editorials in *L'Osservatore Romano.* There is even the text of an interview granted to a French newspaper by Alexandre de Marenches shortly before his death. And soon after Pope John Paul I died in 1978 after his monthlong reign, *Civilita Cristiana,* an integrist publication in Rome, charged intriguingly that Church "liberals" had planned to kill him because they "feared" that he would reverse the reforms mandated by the Vatican Council Two.

T.S.

Washington, D.C.

January 2000